SPHINX

Also by Robin Cook

The Year of the Intern
Coma

SPHINX

by

Robin Cook

G.P. Putnam's Sons
New York

Library of Congress Cataloging in Publication Data

Cook, Robin, date.
  Sphinx.

  I. Title.
PZ4.C76992Sp [PS3553.05545] 813'.5'4 79-1071
ISBN 0-399-12328-8

Printed in the United States of America

Concerning Egypt itself I shall extend my remarks to a great length, because there is no country that possesses so many wonders, nor any that has such a number of works that defy description.

—Herodotus
History

SPHINX

Prologue

1301 B.C.   Tomb of Tutankhamen   Valley of the
Kings   Necropolis of Thebes   Year 10 of His
Majesty, King of Upper and Lower Egypt, Son of
Re, Pharaoh Seti I   fourth month of season of
Inundation, day 10

Emeni thrust his copper chisel through the closely packed
limestone chips directly ahead of him and felt it hit against
solid masonry. He did it again, just to be sure. Without doubt
he had reached the inner door. Beyond lay treasure the likes of
which he could hardly fathom; beyond was the house of
eternity of the young pharaoh, Tutankhamen, buried fifty-one
years previously.

With renewed enthusiasm he dug into the densely packed
rubble. The dust made breathing difficult. Sweat dripped from
his angular face in a steady stream. He was on his stomach in a
pitch-black tunnel barely wide enough even for his thin,
sinewy body. Cupping his hand, he raked the loosened
limestone under him until he could get it past his foot. Then
like a burrowing insect he pushed the chips behind him,
where they were gathered into a reed basket by the water
carrier Kemese. Emeni did not feel any pain as his abraded
hand groped in the blackness for the plastered wall ahead. His
fingertips traced the seal of Tutankhamen on the blocked door,
undisturbed since the young pharaoh had been interred.

9

Resting his head on his left arm, Emeni let his whole body go limp. Pain spread through his shoulders, and behind him he could hear Kemese's labored breathing as he dropped the gravel into the basket.

"We have reached the inner door," Emeni said with a mixture of fear and excitement. More than anything else, Emeni wanted this night to be over. He was not a thief. But there he was, tunneling into the eternal sanctuary of the hapless Tutankhamen. "Have Iramen fetch my mallet." Emeni noticed that his voice had a strange warbling quality within the narrow confines of the tunnel. Kemese squealed delight at the news and scrambled backward out of the tunnel, dragging his reed basket.

Then there was silence. Emeni felt the walls of the tunnel press in upon him. He struggled against his claustrophobic fear, remembering how his grandfather Amenemheb had supervised the digging of this small tomb. Emeni wondered if Amenemheb had touched the surface directly above him. Rolling over, he put his palms against the solid rock, and it reassured him. The plans of Tutankhamen's tomb that Amenemheb had given to his son Per Nefer, Emeni's father, who had, in turn, given them to Emeni, were accurate. Emeni had tunneled exactly twelve cubits from the outer door and had hit the inner door. Beyond lay the antechamber. It had taken two nights of backbreaking labor, but by morning it would be over. Emeni planned to remove only four golden statues, whose location was also pinpointed in the plans. One statue for himself and one for each of his co-conspirators. Then he would reseal the tomb. Emeni hoped the gods would understand. He would not steal for himself. The single golden statue was needed to pay for the complete embalming and funerary preparation of his parents.

Kemese reentered the tunnel, pushing ahead of him his reed basket containing the mallet and an oil lamp. It also contained a bronze dagger with an ox-bone handle. Kemese was a real thief, with no scruples to limit his appetite for gold.

With the mallet and the copper chisel, Emeni's experienced hands made quick work of the mortar holding the stone blocks in front of him. He marveled at the insignificance of Tutankha-

10

men's tomb when compared with the cavernous tomb of Pharaoh Seti I, on which he was currently employed. But the insignificance of Tutankhamen's was a blessing in disguise, for otherwise Emeni would never have been in a position to enter the tomb. Pharaoh Horemheb's formal edict to erase the memory of Tutankhamen had removed the Ka-priests of Amen from standing watch, and Emeni had only to bribe the night watchman of the workers' huts with two measures of grain and beer. Even that was probably unnecessary, since Emeni had planned to enter Tutankhamen's house of eternity during the great feast of Ope. The entire staff of the necropolis, including most of the population of Emeni's own village, the Place of Truth, were all rejoicing in Thebes proper on the east side of the great Nile. Yet, despite the precautions, Emeni was still more anxious than he'd ever been in his entire life, and this anxiety drove him on to frenzied exertion with the mallet and chisel. The block in front of him grated forward, then thudded onto the floor of the chamber beyond.

Emeni's heart stopped as he half-expected to be set upon by demons of the underworld. Instead, his nostrils picked out the aromatic smell of cedar and incense and his ears recorded the solitude of eternity. With a sense of awe he worked his way forward and entered the tomb headfirst. The silence was deafening, the blackness impenetrable. Looking back into the tunnel, he glimpsed faint, attenuated moonlight as Kemese worked his way forward. Groping like a blind man, he sought to give Emeni the oil lamp.

"Can I enter?" asked Kemese to the darkness after handing over the lamp and the tinder.

"Not yet," answered Emeni, busy with the light. "Go back and tell Iramen and Amasis that it'll be about a half-hour before we start refilling the tunnel."

Kemese grumbled and, like a crab, worked his way backward through the tunnel.

A lone spark leaped from the wheel and caught the tinder. Deftly Emeni applied it to the wick of the oil lamp. Light sprang up and pierced the darkness like sudden warmth entering a cold room.

Emeni froze, his legs almost buckling. In the flickering half-light he could make out the face of a god, Amnut, devourer of the dead. The oil lamp shook in his trembling hands, and he stumbled back against the wall. But the god did not advance. Then, as the light played over its golden head, revealing its ivory teeth and its slender, stylized body, Emeni realized he was looking at a funerary bed. There were two others, one with the head of a cow, the other a lion. To the right, against the wall, were two life-size statues of the boy king Tutankhamen, guarding the entrance to the burial chamber. Emeni had already seen similar gilded statues of Seti I being carved in the house of the sculptors.

Emeni carefully avoided a garland of dried flowers dropped on the threshold. He moved quickly, isolating two gilded shrines. With reverence he unlatched the doors and lifted the golden statues from their pedestals. One was an exquisite statue of Nekhbet, a vulture goddess of upper Egypt; the other, Isis. Neither had the name of Tutankhamen. That was important.

Taking the mallet and chisel, Emeni moved under the Amnut funerary bed and quickly made an opening into the side chamber. According to the plans of Amenemheb, the other two statues Emeni wanted were in a coffer in this smaller room. Ignoring a strong sense of foreboding, Emeni entered the room, holding the oil lamp in front of him. To his relief, there were no terrifying objects. The walls were rough-hewn rock. Emeni recognized the chest he wanted from the beautiful image on the top. There, carved in relief, was a young queen offering the pharaoh Tutankhamen bouquets of lotus, papyrus, and poppies. But there was a problem. The lid was locked in some clever way and would not open. Emeni carefully set down the oil lamp on a reddish-brown cedar cabinet and examined the coffer more closely. He was unaware of the activity in the tunnel behind him.

Kemese had already reached its lip, with Iramen right behind him. Amasis, an enormous Nubian, having great difficulty pushing his bulk through the narrow passage, was farther back, but the other two could already see Emeni's shadow dancing grotesquely on the floor and wall of the antechamber. Kemese gripped the bronze dagger in his rotting

12

teeth and oozed headfirst from the tunnel onto the floor of the tomb. Silently he helped Iramen to a standing position beside him. The two waited, scarcely daring to breathe until, with a minor clatter of loose gravel, Amasis finally entered the chamber. Fear quickly metamorphosed to wild-eyed greed as the three peasants eyed the unbelievable treasure spread around them. Never in their lives had they ever seen such marvelous objects, and it was all there for the taking. Like a pack of starved Russian wolves the three launched themselves into the carefully arranged objects. Densely packed coffers were ripped open and dumped. Gold attached to furniture and chariots was ripped off.

Emeni heard the first crash and his heart leaped in his chest. His first thought was that he was caught. Then he heard his companions' cries of excitement and realized what was happening. It was like a nightmare.

"No, no!" he shouted, snatching up the oil lamp and pushing himself through the opening into the antechamber. "Stop, in the names of all the gods, stop!" The sound reverberated in the small room, momentarily startling the three thieves into inaction. Then Kemese snatched up his ox-bone-handled dagger. Seeing the movement, Amasis smiled. It was a cruel smile, the light from the oil lamp reflecting from the surface of his huge teeth.

Emeni lunged for his mallet, but Kemese put his foot on it, pinning it to the floor. Amasis reached out and grabbed Emeni's left wrist, steadying the oil lamp. With his other hand he hit Emeni in the temple, continuing to hold the lamp as the stonecutter collapsed in a heap on the piles of royal linen.

Emeni had no idea how long he was unconscious, but when the blackness receded, the nightmare returned in a tidal wave. At first all he heard were muffled voices. A small amount of gilded light issued from a break in the wall, and turning his head slowly to ease the pain, he stared into the burial chamber. Squatting down between bituminized statues of Tutankhamen, Emeni could make out Kemese's silhouette. The peasants were violating the sacred sanctuary, the Holy of the Holies.

Silently Emeni moved each of his limbs. His left arm and

hand were numb from being twisted underneath him, but otherwise he felt all right. He had to find help. He gauged the distance to the tunnel opening. It was close, but it would be difficult to enter it quietly. Bringing his feet up underneath him, Emeni crouched, waiting for the throbbing in his head to abate. Suddenly Kemese turned, holding up a small golden statue of Horus. He saw Emeni and for a moment he was frozen. Then with a roar he leaped into the center of the anteroom toward the dazed stonecutter.

Ignoring the pain, Emeni dived into the tunnel, scraping his chest and abdomen on the plastered edge. But Kemse moved swiftly and managed to grab an ankle. Bracing himself, he shouted for Amasis. Emeni rolled over onto his back within the tunnel and kicked viciously with his free foot, catching Kemese on his cheekbone. The grip loosened and Emeni was able to scramble forward through the tunnel, mindless of innumerable cuts from the limestone chips. He reached the dry night air and ran toward the necropolis guard station on the road to Thebes.

Behind, in Tutankhamen's tomb, panic ensued. The three thieves knew that their only chance for escape was to leave immediately, even though they had entered only one of the gilded burial shrines. Amasis reluctantly staggered from the burial chamber with a heavy armload of golden statues. Kemese tied a group of solid gold rings in a rag, only to drop the bundle inadvertently on the debris-strewn floor. Feverishly they dumped their spoils into reed baskets. Iramen put down the oil lamp and pushed his basket into the tunnel, climbing in after it. Kemese and Amasis followed, dropping a lotiform alabaster cup on the threshold. Once they were out of the tomb, they began to climb south away from the necropolis guard station. Amasis was overloaded with booty. To free his right hand, he stashed a blue faience cup under a rock, then caught up to the others. They passed the route to Hatshepsut's temple, heading instead for the village of the necropolis workers. Once out of the valley, they turned to the west and entered the vast reaches of the Libyan desert. They were free, and they were rich; very rich.

*   *   *

14

Emeni had never known torture, although on occasion he had fantasized whether he could bear it. He couldn't. The pain ascended, with surprising rapidity, from being tolerable to unbearable. He had been told that he was to be examined with the stick. He had had no idea what that meant until four stout guards of the necropolis forced him down on a low table, holding each of his extremities. A fifth began to beat Emeni unmercifully on the soles of his feet.

"Stop, I will tell all," gasped Emeni. But he had already told everything, fifty times. He wished he could pass out, but he could not. He felt as if his feet were in a fire, pressed against white-hot glowing coals. The agony was intensified by the burning noonday sun. Emeni shrieked like a butchered dog. He tried to bite the arm holding his right wrist, but someone pulled him back by his hair.

When Emeni finally was certain of going crazy, Prince Maya, chief of police of the necropolis, casually waved his manicured hand, indicating the beating should stop. The guard with the club hit Emeni once more before quitting. Prince Maya, enjoying the scent from his customary lotus blossom, turned to his guests: Nebmare-nahkt, mayor of Western Thebes; and Nenephta, overseer and chief architect for his majesty Pharaoh Seti I. No one spoke, so Maya turned to Emeni, who had been released and who was now lying on his back, still feeling the fire in his feet.

"Tell me again, stonecutter, how you knew the way into Pharaoh Tutankhamen's tomb."

Emeni was yanked into a sitting position, the image of the three noblemen swimming before him. Gradually his vision cleared. He recognized the exalted architect Nenephta.

"My grandfather," said Emeni with difficulty. "He gave the plans of the tomb to my father, who gave them to me."

"Your grandfather was a stonecutter for Pharaoh Tutankhamen's tomb?"

"Yes," said Emeni. He went on to explain again that he had wanted only enough money to embalm his parents. He pleaded for mercy, emphasizing that he had given himself up when he saw his companions desecrating the tomb.

Nenephta watched a distant falcon effortlessly spiral in the sapphire sky. His mind wandered from the interrogation. He was troubled by this tomb robber. It was a shock to realize how easily all his efforts to secure his majesty Seti I's house of eternity could be thwarted. Suddenly he interrupted Emeni.

"Are you a stonecutter on Pharaoh Seti I's tomb?"

Emeni nodded. He had stopped his pleading in mid-sentence. He feared Nenephta. Everyone feared Nenephta.

"Do you think the tomb we are building can be robbed?"

"Any tomb can be robbed as soon as it is not guarded."

Anger swept over Nenephta. With great difficulty he refrained from personally thrashing this human hyena who represented everything he hated. Emeni sensed the animosity and cowered back toward his torturers.

"And how would you suggest we protect the pharaoh and his treasure?" asked Nenephta finally in a voice that quivered with restrained anger.

Emeni did not know what to say. He hung his head and endured the heavy silence. All he could think of was the truth. "It is impossible to protect the pharaoh," he said finally. "As it has been in the past, so it will be in the future. The tombs will be robbed."

With a speed that defied his corpulent bulk, Nenephta sprang from his seat and backhanded Emeni. "You filth. How dare you speak so insolently of the pharaoh." Nenephta motioned to hit Emeni again, but the pain in his hand from the first blow stopped him. Instead, he adjusted his linen robe and then spoke. "Since you are an expert in tomb robbing, how is it that your own adventure failed so miserably?"

"I am not an expert in tomb robbing. If I were, I would have anticipated the effect that the treasures of Pharaoh Tutankhamen would have on my peasant helpers. Their greed drove them to madness."

Nenephta's pupils suddenly dilated despite the bright sunlight. His face went flaccid. The change was so apparent that even the somnolent Nebmare-nahkt took notice, stopping a date midway between the bowl and his gaping mouth.

"Is your Excellency all right?" Nebmare-nahkt leaned forward for a better view of Nenephta's face.

But Nenephta's racing mind defied his countenance.

Emeni's words were a sudden revelation. A half-smile emerged from the creases in his cheeks. Turning to the table, he addressed Maya with excitement. "Has Pharaoh Tutankhamen's tomb been resealed?"

"Of course," said Maya. "Immediately."

"Reopen it," said Nenephta, turning back to Emeni.

"Reopen it?" queried a surprised Maya. Nebmare-nahkt dropped his date.

"Yes. I want to enter that pitiful tomb myself. The words of this stonecutter have provided me with an inspiration reminiscent of the great Imhotep. I now know how to guard the treasures of our Pharaoh Seti I for all eternity. I can't believe I never thought of it before."

For the first time Emeni felt a glimmer of hope. But Nenephta's smile vanished as suddenly he turned back to the prisoner. His pupils narrowed and his face darkened like a summer storm.

"Your words have been helpful," said Nenephta, "but they do not atone for your vile deeds. You will be tried, but I will be your accuser. You will die in the prescribed manner. You will be impaled alive in view of your peers, and your body will be left for the hyenas."

Motioning his bearers to bring his chair, Nenephta turned to the other nobles. "You have served the pharaoh well today."

"That is my fervent wish, your Excellency," answered Maya. "But I do not understand."

"It is not for you to understand. The inspiration I have had today shall be the most closely guarded secret in the universe. It will last for all eternity."

November 26, 1922

**Tomb of Tutankhamen   Valley of the
Kings   Necropolis of Thebes**

The excitement was infectious. Even the Sahara sun knifing through the cloudless sky could not diminish the suspense. The fellahin quickened their pace as they brought basket after basket of limestone chips from the entrance to Tutankhamen's tomb. They had reached a second door thirty feet down a corridor from the first. It too had been sealed for three thousand years. What lay beyond? Would the tomb be empty like all the others robbed in antiquity? No one knew.

Sarwat Raman, the beturbaned foreman, climbed the sixteen steps to ground level with a layer of dust clinging to his features like flour. Clutching his galabia, he strode across to the tent marquee, which provided the only bit of shade in the remorselessly sunny valley.

"Beg to inform your Excellency that the entrance corridor has been cleared of rubble," said Raman, bowing slightly. "The second door is now fully exposed."

Howard Carter looked up from his lemonade, squinting from under the black homburg he insisted on wearing despite the shimmering heat. "Very good, Raman. We will inspect the door as soon as the dust settles."

"I will await your honorable instructions." Raman turned and retreated.

"You are a cool one, Howard," said Lord Carnarvon, christened George Edward Stanhope Molyneux Herbert. "How can you sit here and finish your lemonade without knowing what is behind that door?" Carnarvon smiled and winked at his daughter, Lady Evelyn Herbert. "Now I can understand why Belzoni employed a battering ram when he found Seti I's tomb."

"My methods are diametrically opposed to those of Belzoni," said Carter defensively. "And Belzoni's methods were appropriately rewarded with an empty tomb, save for the sarcophagus." Carter's gaze moved involuntarily toward the nearby opening of Seti I's tomb. "Carnarvon, I'm not really certain what we've found here. I don't think we should allow ourselves to get too excited. I'm not even sure it's a tomb. The design is not typical for an eighteenth-dynasty pharaoh. It could be just a cache of Tutankhamen's belongings brought from Akhetaten. Besides, tomb robbers have preceded us, not once but twice. My only hope is that it was robbed in antiquity and someone thought it important enough to reseal the doors. So I truly have no idea what we are going to find."

Maintaining his English aplomb, Carter allowed his eyes to roam about the desolate Valley of the Kings. But his stomach was in knots. He had never been so excited in all of his forty-nine years. In the previous six barren seasons of excavation, he had found nothing. Two hundred thousand tons of gravel and sand had been moved and sifted, for absolutely nothing. Now the suddenness of the find after only five days of excavating was overwhelming. Swirling his lemonade, he tried not to think or hope. They waited. The whole world waited.

The larger dust particles settled in a fine layer on the sloping corridor floor. The group made an effort not to stir the air as they entered. Carter was first, followed by Carnarvon, then his daughter, and finally A. R. Callender, Carter's assistant. Raman waited at the entrance after giving Carter a crowbar. Callender carried a large flashlight and candles.

"As I said, we are not the first to broach this tomb," said Carter, nervously pointing to the upper-left-hand corner. "The door was entered and then resealed in that small area." Then he traced a larger circular area in the middle. "And again in this much larger area here. It is very strange." Lord Carnarvon bent over to look at the royal necropolis seal, a jackal with nine bound prisoners.

"Along the base of the door are examples of the original Tutankhamen seal," continued Carter. The beam of the flashlight reflected the fine dust still suspended in the air, before illuminating the ancient seals in the plaster.

"Now, then," said Carter as coolly as if he were suggesting afternoon tea, "let's see what is behind this door." But his stomach contorted into a tight mass, aggravating his ulcer, and his hands were damp, not so much from the heat as from the unexpressed tension. His body quivered as he lifted the crowbar and made a few preliminary cuts into the ancient plaster. The bits and pieces rained down about his feet. The exertion gave expression to his pent-up emotions, and each lunge was more vigorous than the last. Suddenly the crowbar broke through the plaster, causing Carter to stumble up against the door. Warm air issued from the tiny hole, and Carter fumbled with the matches, lighting a candle and holding a flame to the opening. It was a crude test for the presence of oxygen. The candle continued to burn.

No one dared to speak as Carter gave the candle to Callender and continued working with the crowbar. Carefully he enlarged the hole, making certain that the plaster and stone blocking fell into the corridor and not into the room beyond. Taking the candle again, Carter thrust it through the hole. It burned contentedly. He then put his head to the hole, his eyes straining in the darkness.

In a moment time stood still. As Carter's eyes adjusted, three thousand years disappeared as in a minute. Out of the blackness emerged a golden head of Amnut, ivory teeth bared. Other gilded beasts loomed, the flickering candlelight throwing their exotic silhouettes on the wall.

"Can you see anything?" asked Carnarvon excitedly.

"Yes, wonderful things," answered Carter finally, his voice for the first time betraying emotion. Then he replaced the candle with his flashlight, and those behind him could see the chamber filled with unbelievable objects. The golden heads were part of three funerary beds. Moving the light to the left, Carter gazed at a jumble of gilded and inlaid chariots heaped in the corner. Tracing back to the right, he began to ponder the curiously chaotic state of the room. Instead of the prescribed stately order, objects appeared to have been thrown about without thought. Immediately to the right were two life-size statues of Tutankhamen, each with a kilt of gold, wearing gold sandals, and armed with mace and staff.

Between the two statues was another sealed door.

Carter left the opening so the others could have a better look. Like Belzoni, he was tempted to crash down the wall and dive into the room. Instead, he calmly announced that the rest of the day would be devoted to photographing the sealed door. They would not attempt to enter what was obviously an antechamber until morning.

November 27, 1922

It took more than three hours for Carter to dismantle the ancient blocking of the door to the antechamber. Raman and a few other fellahin helped during this stage. Callender had laid in temporary electric wires, so the tunnel was brightly lit. Lord Carnarvon and Lady Evelyn entered the corridor when the job was almost complete. The last baskets of plaster and stone were hauled away. The moment of entry had arrived. No one spoke. Outside, at the mouth of the tomb, hundreds of reporters from newspapers around the world tensely waited their first view.

For a brief second Carter hesitated. As a scientist he was interested in the minutest detail inside the tomb; as a human being he was embarrassed by his intrusion into the sacred realm of the dead; and as an explorer he was experiencing the exhilaration of discovery. But, British to the core, he merely straightened his bow tie and stepped over the threshold, keeping his eye on the objects below.

Without a sound he pointed at a beautiful lotiform cup of translucent alabaster on the threshold, so Carnarvon could avoid it. Carter then made his way over to the sealed door between the two life-size statues of Tutankhamen. Carefully he began to examine the seals. His heart sank as he realized that this door had also been opened by the ancient tomb robbers, and then resealed.

Carnarvon stepped into the antechamber, his mind reeling

with the beauty of the objects so carelessly scattered around
him. He turned to take his daughter's hand as she prepared to
enter, and in the process noticed a rolled papyrus leaning
against the wall to the right of the alabaster cup. To the left
was a garland of dead flowers, as if Tutankhamen's funeral
had been only yesterday, and beside it a blackened oil lamp.
Lady Evelyn entered, holding her father's hand, followed by
Callender. Raman leaned into the antechamber but did not
enter for lack of space.

"Unfortunately, the burial chamber has been entered and
resealed," said Carter, pointing toward the door in front of
him. Carefully Carnarvon, Lady Evelyn, and Callender moved
over to the archaeologist, their eyes following his finger.
Raman stepped into the antechamber.

"Curiously, though," continued Carter, "it has been entered
only once, instead of twice, like the doors into the antechamber. So there is hope that the thieves did not reach the
mummy." Carter turned, seeing Raman for the first time.
"Raman, I did not give you permission to enter the antechamber."

"I beg your Excellency's pardon. I thought that I could be of
assistance."

"Indeed. You can be of assistance by making sure no one
enters this chamber without my personal approval."

"Of course, your Excellency." Raman silently slipped from
the room.

"Howard," said Carnarvon, "Raman is undoubtedly as
enchanted as we with the find. Perhaps you could be a little
more generous."

"The workers will all be allowed to view this room, but I will
designate the time," said Carter. "Now, as I was saying, the
reason I feel hopeful about the mummy is that I think the tomb
robbers were surprised in the middle of their sacrilege. There
is something mysterious about the way these priceless objects
are haphazardly thrown about. It appears as if someone spent
a little time rearranging things after the thieves, but not
enough to put everything back in its original state. Why?"

Carnarvon shrugged.

"Look at that beautiful cup on the threshold," continued

24

Carter. "Why wasn't that replaced? And that gilded shrine with its door ajar. Obviously a statue was stolen, but why wasn't the door even closed?" Carter stepped back to the door. "And this ordinary oil lamp. Why was it left within the tomb? I tell you, we'd better record the positioning of each object in this room very carefully. These clues are trying to tell us something. It is very strange indeed."

Sensing Carter's tension, Carnarvon tried to look about the tomb through his friend's trained eyes. Indeed, leaving an oil lamp within the tomb was surprising, and so was the disarray of the objects. But Carnarvon was so overwhelmed by the beauty of the pieces he could think of nothing else. Gazing at the translucent alabaster cup abandoned so casually on the threshold, he yearned to pick it up and hold it in his hands. It was so enticingly beautiful. Suddenly he noticed a subtle change in its orientation with regard to the garland of dried flowers and the oil lamp. He was about to say something when Carter's excited voice rang out in the chamber.

"There's another room. Everyone take a look." Carter was squatting down, shining his flashlight beneath one of the funerary beds. Carnarvon, Lady Evelyn, and Callender hurried over to him. There, glittering in the circle of light from the torch, another chamber took form, filled with gold and jeweled treasure. As in the anteroom, the precious objects had been chaotically scattered, but for the moment the Egyptologists were too awed by their find to question what had happened three thousand years in the past.

Later, when they would be ready to explore the mystery, Carnarvon was already fatally ill with blood poisoning. At 2 A.M. on April 5, 1923, less than twenty weeks after the opening of Tutankhamen's tomb and during an unexplainable five-minute power failure throughout Cairo, Lord Carnarvon died. His illness reputedly was started by the bite of an insect, but questions were raised.

Within months four other people associated with the opening of the tomb died under mysterious circumstances. One man disappeared from the deck of his own yacht lying at anchor in the placid Nile. Interest in the ancient robbery of the tomb waned and was replaced by a reassertion of the reputation of the ancient Egyptians in the occult sciences. The specter of the "Curse of the Pharaohs" rose from the shadows of the past. The New York *Times* was moved to write about the deaths: "It is a deep mystery, which it is all too easy to dismiss by skepticism." A fear began to infiltrate the scientific community. There were just too many coincidences.

Day 1

Erica Baron's reaction was pure reflex. The muscles of her back and thighs contracted and she straightened up, twirling to face the molester. She had bent over to examine an engraved brass bowl when an open hand had thrust between her legs, grabbing at her through her cotton slacks. Although she had been the object of a number of lewd stares, and even obviously sexual comments since she had left the Hilton Hotel, she had not expected to be touched. It was a shock. It would have been a shock anywhere, but in Cairo, on her first day, it seemed that much worse.

Her attacker was about fifteen, with a jeering smile that exposed straight rows of yellow teeth. The offending hand was still extended.

Ignoring her canvas tote bag, Erica used her left hand to knock the boy's arm to the side. Then, surprising herself even more than the boy, she clenched her right hand in a tight fist and punched the taunting face, throwing all her weight into the blow.

The effect was astonishing. The punch was like a good karate blow, hurling the surprised boy back against the rickety tables of the brass vendor's shop. Table legs buckled, wares crashed into the cobblestone street. Another boy carrying

27

coffee and water on a metal tray suspended by a tripod was caught in the avalanche, and he too fell, adding to the confusion.

Erica was horrified. Alone in the crowded Cairo bazaar she stood clasping her bag, unable to comprehend that she had actually hit someone. She began to shake, certain the crowds would turn on her, but uncontrollable laughter erupted around her. Even the shopkeeper, whose wares were still rolling in spirals in the street, was chuckling away, holding his sides. The boy pulled himself from the debris, and with his hand to his face, managed a smile.

"*Maareish*," said the shopkeeper, which Erica later learned meant "it can't be helped" or "it doesn't matter." Feigning anger, he waved his ball-peen hammer and chased the boy away. Then, after giving Erica a warm smile, he started retrieving his belongings.

Erica moved on, her heart still beating quickly from the experience, but realizing that she had a lot to learn about Cairo and about modern Egypt. She was trained as an Egyptologist, but unfortunately that meant knowledge of the ancient civilization of Egypt, not the modern one. Her specialty of New Kingdom hieroglyphic writing afforded no preparation for the Cairo of 1980. Ever since her arrival twenty-four hours previously, her senses had been assaulted mercilessly. First it was the smell: a kind of cloying aroma of lamb that seemed to pervade every corner of the city. Then it was the noise: a constant sound of automobile horns mixed with discordant Arabic music blaring from innumerable portable radios. Finally it was the feel of dirt, dust, and sand, which covered the city like the patina of a medieval copper roof, accentuating the unremitting poverty.

The episode with the boy undermined Erica's confidence. In her mind all the smiles of the men in their skullcaps and flowing galabias began to reflect prurient thoughts. It was worse than Rome. Boys not even in their teens followed her, giggling and asking her questions in a mixture of English, French, and Arabic. Cairo was alien, more alien than she had expected. Even the street signs were all written in the decorative but incomprehensible Arabic script. Looking back over her

28

shoulder, up Shari el Muski toward the Nile, Erica thought about returning to the western area of the city. Perhaps the whole idea of coming to Egypt on her own was ridiculous. Richard Harvey, her lover for the last three years, even her mother, Janice, had said as much. She turned again, looking into the heart of the medieval city. The street narrowed, the press of people looked overwhelming.

"Baksheesh," said a little girl no more than six years old. "Pencils for school." The English was crisp and surprisingly clear.

Erica looked down at the child, whose hair was hidden by the same dust that covered the street. She wore a tattered orange print dress and no shoes. Erica bent to smile at her, and suddenly gasped. Clustered around the child's eyelashes were numerous iridescent green house flies. The little girl made no attempt to shoo them away. She just stood there unblinking, holding out her hand. Erica was immobilized.

"Safer!" A white-uniformed policeman, wearing a blue badge that said TOURIST POLICE in bold authoritative letters, pushed his way into the street toward Erica. The child melted into the crowd. The jeering boys vanished. "May I be of assistance?" he said with a distinctive English accent. "You look like you might be lost."

"I'm looking for the Khan el Khalili bazaar," said Erica.

"Tout à droite," said the policeman, gesturing ahead. Then he thumped his forehead with his palm. "Excuse. It is the heat. I've been mixing my languages. Straight ahead, as you'd say. This is El Muski street, and ahead you will cross the main thoroughfare of Shari Port Said. Then the Khan el Khalili bazaar will be on your left. I wish you good shopping, but remember to bargain. Here in Egypt it is a sport."

Erica thanked him and pushed on through the crowd. The minute he was gone, the jeering boys miraculously reappeared and the innumerable street vendors accosted her with their wares. She passed an open-air butcher shop hung with a long row of recently slaughtered lambs, flayed except for the heads, and covered with splotches of pink ink representing government stamps. The carcasses were hung upside down, their unseeing eyes making her flinch and the smell of the offal forcing her lunch into her throat. The stench quickly merged with the decadent smell of overripe mangoes from a neighboring fruit cart and the odor of fresh donkey dung in the street. A few paces beyond, there was the reviving sharpness of herbs and spices and the aroma of freshly brewed Arabic coffee.

The dust from the densely packed narrow street rose and filtered the sun, bleaching the strip of cloudless sky a faint, faraway blue. The sand-colored buildings on each side of the street were shuttered against the blanket of afternoon heat.

As Erica advanced deeper into the bazaar, listening to the sound of ancient wooden wheels on granite cobblestones, she felt herself slipping back in time to medieval Cairo. She sensed the chaos, the poverty, and the harshness of life. She was simultaneously frightened and excited by the throbbing raw fertility, the universal mysteries which are so carefully camouflaged and hidden by Western culture. It was life stripped naked yet mitigated by human emotion; fate was greeted with resignation and even laughter.

"Cigarette?" demanded a boy of about ten. He was dressed in a gray shirt and baggy pants. One of his friends pushed him from behind so that he stumbled closer to Erica. "Cigarette?" he asked again, launching into a kind of Arabic jig and pretending to smoke a make-believe cigarette in exaggerated mime. A tailor, busy ironing with a charcoal-filled iron, grinned, and a row of men smoking intricately embossed water pipes stared at Erica with piercing, unblinking eyes.

Erica was sorry she had worn such obviously foreign clothes. Her cotton slacks and a simple knit blouse made it clear she was a tourist. The other women in Western clothes that Erica had seen had on dresses, not pants, and most of the women in the bazaar still wore the traditional black meliyas. Even Erica's body was different from the local women's. Although she was several pounds heavier than she would have liked, she was a good deal slimmer than Egyptian women. And her face was far more delicate than the round, heavy features crowding the bazaar. She had wide gray-green eyes, luxuriant chestnut hair, and a finely sculptured mouth with a full lower lip that gave her a faintly pouting expression. She knew she was pretty when she worked at it, and when she did, men responded.

Now, picking her way through the crowded bazaar, she regretted she had tried to look attractive. Her attire advertised that she was not protected by local street morality, and even more important, she was alone. She was the perfect catalyst for the fantasies of all the men who watched her.

Clutching her tote bag closer to her side, Erica hurried along as the street narrowed again to cluttered byways jammed with people engaged in every conceivable type of manufacture and commerce. Overhead, carpets and cloth stretched between the buildings to cover the market area, keeping out the sun but increasing the noise and the dust. Erica hesitated again, watching the widely varied faces. The fellahin were heavy-boned, with wide mouths and thick lips, dressed in the traditional galabias and skullcaps. The bedouin were the pure Arabs, with sharp features and slim, wiry bodies. The Nubians were ebony, with tremendously powerful and muscular torsos, often naked to the waist.

The surge of the crowds pushed Erica forward and carried her deeper into the Khan el Khalili. She found herself pressed up against a wide variety of people. Someone pinched her backside, but when she turned around, she couldn't be sure who had done it. She had a following now of five or six persistent boys. She was being hounded like a rabbit in a hunt.

Erica's goal in the bazaar had been the goldsmith section, where she wanted to buy gifts. But her resolve waned, particularly when someone's dirty fingers ran through her hair. She'd had enough. She wanted to return to the hotel. Her passion for Egypt involved the ancient civilization with its art and mysteries. Modern urban Egypt was a little overpowering when taken in all at once. Erica wanted to get out to the monuments, like Saqqara, and above all she wanted to get to Upper Egypt, to the countryside. She knew that was going to be as she dreamed it.

At the next corner she turned to the right, stepping around a donkey that was either dead or dying. It didn't move, and no one paid the poor beast any attention. Having studied a map of the city prior to leaving the Hilton, she guessed she should reach the square in front of the El Azhar mosque if she continued heading southeast. Pushing her way between a clump of shoppers bargaining over scrawny pigeons in reed cages, Erica broke into a jog. She could see a minaret ahead, and a sunlit square.

Suddenly Erica stopped dead in her tracks. The boy who had demanded a cigarette and who was still following her now crashed into her, but bounced off unnoticed. Erica's eyes were riveted to a window display. There in front of her was a piece of pottery in the shape of a shallow urn. It was a morsel of ancient Egypt shining in the middle of modern squalor. Its lip was slightly chipped, but otherwise the pot was unbroken. Even the clay eyelets apparently made to hang the pot were still intact. Aware that the bazaar was filled with fakes, highly priced to attract tourists, Erica still was stunned by the bowl's apparent authenticity. The usual fakes were carved mummiform statues. This was a splendid example of predynastic Egyptian pottery, as good as the best she had seen where she was currently employed, the Boston Museum of Fine Arts. If it were real, it would be more than six thousand years old.

Stepping back in the alleyway, Erica looked at the freshly painted sign over the window. Above were the curious squiggles of Arabic script. Below was printed *Antica Abdul*. The doorway to the left of the window was curtained by a dense row of heavily beaded strings. A tug on her tote bag by one of her hecklers was all the encouragement Erica needed to enter the shop.

The hundreds of colored beads made sharp, crackling noises as they fell back into place behind her. The shop was small, about ten feet wide and twice that deep, and surprisingly cool. The walls were stuccoed and whitewashed, the floor covered with multiple worn Oriental carpets. An L-shaped glass-topped counter dominated most of the room.

Since no one came forward to help her, Erica hiked up the strap of her bag and bent over to look more closely at the amazing piece of pottery that she had seen through the window. It was a light tan, with delicately painted decorations in a shade somewhere between brown and magenta. Crumpled Arabic newspaper had been stuffed inside.

The heavy red-brown curtains in the back of the shop parted, and the proprietor, Abdul Hamdi, emerged, shuffling up to the counter. Erica glanced at the man and immediately

32

relaxed. He was about sixty-five and had a pleasant gentleness of movement and expression.

"I'm very interested in this urn," she said. "Would it be possible for me to examine it more closely?"

"Of course," said Abdul, coming out from behind the counter. He picked up the pot and unceremoniously put it into Erica's trembling hands. "Bring it over to the counter if you'd like." He switched on an unadorned light bulb.

Erica gingerly put the urn on the counter and removed her tote from her shoulder. Then she picked up the pot again, slowly turning it in her fingertips to examine the decorations. Besides purely ornamental designs, there were dancers, antelopes, and crude boats. "How much is this?" Erica looked very carefully at the drawings.

"Two hundred pounds," said Abdul, lowering his voice as if it were a secret. There was a twinkle in his eye.

"Two hundred pounds!" echoed Erica while converting currencies in her mind. That was about three hundred dollars. She decided to bargain a little while trying to determine if the pot were a fake. "I can only afford one hundred pounds."

"One hundred eighty is my best offer," said Abdul, as if making a supreme sacrifice.

"I suppose I could go to one hundred twenty," said Erica, continuing to study the markings.

"Okay, for you . . . He paused and touched her arm. She did not mind. "You are American?"

"Yes."

"Good. I like Americans. Much better than Russians. For you I will do something very special. I will take a loss on this piece. I need the money because this shop is very new. So for you, one hundred and sixty pounds." Abdul reached over and took the pot from Erica and placed it on the table. "A marvelous piece, my best. It is my last offer."

Erica looked at Abdul. He had the heavy features of the fellahin. She noticed that under the worn jacket of his Western suit he was wearing a brown galabia.

Turning the pot over, Erica looked at the spiral drawing on the bottom and let her slightly moist thumb gently rub over the painted design. Some of the burnt-sienna pigment came off. At that moment Erica knew the pot was a fake. It was very cleverly made, but definitely not an antique.

Feeling extremely uncomfortable, Erica put the pot back on the counter and picked up her tote bag. "Well, thank you very much," she said, avoiding looking at Abdul.

"I do have others," said Abdul, opening a tall wooden cabinet against the wall. His Levantine instincts had responded to Erica's initial enthusiasm, and the same instincts sensed a sudden change. He was confused but did not want to lose a customer without a fight. "Perhaps you might like this one." He took a similar piece of pottery from the cabinet and placed it on the counter.

Erica did not want to precipitate a confrontation by telling the seemingly kind old man that he was trying to cheat her. Reluctantly she picked up the second pot. It was more oval than the first and sat on a narrower base. The designs were all left-hand spirals.

"I have many examples of this kind of pottery," continued Abdul, setting out five other pots.

While his back was to Erica she licked her forefinger and rubbed it across the design on the second pot. The pigment did not budge.

"How much is this one?" asked Erica, trying to conceal her excitement. It was conceivable the pot in her hand was six thousand years old.

"They are all different prices according to the workmanship and the condition," said Abdul evasively. "Why not look at them all and pick one that you like. Then we can talk about prices."

Carefully examining each pot in turn, Erica isolated two probable authentic antiques out of seven. "I like these two," she said, her confidence returning. For once her Egyptology expertise had a practical value. She wished Richard were there.

Abdul looked at the two pots, then at Erica. "These are not the most beautiful. Why do you prefer them to the others?"

Erica looked at Abdul and hesitated. Then she said defiantly, "Because the others are fakes."

Abdul's face was expressionless. Slowly a twinkle appeared in his eyes and a smile lifted the corners of his mouth. Finally he broke into laughter, bringing tears to his eyes. Erica found herself grinning.

"Tell me . . ." said Abdul with difficulty. He had to control his laughter before continuing. "Tell me how you know these are fakes." He pointed toward the pots Erica had put aside.

"The easiest way possible. There is no stability to the pigment of the designs. The paint comes off on a wet finger. That never happens to an antique."

Wetting his finger, Abdul tested the pigment. His finger was smudged with burnt sienna. "You are absolutely right." He repeated the test on the two antiques. "The fooler is made the fool. Such is life."

"How much are these two *real* antique pots?" asked Erica.

"They are not for sale. Someday, perhaps, but not now."

Taped to the underside of the glass countertop was an official-looking document with government stamps from the Department of Antiquities. Antica Abdul was a fully licensed antique shop. Next to the license was a printed paper saying that written guarantees on antiquities would be supplied on request. "What do you do when a customer wants a guarantee?" asked Erica.

"I give it to them. For the tourist it makes no difference. They are happy with their souvenir. They never check."

"Doesn't that bother you?"

"No, it does not bother me. Righteousness is a luxury of the wealthy. The merchant always tries to get the highest price for his wares, for himself and for his family. The tourists who come in here want souvenirs. If they want authentic antiquities they know something about them. It is their responsibility. How is it that you know about pigment on ancient pottery?"

"I am an Egyptologist."

"You are an Egyptologist! Allah be praised! Why would a beautiful woman like yourself want to be an Egyptologist? Ah, the world has passed by Abdul Hamdi. I am indeed getting old. So you have been to Egypt before?"

"No, this is my first trip. I wanted to come before, but it was too expensive. It's been a dream of mine for some time."

"Well, I pray that you will enjoy it. You are planning to go to Upper Egypt? To Luxor?"

"Of course."

"I will give you the address of my son's antique shop."

"So he can sell me some fake pottery?" said Erica with a smile.

"No, no, but he can show you some nice things. I too have some wonderful things. What do you think of this?" Abdul lifted a mummiform figure from the cabinet and set it on the counter. It was made of wood covered with plaster and exquisitely painted. A row of hieroglyphic writing ran down the front.

"It is a fake," said Erica quickly.

"No," said Abdul, alarmed.

"The hieroglyphics are not real. It says nothing. It is a meaningless row of signs."

"You can read the mysterious writing as well?"

"That is my specialty, especially writing from the time of the New Kingdom."

Abdul turned the statue around, looking at the hieroglyphics. "I paid plenty for this piece. I'm certain it is real."

"Perhaps the statue is real, but the writing is not. Maybe the writing was added in an attempt to make the piece appear even more valuable." Erica attempted to wipe off some of the black color on the statue. "The pigment seems stable."

"Well, let me show you something else." Abdul reached within the glass-topped cabinet and extracted a small cardboard box. Removing the top of the box, he selected a number of scarabs and placed them in a row on the cabinet. With his forefinger he pushed one toward Erica.

She picked it up and examined it. It was made of a porous material, its top exquisitely carved in the form of the familiar dung beetle revered by the ancient Egyptians. Turning it over, Erica was surprised to see the cartouche of a pharoah, Seti I. The hieroglyphic carving was absolutely beautiful.

"It is a spectacular piece," said Erica, replacing it on the counter.

"So you wouldn't mind having that antique?"

"Not at all. How much is it?"

36

"It is yours. It is a present."

"I can't accept such a gift. Why do you want to give me a present?"

"It is an Arabic custom. But let me warn you, it is not authentic."

Surprised, Erica lifted the scarab to the light. Her initial impression did not change. "I think it is real."

"No. I know it is not real because my son made it."

"It's extraordinary," said Erica, looking again at the hieroglyphics.

"My son is very good. He copied the hieroglyphics from a real piece."

"What is it made of?"

"Ancient bone. There are enormous caches of broken-up mummies in Luxor and Aswan in the ancient public catacombs. My son uses the bone to carve the scarabs. To make the cut surface look old and worn, we feed them to our turkeys. One pass through a turkey gives it a truly venerable appearance."

Erica swallowed, fleetingly sickened by contemplating the scarab's biological journey. But intellectual interest quickly overcame her physical response, and she turned the scarab over and over in her fingers. "I admit, I was fooled, and would be again."

"Don't be upset. Several of these have been taken to Paris, where the curators think they know everything, and they were tested."

"Probably carbon-dated," interjected Erica.

"Whatever. Anyway, they were declared truly ancient. Well, obviously the bone was ancient. Now my son's scarabs are in museums around the world."

A cynical laugh escaped from Erica. She knew she was dealing with an expert.

"My name is Abdul Hamdi, so please call me Abdul. What is your name?"

"Oh, I beg your pardon. Erica Baron." She placed the scarab on the counter.

"Erica, I would be pleased if you joined me for some mint tea."

Abdul put the other pieces back into their places, then drew aside the heavy red-brown drapes. Erica had enjoyed talking with Abdul, but she hesitated a moment before picking up her bag and advancing toward the opening. The back room was about the same size as the front part of the shop, but it appeared to have no doors or windows. The walls and floor were covered with Oriental carpets, giving the area the appearance of a tent. In the center of the room were cushions, a low table, and a water pipe.

"One moment," said Abdul. The curtain fell back into place, leaving Erica to stare at several large objects that were completely draped with cloth. She could hear the crackling noises of the beads in the front entrance, and muffled shouts as Abdul ordered tea.

"Please sit down," Abdul said when he returned, indicating the large cushions on the floor. "It is not often I have the pleasure of entertaining a lady so beautiful and so knowledgeable. Tell me, my dear, where are you from in America?"

"Originally I'm from Toledo, Ohio," said Erica somewhat nervously. "But I live in Boston now, or actually Cambridge, which is right next to Boston." Erica's eyes slowly moved around the small room. The single incandescent bulb hanging in the center gave the deep reds of the Oriental carpets an incredibly rich softness, like red velvet.

"Boston, yes. It must be beautiful in Boston. I have a friend there. We write occasionally. Actually, my son writes. I cannot write in English. I have a letter from him here." Abdul rummaged through a small chest by the cushion, producing a typed letter addressed to Abdul Hamdi, Luxor, Egypt. "Perhaps you know him?"

"Boston is a very big city . . ." began Erica before she caught sight of the return address: Dr. Herbert Lowery, her boss. "You know Dr. Lowery?" she asked incredulously.

"I've met him twice and we write occasionally. He was very interested in a head of Ramses II that I had about a year ago. A wonderful man. Very clever."

"Indeed," said Erica, amazed that Abdul would be corresponding with such an eminent figure as Dr. Herbert Lowery, chairman of the Department of Near Eastern Studies at the

Boston Museum of Fine Arts. It made her considerably more at ease.

As if sensing Erica's thoughts, Abdul fished several other letters from his little cedar chest. "Here are letters from Dubois, at the Louvre, and Caufield, at the British Museum."

The beads clacked in the outer room. Abdul reached back and drew the curtains aside, speaking a few words of Arabic. A young boy in a once-white galabia and bare feet slipped noiselessly into the room. He was carrying one of those trays supported by a tripod. Silently he placed the glasses with metal holders next to the water pipe. He did not look up from his task. Abdul dropped a few coins onto the boy's tray and held the curtains back for the boy to leave. Turning back to Erica, he smiled and stirred his tea.

"Is this safe for me to drink?" asked Erica, fingering her glass.

"Safe?" Abdul was surprised.

"I've been warned so much about drinking water here in Egypt."

"Ah, you mean for your digestion. Yes, it is completely safe. The water boils constantly in the tea shop. Enjoy. This is a hot, parched land. It is an Arabic custom to drink tea or coffee with your friends."

They sipped in silence. Erica was pleasantly surprised by the taste, and by the tingling freshness the drink left in her mouth.

"Tell me, Erica . . .", said Abdul, breaking the silence. He pronounced her name in a strange way, placing the accent on the second syllable. "Provided, of course, you do not object to my asking. Tell me why you have become an Egyptologist."

Erica looked down into her tea. The flecks of mint slowly swirled in the warm fluid. She was accustomed to the question. She had heard it a thousand times, especially from her mother, who never could understand why a beautiful young Jewish girl who "had everything" would choose to study Egyptology and not education. Her mother had tried to change her mind, first by gentle conversation ("What are my friends going to think?"), then by forcible debate ("You'll never be able to support yourself!"), finally by threatening to withdraw financial support. It was all in vain. Erica continued her studies, possibly in part because of her mother's opposition, but mostly because she loved everything about the field of Egyptology.

It was true she did not think in practical terms of what kind of job would be waiting for her when she finished, and it was also true that she "lucked out" by being hired by the Boston Museum of Fine Arts, when most of her fellow students were still unemployed with little immediate hope in sight. Nonetheless she loved the study of ancient Egypt. There was something about the remoteness and the mystery, combined with incredible wealth and value of the material already discovered, that fascinated her. She was particularly fond of the love poetry, which made the ancient people come alive. It was through the poems that Erica could feel the emotion spanning the millennia, reducing the meaning of time and making her wonder if society had progressed at all.

Looking up at Abdul, Erica finally said, "I studied Egyptology because it fascinated me. When I was a little girl and my family took a trip to New York City, the only thing I remembered was seeing a mummy at the Metropolitan Museum. Then when I was in college I took a course in ancient history. I really enjoyed studying about the culture." Erica shrugged and smiled. She knew she could never give a complete explanation.

"Very strange," said Abdul. "For me, it is a job, better than breaking my back in the field. But for you . . ." He shrugged. "As long as you are happy, it is good. How old are you, my dear?"

"Twenty-eight."

"And your husband, where is he?"

Erica smiled, fully conscious that the old man had no idea why she was smiling. The whole complex of problems surrounding Richard cascaded out of her unconscious. It was like opening a floodgate. She was almost tempted to try to explain her problems to this sympathetic stranger, but she didn't. She had come to Egypt to get away and to use her knowledge of Egyptology. "I'm not yet married," she said at length. "Are you interested, Abdul?" The smile returned.

"Me, interested? I'm always interested." Abdul laughed.

"After all, Islam lets the faithful have four wives. But for me I could not handle four times the joy of my only wife. Still, twenty-eight and not married. It is a strange world."

Watching Abdul drink, Erica thought about how much she was enjoying this interlude. She wanted to remember it.

"Abdul, would you mind if I took your picture?"

"I am pleased."

While Abdul straightened himself on his pillow and smoothed his jacket, Erica extracted her small Polaroid and attached the flash bar. A moment after the flash washed the room with an unnatural light, the camera spit out the un-developed photo.

"Ah, if only the Russian rockets would have worked as well as your camera," said Abdul, relaxing. "Since you are the most beautiful and the youngest Egyptologist I have ever had in my shop, I would like to show you something very special."

Abdul slowly got to his feet. Erica glanced at the photo. It was developing nicely.

"You are lucky to see this piece, my dear," said Abdul, carefully lifting the cloth cover on an object about six feet tall.

Erica looked up and gasped. "My God," she said in disbelief. In front of her was a life-size statue. She scrambled to her feet to look more closely. Abdul proudly stepped back like an artist unveiling his life's work. The face was made of beaten gold reminiscent of the mask of Tutankhamen, but more finely crafted.

"It is Pharaoh Seti I," said Abdul. He put down the cloth cover and sat, letting Erica enjoy her find.

"This is the most beautiful statue I have ever seen," whispered Erica, gazing into the stately, calm face. The eyes were made of white alabaster set with green feldspar. The eyebrows were made of translucent carnelian. The traditional ancient Egyptian headdress was made of gold inlaid with bands of lapis lazuli. Around the neck was an opulent pectoral in the form of the vulture representing the Egyptian goddess Nekhbet. The necklace was made of gold and set with hundreds of pieces of turquoise, jasper, and lapis lazuli. The beak and the eyes were made of obsidian. At the girdle was a sheathed gold dagger whose handle was finely crafted and encrusted with precious stones. The left hand was extended, holding a mace that was also covered with inlaid jewels. The total effect was dazzling. Erica was overwhelmed. This statue was no fake, and its value was unbelievable. Indeed, any piece of the jewelry was priceless. Standing amid the warm red glow of the Oriental carpets, the statue radiated a light as pure and clear as a diamond. Slowly circling the piece, Erica finally could speak.

"Where on earth did this come from? I've never seen anything like it."

"It came from beneath the sands of the Libyan desert, where all our treasures are hidden," said Abdul, cooing like a proud parent. "It is only resting here for a few hours before it resumes its journey. I thought you'd like to see it."

"Oh, Abdul. It is so beautiful, I'm speechless. Truly." Erica came back around the front of the statue, noting for the first time the hieroglyphics cut into the base. Immediately she recognized the name of Pharaoh Seti I, contained within the enclosure called a cartouche. Then she saw another cartouche with another name. Thinking it an alternate name for Seti I, she began to translate. To her astonishment, the name was Tutankhamen. It didn't make sense. Seti I was an extremely important and powerful pharaoh who had ruled some fifty years after the insignificant boy king Tutankhamen. The two pharaohs were in different dynasties from totally separate families. Erica was sure that she must have made a mistake, but checking again, she realized she had been right. The hieroglyphics contained both names.

The sharp crackling noise from the beads in the outer part of the shop brought Abdul instantly to his feet. "Erica, please excuse, but I must be reasonably careful." The dark cloth cover settled back over the fabulous statue. For Erica it was like being prematurely awakened from a wonderful dream. In front of her was a nondescript shapeless mass. "Let me attend to the customers. I will be right back. Enjoy your tea . . . perhaps you'd like a little more?"

"No, thank you," said Erica, who wanted to see the statue again, not drink more tea.

As Abdul shuffled over to the curtain and carefully peered

out, Erica picked up the now-developed Polaroid picture. Except for missing part of Abdul's head, the snapshot was fine. She thought about taking a shot of the statue if Abdul would agree.

Apparently whoever was outside was in no rush, because, letting the curtains go, Abdul moved back over to his cedar chest. Erica sat down on her cushion.

"Do you have a guidebook for Egypt?" asked Abdul in a quiet voice.

"Yes," said Erica. "I managed to get a Nagel's guide."

"I have something better," said Abdul, pulling a small aging book from among his correspondence. "Here is a Baedeker, 1929 edition. It is the best for touring the monuments of Egypt. I'd be pleased if you'd use it during your stay here in my country. It is far superior to the Nagel's."

"You are so kind," said Erica, taking the book. "I'll be very careful with it. Thank you."

"It pleases me to make your visit more enjoyable," said Abdul, walking back to the curtain, where he hesitated again. "If you have difficulty getting the book to me when you leave Egypt, return it to the man whose name and address are written in the flyleaf. I travel a lot and might not be in Cairo at the time." He smiled and walked through to the store. The heavy drapes snapped back into place.

Erica flipped through the guidebook, noting the plethora of drawings and fold-out maps. The description of the Temple of Karnak, given Baedeker's highest rating of four stars, was almost forty pages. It looked superb. The next chapter commenced with a series of copper engravings of Queen Hatshepsut's temple, followed by a long description, which Erica was particularly interested in reading. She slipped the snapshot of Abdul into the book, both to mark the place and to preserve the photograph, and put both into her tote bag.

Alone in the room, she let her attention wander back to the fabulous statue of Seti I. She had all she could do to keep herself from reaching over and lifting the veil to look at the curious row of hieroglyphics. She wondered if it would really be a violation of trust if she looked at the statue. Reluctantly she decided it would be, and she was about to take out the guidebook when she heard a definite change in the muffled conversation coming from the outer part of the shop. The voices weren't louder, but they sounded angry. At first she thought they were merely bargaining. Then the sound of shattering plate glass cut through the silence of the dimly lit room, followed by a scream that was quickly choked off. Erica felt a sensation of pure panic spread up from her chest and pound in her temples. A single voice recommenced, lower, more threatening.

As silently as possible, Erica moved over to the curtain, and imitating Abdul a few minutes earlier, spread the edges to look into the outer part of the shop. The first thing she saw was the back of an Arab dressed in a ragged, dirty galabia, holding aside the beaded strings at the entranceway, apparently watching for intruders. Then, looking a little to the left, Erica stifled a scream. Abdul was pulled backward over the broken glass-topped counter by another Arab, also dressed in a torn, dirty galabia. In front of Abdul stood a third Arab, dressed in a clean white-and-brown-striped robe and a white turban, who was brandishing a gleaming scimitar. The light from the single overhead bulb reflected its razor-sharp edge as it was raised in front of Abdul's terrified face.

Before Erica could allow the curtain to hide the grisly scene, Abdul's head was yanked back and the scimitar was viciously drawn across the base of his neck, slicing through the soft tissues to the spine. A gasping sound escaped from the severed windpipe before the spurting bright red blood drenched the area.

Erica's legs buckled and she dropped to her knees, the heavy drapes masking the sound of her fall. Terrified, she scanned the room for some concealment. The cabinets? There was no time to try to get inside. Pulling herself to her feet, she pressed into the far corner between the last cabinet and the wall. It was hardly a hiding place. At best it hid her own view, like a child covering his eyes in the dark. But the beak-nosed face of the man who had held Abdul down seemed burned in her mind. She kept picturing his cruel black eyes and his snarling mouth under his mustache, revealing sharp, gold-tipped teeth.

There was more commotion from the outer part of the shop, some sounds like the movement of furniture, followed by a terrifying silence. Time passed agonizingly slowly. Then Erica heard voices coming toward her. The men were entering the back room. She almost stopped breathing, her skin crawling with fear. The Arabic conversation was right behind her. She could feel the presence of the people, could hear them moving about. There were footsteps, a thud. Someone cursed in Arabic. Then the footsteps moved away and Erica heard the familiar crackling noises of the beads in the entranceway.

Erica let out her breath but stayed pressed into the corner as if she were poised on a ledge on a thousand-foot precipice. Time passed, but she had no idea if she had waited five minutes or fifteen. Silently she counted to fifty. Still no sounds. Slowly she turned her head and backed slightly away from the corner. The room was empty, her tote bag undisturbed on the carpet, her cup of tea waiting. But the magnificent statue of Seti I was gone!

The sound of beads hitting against each other in the entranceway sent a new chill plunging down Erica's spine. As she turned back toward the corner in a panic, her foot hit her unfinished tea. The glass fell over and tumbled free from its metal frame. The carpet absorbed the fluid and the sound until the glass rolled against the table with a dull thud. Erica pressed herself against the corner once again. She heard the heavy curtain yanked aside. Even though her eyes were closed, she could see the effect of natural light in the room. Then the light disappeared. She was alone with whoever was in the room. There were several muted noises and the sound of footsteps coming closer. She held her breath again.

Suddenly a hand with an iron grip grabbed her left arm and yanked her from the corner, pulling her stumbling into the center of the room.

Boston   8:00 A.M.

The sound of the alarm clock shattered Richard Harvey's dream, forcing him to acknowledge the arrival of another day. He had tossed and turned fitfully the whole night. The last time he remembered looking at the clock it was almost five A.M. He had twenty-seven scheduled patients that day at the office, and he felt like he'd been run over.

"Christ," he said angrily as he brought his fist down on the top of the alarm clock. The force of the blow not only compressed the snooze button but also popped out the plastic cover over the dial. It had happened before, and the cover could be easily replaced into its housing, but still it tended to symbolize for Richard his life of late. Things were out of control, and he was not used to that.

He swung his legs over the side of the bed and sat up, looking at the clock. Rather than deal with the alarm again, he bent over and yanked out the plug. The almost imperceptible grinding noise of the electric clock stopped. So did the sweep of the second hand. Next to the clock was a photo of Erica on skis. Instead of smiling, she was gazing into the camera with her full lower lip thrust out in that pouting expression that alternately enraged Richard and filled him with desire. He reached over and turned the picture around, breaking the spell. How could any girl as beautiful as Erica be in love with a civilization that had been dead more than three thousand years? Still, he missed her terribly, and she'd only been gone for two nights. How was he going to deal with four weeks?

Richard got up and padded to the toilet stark naked. At age thirty-four he was in very good shape. He'd always been athletic, even through medical school, and now that he'd been in private practice for three years, he still played tennis and racket ball regularly. His six-foot frame was lean and well-muscled. As Erica had told him, even his ass had definition.

From the bathroom he ventured into the kitchen, putting on water to boil and pouring a glass of juice. In the living room he opened the shutters that gave out onto Louisburg Square. The mid-October sunlight filtered down through the golden leaves of the elms, taking the chill off the air. Richard smiled wearily, deepening the lines at the corners of his eyes and accentuating his dimples. He was a pleasantly handsome man with a square, somewhat impish face under thick honey-colored hair. His blue eyes, deeply set, had a frequent twinkle.

"Egypt. Christ, it's like going to the moon," Richard said forlornly to the beautiful morning. "Why the hell did she have to go to Egypt?"

He showered, shaved, dressed, and breakfasted in a long-established, efficient pattern. The only interruption of the usual routine was his socks. He didn't have any clean socks, so he was forced to find some in the hamper. It was going to be a terrible day. Meanwhile, he could think of nothing but Erica. Finally, in desperation, he put a call through to Erica's mother in Toledo, with whom he got along splendidly. It was eight thirty and he knew he'd catch her before she left for work.

After some small talk, Richard got to the point.

"Have you heard from Erica yet?"

"My God, Richard, she'd only been gone a day."

"True. I just thought there was a chance. I'm worried about her. I don't understand what's going on. Everything was fine until we started talking about marriage."

"Well, you should have done it a year ago."

"I couldn't have done it a year ago. My practice was just getting started."

"Of course you could have. You just didn't want to then. It's that simple. And if you're worried about her now, you should have kept her from going to Egypt."

"I tried."

"If you had tried, Richard, she'd be in Boston right now."

"Janice, I really tried. I told her that if she went to Egypt I didn't know what would happen to our relationship. It was going to be different."

"And what did she say to that?"

"She said she was sorry, but that it was important for her to go."

"It's a stage, Richard. She'll get over it. You're just going to have to relax."

"I'm sure you're right, Janice. At least I hope so. If you hear from her, let me know."

Richard hung up the phone, acknowledging that he didn't feel much better. In fact, he felt a certain panic, as if Erica was slipping away from him. Impulsively he called TWA and checked on connections to Cairo, as if the mere act of doing so would make him feel closer. It didn't, and he was already late for the office. Thinking of Erica enjoying herself while he was suffering a depression made him angry. But there was little he could do.

Cairo   3:30 P.M.

Erica had not been able to speak for some time. When she had looked up expecting to face the Arab killer, she had found herself standing in front of a European dressed in an expensive three-piece beige suit. They had looked at each other for what seemed like an eternity, both confused. But Erica was also terrified. As a result, it had taken a quarter of an hour for Yvon Julien de Margeau to convince her that he meant her no harm. Even then Erica had trouble speaking, because she was trembling so violently. Finally, and with great difficulty, she had communicated to Yvon that Abdul was in the outer part of the shop, either dead or dying. Yvon, who had explained that the shop had been empty when he entered, agreed to check after loudly insisting that Erica sit down. He returned quickly.

"There is no one in the shop," said Yvon. "There is broken glass and some blood on the floor. But there is no body."

"I want to get away from here," said Erica. It was her first whole sentence.

"Of course," soothed Yvon. "But first tell me what happened."

"I want to go to the police," continued Erica. The trembling recommenced. When she closed her eyes, she saw the image of the knife cutting into Abdul's throat. "I saw someone killed. Just a few moments ago. It was terrible. I've never even seen someone injured. Please, I want to go to the police!"

With her mind beginning to function, Erica looked at the

man in front of her. Tall and thin, he was in his late thirties, with a tanned and angular face. There was an air of authority about him, heightened by the intense blue of his hooded eyes. More than anything else, after seeing the ragged Arabs, Erica was reassured by his impeccable tailoring.

"I had the misfortune of watching a man murdered," she said at length. "I looked out through the curtain and saw three men. One was in the doorway, another was holding the old man, and the other . . ."Erica had trouble continuing—"and the other slit the old man's throat."

"I see," said Yvon thoughtfully. "What were these three men wearing?"

"I'm not sure you do see," said Erica, raising her voice. "What were they wearing? I'm not talking about some purse-snatchers. I'm trying to tell you that I saw a man murdered. Murdered!"

"I believe you. But were these men Arabic or European?"

"They were Arab, dressed in galabias. Two of them were filthy, the other appeared considerably better off. My God, to think I came here for a vacation." Erica shook her head and began to get up.

"Could you recognize them?" asked Yvon calmly. He put his hand on Erica's shoulder, both to reassure her and to encourage her to remain seated.

"I'm not sure. It happened so fast. Maybe I could recognize the man with the knife. I don't know. I never did see the face of the man by the door." Raising her hand, Erica was amazed to see how violently it was trembling. "I'm not sure I believe any of this myself. I was talking with Abdul, who owns the store. In fact, we had been talking for some time, drinking tea. He was full of wit, a real person. God . . ." Erica ran her fingers through her hair. "And you say there's no body out there?" Erica pointed through the curtain. "There really was a murder."

"I believe you," said Yvon. His hand still rested on Erica's shoulder, and she felt curiously comforted.

"But why would they take the body, too?" asked Erica.

"What do you mean, too?"

"They took a statue that was right here," said Erica,

pointing. "It was a fabulous statue of an ancient Egyptian pharoah—"

"Seti I," interjected Yvon. "That crazy old man had the Seti statue here!" Yvon rolled his eyes in disbelief.

"You knew about the statue?" asked Erica.

"I did. In fact, I was coming here specifically to discuss it with Hamdi. How long ago did all this happen?"

"I'm not sure. Fifteen, twenty minutes. When you came in, I thought you were the killers returning."

"*Merde*," said Yvon, pulling away from Erica to pace the room. He took off his beige jacket and dropped it on one of the cushions. "So close." He stopped pacing, turning back to Erica. "Did you actually see the statue?"

"Yes, I did. It was unbelievably beautiful, by far the most impressive piece I've ever seen. Even the finest of Tutankhamen's treasures could not compare. It showed the heights that New Kingdom craftsmanship had reached by the nineteenth dynasty."

"Nineteenth dynasty? How did you know that?"

"I'm an Egyptologist," said Erica, regaining some of her composure.

"An Egyptologist? You do not look like an Egyptologist."

"And how is an Egyptologist supposed to look?" asked Erica testily.

"Okay, let us just say that I would not have guessed," Yvon said. "Was your being an Egyptologist the reason Hamdi showed you the statue?"

"I presume so."

"Still, it was foolish. Very foolish. I cannot understand why he would be willing to take such risks. Do you have any idea what the value of that statue is?" asked Yvon almost angrily.

"Priceless," returned Erica. "It is all the more reason to go to the police. That statue is an Egyptian national treasure. As an Egyptologist I am aware of the black market in antiquities, but I had no idea that pieces of such value were involved. Something has to be done!"

"Something has to be done!" Yvon laughed cynically. "American self-righteousness. The biggest market for antiquities is America. If the objects could not be sold, there would be no black market. It is the buyer who is ultimately at fault."

"*American* self-righteousness!" said Erica indignantly. "What about the French? How can you say something like that, knowing that the Louvre is brimming with priceless objects, essentially stolen, like the Zodiac from the Temple of Dendera? People travel thousands of miles to come to Egypt, and end up looking at a plaster cast of the Zodiac."

"It was safer for the Zodiac stone to remove it," said Yvon.

"Come on, Yvon. You can think of a better excuse than that. It had a certain validity in the past, but not today." Erica couldn't believe that she had recovered enough to involve herself in a nonsensical argument. She also noticed that Yvon was incredibly attractive and that she was baiting him into some kind of emotional response.

"Okay," said Yvon coolly, "we agree in principle. The black market must be controlled. But we disagree in method. For instance, I do not think we should go immediately to the police."

Erica was shocked.

"So you disagree?" asked Yvon.

"I'm not sure," stammered Erica, frustrated by her own transparency.

"I understand your concern. Let me explain to you where you are. I'm not trying to be patronizing, just realistic. This is Cairo, not New York or Paris or even Rome. I say that because even Italy is run incredibly efficiently when compared with Egypt, which is saying a lot. Cairo suffers from a gargantuan bureaucracy. Oriental intrigue and bribery are the rule, not the exception. If you go to the police with your story, you will be the prime suspect. Consequently, you will be jailed or at the very least placed under house arrest. Six months to a year could go by before even the appropriate papers are filled out. Your life will be pure hell." Yvon paused. "Am I making any sense? I'm telling you this for your own protection."

"Who are you?" asked Erica, reaching for her bag to get a cigarette. In truth, she did not really smoke; Richard hated it when she did, and she'd purchased a carton of cigarettes in the duty-free shop as a gesture of rebellion. But at the moment, she wanted to do something with her hands.

Watching her fumble in her bag, Yvon took out a gold case and held it open. Erica took a cigarette self-consciously. He lit it with a gold Dior lighter, then took one for himself. They smoked in silence for a few moments. Erica puffed without inhaling.

"I am what you call in your country a concerned citizen," said Yvon, brushing back his dark brown hair, which was already neatly in place. "I have deplored the destruction of antiquities and archaeological sites, and I've decided to do something about it. Knowledge of this Seti I statue was the biggest . . . what do you say . . ." Yvon searched for a word.

Erica tried to help by suggesting "find."

Yvon shook his head, but he moved his hand in a circle to encourage Erica. Erica shrugged and suggested "break."

"To solve a mystery," added Yvon, "you need a . . ."

"Clue or lead," said Erica.

"Ah, lead. Yes. It was the biggest lead. But now, I don't know. The statue may be gone forever. Maybe you can help if you could identify the killer, but here in Cairo it will be difficult. And if you go to the police, it will be definitely impossible."

"How did you learn about the statue in the first place?" asked Erica.

"From Hamdi himself. I'm sure he wrote to a number of people besides me," said Yvon, looking around the room. "I came here as soon as possible. In fact, I arrived in Cairo only a few hours ago." He walked over to one of the large wooden cabinets and pulled open the door. It was filled with small artifacts. "It would be helpful if his correspondence was here," said Yvon, picking up a small wooden mummy figure. "Most of these pieces are fake," he added.

"There are letters in that chest," said Erica, pointing.

Yvon followed Erica's finger and walked over and opened the chest.

"Very good," said Yvon, pleased. "Perhaps there will be something in this material to help us. But I'd like to make certain there isn't more correspondence hidden here." He walked to the curtain and pulled it open. A small amount of daylight entered the area. "Raoul," Yvon called loudly. The beads in the entranceway clacked. Yvon held open the curtain and Raoul entered.

He was younger than Yvon, in his late twenties, with olive skin and black hair and a carefree air of self-assured masculinity. He reminded Erica of Jean-Paul Belmondo.

Yvon introduced him, explaining that he was from the south of France and that though he spoke fluent English, his heavy accent made him a little hard to understand. Raoul shook Erica's hand and smiled broadly. Then, ignoring Erica, the two men conversed rapidly in French before beginning to search the shop to see if there were any more records.

"This will take only a few minutes, Erica," said Yvon, carefully going through one of the upright cabinets.

Erica sank to one of the large cushions in the center of the room. She felt numbed by the whole experience. She knew that searching the premises was illegal, but she did not protest. Instead she vacantly watched the two men. They had finished with the cabinets and were starting to take down all the carpets hanging on the walls.

While they worked, their differences were apparent. It was more than physical appearance. It was the way they moved and handled things. Raoul was blunt and direct, often relying on sheer strength. Yvon was careful and contemplative. Raoul was in constant motion, often bending, his head slightly drooped between his powerful shoulders. Yvon stood erect, and he regarded objects from a comfortable distance. He had rolled up his sleeves, revealing smooth forearms that emphasized his small sculptured hands. All at once Erica recognized what was so different about Yvon. He had the sheltered, pampered look of a nineteenth-century aristocrat. An air of elegant authority hovered over him like a halo.

With her pulse still racing, Erica abruptly found sitting intolerable. She stood up and walked over to the heavy drapes. She wanted some air but realized she was reluctant to look into the outer part of the shop, despite Yvon's assurance that the body was gone. Finally she reached out and pulled open the curtain.

Erica screamed. Only two feet from her was a face that had whirled to look at her when she pulled open the curtain. There was a crash of pottery as the figure in the shop dropped his armload, obviously as frightened as Erica.

Raoul responded instantaneously, pushing past Erica into the front room. Yvon followed. The thief stumbled over the pottery and tried to reach the doorway, but Raoul was like a cat, and with a sharp karate chop between the shoulders brought the intruder to the floor. He rolled over, a boy about twelve.

Yvon took one look and walked back to Erica.

"Are you all right?" he asked softly.

Erica shook her head. "I'm not accustomed to this sort of thing." She was still holding onto the drapes, her head down.

"Take a look at this boy," said Yvon. "I want to be sure he wasn't one of the three." He put his arm around her, but she politely pushed him away.

"I'm okay," she said, realizing she had overreacted because she had suppressed her earlier fright and then exploded at this latest happening.

Taking a deep breath, she went over and looked down at the cowering child.

"No," she said simply.

Yvon spoke sharply in Arabic to the boy, who responded by scrambling to his feet and bolting through the entranceway, leaving the beaded strips dancing behind him. "The poverty in this place makes some of these people act like vultures. They sense when there is trouble."

"I want to leave," said Erica as calmly as possible. "I'm not sure where I want to go, but I want to get out of here. And I still feel the police should be told."

Yvon reached out and put a hand on Erica's shoulder. He spoke paternally. "The police can be informed, but without involving yourself. The decision is yours to make, but believe me, I know what I'm talking about. Egyptian jails rival those in Turkey."

Erica studied Yvon's steady eyes before looking down at her still-trembling hands. With the poverty and overwhelming disorder she'd already seen in Cairo, Yvon's comments made sense. "I want to return to my hotel."

"I understand," said Yvon. "But please allow us to accompany you, Erica. Just let me get the letters we've found. It will only be a moment." Both men disappeared through the heavy curtains.

Erica stepped over to the broken counter and stared at the mixture of shattered glass and dried blood. It was difficult to stifle a feeling of nausea, but with luck she quickly found what she was searching for—the fake scarab Abdul had given to her, the one that had been so exquisitely carved by his son. She slipped it into her pocket, at the same time gently touching the broken pottery on the floor with her toe. The two authentic antiques were among the rubble. After lasting six thousand years, they were broken needlessly, smashed on the floor of this pitiful shop by a twelve-year-old thief. The waste made her physically ill. Her gaze went back to the blood, and she had to close her eyes to check the tears. A sensitive human life snuffed out because of greed. Erica tried vainly to recall the appearance of the man who had wielded the scimitar. His features had been sharp, like the typical bedouin's, his skin the color of burnished bronze. But she could not form a definite mental image of the man. She opened her eyes again and looked around the shop. Anger began to supplant the incipient tears. She wanted to go to the police for Abdul Hamdi so that the killer would be brought to justice. But Yvon's admonition about the police in Cairo was undoubtedly correct. And if she couldn't even be sure she'd recognize the killer if she saw him again, then the risk of going to the police was not worth it.

Erica bent down and picked up one of the larger shards of pottery. Her expertise was in the past, and with impressive facility her mind conjured up the image of the Seti statue, with its alabaster-and-feldspar eyes. There was no doubt in her mind that the statue had to be recovered. She had never known that objects of such importance were involved in the black market.

Erica walked over to the curtain and drew it aside. Yvon and Raoul were in the process of rolling up the floor carpets. Yvon looked up and motioned that it would be only a moment longer. Erica watched them work. Yvon was obviously interested in trying to do something about the black market. The

French had done a great deal to curb looting of Egyptian treasures, at least the stuff they didn't carry off to the Louvre. If her not going to the police could help recover the statue, then perhaps it was the best thing to do. Erica decided she'd go along with Yvon, but she knew there was a degree of rationalization in her thinking.

Leaving Raoul to replace the carpets, Yvon guided Erica out of Antica Abdul. Moving through the Khan el Khalili with Yvon was a totally different experience than trying to walk through it alone. No one bothered her. As if trying to distract her from the events of the last hour, Yvon talked continuously about the bazaar and about Cairo. He was obviously quite familiar with the history of the city. He had removed his tie, and his shirt was open at the collar.

"How about a bronze head of Nefertiti?" he asked, holding up one of the ugly tourist souvenirs he had taken from a vendor's cart.

"Never!" said Erica, horrified. She remembered the scene after the molester had attacked her.

"You must have one," said Yvon, beginning to bargain in Arabic. Erica tried to interfere, but he bought the statue and gave it to her with great ceremony. "A souvenir of Egypt to cherish. The only problem is, I believe they are made in Czechoslovakia."

Smiling, Erica took the small statue. The charm of Cairo began to filter through the heat, dirt, and poverty, and she relaxed a little.

The narrow alleyway on which they were walking opened up and they stepped into the sunlight of the Al Azhar square. With a cacophony of auto horns, traffic had come to a standstill. To the right Yvon pointed out an exotic building with a square minaret and surmounted by five onion-shaped turrets. Then he turned her around. To the left, almost concealed by the traffic and an open market, was the entrance to the famous Al Azhar mosque. They walked toward the mosque, and the closer they got, the easier it became to appreciate the elaborate entrance with its two arches and intricate arabesque decorations. It was the first example of medieval Muslim architecture Erica had approached since her arrival. In truth, she did not know much about Islam, and the buildings had a particularly exotic feel for her. Yvon sensed her interest and pointed out the various minarets, particularly those with domes and stone filagree. He continued a running commentary on the mosque's history, including which sultans had added to it.

Erica tried to concentrate on Yvon's monologue, but it became impossible. The area directly in front of the building served as a busy market and was jammed with people. Besides, her mind kept returning to Abdul and the image of his sudden and horrible death. When Yvon changed the subject, Erica did not respond. He had to say again: "This is my car. May I give you a lift to your hotel?" It was a black Egyptian-built Fiat, relatively new, but with a full complement of dents and scrapes. "It is not a Citroën, but it is okay."

Erica was momentarily flustered. She had not expected a private auto. A taxi would have been fine; she liked Yvon, but he was a stranger in a strange land. Her eyes betrayed her thoughts.

"Please understand my position," said Yvon. "I feel that you were caught in a very unfortunate circumstance. I am glad I happened by, wishing only that I'd been twenty minutes earlier. I merely want to help you. Cairo can be difficult, and with the kind of experience you've had, it could be over-whelming. At this time of day you will not catch a taxi. There simply are not enough. Let me give you a ride to your hotel."

"What about Raoul?" asked Erica, trying to stall.

Yvon unlocked the passenger door and opened it. Instead of trying to pressure Erica, he walked over to a turbaned Arab who had been apparently watching the car, spoke some words of Arabic, and dropped a few coins in the man's open palm. Then he opened the driver's door and got in, leaning across to smile up at Erica. His blue eyes appeared soft in the afternoon sun. "Don't worry about Raoul. He can take care of himself. It's you I am worried about. If you have the fortitude to wander around Cairo by yourself, you certainly shouldn't mind riding with me as far as your hotel. But if not, tell me where you are staying and I'll meet you there in the lobby. I'm not ready to give up on this Seti I statue, and you may be able to help."

Yvon busied himself with his seat belt. Erica glanced around the square, sighed, and got into the car. "The Hilton," she said.

The ride was not relaxing. Prior to pulling away from the curb, Yvon had donned soft kid driving gloves, pulling the leather over each finger with great care. When he did put the car in gear, it was with a vengeance, and the small auto leaped into the traffic with squealing wheels. Because of the snarled traffic, the brakes had to be applied immediately, with the result that Erica had to brace herself against the dash. And so the ride continued in sudden fits and stops, throwing Erica forward and backward. They went from what she thought was one near-accident to the next, often clearing other autos, trucks, donkey carts, and even buildings by millimeters. Animals and people fled before them as Yvon, gripping the steering wheel with both hands, drove as if he were engaged in a competitive sport. He was determined and aggressive, although he did not become angry or exasperated at the performance of others. If another car or cart snaked in front of him, he did not mind. He would wait patiently until a slot opened, then race forward.

They headed southwest out of the bustling center, passing the remains of the old city walls and the magnificent citadel of Saladin. Within the citadel the domes and minarets of the Muhammad Ali mosque soared heavenward in a bold affirmation of the worldly power of Islam. They reached the Nile at the level of the northern tip of the island of Roda. Turning to the right, they headed up the broad avenue that ran along the east bank of the mighty river. The sparkling cool blue of the water, reflecting the afternoon sunlight in a million diamonds, provided a refreshing contrast to the heat and squalor of downtown Cairo. When Erica had first seen the Nile the day before, she had been impressed by its history and the fact that its waters came from distant equatorial Africa. Today she could really understand that Cairo and all of inhabited Egypt could not exist without the river. The oppressive dust and heat proclaimed the power and harshness of the desert that pressed constantly at Cairo's back door, threatening like a plague.

Yvon drove directly to the front entrance of the Hilton. Leaving the keys in the car, he managed to beat the turbaned doorman to the passenger side and chivalrously helped Erica out of the car. Erica, who had just witnessed the most violent scenes of her life, smiled at the unexpected gallantry. Coming from America, she was unaccustomed to seeing such an obviously masculine man concerned with the details of courtesy. It was a unique European combination, and one which, even exhausted as she was, Erica could not help but find charming.

"I will wait for you if you would like to go to your room and freshen up before we talk," said Yvon as they entered the busy lobby. The afternoon international flights had arrived.

"I think I need a drink first," said Erica without a moment's hesitation.

The temperature of the air-conditioned cocktail lounge was delicious, like sliding into a pool of crystal water. They sat in a corner booth and ordered. When the drinks came, Erica held the frosted glass of her vodka and tonic to her cheek for a moment to appreciate its coolness.

Looking at Yvon calmly sipping his Pernod, she realized how quickly he could adapt to his environment. He was as comfortable within the depths of the Khan el Khalili as he was in the Hilton. There was the same confidence, the same control. Looking more carefully at his clothes, Erica recognized how fastidiously they were tailored to his body. Comparing their elegance to Richard's unchanging Brooks Brothers look made her smile, but she knew that Richard was not interested in clothes and that the comparison wasn't fair.

Erica took a taste of her drink and began to relax. She took another sip, a bigger one, and breathed in deeply before swallowing. "God, what an experience," she said. She rested her head in her hand and massaged her temples. Yvon remained silent. After a few minutes she sat up and straightened her shoulders. "What are you going to do about the Seti statue?"

"I'm going to try to find it," said Yvon. "I must find it before it gets out of Egypt. Did Abdul Hamdi say anything to you about where it was going? Anything?"

"Only that it was in the shop for a few hours and it would soon resume its journey. Nothing else."

"About a year ago, a similar statue appeared and—"

"What do you mean, similar?" asked Erica excitedly.

"It was a gilded statue of Seti I," said Yvon.

"Did you actually see it, Yvon?"

"No. If I had, it would not be in Houston today. It was bought by an oil man through a bank in Switzerland. I tried to trace it, but Swiss banks are very uncooperative. I got nowhere."

"Do you know if the Houston statue had hieroglyphics carved in the base?" asked Erica.

Yvon shook his head while lighting a Gauloise. "I haven't the slightest idea. Why do you ask?"

"Because the statue I saw had hieroglyphics cut into the base," said Erica, warming to the subject. "And the thing that caught my eye was the fact that there were the names of two pharaohs. Seti I and Tutankhamen!"

Inhaling deeply on his cigarette, Yvon regarded Erica questioningly. His thin lips pressed together tightly as he blew the smoke from his nostrils.

"Hieroglyphics are my specialty," said Erica defensively.

"It's impossible for Seti's and Tutankhamen's names to be on the same statue," said Yvon flatly.

"It is strange," continued Erica, "but there is no doubt in my mind. Unfortunately, I did not have time to translate the rest. My first thought was that the statue was a fake."

"It was no fake," said Yvon. "Hamdi would not have been killed for a fake. Couldn't you have mistaken Tutankhamen's name for another?"

"Never," said Erica. She found a pen in her bag, drew the coronation name of Tutankhamen on her cocktail napkin, and pushed it toward Yvon defiantly. "That was carved in the base of the statue I saw."

Looking at the drawing, Yvon smoked in thoughtful silence. Erica watched him.

"Why was the old man killed?" she said finally. "That's what seems so senseless. If they wanted the statue, they could have taken it. Hamdi was there by himself."

"I have no idea," admitted Yvon, looking up from the drawing of Tutankhamen's name. "Perhaps it has something to do with the curse of the pharaohs." He smiled. "About a year ago I'd traced a route for Egyptian antiquities to a middleman in Beirut, who obtained the pieces from Egyptian pilgrims going to Mecca. No sooner had I made the contact than the gentleman was killed. I'm wondering if it has something to do with me!"

"Do you think he was killed for the same reasons as Abdul Hamdi?" asked Erica.

"No. Actually, he was caught between Christian and Muslim bullets. Still, I was on my way to see him when it happened."

"It is such a senseless tragedy," said Erica sadly, again thinking of Abdul.

"It is indeed," agreed Yvon. "But remember, Hamdi was no innocent bystander and he knew the stakes. That statue was priceless, and in the middle of all this poverty, money can move mountains. That's the real reason it would be a mistake for you to go to the authorities. It's hard to find someone you can trust under the best of circumstances, and when that kind of money is involved, the police themselves may not act with honesty."

"I'm not sure what I should do," said Erica. "But what are your plans, Yvon?"

Taking another draw on his Gauloise, he let his gaze wander around the tastelessly decorated lounge. "Hopefully, there will be some information in Hamdi's correspondence. It's not much, but it's a start. I've got to find out who killed him." Turning back to Erica, his face took on a more serious expression. "I very well might need you to make the final identification. Would you do that?"

"Of course, if I can," said Erica. "I really didn't get a very good look at the killers, but I'd really like to help." Erica thought about what she'd said. The words sounded so trite. But Yvon did not seem to notice. Instead, he reached across and gently grasped her wrist.

"I am very pleased," he said warmly. "Now I must go. I'm

staying at the Meridien Hotel, suite 800. That's on the island of Roda." Yvon paused, but his hand still lightly gripped Erica's wrist. "I would be quite happy if you would agree to have dinner with me tonight. This day must have given you a terrible impression of Cairo, and I would like to show you the other side."

The unexpected offer flattered Erica. Yvon was unreasonably charming and could probably dine with any one of a thousand women. His interest was obviously the statue, but her own reactions were confusing.

"Thank you, Yvon, but I'm exhausted. I'm still suffering from jet lag, and I didn't sleep well yesterday. Some other night, perhaps."

"We could have an early dinner. I'll have you back here by ten. After your experience today, I just don't think you should be sitting in your hotel room by yourself."

Looking at her watch, Erica saw that it was not quite six P.M.. Ten would not be too late, and she had to eat anyway.

"If it would not be a bother to have me back by ten, then I'd like to have dinner with you."

Yvon tightened his grip on her wrist for an instant, then let go. "*Entendu*," he said, and motioned for the check.

Boston 11:00 A.M.

Richard Harvey looked down at the corpulent bulk of Henrietta Olson's abdomen. The upper and lower sheets had been separated to expose the area of the gall bladder. The rest of Henrietta's body was covered to preserve her dignity.

"Now, Mrs. Olson, please point to where you felt the pain," said Richard.

A hand snaked out from beneath the sheets. With her index finger Henrietta indented her belly just under the right rib cage.

"And also back here, Doctor," said Henrietta, rolling over on her right side and jabbing her finger in the middle of her back. "Right about here," said Henrietta, poking Richard with her finger at the level of his kidney.

Richard rolled his eyes so that only Nancy Jacobs, his office nurse, could see, but she shook her head, feeling that Richard was being unusually short with his patients.

Richard looked up at the clock. He knew he had three more patients to see before lunch. Although his three-year-old practice of internal medicine was doing amazingly well and he liked his work, some days were a little trying. Problems relating to smoking and obesity comprised ninety percent of his cases. It was a far cry from the intellectual intensity of his residency at the general. And now, on top of this problem, was the situation with Erica. It made concentrating on problems like Henrietta's gall bladder almost impossible.

There was a quick knock, and Sally Marinski, the receptionist, poked her head in. "Doctor, your call is on one." Richard's face brightened. He'd asked Sally to ring up Janice Baron, Erica's mother.

"Excuse me, Mrs. Olson," said Richard. "I must take this call. I'll be right back." He motioned for Nancy to stay.

Closing the door to his office, Richard picked up the phone and pressed the connecting button.

"Hello, Janice."

"Richard, Erica hasn't written yet."

"Thanks a lot. I know she hasn't written yet. The reason I called is to tell you I'm really going crazy. I want to know what you think I should do."

"I don't think you have a lot of choices right now, Richard. You're just going to have to wait until Erica gets back."

"Why do you think she went?" asked Richard.

"I haven't the faintest idea. I've never understood this Egypt thing, right from the time she announced that she was going to major in it. If her father hadn't died, he would have been able to talk some sense into her."

Richard paused before speaking. "I mean, I'm glad she has interests, but a hobby should not threaten the rest of your life."

"I agree, Richard."

There was another pause, and Richard absentmindedly toyed with his desk set. He had a question for Janice, but he was afraid to ask.

"What do you think of me going to Egypt?" he said finally.

There was a silence.

"Janice?" said Richard, wondering if the connection had been broken.

"Egypt! Richard, you can't leave your office like that."

"It would be difficult, but if it's necessary, I can do it. I can get coverage."

"Well . . . maybe it's a good idea. But I don't know. Erica has always had a mind of her own. Did you talk to her about going?"

"No, we never discussed it. I think she just assumed I couldn't leave right now."

"Maybe it would show her that you care," said Janice thoughtfully.

"Know that I care! My God, she knows I put a down payment on that house in Newton."

"Well, that may not be exactly what Erica has in mind, Richard. I do think that the problem is that you dragged your feet too long, so maybe going to Egypt is a good idea."

"I don't know what I'll do, but thanks, Janice."

Richard replaced the receiver and looked on his blotter at the patient list for the afternoon. It was going to be a long day.

Cairo 9:10 P.M.

Erica leaned back as the two attentive waiters cleared away their dishes. Yvon had been so crisp and short with them that Erica had almost been embarrassed, but it was obvious that Yvon was accustomed to efficient servants with whom, the less said, the better. They had dined sumptuously by candle-light on spicy local dishes that Yvon had ordered with great authority. The restaurant was romantically although inappropriately called the Casino de Monte Bello, and it was situated on the crest of the Mukattam Hills. From where Erica was sitting on the veranda she could look east into the rugged Arabian mountains that ran across the Arabian peninsula to China. To the north she could see the spreading veins of the delta as the Nile fanned out searching for the Mediterranean, and to the south she could see the river coming from the heart of Africa like a flat, shiny snake. But by far the most impressive vista was to the west, where the minarets and domes of Cairo thrust their heads through the mist that covered the city. Stars were emerging in the darkening silver sky just like the lights of the city below. Erica was obsessed with images of the Arabian Nights. The city projected an exotic, sensuous, and mysterious quality that forced the sordid events of the day to recede.

"Cairo has a very powerful, bitter charm," said Yvon. His face was lost in the shadows until the ember of his cigarette became fiery red as he inhaled, illuminating his sharply cut features. "It has such an unbelievable history. The corruption, the brutalities, the continuity of violence, are so fantastic, so grotesque as to defy comprehension.

"Has it changed much?" asked Erica, thinking of Abdul Hamdi.

"Less than people think. The corruption is a way of life. The poverty is the same."

"And bribery?" asked Erica.

"That hasn't changed at all," said Yvon, carefully tapping his cigarette over the ashtray.

Erica took a sip of wine. "You've convinced me not to go to the police. I really have no idea if I could identify the killers of Mr. Hamdi, and the last thing I want to do is get caught up in a morass of Asian intrigue."

"It's the smartest thing you can do. Believe me."

"But it still bothers me. I can't help but feel I'm shirking my responsibility as a human being. I mean, to see a murder and then not do anything. But you think that my not going to the police will help your crusade against the black market?"

"Absolutely. If the authorities find out about this Seti statue before I can locate it, then any chance of its helping me penetrate the black market will be lost." Yvon reached over and reassuringly squeezed her hand.

"While you're trying to find the statue, will you try to find out who killed Abdul Hamdi?" Erica asked.

"Of course," said Yvon. "But don't misunderstand me. My motive is the statue and controlling the black market. I don't fool myself into thinking I will be able to influence moral attitudes here in Egypt. But if I do find the killers, I will alert the authorities. Will that help assuage your conscience?"

"It will," said Erica.

Immediately below, lights came on, illuminating the citadel. The castle fascinated Erica, evoking images of the Crusades.

"One thing you said this afternoon surprised me," she said, turning back to Yvon. "You mentioned the 'Curse of the Pharaohs.' Surely you don't believe in such nonsense."

Yvon smiled, but allowed the waiter to serve the aromatic Arabic coffee before speaking. "Curse of the Pharaohs! Let's say I don't dismiss such ideas totally. The ancient Egyptians spent great efforts on preserving their dead. They were

72

renowned for their interest in the occult, and they were experts with all sorts of poisons. *Alors . . .*" Yvon sipped his coffee. "Many of the people dealing with treasures from pharaonic tombs have died mysteriously. There's no doubt about that."

"The scientific community has a lot of doubt," said Erica.

"Certainly the press has been quick to exaggerate various stories, but there have been some very curious deaths related to Tutankhamen's tomb, starting with Lord Carnarvon himself. There has to be something to it; how much, I do not know. The reason I mentioned the curse was that it seems two merchants who were good 'leads,' as you say, were killed just prior to my meeting with them. Coincidence? Probably."

After their coffee they strolled along the crest of the mountain to a hauntingly beautiful ruined mosque. They didn't speak. The beauty cradled and awed them. Yvon offered his hand as they climbed over some rocks to stand within the towering roofless walls of the once-proud building. Above, the Milky Way was splattered against the midnight-blue sky. For Erica the magical charm of Egypt lay in its past, and there in the darkness of the medieval ruins she could feel it.

On the way back to the car, Yvon put his arm around her, but he continued to talk placidly about the mosque and deposited her at the entrance to the Hilton very close to ten o'clock, as promised. Still, riding up in the elevator, Erica admitted to herself that she was mildly infatuated. Yvon was a charming and devilishly attractive man.

Reaching her room, she inserted the key, opened the door, and flipped on the light, dropping her tote bag on the luggage rack in the small foyer. She closed the door and double-latched it. The air-conditioning was on full blast, and preferring not to sleep in an artificially cooled room, she headed toward the switch near the balcony to turn it off.

Halfway there she stopped and bit back a scream. A man was sitting in her easy chair in the corner of the room. He did not move or speak. He had pure bedouin features but was carefully dressed in a gray silk European suit, white shirt, and black tie. His total immobility and piercing eyes paralyzed her.

He was like a terrifying sculpture in deep bronze. Although back home Erica had fantasized how violently she would react if she were ever threatened with rape, now she did nothing. Her voice failed her; her arms hung limply.

"My name is Ahmed Khazzan," said the figure at last in a voice that was deep and fluid. "I am the director general of the Department of Antiquities of the Egyptian Arab Republic. I apologize for this intrusion, but it is necessary." Reaching into his jacket pocket, he extracted a black leather wallet. It fell open in his outstretched hand. "My official credentials, if you wish."

Erica's face blanched. She had wanted to go to the police. She knew she should have gone to the police. Now she was in very deep trouble. Why had she listened to Yvon? Still paralyzed by the man's hypnotic gaze, Erica could not speak.

"I am afraid you must come along with me, Erica Baron," said Ahmed, standing up and walking over to her. Erica had never seen such piercing eyes. In a face objectively as handsome as Omar Sharif's, they absorbed and terrified her.

Erica stammered incoherently, but managed to finally look away. Beads of cold sweat had appeared on her forehead. She could feel her underarms were damp. Having never been in trouble with any authorities anywhere, she was totally unnerved. Mechanically she put on a sweater and picked up her bag.

Ahmed remained silent as he opened the door into the hallway; his expression of intense concentration did not alter. Erica conjured up images of dank, horrible jail cells as she walked beside him through the lobby. Boston suddenly seemed very far away.

Ahmed waved at the entrance to the Hilton, and a black sedan pulled up. He opened the rear door and motioned for Erica to enter, which she did quickly, hoping that her cooperation would atone for her having failed to report Abdul's murder. As the car drove off, Ahmed maintained the oppressive and intimidating silence, fixing Erica from time to time with his unwavering gaze.

Erica's imagination raced in anxious circles. She thought about the United States embassy and the consulate. Should she demand the opportunity to call, and if so, what would she say? Looking out the car window, she noticed the city was still very much alive with other vehicles and pedestrians, although the great river looked like a pool of stagnant black ink.

"Where are you taking me?" asked Erica, her voice sounding strange, even to herself.

Ahmed did not answer immediately. Erica was about to ask again when he spoke. "To my office in the Ministry of Public Works. It is a short ride."

True to his word, the black sedan soon pulled off the main street into a semicircle of concrete in front of a pillared government building. A night watchman opened the massive entrance door as they mounted the steps.

Then began a walk that seemed as long as the ride from the Hilton. With only the hollow sounds of their shoes on the stained marble floor, they crossed a bewildering number of deserted corridors, leading them deeper and deeper into the labyrinthine reaches of a prodigious bureaucracy. At last they reached the proper office. Ahmed unlocked the door and led the way through the anteroom jammed with metal desks and antique typewriters. Entering a spacious office beyond, he indicated a chair for Erica. It faced an old mahogany desk neatly arranged with carefully sharpened pencils and a new green blotter. Ahmed maintained his silence as he removed his silk jacket.

Erica felt like a cornered animal. She had expected to be taken to a room full of accusing faces where she would be subjected to the usual bureaucratic red tape, like fingerprinting. She had anticipated trouble over the fact that she did not have her passport, which the hotel people had demanded on registration, saying that it had to be stamped and would not be back for twenty-four hours. But this empty room was proving more frightening. Who would know where she was? She thought of Richard and her mother and wondered if she might make a long-distance call.

She glanced nervously around the office. It was Spartanly appointed and extremely tidy. Framed photos of various archaeological monuments adorned the walls, along with a modern poster of the funerary mask of Tutankhamen. Two large maps covered the right wall. One was of Egypt, and small red-topped pins had been inserted at various locations. The other map was of the Necropolis of Thebes, with the tombs marked with Maltese crosses.

Biting her lip to hide her anxiety, Erica looked back at Ahmed. To her surprise, he was busy with an electric hot plate.

"Would you care for some tea?" he asked, turning around.

"No, thank you," said Erica, numbed by the weird circumstances. Gradually her mind began to suggest that she had jumped to conclusions, and she thanked heaven that she had not blurted out a confession before hearing what the Arab had to say.

Ahmed poured himself a cup of tea and brought it over to the desk. Slowly stirring in two sugars, he once more brought his powerful gaze to bear on Erica. She quickly lowered her eyes to avoid the impact, speaking without looking up. "I would like to know why I have been brought to this office."

Ahmed didn't answer. Erica looked up to make sure he'd heard her, and as their eyes met, Ahmed's voice lashed out like a whip.

"I want to know what you are doing in Egypt," he said, practically shouting.

His anger took Erica by surprise, and she stumbled over her words. "I'm . . . I'm here . . . I'm an Egyptologist."

"And you are Jewish, aren't you?" snapped Ahmed.

Erica was smart enough to realize that Ahmed was trying to push her off balance, but she wasn't sure she was strong enough to resist his attack. "Yes," she said simply.

"I want to know why you are in Egypt," repeated Ahmed, raising his voice again.

"I came here—" said Erica defensively.

"I want to know what the purpose of your trip is and who you work for."

"I don't work for anyone, and there was no purpose for my trip," said Erica nervously.

"You expect me to believe there was no purpose for your trip?" Ahmed said cynically. "Come, now, Erica Baron." He smiled, and his swarthy complexion enhanced the whiteness of his teeth.

"Of course there was a purpose," said Erica, her voice breaking. "What I meant was that I didn't come here for some ulterior motive." Her voice trailed off as she remembered her complicated problems with Richard.

"You are not convincing," said Ahmed. "Not at all."

"I'm sorry," said Erica. "I'm an Egyptologist. I've studied about ancient Egypt for eight years. I work in an Egyptology department in a museum. I've always wanted to come. I had had plans to come years ago, but my father's death made it impossible. It wasn't until this year that I could manage it. I've made arrangements to do a little work while I'm here, but mostly it is a vacation."

"What kind of work?"

"I plan to do some on-site translation of New Kingdom hieroglyphics in Upper Egypt."

"You're not here to buy antiquities?"

"Heavens, no," said Erica.

"How long have you known Yvon Julien de Margeau?" He leaned forward, his eyes riveted to Erica's.

"I met him for the first time today," Erica blurted.

"How did you meet?"

Her pulse quickened, and perspiration reappeared on her forehead. Did Ahmed know about the murder after all? A moment earlier she would have said no, but now she wasn't certain. "We met in the bazaar," stammered Erica. She held her breath.

"Do you know that Monsieur de Margeau has been known to purchase valuable Egyptian national treasures?"

Erica was afraid her relief was apparent. Obviously Ahmed did not know about the murder. "No," she said. "I had no idea."

"Do you have any comprehension," continued Ahmed, "of the extent of the problem we face trying to stop the black market in antiquities?" He stood up and walked over to the map of Egypt.

"I have some idea," said Erica, confounded by the multiple directions of the conversation. She still did not know why she had been brought to Ahmed's office.

"The situation is very bad," said Ahmed. "Take, for instance, the highly destructive theft in 1974 of ten slabs of hieroglyphic relief from the Temple of Dendera. A tragedy, a national disgrace." Ahmed's index finger rested on the red-topped pin stuck in the map at the location of the Temple of Dendera. "It had to be an inside job. But the case was never broken. The poverty works against us here in Egypt." Ahmed's voice trailed off. His face reflected strain and commitment. Carefully his index finger touched the red tops of other pins. "Each one of these indicates a major antiquities theft. If I had a reasonable-sized staff, and if I had some money to pay the guards a decent wage, then I could do something about all this." Ahmed was speaking more to himself than to Erica. Turning, he seemed almost surprised to see her in his office. "What is Monsieur de Margeau doing in Egypt?" he asked, his anger returning.

"I don't know," said Erica. She thought about the Seti statue and Abdul Hamdi. She knew if she talked about the statue she'd have to talk about the murder.

"How long is he staying?"

"I haven't the faintest idea. I only met the man today."

"But you had dinner with him tonight."

"That's right," said Erica defensively.

Ahmed walked back toward the desk. He leaned forward and looked down threateningly into Erica's gray-green eyes. She could sense his intensity and tried to return his gaze, but without much success. She did feel a little more confident, realizing that Ahmed was interested in Yvon, not her, but she was still afraid. Besides, she had lied. She knew Yvon was there for the statue.

"What did you learn about Monsieur de Margeau during your dinner?"

"That he is a charming man," said Erica evasively.

Ahmed slammed his hand down on his desk, sending some of the carefully sharpened pencils flying and making Erica flinch.

"I'm not interested in his personality," said Ahmed slowly. "I want to know why Yvon de Margeau is in Egypt."

"Well, why don't you ask him?" said Erica finally. "All I did was go to dinner with the man."

"Do you often go to dinner with men you just meet?" asked Ahmed.

Erica studied Ahmed's face very carefully. The question surprised her, but then, almost everything had been surprising. His voice suggested a kind of disappointment, but Erica knew that was absurd.

"I very rarely go to dinner with strangers," she said defiantly, "but I felt immediately comfortable with Yvon de Margeau and I thought he was charming."

Ahmed walked over to his jacket and carefully put it on. Taking the last of his tea in a gulp, he looked back to Erica. "For your own good, I would ask you to keep this conversation confidential. Now I will take you back to your hotel."

Erica was more confused than ever. Watching Ahmed retrieve the pencils that had fallen from the desk, Erica suddenly was overcome with guilt. The man was obviously sincere in his desire to contain the black market in antiquities, and she was withholding information. At the same time, the experience with Ahmed was frightening; as Yvon had warned her, he certainly did not behave like any American officials she had known. She decided to let him take her back to the hotel without saying anything. After all, she could always contact him if she felt she had to.

Cairo 11:15 P.M.

Yvon Julien de Margeau had on a red silk Christian Dior robe tied loosely at the waist, exposing most of his silver-haired chest. The sliding glass doors of suite 800 were all open, allowing the cool desert breeze to rustle gently through the room. A table had been placed on the wide balcony, and from where Yvon was sitting he could look north across the Nile toward the delta. Gezira island, with its slender phallic observation tower, loomed in the mid-distance. On the right bank, Yvon could see the Hilton, and his mind kept returning to Erica. She was very different from any of the women he had known. He was both shocked and attracted by her passionate interest in Egyptology and was confused by her talk of career. After a moment he shrugged, considering her in the context with which he was most familiar. She was not the most beautiful woman he'd been with of late, and yet there was something about her that had suggested a subtle yet powerful sensuality.

On the center of the table Yvon had placed his attaché case filled with the voluminous papers he and Raoul had found at Abdul Hamdi's. Raoul was stretched out on the couch double-checking letters Yvon had already perused.

"*Alors,*" said Yvon suddenly, slapping the letter he was reading with his free hand. "Stephanos Markoulis. Hamdi corresponded with Markoulis! The travel agent from Athens."

"That could be what we are looking for," said Raoul

81

expectantly. "Do you think there is a threat involved?"

Yvon continued reading the text. After a few minutes he looked up. "Can't be sure of any threat. All he says is that he is interested in the matter and he would like to come to some sort of a compromise. But he doesn't say what the matter is."

"He could have been referring only to the Seti statue," said Raoul.

"Possibly, but my intuition says no. Knowing Markoulis, he would have been more direct if it only concerned the statue. It had to be more. Hamdi must have threatened him."

"If that's the case, Hamdi was no fool."

"He was the ultimate fool," said Yvon. "He's dead."

"Markoulis had also been in correspondence with our murdered contact in Beirut," said Raoul.

Yvon looked up. He had forgotten about Markoulis' connection with the Beirut contact. "I think Markoulis is where we should start. We know he deals in Egyptian antiquities. See if you can get a call through to Athens."

Raoul lifted himself from the couch and gave the orders to the hotel operator. After a minute he said, "Telephone traffic is surprisingly light tonight, or so the operator says. There should be no trouble with the call. For Egypt, that is a miracle."

"Good," said Yvon, reaching out to shut his attaché case. "Hamdi corresponded with every major museum in the world, but Markoulis is still a long shot. The only real hope we have is Erica Baron."

"And I don't see her being much help," said Raoul.

"I have an idea," said Yvon, lighting a cigarette. "Erica did see the faces of two of the three men involved in the killing."

"That might be so, but I doubt if she could recognize them again."

"True. But I don't think it matters, if the killers think she can."

"I'm not following you," said Raoul.

"Would it be possible to let the Cairo underworld know that Erica Baron watched the murder and can easily identify the killers?"

"Ah," said Raoul, his face reflecting sudden understanding.

"I see what you are thinking. Using Erica Baron as a decoy to flush the killers into the open."

"Precisely. There's no way the police are going to do anything about Hamdi. The Department of Antiquities won't do anything unless they've heard of the Seti statue, so Ahmed Khazzan won't be involved. He's the only official who could make it difficult for us."

"There's one major problem," said Raoul seriously.

"What is that?" asked Yvon, drawing on his cigarette.

"It's a very dangerous course. It probably means signing a death warrant for Mademoiselle Erica Baron. I'm sure they will kill her."

"Could one protect her?" asked Yvon, remembering Erica's narrow waist, her warmth, and her appealing earthiness.

"Probably, if we used the right person."

"Are you thinking of Khalifa?"

"I am."

"He's trouble."

"Yes, but he's the best. If you want to protect the girl plus get the killers, you need Khalifa. The real problem is that he's expensive. Very expensive."

"That I don't mind. I want and need that statue. I'm certain it will be the fulcrum I need. In fact, at this point I believe it's the only way. I've been through all of Abdul Hamdi's stuff that we have. Unfortunately, there is almost nothing about the black market."

"Did you really think there would be?"

"It was a little too much to ask, I admit. From what Hamdi said in his letter to me, I thought it was possible. But get Khalifa. I want him to start tailing Erica Baron in the morning. Also, I think I'll even spend some time with her myself. I'm not sure she's told me everything."

Raoul regarded Yvon with a disbelieving smile.

"Okay," said Yvon. "You know me too well. There's something I find very attractive about the woman."

Athens   11:45 P.M.

Reaching back over his shoulder, Stephanos Markoulis flipped off the lamp. The room was bathed in the soft blue glow of the moon that fell into the room through the French doors leading to the balcony.

"Athens is such a romantic city," said Deborah Graham, pulling away from Stephanos' embrace. Her eyes sparkled in the half-light. She was intoxicated by the atmosphere as well as the bottle of Demestica wine that lay empty on the nearby table. Her straight blond hair tumbled over her shoulders, and with a coquettish twist of her head she pulled it behind her ears. Her blouse was unbuttoned and the whiteness of her breasts contrasted sharply with her deep Mediterranean tan.

"I agree," said Stephanos. His large hand reached out to massage her breasts. "That's why I choose to live in Athens. Athens is for lovers." Stephanos had heard the expression from another girl on another night and had said to himself at the time that he wanted to use the phrase himself. Stephanos' shirt was also open, but it was always open. He had a broad chest covered with dark hair that served to set off his collection of solid gold chains and medallions.

Stephanos was very eager to get Deborah into his bed. He had always found Australian girls to be uncommonly easy and good lays. A number of people had told him that in Australia they acted very differently, but he did not care. He was content to ascribe his luck to the romantic atmosphere and his own prowess, but mostly the latter.

"Thank you for inviting me here, Stephanos," said Deborah sincerely.

"My pleasure," said Stephanos, smiling.

"Would you mind if I went out on your balcony for a moment?"

"Not at all," said Stephanos, silently groaning at the delay.

Holding her blouse together, Deborah bounced toward the French doors.

Stephanos watched the undulating movement of her buttocks beneath her faded jeans. He guessed she was about nineteen. "Don't get lost out there," he called.

"Stephanos, this balcony is only three feet wide."

"I see you pick up quickly on sarcasm," said Stephanos. All at once he felt a flicker of doubt whether Deborah was going to come through. Impatiently he lit a cigarette, blowing the smoke forcefully toward the ceiling.

"Stephanos, come out here and tell me what I'm looking at."

"Christ," said Stephanos to himself. Reluctantly he got up and joined her. Deborah was leaning as far out as possible, pointing down Ermon Street.

"Is that Constitution Square I can just see?"

"That's right."

"And that's the corner of the Parthenon," said Deborah, pointing in the opposite direction.

"You've got it."

"Oh, Stephanos, this is beautiful." Gazing up at him, she put her arms around his neck and looked into his broad face. She had been excited by his appearance from the first moment he'd stopped her in the Plaka. He had deep laugh lines, which gave his face character, and a heavy beard that Deborah thought enhanced his masculinity.

She was still a little afraid of having agreed to come to this stranger's apartment, yet there was something about being in Athens and not Sydney that made it all right. Besides, the fear added to the mood, and she was already incredibly excited.

"What kind of work do you do, Stephanos?" she asked, the delay increasing her anticipation.

"Does it matter?"

"I'm just interested. But you don't have to tell me."

"I own a travel agency, Aegean Holidays, and I do some smuggling on the side. But mostly I chase women."

"Oh, Stephanos. Be serious."

"I am. I have a comfortable travel business, but I also smuggle machine parts into Egypt, antiquities out. But as I said, I mostly chase women. It's the one thing I never get tired of."

Deborah regarded Stephanos' dark eyes. To her surprise, the fact that he admitted to being a womanizer enhanced the forbidden exhilaration of the experience. She threw herself against him.

Stephanos was good at almost everything he did. He could feel her inhibitions relax. With a sense of satisfaction he lifted her and carried her into the apartment. Bypassing the living room, he took her directly into the bedroom. Without resistance he removed her clothes. She looked delicious totally naked in the blue room light.

Stepping out of his own trousers, Stephanos bent down and kissed Deborah gently on the lips. She reached out, wanting him to take her.

With shattering suddenness the phone next to the bed began to ring. Stephanos switched on the light to glance at the clock. It was almost midnight. Something was wrong.

"You answer it," commanded Stephanos.

Deborah looked at him with surprise, but quickly picked up the receiver. She said hello in English, and immediately tried to give the phone to Stephanos, saying it was an international call. Stephanos motioned for her to keep the phone and silently told her to find out who was calling. Deborah obediently listened, asked who was calling, and then put her hand over the phone.

"It's Cairo. A Monsieur Yvon Julien de Margeau."

Stephanos snatched the phone, his face reflecting a sudden change from seeming playfulness to calculation. Deborah shrank back, covering her nakedness. Looking at his face now, Deborah realized she'd made a mistake. She tried to gather her clothes, but Stephanos was sitting on her jeans.

"You're not going to convince me you just wanted to have a friendly conversation in the middle of the night," said Stephanos with uncamouflaged irritation.

"You're right, Stephanos," said Yvon calmly. "I wanted to ask you about Abdul Hamdi. Do you know him?"

"Of course I know the bastard. What about him?"

"Have you done any business with him?"

"That's a pretty personal question, Yvon. What are you driving at?"

"Hamdi was murdered today."

"That's too bad," said Stephanos sarcastically. "But why would that concern me?"

Deborah was still trying to rescue her jeans. Gingerly she put one hand on his back and pulled with the other. Stephanos was aware of the distraction but not the purpose. Savagely he lashed out and hit her with the back of his hand, knocking her off the other side of the bed. With trembling hands she dressed in the clothes she had.

"Do you have any idea who killed Hamdi?" asked Yvon.

"There are a lot of people who wanted that bastard dead," said Stephanos angrily. "Myself included."

"Did he try to blackmail you?"

"Listen, de Margeau, I don't think I want to answer any of these questions. I mean, what is in all this for me?"

"I'm willing to trade you information. I know something you'd like to find out."

"Try me."

"Hamdi had a Seti I statue like the one in Houston."

Stephanos' face went bloodred. "Jesus Christ!" he shouted jumping to his feet, oblivious of his own nakedness. Deborah saw her chance and retrieved her jeans. Finally dressed, she cowered on the other side of the bed with her back to the wall.

"How did he get a Seti statue?" asled Stephanos, controlling his anger.

"I have no idea," said Yvon.

"Has there been any official publicity?" asked Stephanos.

"None. I happened on the scene immediately after the murder. I got all of Hamdi's papers and correspondence, including your last letter."

88

"What are you going to do with it?"

"Nothing for the moment."

"Was there anything about the black market in general? Was he trying some sort of grand exposé?"

"Um, so he did try to blackmail you," said Yvon triumphantly. "The answer is no. There was no grand exposé. Did you kill him, Stephanos?"

"If I did, do you honestly think I'd tell you, de Margeau? Be realistic."

"Just thought I'd ask. Actually we have a good lead. The murder was seen at close range by an expert witness."

Stephanos stopped by the doorway, looking through the living room to the balcony, thinking. "This witness, can he identify the killers?"

"Absolutely. And he happens to be a very nicely endowed she, who also happens to be an Egyptologist. Her name is Erica Baron, and she's at the Hilton."

Pushing the button to disconnect, Stephanos dialed a local number. He tapped on the phone impatiently while the connection went through. "Evangelos, pack your bag. We're going to Cairo in the morning." He hung up before Evangelos could respond. "Shit," he shouted to the night. At that moment he caught sight of Deborah. For an instant he was bewildered, having forgotten her presence. "Get out of here," he yelled. Deborah scrambled to her feet and rushed from the room. Freedom in Greece appeared to be as dangerous and unpredictable as she had been told back home.

Cairo   12:00 Midnight

Emerging from the smoke-filled Taverne cocktail lounge, Erica blinked in the bright light of the Hilton lobby. The experience with Ahmed and the intimidating feeling of the huge government building had so unnerved her that she had decided to have a drink. She had wanted to relax, but going into the bar had not been a good idea. She had been unable to enjoy her drink in peace; several American architects had decided she was just the antidote to a boring evening. No one had been willing to believe she wanted to be alone. So she'd finished her drink and left.

Standing at the periphery of the lobby, she could feel the physical effects of the Scotch, and she stopped for a moment to allow her equilibrium to return to normal. Unfortunately the alcohol had not affected her anxiety. If anything, it had increased it, and the watchful eyes of the men in the bar had played on her incipient paranoia. She wondered if she were being followed. Slowly she let her eyes roam around the grand foyer. On one of the couches a European man was obviously looking at her over the tops of his reading glasses. A bearded Arab dressed in flowing white robes standing near a jewelry display case was also staring at her with unblinking coal-black eyes. An enormous black who looked like Idi Amin smiled at her from in front of the registration desk.

Erica shook her head. She knew her exhaustion was getting the better of her. If she were in Boston wandering around alone at midnight, she would be stared at. She took a deep breath and headed for the bank of elevators.

When she reached her door, Erica vividly remembered the shock of seeing Ahmed in her room. Her pulse quickened as she pushed open the door. Gingerly she switched on the light. Ahmed's chair was empty. Next she looked in the bathroom. It too was empty. Double-latching the door, she noted an envelope on the floor of the foyer.

It was Hilton stationery. Walking toward the balcony, she opened the envelope and read that Monsieur Yvon Julien de Margeau had phoned and that she was to call back, regardless of the hour. Below the message was a printed square followed by the word "urgent."

Breathing in the cool night air, Erica began to relax. The spectacular view helped. She'd never been in the desert before and was astounded to see as many stars at the horizon as directly above. Immediately in front of her the broad black ribbon of the Nile stretched out like the wet black pavement of a huge highway. In the distance she could see illuminated the mysterious sphinx, silently guarding the riddles of the past. Next to the mythical creature the fabled pyramids thrust their granular hulks skyward. Despite their antiquity, their crisp geometry suggested something futuristic, twisting the context of time around. Looking to the left, Erica could see the island of Roda, which looked like an ocean liner in the Nile. On its near tip she could see the lights of the Hotel Meridien, and her thoughts returned to Yvon. She read the message again and wondered if Yvon could possibly know about Ahmed's visit. She also pondered if she should tell him if he didn't already know. But she felt a strong urge not to involve herself as far as the authorities were concerned, and it seemed to her that telling Yvon about Ahmed could possibly do just that. If there were something between Ahmed and Yvon, it was their business. Yvon could handle it.

Sitting on the edge of the bed, Erica asked to be connected with the Meridien Hotel, suite 800. With the receiver held between her head and shoulder, Erica removed her blouse. The cool air felt good. It took almost fifteen minutes to establish the connection, and Erica realized that the Egyptian phones were atrocious, as she had been warned.

"Hello." It was Raoul.

"Hello. This is Erica Baron. May I speak with Yvon?"

"One moment."

There was a pause, and Erica removed her shoes. There was a line of Cairo dust across her instep.

"Good evening," said Yvon cheerfully.

"Hello, Yvon. I got a message to call you. It said 'urgent.'"

"Well, I wanted to speak to you as soon as possible, but there is no emergency. I just had a wonderful evening tonight and I wanted to thank you."

"That's very nice of you to say," said Erica, slightly flustered.

"As a matter of fact, I thought you looked very beautiful tonight, and I am very anxious to see you again."

"You are?" asked Erica before thinking.

"Absolutely. In fact, I'd be delighted to have breakfast with you in the morning. They serve wonderful eggs here at the Meridien."

"Thank you, Yvon," said Erica. She had enjoyed Yvon's company, but she had no intention of wasting her time in Egypt on a flirtation. She had come to see the objects of her years of study firsthand, and she did not want to be distracted. More important, she still had not decided exactly what her responsibility was to the fabulous statue of Seti I.

"I can have Raoul pick you up whenever you wish," Yvon said, interrupting her thoughts.

"Thank you, Yvon, but I'm exhausted. I don't want to get up at a certain time."

"I understand. You could just call me when you wake up."

"Yvon, I enjoyed myself tonight, especially after this afternoon. But I think I need some time to myself. I'd like to sightsee a little."

"I'd be glad to show you more of Cairo," said Yvon persistently.

Erica did not want to spend the day with Yvon. Her interest in Egypt was too personal to share. "Yvon, how about dinner again? That would be the best for me."

"Dinner would have been included in the day, but I

understand, Erica. Dinner will be fine, and I will look forward to it very much. But let's set a time. Say, nine o'clock."

After a friendly good-bye, Erica hung up the phone. She was surprised at Yvon's persistence. She had not felt that she looked very good that evening. She got up and looked at herself in the bedroom mirror. She was twenty-eight, but some people thought she looked younger. She noticed again the minute wrinkles that had miraculously appeared beside her eyes on her last birthday. Then she noticed a small pimple just forming on her skin. "Damn," she said as she tried to squeeze it. It wouldn't squeeze. Erica looked at herself and wondered about men. She wondered what it was that they really liked.

She removed her bra, then her skirt. Waiting for the shower to run hot, she stared at the bathroom mirror. Turning her head to the side, she touched the slight bump on her nose and wondered if she should do something about it. Stepping back to get the whole effect, she was reasonably pleased with her body, although she thought she needed more exercise. Suddenly she felt very lonely. She thought about the life she had willfully left in Boston. There were problems, but maybe running away to Egypt was not the answer. She thought about Richard. With the shower running, Erica returned to the bedroom and looked at the telephone. Impulsively she put a call through to Richard Harvey and was disappointed when the operator told her it would be at least two hours, maybe more. Erica complained, and the operator said that she should be happy because the lines were not very busy. Usually it would take several days to call long distance from Cairo; it was easier to call into the city. Erica thanked her and hung up. Staring at the silent phone, she felt a sudden rush of emotion. She fought back undirected tears, knowing she was too exhausted to think about anything more until she had some sleep.

Cairo   12:30 A.M.

Ahmed watched the reflected lights forming patterns on the Nile as his car crossed the 26 July bridge to Gezira island. His driver kept leaning on the horn, but Ahmed no longer tried to interfere. Drivers in Cairo believed continuous honking was as necessary as steering.

"I will be ready at eight A.M.," said Ahmed, emerging from his car in front of his home on Shari Ismail Muhammad in the district of Zamalek. The driver nodded, made a quick U-turn, and disappeared into the night.

Ahmed's steps were slow as he entered his empty Cairo apartment. He much preferred his small house by the Nile in his native Luxor in Upper Egypt, and he went as often as possible. But the burden of office as director of the antiquities service kept him in town more than he liked. Perhaps more than anyone, Ahmed was aware of the negative consequences of the huge bureaucracy Egypt had created. In order to encourage education, every graduate of the university was guaranteed a job in the government. Consequently there were too many people with not enough to do. Insecurity in such a system was rampant, and most individuals spent their time plotting ways of ensuring the perpetuation of their positions. If it weren't for the subsidy from Saudi Arabia, the entire top-heavy mess would crumble overnight.

Such thoughts depressed Ahmed, who had sacrificed everything in order to rise to his present position. He had set out to control the antiquities service, and now that he did, he had to face the gross inefficiencies of the department. And so far his attempts at reorganization had met with fierce opposition.

He sat on his Egyptian rococo couch and pulled some memoranda from his attaché case. He read the titles: "Revised Security Arrangements for the Necropolis of Luxor, Including Valley of the Kings" and "Underground Bombproof Storage Chambers for Tutankhamen Treasures." He opened the first because that was the one he was particularly interested in. He had recently totally reorganized the security for the Necropolis of Luxor. It had been his first priority after reaching office.

Ahmed read the first paragraph twice before he acknowledged that his mind was not on the subject. He kept remembering Erica Baron's exquisitely molded face. He had been startled by her beauty when he first caught sight of her in her room. It had been his plan to throw her off balance for the interrogation, but it had been he who had been initially thrown. There was a similarity, not in appearance, but in demeanor, between Erica and a woman Ahmed had fallen in love with during his three-year stay at Harvard. It had been Ahmed's only real love affair, and being reminded of it was painful. The anguish he'd felt when leaving for Oxford still haunted him. Knowing he would never see her again made it the most difficult experience he'd ever had. And it had affected him greatly. From that time he had avoided romance so that he could accomplish the goals his family had set for him.

Leaning his head back against the wall, Ahmed allowed his memory to conjure up an image of Pamela Nelson, the girl from Radcliffe. He could see her clearly through the mist of fourteen years. Instantly he remembered those moments of awakening on a Sunday morning, the cold of Boston effectively screened out by their love. He could remember how he enjoyed watching her sleep, and how he would ever so carefully stroke her forehead and cheeks with his hand until she stirred and smiled.

Ahmed heaved himself to his feet and walked into the kitchen. He busied himself making tea, trying to escape from the memories that Erica had so effectively awakened. It seemed like only yesterday that he had left for America. His parents had taken him to the airport, full of instructions and encouragement, unaware of their son's fears. The idea of America had been overwhelmingly exciting for a boy from Upper Egypt, but Boston had turned out to be just horribly lonely. At least until he'd met Pamela. Then it had been enchanting. Basking in Pamela's companionship, he had hungrily devoured his studies, finishing Harvard in three years.

Bringing the tea back into the living room, Ahmed returned to his rock-hard couch. The warm fluid soothed his tense stomach. After careful thought he understood why Erica Baron reminded him of Pamela Nelson. He had sensed in Erica the same intelligence and personal generosity that Pamela had used to veil her sensuous inner self. It had been the hidden woman that Ahmed had fallen in love with. Ahmed closed his eyes and remembered Pamela's naked body. He sat perfectly still. The only sound was the ticking of the marble clock on the buffet.

Suddenly he opened his eyes. The official portrait of a smiling Sadat erased the warm memories. The present reasserted itself, and Ahmed sighed. He then laughed at himself. Indulging in such memories was unusual for him. He knew that his responsibilities in the department and within his family offered little room for such sentimental thoughts. To get to his present position had been a struggle, and now he was very close to his ultimate goal.

Ahmed picked up the memorandum about the Valley of the Kings and again tried to read. But his mind would not cooperate; it kept wandering back to Erica Baron. He thought of her transparency during the interrogation. He knew that such responses were not weaknesses but rather evidence of sensitivity. At the same time, he was thoroughly convinced that Erica knew nothing of importance.

Suddenly Ahmed remembered the words of the assistant who had originally reported that Yvon de Margeau had dined with Erica. He'd said that de Margeau had taken her to the Casino de Monte Bello and that the setting looked very romantic.

Ahmed stood up and paced the room. He felt angry without

knowing why. What was de Margeau doing in Egypt? Was he going to buy more antiquities? On his previous visits, Ahmed had not been able to keep him under adequate observation. Now there was possibly a way. If Erica's relationship with de Margeau grew, he could follow the man through Erica.

He picked up the phone and called his second in command, Zaki Riad, and ordered him to have Erica Baron followed twenty-four hours a day, starting in the morning. He also told Riad that he wanted the individual assigned to report directly to him. "I want to know where she goes and whom she meets. Everything."

Cairo   2:45 A.M.

It was an unfamiliar jangle that made Erica sit bolt upright.
At first she had no idea where she was: there was a sound of
water, and she was dressed only in her underpants. The harsh
metallic sound recurred, and she realized she was in her hotel
and that the phone was ringing. The sound of water was the
shower, still running. She had fallen asleep on top of the
bedspread with all the lights blazing.

Her mind was still foggy when she picked up the receiver.
The operator said that her call to America was ready. After
several distant sounds the phone went dead. She shouted
hello several times; then, shrugging her shoulders, she hung
up and went into the bathroom to turn off the shower. A
casual glance in the mirror unnerved her. She looked terrible.
Her eyes were red, her lids puffy, and the pimple on her chin
had come to a head.

The phone rang again, and she ran back to the bedroom to
pick it up.

"I'm so glad you called, dear. How was the trip?" Richard
sounded pleased on the other end.

"Terrible," said Erica.

"Terrible? What's wrong?" Richard was instantly alarmed.
"Are you all right?"

"I'm fine. It just hasn't been what I expected," said Erica. At
once, sensing Richard's overprotectiveness, she decided that it

probably had been a mistake to call him. But having already committed herself, she told him about the statue and the murder, about her terror, about Yvon and then Ahmed.

"My God," said Richard, obviously aghast. "Erica, I want you to come home immediately, the next flight!" There was a pause. "Erica, did you hear me?"

Erica pushed her hair back. Richard's command had a negative effect. He was not in a position to give her orders, no matter what his motivation.

"I'm not ready to leave Egypt," she said evenly.

"Look, Erica, you've made your point. There's no need to drag it out, especially if you are in danger."

"I'm not in danger," Erica said flatly, "and what point are you referring to?"

"Your independence. I understand. You don't have to continue your acting-out."

"Richard, I don't think you understand. It's not that simple. I'm not acting-out. Ancient Egypt means a great deal to me. I've dreamed of visiting the pyramids since I was a child. I'm here because I want to be here."

"Well, I think you are being foolish."

"Frankly, I don't think this is a proper topic for a transatlantic call. You keep forgetting that besides being a woman I'm an Egyptologist. I've spent eight years of my life studying for my degree, and I'm vitally interested in what I'm doing. It's important to me." Erica could feel herself getting angry all over again.

"More important than our relationship?" asked Richard somewhere between being hurt and being angry.

"As important as your medicine is to you."

"Medicine and Egyptology are very different."

"Of course, but what you forget is that people can approach Egyptology with the same commitment that you apply to medicine. But I'm not going to talk any more about this now, and I'm not coming back to Boston. Not yet."

"Then I will come over to Egypt," said Richard magnanimously.

"No," said Erica simply.

100

"No?"

"That's what I said—no. *Do not come to Egypt.* Please. If you want to do something for me, phone my boss, Dr. Herbert Lowery, and ask him to call me here as soon as possible. Apparently it is much easier to call into Egypt than out."

"I'd be happy to call Lowery, but are you sure you don't want me to join you?" asked Richard, amazed at the rebuff.

"I'm sure," said Erica before saying good-bye and terminating the conversation.

When the phone rang again just after four A.M., Erica was not jolted as she had been earlier. However, she was afraid it was Richard calling back, and she let it ring several times, deciding exactly what she would say. But it wasn't Richard. It was Dr. Herbert Lowery.

"Erica, are you all right?"

"I'm fine, Dr. Lowery. Just fine."

"Richard seemed very upset when he called about an hour ago. He said you wanted me to call."

"That's right, Dr. Lowery. I can explain," said Erica, sitting up to help herself wake up. "I wanted to talk to you about something astounding, and I was told that it was easier to call into Cairo than out. Did Richard tell you anything about my first day here?"

"No. He said you'd had some trouble. That was all."

"Trouble is hardly the word," said Erica. She quickly sketched the events of the day for Dr. Lowery. Then, with as much detail as she could remember, she described the Seti I statue.

"Unbelievable," said Dr. Lowery when Erica had finished. "Actually, I have seen the Houston statue. The man who bought it is indecently rich, and he had both Leonard from the Met and me flown down to Houston in his 707 to authenticate it. We both agreed it was the finest sculpture ever found in Egypt. I thought it probably came from Abydos or Luxor. Its condition was astounding. It was hard to believe it had been buried for three thousand years. Anyway, what you describe sounds like a mate."

"Did the Houston statue have hieroglyphics cut into the base?" asked Erica.

"It did, indeed," said Dr. Lowery. "It had some very typical religious exhortation, but it also had a very curious bit of hieroglyphics at the base."

"So did the one I saw," added Erica excitedly.

"It was very difficult to translate," said Lowery, "but it said something like 'Eternal peace granted to Seti I, who ruled after Tutankhamen.'"

"Fantastic," said Erica. "The one I saw also had the names Seti I and Tutankhamen. I was sure of it, but it's so weird."

"I agree it doesn't make any sense for Tutankhamen's name to appear. In fact, Leonard and I wondered about the authenticity of the statue when we saw that. But there was no doubt it was real. Did you notice which of Seti I's names was used.?"

"I think it was his name associated with the god Osiris," said Erica. "Wait, I can tell you for sure." Erica suddenly remembered the scarab Abdul Hamdi had given her. She ran over to the pants she'd draped over a chair. The scarab was still in the pocket.

"Yes, it was his Osiris name," said Erica. "I remembered it was the same as I've seen on a clever fake scarab. Anyway, Dr. Lowery, could you possibly get a photo of the hieroglyphics on the Houston statue and send it to me?"

"I'm sure I can. I remember the man, a Jeffrey Rice. He will be extremely interested that there is another statue like his, and I think he'll be cooperative in exchange for the news."

"It is a tragedy," said Erica, "that the statue could not be studied at the site it was found."

"Indeed," said Dr. Lowery. "That's the real problem with the black market. The treasure hunters destroy so much information."

"I've known about the black market, but I never realized its true power," said Erica. "I'd really like to do something about it."

"That's a wonderful goal. But the stakes are high, and as Abdul Hamdi learned too late, it is a deadly game."

Erica thanked Dr. Lowery for calling, and told him that she

would soon be heading up to Luxor to get to work on her translations. Dr. Lowery told her to be careful and to enjoy herself.

Hanging up, Erica relished the feeling of excitement. It made her remember why she had studied Egypt in the first place. Settling herself back to sleep, she felt all her initial enthusiasm for her trip return.

Day 2

Cairo awakened early. From the nearby villages the donkey carts laden with produce had begun their trek into the city before the eastern sky had even bleached from its nighttime blackness. The sounds were those of the wooden wheels, the jangle of the harness fittings, and the bells of the lambs and goats trotting into market. As the sun brightened the horizon, the animal carts were joined by a medley of petroleum-powered vehicles. Bakeries stirred and the air was filled with the delicious aroma of baking bread. By seven the taxis emerged like insects and the honking began. People appeared on the streets and the temperature climbed.

Having left her balcony door ajar, Erica was soon assaulted by the sounds of the traffic on the El Tahrir bridge and on the broad boulevard, Korneish el-Nil, that ran along the Nile in front of the Hilton. Rolling over, she looked out at the pale blue of the morning sky. She felt much better than she had expected. Glancing at her watch, she was surprised she had not slept longer. It wasn't even quite eight o'clock.

Erica pushed herself up to a sitting position. The fake scarab was lying on the table next to the phone. She picked it up and pressed it as if to test its reality. After a night's rest the events of the previous day seemed like a dream.

Ordering breakfast in her room, Erica began to plan her day. She decided to visit the Egyptian Museum and view some of

105

the Old Kingdom exhibits, then head out to Saqqara, the necropolis of the Old Kingdom capital of Mennofer. She would avoid the usual tourist habit of rushing directly to the pyramids of Giza.

Breakfast was simple: juice, melon, fresh croissants and honey, and sweet Arabic coffee. It was served elegantly on her splendid balcony. With the pyramids reflecting the sun in the distance and the Nile silently slipping by, Erica experienced a sense of euphoria.

After pouring herself more coffee, Erica brought out her Nagel's guide to Egypt and turned to the section on Saqqara. There was much too much to see in any one day, and she intended to plan her itinerary carefully. Suddenly she remembered Abdul Hamdi's guidebook. It was still nestled deep within her canvas tote bag. Gingerly she opened the cover, which was no longer securely attached, and gazed at the name and address in the flyleaf: Nasif Malmud, 180 Shari El Tahir. It made her think of the cruel irony of Abdul Hamdi's last words. "I travel a lot and might not be in Cairo at the time you leave." She shook her head, realizing that the old man had been right. Turning to the section on Saqqara, she began to compare the older Baedeker with the newer Nagel's.

Overhead, a black falcon hovered on the wind, then plunged down on a rat scuttling through an alley.

Nine floors below, Khalifa Khalil reached over in his rented Egyptian Fiat and pressed the lighter button. He waited patiently until it popped out. Leaning back, he lit his cigarette with obvious pleasure, inhaling deeply. He was an angular and muscular man with a large hooked nose that seemed to pull his mouth into a perpetual sneer. He moved with restrained grace, like a jungle cat. Glancing up at the balcony of 932, he could make out his quarry. With his powerful field glasses he could see Erica very well and allowed himself to enjoy the view of her legs. Very nice, he thought, congratulating himself on obtaining such a pleasurable assignment. Erica shifted her legs toward him, and he grinned: this gave him a distinctively startling appearance, because one of his upper front incisors had been broken in such a way that it came to a sharp point. In his customary black suit and black tie, many people thought he looked like a vampire.

Khalifa was an unusually successful soldier of fortune, experiencing no problem with unemployment in the turbulent Middle East. He had been born in Damascus and raised in an orphanage. He had been trained as a commando in Iraq but had been phased out because he could not work with a team. He also lacked a conscience. He was a sociopathic killer who could be controlled only by money. Khalifa laughed happily when he thought that he was being paid the same for baby-sitting a beautiful American tourist as for running AK assault rifles to the Kurds in Turkey.

Scanning Erica's neighboring balconies, Khalifa saw nothing suspicious. His orders from the Frenchman had been simple. He was to protect Erica Baron from a possible murder attempt and catch the perpetrators. Swinging his binoculars away from the Hilton, he slowly scanned the people along the banks of the Nile. He knew it could be difficult to protect against a long-distance shot by a high-powered rifle. No one looked suspicious. By reflex his hand reassuringly patted the Stechkin semiautomatic pistol holstered beneath his left arm. It was his prized possession. He had taken it from a KGB agent he'd murdered in Syria for the Mossad.

Turning back to Erica, Khalifa had trouble believing someone would want kill such a fresh-looking girl. She was like a peach ready for picking, and he wondered if Yvon's motives were strictly business.

Suddenly the girl stood up, gathered her books, and disappeared within her room. Khalifa lowered the glasses to view the Hilton entrance. There was the usual line of taxis and early-morning activity.

Gamal Ibrahim struggled with the *El Ahram* newspaper, trying to fold over the first page. He was sitting in the rear seat of a taxi he'd hired for the day, parked in the Hilton driveway on the side opposite the entrance. The doorman had complained, but had relented when he saw Gamal's Department of Antiquities identification. On the seat next to Gamal was a blown-up passport photo of Erica Baron. Each time a woman emerged from the hotel, Gamal would compare the face with the photo.

Gamal himself was twenty-eight. He was a little more than five-feet-four and slightly overweight. Married with two children, aged one and three, he had been hired by the Department of Antiquities just prior to receiving his doctorate in public administration from the University of Cairo that spring. He started work in mid-July, but things had not gone as smoothly as he would have liked. The staff in the department was so large that the only assignments he had been given were odd jobs such as this one, following Erica Baron and reporting where she went. Gamal picked up Erica's photo as two women emerged and entered a taxi. Gamal had never followed anyone, and he felt the job demeaning, but he was in no position to refuse, especially since he was to report directly to Ahmed Khazzan, the director. Gamal had lots of ideas for the department and felt that now he might have a chance to be heard.

Dressing sensibly for the heat she expected at Saqqara, Erica put on a light beige cotton blouse with short sleeves and cotton pants of a slightly darker shade cut full with a drawstring waist. In her tote bag she deposited her Polaroid, her flashlight, and the 1929 Baedeker guidebook. After careful comparison she had agreed with Abdul Hamdi. The Baedeker was far better than Nagel's.

At the front desk she was able to retrieve her passport, which apparently had been duly recorded. She was also introduced to her guide for the day, Anwar Selim. Erica did not want a guide, but the hotel had suggested it, and after being tormented by hecklers the day before, she had finally relented, agreeing to pay seven Egyptian pounds for the guide and ten for the taxi and driver. Anwar Selim was a gaunt man in his middle forties, who wore a metal pin with the number 113 on the lapel of his gray suit, proving he was a government-licensed guide.

"I have a wonderful itinerary," said Selim, who had an affectation of smiling in the middle of his sentences. "First we will visit the Great Pyramid in the coolness of the morning. Then—"

"Thank you," said Erica, interrupting. She backed away. Selim's teeth were in sorry shape, and his breath was capable of stopping a charging rhinoceros. "I have already planned the day. I want to go to the Egyptian Museum first for a short visit, then go on to Saqqara."

"But Saqqara will be hot in the middle of the day," protested Selim. His mouth was set in a hardened smile, the skin of his face taut from continuous exposure to Egyptian sun.

"I'm sure it will be," announced Erica, trying to cut off this dialogue, "but it is the itinerary I would like to follow."

Without altering his facial expression Selim opened the door of the battered taxi that had been retained for her. The driver was young, with a three-day stubble on his face.

As they pulled away for the short hop to the museum, Khalifa put his field glasses on the floor of the car. He allowed Erica's taxi to pull out into the street before he started his engine, wondering if there was some way he could get some information about the guide and the taxi driver. As he put his car into gear, he noted another taxi pull out from the Hilton directly behind Erica's. Both cars turned right at the first intersection.

Gamal had recognized Erica when she had appeared, without having to refer to the photo. Hastily he had written the guide's number, 113, in the margin of his newspaper before telling his driver to follow Erica's taxi.

When they reached the Egyptian Museum, Selim helped Erica out of the car, and the taxi proceeded to the shade of a sycamore to wait. Gamal had his driver stop under a nearby tree that afforded a view of Erica's taxi. Opening his newspaper, he went back to a long article on Sadat's proposals for the West Bank.

Khalifa parked outside the museum compound and purposely walked past Gamal's taxi to see if he recognized the man. He did not. For Khalifa, Gamal's movements were already suspicious, but following orders, he entered the museum behind Erica and her guide.

Erica had walked into the famed museum with great enthusiasm, but even her knowledge and interest could not overcome the oppressive atmosphere. The priceless objects looked as out-of-place in the dusty rooms as they did in the Boston Museum on Huntington Avenue. The mysterious statues and stony faces had the look of death, not immortality. The guards were dressed in white uniforms and black berets, reminiscent of the colonial era. Sweepers with thatched brooms pushed the dust from room to room without ever carrying it away. The only workers who were really busy were the repairmen who stood in small roped-off areas plastering or doing simple carpentry with tools similar to those pictured in the ancient Egyptian murals.

Erica tried to ignore the surroundings and concentrate on the more-renowned pieces. In room 32 she was astounded at the lifelike quality of the limestone statues of Rahotep, brother of Khufu, and Nofritis, his wife. They had a serene contemporary look. Erica was content to merely gaze at the faces, but her guide felt compelled to offer the full benefit of his knowledge. He told Erica what Rahotep had said to Khufu when he had first seen the statue. Erica knew it was pure fiction. Politely she told Selim to only answer her questions and that she was actually familiar with most of the objects.

As Erica rounded the Rahotep statue, her eyes wandered across the entranceway of the gallery before returning to the back of the statue. An image of a dark man with a tooth that looked like a fang hovered in her mind, but when she turned again there was no figure in the doorway. It had happened so quickly that it gave her an uneasy feeling. The events of the previous day made her wary, and as she walked around the Rahotep statue she looked at the doorway several times but the dark figure did not reappear. Instead a very noisy group of French tourists entered the room.

Motioning for Selim to leave, Erica stepped from room 32 into the long gallery that ran along the whole western edge of the building. The corridor was empty of people, but as she looked through a double arch to the northwest corner, Erica again saw a fleeting dark figure.

With Selim trying to get her to view various famous objects

along the way, Erica quickly walked down the long gallery toward the spot where it intersected a similar gallery on the north side of the museum. Exasperated, Selim doggedly followed the fast-paced American, who seemed to want to view the museum at the speed of light.

She stopped abruptly just short of the intersection. Selim halted behind her, gazing around to see what could have caught her attention. She was standing next to a statue of Senmut, steward of Queen Hatshepsut, but rather than studying it, she was carefully looking around the corner into the north gallery.

"If there is something in particular you'd like to see," said Selim, "please—"

Erica angrily motioned for Selim to be still. Stepping out into the middle of the gallery, Erica searched for the dark figure. She saw nothing, and felt a little foolish. A German couple walked by, arm in arm, arguing over the floor plan of the museum.

"Miss Baron," said Selim, obviously struggling to be patient, "I am very familiar with this museum. If there is something you'd like to see, just ask."

Erica took pity on the man and tried to think of something to ask him so he'd feel more useful.

"Are there any Seti I artifacts in the museum?"

Selim put his index finger on his nose, thinking. Then, without speaking, he lifted the finger in the air and motioned for Erica to follow. He led her up to the second floor to room 47 over the entrance foyer. He stood beside a large piece of exquisitely carved quartzite, labeled 388.1. "The lid to Seti I's sarcophagus," he said proudly.

Erica looked at the piece of stone, mentally comparing it with the fabulous statue she'd seen the day before. It wasn't much of a comparison. She also remembered that Seti I's sarcophagus itself had been pirated off to London and rested in a small museum there. It was painfully obvious how much the black market shortchanged the Egyptian Museum.

Selim waited until Erica looked up. He then pulled her by the hand to the entrance of another room, directing her to pay the guard at the door another fifteen piasters so that they could enter. Once in the room, Selim navigated between the long low glass cases until he reached one by the wall. "The mummy of Seti I," said Selim smugly.

Looking down at the dried-up face, Erica felt a little sick. It was the kind of image Hollywood makeup artists strove to imitate for countless horror movies, and she noticed that the ears had fragmented and that the head was no longer attached to the torso. Instead of ensuring immortality, the remains suggested that the horror of death was permanent.

Glancing around at the other royal mummies contained within the room, Erica thought that instead of making ancient Egypt come alive, the petrified bodies emphasized the enormous time that had elapsed and the remoteness of ancient Egypt. She looked back at the face of Seti I. It looked nothing like the beautiful statue she'd seen the day before. There was no resemblance whatsoever. The statue had had a narrow jaw with a straight nose, whereas the mummy had a very wide jaw and a hawklike hooked nose. It gave her the creeps, and she shivered before turning away. Motioning to Selim to follow, she walked out of the room, eager to be leaving the dusty museum for the field.

Erica's taxi whisked her out into the Egyptian countryside, leaving the confusion of Cairo behind. They drove south on the west bank of the Nile. Selim had tried to continue conversation by telling Erica what Ramses II had said to Moses, but had finally fallen silent. Erica did not want to hurt Selim's feelings and had tried to ask him about his family, but the guide did not seem to want to talk about that. So they drove in silence, leaving Erica at peace to enjoy the view. She loved the color contrast between the sapphire blue of the Nile and the brilliant green of the irrigated fields. It was time for the date harvest, and they passed donkey loads of palm branches festooned with the red fruit. Opposite the industrial city of Hilwan, which was on the east side of the Nile, the asphalt road forked. Erica's taxi careened to the right, its horn honking several times despite the fact that the road ahead was clear.

Gamal was only five or six car lengths behind. He was literally on the edge of his seat, making small talk with his driver. He had removed his gray suit jacket in deference to the heat, which he knew was only going to get worse.

Almost a quarter of a mile back, Khalifa had his radio blaring, and the discordant music filled the car. He was now convinced that Erica was already being followed, but the method was peculiar. The taxi was much too close. At the museum entrance he had gotten a good look at the occupant, who appeared to be a university student, but Khalifa had dealt with student terrorists. He knew that their simple appearance was often a cover for ruthlessness and daring.

Erica's taxi entered a grove of palms that grew so close together it gave the appearance of a coniferous forest. A cool shade replaced the stark sunlight. They came to a halt at a small brick village. On one side was a miniature mosque. On the other was an open area with an eighty-ton alabaster sphinx, lots of pieces of broken statuary, and a huge fallen limestone statue of Ramses II. At the edge of the clearing was a small refreshment stand called the Sphinx Café.

"The fabled city of Memphis," said Selim solemnly.

"You mean Mennofer," said Erica, looking out at the meager remains. Memphis was the Greek name. Mennofer was the ancient Egyptian name. "I'd like to buy us all a coffee or a tea," said Erica, seeing she'd hurt his feelings.

Walking to the refreshment stand, Erica was glad she had been prepared for pitiful remains of this once-mighty capital of ancient Egypt, because otherwise she would have been very disappointed. A large group of ragged young boys approached with their collections of fake antiquities but were effectively driven off by Selim and the taxi driver. They mounted a small veranda with round metal tables and ordered drinks. The men had coffee. Erica ordered Orangina.

Perspiration running down his face, Gamal got out of his taxi clutching his *El Ahram*. Although he had been initially indecisive, he finally convinced himself he needed a drink. Avoiding looking at Erica's group, he took a table near the kiosk. After obtaining a coffee, he disappeared behind his newspaper.

Khalifa kept his telescopic sight on Gamal's chubby torso, but he allowed the fingers of his right hand to relax. He had stopped seventy-five yards short of the Memphis clearing and had quickly unsheathed his Israeli FN sniper's rifle. He was sitting low in the back seat of his car with the rifle barrel resting on the open driver's window. From the moment Gamal had emerged from his car, Khalifa had had him squarely in his sights. If Gamal had made any sudden movement toward Erica, Khalifa would have shot him in the ass. It wouldn't have killed him, but, as Khalifa told himself, it would have slowed him down considerably.

Erica did not enjoy her drink because of the swarm of flies that inhabited the veranda. They were not deflected by a waving hand, and on several occasions they had actually landed on her lips. She got up, told the men not to hurry, and wandered in the clearing. Before getting back in the taxi, Erica stopped to admire the alabaster sphinx. She wondered what kind of mysteries it would tell if it could talk. It was very ancient. It had been made during the Old Kingdom.

Back in the car, they drove on through the dense palm forest until it thinned. Cultivated fields reappeared, along with irrigation canals choked with algae and water plants. Suddenly the Step Pyramid of Pharaoh Zoser reared its familiar profile above a row of palms. Erica felt a thrill of excitement. She was about to visit the oldest stone structure built by man, and for Egyptologists the most important site in Egypt. Here the famed architect Imhotep had built a celestial stairway of six enormous steps rising to a height of about two hundred feet, inaugurating the pyramid age.

Erica felt like an impatient child on her way to the circus. She hated the delay of bouncing through a small mud-brick village before crossing a large irrigation canal. Just beyond the bridge the cultivated land stopped and the arid Libyan desert began. There was no transition. It was like going from noon to midnight without a sunset. Suddenly on either side of the road Erica saw only sand and rock and shimmering heat.

As the taxi came to a halt in the shade of a large tour bus, Erica was the first one out. Selim had to run to keep up with her. The driver opened all four doors of his small car to encourage ventilation while he waited.

Khalifa was becoming more and more confused about

Gamal's behavior. Ignoring Erica, the man had taken his newspaper into the shade of the pyramid's enclosure wall. He had not even bothered to follow Erica inside. Khalifa deliberated for a few minutes, wondering what would be best for him to do. Thinking that Gamal's presence could possibly be some sort of clever ruse, he elected to stick close to Erica. He removed his jacket and shifted his Stechkin semiautomatic to his right hand with his jacket draped over it.

For the next hour Erica was intoxicated by the ruins. This was the Egypt she had dreamed about. Her knowledge was capable of translating the debris of the necropolis into the prodigious achievement that it had been five thousand years previously. She knew she could not see everything in one day, and was content to touch the highlights and enjoy the unexpected, like the cobra reliefs she'd never read about. Selim finally accepted his role and stayed mostly in the shade. He was pleased, however, when Erica motioned about noon that she was ready to move on.

"There is a small café/rest-house here," said Selim hopefully.

"I'm very excited to see some of the nobles' tombs," said Erica. She was too excited to stop.

"The rest house is right next to the mastaba of Ti and the serapeum," said Selim.

Erica's eyes brightened. The serapeum was one of the most unusual ancient Egyptian monuments. Within the catacombs the mummified remains of Apis bulls had been interred with pomp and circumstance befitting kings. It had been with enormous effort that the serapeum had been dug by hand into the solid rock. Erica could understand the effort devoted to construction of human tombs, but not for the bulls. She was convinced that there was a mystery associated with the tomb of the Apis bulls that had yet to be unraveled. "I'm ready for the serapeum," she said with a smile.

Being overweight, Gamal did not fare well in the heat. Rarely, even in Cairo, did he wander outside at midday. Saqqara at noon was almost beyond his capabilities. As his driver followed Erica's taxi, he tried to think of ways to survive. Perhaps he could find some shade and have the driver follow Erica until she was ready to return to Cairo. Ahead, Erica's taxi pulled up and parked at the Saqqara rest house. Looking around, Gamal remembered that when he'd visited the area as a child with his parents he had walked through a scary, dark subterranean cave for bulls. Although the cave had frightened him, he still remembered that it had been deliciously cool.

"Isn't this the site of the serapeum?" he asked, touching his driver's shoulder.

"Right over there," said the driver, pointing toward the beginning of a trench that served as an access ramp.

Gamal looked over at Erica, who had gotten out of her car and was examining the row of sphinxes leading toward the ramp. All at once Gamal knew how he'd cool off. Besides, he thought, it would be fun to see the serapeum again after so many years.

Khalifa was not happy, and he ran his hand nervously through his greasy hair. He'd decided that Gamal was not the amateur he pretended to be. He was far too nonchalant. If he had only been sure of the boy's ultimate intention, he would have shot and delivered him alive to Yvon de Margeau. But he had to wait for Gamal to make a move. The situation was more complicated and more dangerous than he had anticipated. Khalifa screwed the silencer on the barrel of his automatic and was about to get out of the car when he saw Gamal entering a trench leading to a subterranean opening. He consulted a map. It was the serapeum. Looking back at Erica happily photographing a limestone sphinx, Khalifa knew there was only one reason why Gamal would enter the serapeum first. In one of the dark, vaulted galleries or in one of the narrow passageways, Gamal was going to wait like a poisonous snake and strike when least expected. The serapeum was a perfect assassination spot.

Despite his many years of experience, Khalifa was unsure of what to do. He too could enter before Erica Baron and try to find Gamal's hiding place, but that could be too risky. He decided he had to enter with Erica and strike first.

Erica walked down the ramp approaching the entrance. She was not fond of caves and in truth did not care for closed spaces. Even before stepping into the serapeum she could feel the damp coolness, and a tingling sensation announced the appearance of gooseflesh on her thighs. She had to force herself forward. A bedraggled Arab with a face like a hatchet took her money. The serapeum had an ominous feel.

Once inside the gloomy entrance gallery, Erica could sense the mysterious grip that aspects of ancient Egyptian culture had exerted on people through the ages. The darkened passageways looked like tunnels to the netherworld, suggesting the eerie power of the occult. Following Selim, she walked deeper and deeper into the bizarre environment. They went down an unendingly long corridor with irregular and rough-hewn walls, meagerly illuminated by infrequent low-wattage light bulbs. In the areas between the lights, dark shadows made vision difficult. Other tourists had a way of suddenly emerging out of the gloom; voices sounded hollow and echoed repeatedly. At right angles to the main corridor were separate galleries, each containing a mammoth black sarcophagus covered with hieroglyphics. Very few of the side galleries were illuminated. Erica quickly felt she had seen enough, but Selim was insistent, saying that the best sarcophagus was at the far end and that a wooden stairway had been built, so she could even see the carvings inside. Reluctantly Erica continued behind Selim. Finally they reached the gallery in question, and Selim stepped aside for Erica to pass. She reached out to grasp the wooden handrail leading to the viewing platform.

Khalifa was a bundle of raw nerves, following close behind Erica. He had released the safety catch on his semiautomatic and again held it in his right hand beneath his jacket. He'd come within a hairbreath of shooting several tourists when they had suddenly appeared out of the darkness.

As he rounded the corner of the last gallery, he was only fifteen feet behind Erica. The moment he saw Gamal he acted by reflex. Erica was climbing the short wooden stairway built along the side of the highly polished granite sarcophagus. Gamal was on top of the platform looking down at Erica as she climbed. He had stepped back from the edge. Unfortunately for Khalifa, she was directly between him and Gamal, shielding his view and making a quick shot impossible. In a panic

Khalifa surged forward, thrusting Selim to the side. He charged up the short stairway, knocking Erica down on her knees, sending her sprawling toward the surprised Gamal.

Spurts of fiery light leaped from Khalifa's covered pistol, and the deadly slugs tore into Gamal's chest, piercing his heart. His hands started to rise. His small features twisted in pain and confusion as he teetered and fell forward on top of Erica. Khalifa vaulted over the wooden banister, pulling his knife from his belt. Selim screamed before trying to run. The tourists on the platform still had not comprehended what had happened. Khalifa dashed across the corridor toward the electric wires responsible for the primitive lights. Gritting his teeth against a possible shock, he sliced through the wire, plunging the entire serapeum into utter darkness.

Cairo 12:30 P.M.

Stephanos Markoulis ordered another Scotch for himself and Evangelos Papparis. Both men were dressed in open-necked knit shirts and were sitting in a corner booth of the La Parisienne lounge in the Meridien Hotel. Stephanos was in a sour, nervous mood, and Evangelos knew his boss well enough to keep still.

"Goddamned Frenchman," said Stephanos, looking at his watch. "He said he'd be right down, and it's been twenty minutes."

Evangelos shrugged. He didn't say anything because he knew no matter what he said, it would only inflame Stephanos further. Instead he reached down and adjusted the small pistol strapped to his leg just within the top of his right boot. Evangelos was a brawny man with oversized features, particularly his brows, which made him look a little like a Neanderthal, except that his head was completely bald.

Just then Yvon de Margeau appeared in the doorway, carrying his attaché case. He was dressed in a blue blazer with an ascot, and was followed by Raoul. The two men surveyed the room.

"These rich guys always look like they're on their way to a polo match," said Stephanos sarcastically. He waved to catch Yvon's attention. Evangelos shifted the table slightly to give his right hand free range of motion. Yvon saw them and

119

walked over. He shook hands with Stephanos and introduced Raoul before sitting down.

"How was your flight?" asked Yvon with restrained cordiality as soon as they had ordered.

"Terrible," said Stephanos. "Where are the old man's papers?"

"You don't spare words, Stephanos," said Yvon with a smile. "Perhaps it is best. In any case, I want to know if you killed Abdul Hamdi."

"If I had killed Hamdi, do you think I'd come down here to this hellhole?" said Stephanos with scorn. He despised men like Yvon who had never had to work a day in their lives.

Believing that silence could be useful with a person like Stephanos, Yvon made a big production out of opening a new pack of Gauloises. He offered them around, but Evangelos was the only taker. He reached for the cigarette, but Yvon teased him by keeping the cigarettes just out of his grasp so that he could make out the tattoo on Evangelos' hairy, muscular forearm. It was a hula dancer with the word "Hawaii" just below it. Finally letting Evangelos take a cigarette, Yvon asked, "Do you go to Hawaii frequently?"

"I worked the freighters when I was a kid," said Evangelos. He lit the Gauloise from a small candle on the table and sat back.

Yvon turned to Stephanos, whose impatience was showing. With careful movements Yvon lit his cigarette with his gold lighter before speaking. "No," said Yvon. "No, I don't think you'd come to Cairo if you'd killed Hamdi, unless you were worried about something, unless something went wrong. But to tell you the truth, Stephanos, I don't know what to believe. You did come here very quickly. That's a little suspicious. Besides, I have learned that Hamdi's killers were not from Cairo."

"Ah," snapped Stephanos, exasperated. "Let me see if I get this right. You learn the killers weren't from Cairo. From that information you decide that they obviously have to be from Athens. Is that your reasoning?" Stephanos turned toward Raoul. "How can you work for this man?" He tapped his forehead with his index finger.

120

Raoul's dark eyes did not blink. His hands rested on his knees. He was prepared to move in a fraction of a second.

"I'm sorry to disappoint you, Yvon," said Stephanos, "but you'll have to look elsewhere for Hamdi's killer. It wasn't me."

"Too bad," said Yvon. "It would have answered a lot of questions. Do you have any thoughts as to who might have done it?"

"I haven't the slightest idea," said Stephanos, "but I have a feeling that Hamdi made himself a number of enemies. How about letting me see Hamdi's papers?"

Yvon lifted his attaché case to the top of the table and put his finger on the latch. He paused. "One other question. Do you have any idea where the Seti I statue is?"

"Unfortunately, no," said Stephanos, looking hungrily at the case.

"I want that statue," said Yvon.

"If I hear anything about it, I will let you know," said Stephanos.

"You never gave me a chance to see the Houston statue," said Yvon, watching Stephanos carefully.

Looking up from the case, Stephanos' face gave a hint of surprise. "What makes you think I was involved with the Houston statue?"

"Let's just say I know," said Yvon.

"Did you learn that from Hamdi's papers?" asked Stephanos angrily.

Instead of answering, Yvon flipped the latch of his case and dumped Hamdi's correspondence onto the table. Leaning back, he casually sipped his Pernod as Stephanos quickly shuffled through the letters. He found his own to Abdul Hamdi and put it aside. "Is this all?" he asked.

"That was all we found," answered Yvon, turning his attention back to the group.

"Did you search the place well?" asked Stephanos.

Yvon glanced over at Raoul, who nodded affirmatively. "Very well," said Raoul.

"There has to have been more," said Stephanos. "I cannot imagine the old bastard was bluffing. He said he wanted five thousand dollars in cash or he was going to turn the papers over to the authorities." Stephanos went through the papers again, more slowly.

"If you had to guess, what would you think happened to the Seti statue?" asked Yvon, taking another drink of Pernod.

"I don't know," said Stephanos without looking up from a letter addressed to Hamdi from a dealer in Los Angeles. "But if it's any help, I can assure you it's still here in Egypt."

An awkward silence prevailed. Stephanos was busy reading. Raoul and Evangelos glared at each other over their drinks. Yvon looked out the window. He too thought the Seti statue was still in Egypt. From where he was sitting, he could see the pool area, beyond which was the expanse of the Nile. In the middle of the river the Nile fountain was operating, sending a stream of water straight into the air. Multiple miniature rainbows appeared along the sides of the enormous jet of water. Yvon thought about Erica Baron and hoped that Khalifa Khalil was as good as Raoul said he was. If Stephanos had killed Hamdi and made a move against Erica, Khalifa was going to earn his pay.

"What about this American woman?" said Stephanos, seemingly reading Yvon's thoughts. "I want to see her."

"She's staying at the Hilton," said Yvon. "But she's a bit edgy about the whole affair. So treat her gently. She's the only connection I have with the Seti statue."

"The statue is not my current interest," said Stephanos, pushing the correspondence away. "But I want to talk to her, and I promise I'll be my usual tactful self. Tell me, have you learned anything at all about this Abdul Hamdi?"

"Not much. He was originally from Luxor. He came to Cairo a few months ago to establish a new antiquities shop. He had a son who still has an antique business in Luxor."

"Have you visited this son?" asked Stephanos.

"No," said Yvon, rising. He'd had enough of Stephanos. "Remember to tell me if you learn anything about the statue. I can afford it." With a slight smile, Yvon turned. Raoul stood up and followed.

"Do you believe him?" asked Raoul when they were outside.

"I don't know what to think," said Yvon, continuing to

walk. "Whether I believe him is one question, whether I trust him is another. He is the biggest opportunist I've ever met, bar none. I want Khalifa to be briefed that he must be extremely careful when Stephanos meets with Erica. If he tries to hurt her, I want him shot."

Saqqara Village 1:48 P.M.

There was one fly in the room that repeatedly flew an erratic course between the two windows. It sounded noisy in the otherwise still enclosure, especially when it slammed against the glass. Erica looked around the chamber. The walls and ceiling were whitewashed. The only decoration was a smiling poster of Anwar Sadat. The single wooden door was closed.

Erica was sitting in a straight-backed chair. Above her was a light bulb suspended from the ceiling by a frayed black wire. Near the door was a small metal table and another chair like the one she was sitting on. Erica looked a mess. Her pants were torn at the right knee, with an abrasion beneath. A large stain of dried blood covered the back of her beige blouse.

Holding out her hand, she tried to judge whether her trembling was lessening. It was hard to say. At one point she had thought she was going to throw up, but the nausea had passed. Now she felt intermittent waves of dizziness, which she was able to disperse by closing her eyes tightly. There was no doubt she was still in a state of shock, but she was beginning to think more clearly. She knew, for example, that she had been taken to a police station in the village of Saqqara.

Erica rubbed her hands together, noticing that they became moist as she remembered the events in the serapeum. When Gamal first fell on her, she had thought she was trapped in a cave-in. She had made frantic attempts to free herself, but it had been impossible because of the narrow confines of the

125

wooden stairway. Besides, the blackness had been so complete she hadn't even been sure she had her eyes open. And then she had felt the warm, sticky fluid on her back. Only later did she find out it had been blood from the dying man on top of her.

Erica shook herself past another bout of nausea and looked up as the door opened. The same man who earlier had taken thirty minutes to fill out some sort of government form with a broken pencil reappeared. He spoke little English, but elaborately motioned Erica to follow him. The aged pistol holstered at his belt did not reassure her. She had already experienced the bureaucratic chaos Yvon had feared: obviously she was being considered a suspect rather than an innocent victim. From the moment the "authorities" had arrived on the scene, pandemonium had reigned. At one point two policemen had had such an argument over some piece of evidence that they had almost come to blows. Erica's passport had been taken and she had been driven to Saqqara in a locked van that was as hot as an oven. She had asked on numerous occasions if she could call the American consulate but had received only shrugs in return as the men continued to argue over what to do with her.

Now Erica followed the man with the old gun through the dilapidated police station out to the street. The same van that had driven her from the serapeum to the village was waiting, its engine idling. Erica tried to ask for her passport, but instead of answering, the man hurried her inside the truck. The door was closed and locked.

Anwar Selim was already crouched on the wooden seat. Erica had not seen him since the catastrophe in the serapeum, and was so pleased to find him again she almost threw her arms around him, begging him to tell her everything was going to be all right. But as she moved into the van, he glowered at her and turned his head.

"I knew you were going to be trouble," he said without looking at her.

"Me, trouble?" She noticed he was handcuffed, and shrank back.

The van lurched forward, and both passengers had to steady

themselves. Erica felt perspiration run down her back.

"You acted strangely from the first moment," said Selim, "especially in the museum. You were planning something. And I'm going to tell them."

"I . . ." began Erica. But she did not continue. Fear clouded her brain. She should have reported Hamdi's murder.

Selim looked at her and spit on the floor of the van.

Cairo 3:10 P.M.

When Erica got out of the van, she recognized the corner of El Tahrir Square. She knew she was close to the Hilton, and she wished she could go back to her room to make some calls and find help. Seeing Selim in shackles had increased her anxiety, and she wondered if she were under arrest.

She and Selim were hurried inside the General Security Police Building, which was jammed with people. Then they were separated. Erica was fingerprinted, photographed, and finally escorted to a windowless room.

Her escort smartly saluted an Arab reading a dossier at a plain wooden table. Without looking up he waved his right hand and Erica's escort departed, closing the door quietly. Erica remained standing. There was silence except when the man turned a page. The fluorescent lights made his bald head shine like a polished apple. His lips were thin and moved slightly as he read. He was impeccably attired in a white martial uniform with a high collar. A black leather strap ran through the epaulet on the left shoulder and was attached to a broader black leather belt that supported a holstered automatic pistol. The man turned to the last page, and Erica caught sight of an American passport clipped to the dossier and hoped that she would be speaking to someone reasonable.

"Please sit down, Miss Baron," said the policeman, still without looking up. His voice was crisp, emotionless. He had a mustache trimmed to a knifelike line. His long nose curled under at the tip.

Quickly Erica sat in the wooden chair facing the table. Beneath it she could see, next to the policeman's polished boots, her canvas tote bag. She'd been worried that she'd seen the last of it.

The policeman put down the dossier, then picked up the passport. He opened it to the photo of Erica, and his eyes traveled back and forth between her and the photo several times. He then reached out and put the passport on the table next to the telephone.

"I am Lieutenant Iskander," said the policeman, clasping his hands together on the table. He paused, looking intently at Erica. "What happened in the serapeum?"

"I don't know," stammered Erica. "I was walking up some stairs to view a sarcophagus, and then I was knocked down from behind. Then someone fell on top of me, and the lights went out."

"Did you see who it was that knocked you down?" He spoke with a slight English accent.

"No," said Erica. "It all happened so quickly."

"The victim was shot. Didn't you hear shots?"

"No, not really. I heard several sounds like someone beating a rug, but no shots."

Lieutenant Iskander nodded and wrote something in the dossier. "Then what happened?"

"I could not get out from beneath the man who fell on me," said Erica, remembering again the feeling of terror. "There were some shouts, I think, but I'm not really sure. I do remember that someone brought candles. They helped me up, and someone said the man was dead."

"Is that all?"

"The guards arrived, then the police."

"Did you look at the man who was shot?"

"Sort of. I had trouble looking at him."

"Had you ever seen him before?"

"No," said Erica.

Reaching down and lifting the tote bag, Iskander pushed it over to Erica. "See if anything is missing."

130

Erica checked the bag. Camera, guidebook, wallet—all seemed to be untouched. She counted her money and checked her traveler's checks. "Everything seems to be here."

"Then you weren't robbed."

"No," said Erica. "I suppose not."

"You are trained as an Egyptologist. Is that correct?" asked Lieutenant Iskander.

"Yes," said Erica.

"Does it surprise you to know that the man who was killed worked for the Department of Antiquities?"

Glancing away from Iskander's cold eyes, Erica looked down at her hands, realizing for the first time that they had been busy working at each other. She held them still, thinking. Although she felt the urge to answer Iskander's questions rapidly, she knew that the question he'd just asked her was important, perhaps the most important of the interview. It reminded her of Ahmed Khazzan. He'd said he was director of the Department of Antiquities. Maybe he could help.

"I'm not sure how to answer," she said finally. "It doesn't surprise me the man worked for the Department of Antiquities. He could have been anyone. I certainly did not know him."

"Why did you visit the serapeum?" asked Lieutenant Iskander.

Remembering Selim's accusing comments in the van, Erica thought carefully about her answer. "The guide I'd hired for the day suggested it," said Erica.

Opening the dossier, Lieutenant Iskander again wrote.

"May I ask a question?" asked Erica in an uncertain voice.

"Certainly."

"Do you know Ahmed Khazzan?"

"Of course," said Lieutenant Iskander. "Do you know Mr. Khazzan?"

"Yes, and I'd like very much to speak with him," said Erica.

Lieutenant Iskander reached out and picked up the phone. He watched Erica as he dialed. He did not smile.

Cairo 4:05 P.M.

The walk seemed endless. Corridors stretched in front of her until perspective reduced them to pinpoints. And they were jammed with people. Egyptians wearing everything from silk suits to ragged galabias were lined up in front of doors or spilling out of offices. Some were sleeping on the floor, so that Erica and her escort had to step over them. The air was heavy with cigarette smoke, garlic, and the greasy smell of lamb.

When Erica reached the outer office of the Department of Antiquities she remembered the multitude of desks and antique typewriters from the night before. The difference was that now they were occupied with ostensibly busy civil servants. After a short wait Erica was shown into the inner office. It was air-conditioned, and the coolness was a welcome relief.

Ahmed was standing behind the desk peering out the window. A corner of the Nile could be seen between the Hilton and the skeleton of the new Intercontinental Hotel. He turned when Erica entered.

She had been prepared to pour out her problems like an overflowing river and plead with Ahmed to help her. But something in his expression made her hold back. There was a sadness about his face. His eyes were veiled and his thick dark hair was disheveled, as if he had been repeatedly running his fingers over his scalp.

"Are you all right?" asked Erica, genuinely concerned.

"Yes," said Ahmed slowly. His voice was hesitant, depressed. "I never imagined what the strain of running this department was going to be like." He flopped down in his chair, eyes momentarily closed.

Before, Erica had only guessed at his sensitivity. Now she wanted to walk around the desk and comfort the man.

Ahmed's eyes opened. "I'm sorry," he said. "Please sit down."

Erica complied.

"I've been briefed about what happened at the serapeum, but I'd like to hear the story in your own words."

Erica began at the beginning. Wanting to tell everything, she even mentioned the man in the museum who had made her nervous.

Ahmed listened intently. He did not interrupt. Only after she stopped did he speak. "The man who was shot was named Gamal Ibrahim and he worked here at the Department of Antiquities. He was a fine boy." Ahmed's eyes glistened with tears. Seeing such an obviously strong man so moved, unlike the American men she knew, made Erica forget her own troubles. This ability to reveal emotion was a powerfully attractive quality. Ahmed looked down and composed himself before he continued. "Had you seen Gamal at all during the morning?"

"I don't believe so," said Erica, but not convincingly. "There is a chance I saw him at a refreshment stand in Memphis, but I'm not sure."

Ahmed ran his fingers through his thick hair. "Tell me," he said. "Gamal was already upon the wooden platform in the serapeum when you started up the stairs."

"That's right," said Erica.

"I find that curious," said Ahmed.

"Why?" questioned Erica.

Ahmed looked slightly flustered. "I'm just thinking," he said evasively, "nothing makes sense."

"I feel the same way, Mr. Khazzan. And I want to assure you that I had nothing to do with the affair. Nothing. And I think I should be able to call the American embassy."

134

"You may call the American embassy," said Ahmed, "but frankly there is no need to do so."

"I think I need some help."

"Miss Baron, I'm sorry you were inconvenienced today. But actually this is our problem. You can call whomever you'd like when you get back to your hotel."

"I'm not going to be detained here?" asked Erica, almost afraid to believe what she was hearing.

"Of course not," said Ahmed.

"That is good news," said Erica. "But there is one other thing I must tell you about. I should have told you last night, but I was afraid. Anyway . . ." She breathed in deeply. "I've had two very strange and upsetting days. I'm not sure which was worse. Yesterday afternoon I inadvertently witnessed another murder, incredible as it may sound." Erica involuntarily shivered. "I happened to see an old man by the name of Abdul Hamdi killed by three men, and—"

Ahmed's chair thudded to the floor. He had been leaning back. "Did you actually see the faces?" His surprise and concern were apparent.

"Two of them, yes. The third, no," said Erica.

"Could you identify those whom you did see?" asked Ahmed.

"Possibly. I'm not sure. But I do want to apologize about not telling you last night. I really was afraid."

"I understand," said Ahmed. "Don't worry. I will take care of that. But undoubtedly we will have more questions."

"More questions . . ." said Erica forlornly. "Actually, I would like to leave Egypt as soon as possible. This trip is nothing like I'd planned."

"I'm sorry, Miss Baron," said Ahmed, regaining the composure Erica remembered from the night before. "Under the circumstances, you will not be allowed to leave until these issues are cleared up or we are sure you cannot contribute any more. I really am sorry that you have become involved like this. But you may feel free to move about as much as you'd like—just let me know if you plan to leave Cairo. Again, you should feel free to discuss the problem with the American

135

embassy, but remember they have little say over our internal affairs."

"Being detained within the country is far better than being in jail," said Erica, smiling weakly. "How long do you think it will be before I will be allowed to leave?"

"It's hard to say. Perhaps a week. Although it might be difficult, I suggest that you try to regard your experiences here as unfortunate coincidences. I think you should try to enjoy Egypt." Ahmed toyed with his pencils before continuing. "As a representative of the government, I'd like to offer you dinner tonight and show you that Egypt can be very pleasurable."

"Thank you," said Erica, genuinely moved by Ahmed's concern, "but I'm afraid I already have plans with Yvon de Margeau."

"Oh, I see," said Ahmed, looking away. "Well, please accept my apologies from my government. I will have you driven to your hotel, and I promise I will be in touch."

He stood up and shook hands with Erica across his desk. His grip was pleasantly strong and firm. Erica walked from the room, surprised that the conversation had ended so abruptly and stunned to be free.

As soon as she left, Ahmed summoned Zaki Riad, the assistant director, to his office. Riad had fifteen years' seniority in the department but had been passed over during Ahmed's meteoric rise to director. Although he was an intelligent, quick-witted man, his physical type was the exact opposite of Ahmed's. He was obese, with bloated features, and his hair was as dark and tightly curled as a karakul lamb's.

Ahmed had walked to the giant map of Egypt, turning when his assistant had seated himself. "What do you make of all this, Zaki?"

"I haven't the slightest idea," answered Zaki, wiping his brow, which sweated despite the air conditioning. He enjoyed seeing Ahmed under pressure.

"I cannot for the life of me figure out why Gamal was shot," said Ahmed, slamming his fist against his open palm. "God, a young man with children. Do you think his death had anything to do with the fact he was following Erica Baron?"

"I cannot see how," said Zaki, "but I guess there's always a chance." The last comment was intended to sting. Zaki stuck an unlit pipe in his mouth, mindless of the ashes that drifted down onto his chest.

Ahmed covered his eyes with his hand and massaged his scalp; then slowly he let his hand slide down his face to stroke his luxuriant mustache. "It just doesn't make sense." He turned and looked at the large map. "I wonder if there is something going on in Saqqara. Maybe some new tombs have been illicitly discovered." He walked back and sat down behind his desk. "More disturbing, the immigration authorities notified me that Stephanos Markoulis arrived in Cairo today. As you know, he does not come here often." Ahmed leaned forward, looking directly at Zaki Riad. "Tell me, what have the police reported about Abdul Hamdi?"

"Very little," said Zaki. "Apparently he was robbed. The police were able to learn that the old man had recently experienced a marked change in fortune, moving his antique business from Luxor to Cairo. At the same time, he'd been able to purchase more valuable pieces. He must have had some money. So he was robbed."

"Any idea where his money came from?" asked Ahmed.

"No, but there is someone who might. The old man does have a son in the antique business in Luxor."

"Have the police spoken to the son?" asked Ahmed.

"Not that I know of," said Zaki. "That would be too logical for the police. Actually, they're not all that interested."

"I'm interested," said Ahmed. "Arrange air transportation for me to go to Luxor tonight. I will pay Abdul Hamdi's son a visit in the morning. Also, send several additional guards to the Necropolis of Saqqara."

"Are you sure this is the right time for you to leave Cairo?" asked Zaki, pointing with the stem of his pipe. "As you indicated, with Stephanos Markoulis in Cairo, something is happening."

"Perhaps, Zaki," said Ahmed, "but I think I need to get away and spend a day or so in my own house by the Nile. I cannot help but feel a tremendous responsibility for poor Gamal. When I feel this depressed, Luxor is an emotional balm."

"And what about the American woman, Erica Baron?" Zaki lit his pipe with a stainless-steel lighter.

"She's fine. She's scared, but she seemed to have pulled herself together by the time she left. I'm not sure how I'd react if I'd witnessed two murders in twenty-four hours, especially if one of the victims fell on top of me."

Zaki took several thoughtful puffs on his pipe before continuing. "Strange. But, Ahmed, when I asked about Miss Baron, I wasn't inquiring about her health. I want to know if you want her followed."

"No," said Ahmed angrily. "Not tonight. She's going to be with de Margeau." Almost the instant the words left his mouth, Ahmed felt embarrassed. His emotion was out of place.

"This is not like you, Ahmed," said Zaki, watching the director very closely. He'd known Ahmed for several years, and Ahmed had never shown any interest in women. Now, suddenly it seemed that Ahmed was jealous. Finding a potential human weakness in Ahmed made Zaki feel inwardly pleased. He'd grown to hate Ahmed's perfect record. "Perhaps it is best if you go to Luxor for a few days. I will certainly be happy to keep things under control here in Cairo, and I will look into Saqqara personally."

Cairo   5:35 P.M.

As the government car pulled up to the Hilton, Erica still could not quite believe she had been released. She opened the door before the vehicle had come to a complete stop and thanked the driver as if he'd had something to do with her release. Entering the Hilton was a little like coming home.

Once again the lobby was extremely busy. The afternoon international flights had been discharging passengers in a steady stream. Most of them were waiting perched on their luggage as the inefficient hotel tried to deal with the daily onslaught.

Erica realized how out-of-place she must look. She was hot, sweaty, and a mess. The large bloodstain was still on her back, and her cotton pants were in sorry shape, smeared with dirt and torn on her right knee. If there had been an alternate route to her room she would have taken it. Unfortunately, she had to walk directly across the large red-and-blue Oriental rug beneath the main crystal chandelier. It was like being in a spotlight, and people began to stare.

One of the men at the registration desk caught sight of her and waved with his pen, pointing in her direction. Erica quickened her step, gaining on the elevator. She pressed the button, afraid to look behind her in case someone was coming to stop her. She pushed the elevator button several more times while the floor indicator slowly came toward Ground. The door opened and she entered the car, asking the operator for the ninth floor. He nodded silently. The door began to close, but before it sealed, a hand wrapped around its lead edge, forcing the elevator man to reopen it. Erica backed against the rear of the car and held her breath.

"Hello, there," said a large man wearing a stetson and cowboy boots. "Are you Erica Baron?"

Erica's mouth opened, but no words came out.

"My name is Jeffrey John Rice, from Houston. You are Erica Baron?" The man continued to keep the door from closing. The elevator operator stood like a stone statue.

Like a guilty child Erica nodded in affirmation.

"So nice to meet you, Miss Baron." Jeffrey Rice held out his hand.

Erica lifted her own like an automaton. Jeffrey Rice pumped it exuberantly. "It's a pleasure, Miss Baron. I'd like you to meet my wife."

Without letting go of her hand, Jeffrey Rice yanked Erica from the elevator. She stumbled forward, rescuing her tote as the strap slipped off her shoulder.

"We've been waiting for you for hours," said Rice, pulling Erica toward the lobby.

After four or five clumsy steps she managed to extract her hand. "Mr. Rice," she said, coming to a stop, "I'd like to meet your wife, but some other time. I've had a very strange day."

"You do look a little ragged, dear, but let's have one drink." He reached out again and took Erica's wrist.

"Mr. Rice!" said Erica sharply.

"Come on, honey. We've come halfway around the world to see you."

Erica looked into Jeffrey Rice's tanned, immaculately barbered face. "What do you mean, Mr. Rice?"

"Exactly what I said. My wife and I have come from Houston to see you. We flew all night. Luckily I've my own plane. Least you can do is have a drink with us."

Suddenly the name registered. Jeffrey Rice had the Houston statue of Seti I. It had been late at night when she'd spoken to Dr. Lowery, but now she remembered.

"You've come from Houston?"

140

"That's right. Flew over. Landed a few hours ago. Now, come over and meet my wife, Priscilla."

Erica allowed herself to be pulled back through the lobby to be introduced to Priscilla Rice, a Southern belle with a deep décolletage and a very large diamond ring that effectively competed for sparkle with the enormous chandelier. Her Southern accent was even more pronounced than her husband's.

Jeffrey Rice herded his wife and Erica into the Taverne lounge. His officious manner and loud voice got rapid service, especially since he freely passed out Egyptian one-pound notes as tips. Within the dim light of the cocktail lounge Erica felt a little less conspicuous. They sat in a corner booth, where Erica's torn and soiled clothes could not be seen.

Jeffrey Rice ordered straight bourbon for both himself and wife and a vodka and tonic for Erica, who found herself relaxing, even laughing at the Texan's tall stories about their experiences at customs. Erica allowed herself a second vodka and tonic.

"Well, to business," said Jeffrey Rice, lowering his voice. "I certainly don't want to spoil this party, but we have come a long way. Rumor has it that you've seen a statue of Pharaoh Seti I."

Erica noticed that Rice's demeanor changed dramatically. She guessed that he was a shrewd businessman beneath the playful-Texan guise.

"Dr. Lowery said that you wanted some photos of my statue, particularly of the hieroglyphics in the base. I have those photos right here." Jeffrey Rice drew an envelope from his jacket pocket and held it straight up in the air. "Now, I'm happy to give these to you, provided you tell me where you saw the statue you told Dr. Lowery about. You see, I was planning on giving my statue to my city of Houston, but it's not going to be so special if there's a whole bunch of them floating around. In other words, I want to buy that statue you saw. I want to buy it bad. In fact, I'm willing to give ten thousand dollars to anyone who can just tell me where it is so that I can buy it. Yourself included."

Putting her drink down, Erica stared at Jeffrey Rice. Having seen Cairo's unmitigated poverty, she knew that ten thousand dollars here would have the same effect as a billion dollars in New York. It would create unbelievable pressure in the Cairo underworld. Since Abdul Hamdi's death was doubtless related to the statue, the ten thousand dollars offered just for information could cause numerous additional deaths. It was a frightening thought.

Erica rapidly described her experience with Abdul Hamdi and the statue of Seti I. Rice listened intently, writing down Abdul Hamdi's name. "Do you know if anyone else has seen the statue?" he asked, tilting back his stetson.

"Not that I know of," said Erica.

"Is there anyone else that knows Abdul Hamdi had the statue?"

"Yes," said Erica. "A Monsieur Yvon de Margeau. He's staying at the Meridien Hotel. He indicated that Hamdi had corresponded with potential buyers around the world, so there are probably a lot of people that knew Hamdi had the statue."

"Looks like this is going to be more fun than we expected," said Rice, leaning across the table and patting his wife's slim wrist. Turning back to Erica, he handed her the envelope of photos. "Do you have any idea where the statue could be?"

Erica shook her head. "No idea whatsoever," she said, taking the envelope. Despite the poor light, she could not wait to see the pictures, so she pulled them out and looked closely at the first one.

"That's some statue, isn't it?" said Rice, as if he were showing Erica pictures of his firstborn child. "It makes all that Tut stuff look like a child's toys."

Jeffrey Rice was right. Looking at the photos, Erica admitted the statue was stunning. But she also noticed something else. As far as she could recall, the statue was identical with the one she'd seen. Then she hesitated. Looking at Rice's statue, she saw that the right hand was holding the jewel-encrusted mace. She remembered that Abdul's statue held the mace in its left hand. The statues were not the same, they were mirror images! Erica shuffled through the rest of the photographs.

There were pictures of the statue from every angle, very good photos, obviously professional. Finally, toward the bottom of the stack, were the close-ups. Erica felt her pulse quicken when she saw the hieroglyphics. It was too dark to see the symbols clearly, but by tilting the photo she was able to see the two pharaonic cartouches. There were the names, Seti I and Tutankhamen. Amazing.

"Miss Baron," said Jeffrey Rice, "it would be our pleasure to have you join us for dinner." Priscilla Rice smiled warmly as her husband extended the invitation.

"Thank you," said Erica, replacing the photos in the envelope. "Unfortunately, I already have plans. Perhaps some other evening, if you are staying in Egypt."

"Of course," said Jeffrey Rice. "Or you and your guests could join us tonight."

Erica thought for a moment, then declined. Jeffrey Rice and Yvon de Margeau would mix like oil and water. Erica was about to excuse herself when she thought of something else. "Mr. Rice, how did you buy your Seti I statue?" Her voice was hesitant, since she didn't know the propriety of the question.

"With money, my dear!" Jeffrey Rice laughed, slapping the table with an open hand. He obviously thought his joke was hilarious. Erica smiled weakly and waited, hoping there would be more.

"I heard about it from an art-dealer friend in New York. He called me up and said that there was an amazing piece of Egyptian sculpture that was going to be auctioned behind closed doors."

"Closed doors?"

"Yeah, no publicity. Kinda hush-hush. Happens all the time."

"Was it here in Egypt?" asked Erica.

"Nope, Zurich."

"Switzerland," said Erica incredulously. "Why Switzerland?"

Jeffrey Rice shrugged. "At that kind of auction you don't ask questions. There's a certain etiquette."

"Do you know how it got to Zurich?" asked Erica.

"No," said Jeffrey Rice. "As I said, you don't ask questions.

It was arranged by one of the big banks there, and they tend to be very closemouthed. All they want is the money." Smiling, he got up and offered to escort Erica back to the elevator. He obviously had no intention of saying more.

Erica entered her room with her head reeling. Jeffrey Rice's statements were as much to blame as the two drinks. While he had waited with her for the elevator, he had casually mentioned that the statue was not the first Egyptian antiquity he'd purchased in Zurich. He'd gotten several gold statues and a wonderful pectoral necklace, all possibly dating from the time of Seti I.

Putting the envelope with the photos down on the bureau, Erica thought about her earlier conception of the black market: somebody would find a small artifact in the sand and would sell it to someone who wanted it. Now she was forced to admit that the final transacting took place in the paneled conference rooms of international banks. It was incredible.

Erica removed her blouse, looked at the bloodstain, and impulsively threw it away. Her pants followed the blouse to the same wastebasket. Removing her bra, she noticed the blood had even soaked through to the back strap. But she could not cavalierly discard her bra. Bras were difficult for Erica to buy, and there were only a few brands that were comfortable. Before doing something rash, she opened the top drawer of the bureau to count how many she'd brought along. But instead of counting, she found herself just looking at her underclothes. Lingerie was an extravagance that Erica had allowed herself even during her financially lean years as a full-time student. She enjoyed the reassuring feminine feel of expensive underwear. Consequently she was careful with them, and when she had unpacked, she had taken the time to lay things out neatly. But now the drawer looked different. Someone had been in her belongings!

Erica stood up and looked around the room. The bed was made, so obviously housekeeping had been in, but would they go into her clothes? It was possible. Quickly she checked the middle drawer, pulling out her Levi's. In the side pocket were her diamond earrings, the last gift she'd received from her

144

father. In the back pocket was her return airline ticket and the bulk of her traveler's checks. After finding everything in its place, she heaved a sigh of relief and returned the jeans.

Looking back into the top drawer, she wondered if she could have disturbed her own belongings that morning. Walking into the bathroom, she picked up her plastic makeup bag and examined its contents. Obviously she did not organize her makeup, yet she used the various articles in an orderly fashion, dropping each into the bag after using it. Her moisturizer should have been close to the bottom; instead it was on the top. Also on the top were her birth-control pills, which she always took in the evening. Erica looked at herself in the mirror. Her eyes reflected a feeling of violation, similar to that generated by the boy who had felt her up the day before. Someone had had his hands in her things. Erica wondered if she should report the incident to the hotel management. But what would she say, since nothing was taken?

Returning to the foyer, Erica nervously locked her door with the dead bolt. Then she walked over and looked out through the sliding glass door, where the fiery Egyptian sun was reaching for the western horizon. The sphinx looked like a hungry lion ready to pounce. The pyramids thrust their massive shapes against a bloodred sky. Erica wished she felt happier to be within their shadow.

Cairo 10:00 P.M.

Dinner with Yvon turned out to be a soothingly romantic interlude. Erica surprised herself with her resilience; despite the harrowing day and despite the guilty feeling she had had since her call to Richard, she was able to enjoy the evening. Yvon had picked her up at her hotel while the spot where the sun had set still glowed like a dying ember. They had driven south along the Nile out of the dusty heat of Cairo toward the town of Maadi. As the stars had emerged in the darkening sky, Erica's tension had evaporated into the cool evening air.

The restaurant was called the Sea Horse, and it was situated directly on the Nile's eastern bank. Taking advantage of the perfect Egyptian nighttime climate, the dining room was open on all four sides. Across the river and above a line of palms were the illuminated pyramids of Giza.

They dined on fresh fish and giant prawns from the Red Sea, grilled on an open fire and washed down with a chilled white wine called Gianaclis. Yvon thought it was terrible and cut it with mineral water, but Erica liked its slightly sweet, fruity taste.

She watched him drink, admiring his closely fitted dark blue silk shirt. Reminding her of her silk tops, which she prized and wore on special occasions, it should have seemed feminine, but it didn't. In fact the silvery sheen seemed to emphasize his masculinity.

Erica herself had taken a long time to get ready, and the

effort had paid off. Her freshly washed hair was loosely pulled back on the sides and held with tortoiseshell combs. She had chosen to wear a one-piece chocolate-brown jersey with a scooped neck, cap sleeves, and elastic waist. Beneath she had on hose for the first time since she had gotten off the plane. She knew that she looked as good as she could, and the whole effect pleased her as the soft Nile breeze caressed the nape of her neck.

Their conversation started lightly but soon switched to the murders. Yvon had been frustrated in his attempts to discover who had killed Abdul Hamdi. He told Erica that the only thing he'd learned was that the murderers were not from Cairo. Then Erica described her harrowing episode in the serapeum and the subsequent experience with the police.

"I wish you had allowed me to accompany you today," said Yvon, shaking his head in wonderment when Erica had finished her story. He reached across the table and lightly pressed her hand.

"So do I," admitted Erica, looking down at their barely touching fingers.

"I have a confession," said Yvon softly. "When I first met you, I was only interested in the Seti statue. But now I find you irresistibly charming." His teeth gleamed in the candlelight.

"I don't know you well enough to know when you are teasing," said Erica, acknowledging an adolescent thrill.

"I'm not teasing, Erica. You are very different from any woman I've ever met."

Erica looked out across the darkened Nile. Faint movement on the near bank caught her eye, and she could just make out several fishermen working on a sailboat. They were apparently naked and their skin glistened like polished onyx in the darkness. With her eyes momentarily captured by the scene, Erica thought about Yvon's comment. It sounded like such a cliché, and in that sense a little demeaning. Yet it was possible there was some truth in it, because Yvon was different from any man she'd ever met.

"The fact that you are trained as an Egyptologist," continued Yvon, "I find fascinating, because—and I mean this as a

148

compliment—you have an East European sensuality that I love. Besides, I think you share some of Egypt's mysterious vibrancy."

"I think I'm very American," said Erica.

"Ah, but Americans have ethnic origins, and I think yours are apparent. I find it very attractive. To tell you the truth, I am tired of the cold, blond Nordic look."

As strange as it seemed to her, Erica found herself at a loss for words. The last thing she expected or wanted was an infatuation making her emotionally vulnerable.

Yvon seemed to sense her discomfort and changed the subject while their dinner dishes were cleared. "Erica, could you possibly identify the killer in the serapeum today? Did you get to see his face?"

"No," said Erica, "it was as if the sky had fallen in. I didn't see anyone."

"God, what an awful experience. I can't think of anything worse. And falling on top of you! Unbelievable. But you know that assassinations of government officials are a daily occurrence in the Middle East. Well, at least you weren't hurt. I know it will be difficult but I wouldn't give it any more thought. It was just such a crazy coincidence. And coming on top of Hamdi's death makes it that much worse. Two murders in two days. I don't know if I could take it."

"I know it was probably a coincidence," said Erica, "but there is one thing that concerns me. The poor man who was shot didn't just work for the government; he worked for the Department of Antiquities. So both victims dealt with ancient artifacts, but from supposedly opposite sides of the issue. Still, what do I know?" Erica smiled weakly.

The waiter brought out Arabic coffee and served the dessert. Yvon had ordered a coarse semolina cake coated in sugar and sprinkled with walnuts and raisins.

"One of the amazing aspects of your adventure," said Yvon, "was that you were not detained by the police."

"That's not totally correct. I was detained for a number of hours, and I'm not permitted to leave the country." Erica tasted the dessert but decided it wasn't worth the calories.

"That's nothing. You're lucky you're not in jail. I'd be

willing to wager that your guide still is."

"I think I have Ahmed Khazzan to thank for my release," said Erica.

"You know Ahmed Khazzan?" asked Yvon. He stopped eating.

"I don't know how to categorize our relationship," said Erica. "After you left me last night, Ahmed Khazzan was waiting for me in my room."

"This is true?" Yvon's fork clattered as it hit the table.

"If you think you're surprised, try to imagine how I felt. I thought I was being arrested for not reporting Hamdi's murder. He took me to his office and questioned me for an hour."

"That's incredible," said Yvon, wiping his mouth with his napkin. "Ahmed Khazzan already knew about Hamdi's murder?"

"I don't know if he did or not," said Erica. "Initially I thought he did. Why else would he have taken me to his office? But he never said anything about it, and I was afraid to bring it up."

"Then what did he want?"

"Mostly he wanted to know about you."

"Me!" Yvon assumed a playfully innocent expression and poked his chest with his index finger. "Erica, you have had a most amazing two days. I've never even met Ahmed Khazzan, and I've been coming here to Egypt for a number of years. What did he ask you about me?"

"He wanted to know what you are doing in Egypt."

"And what did you tell him?"

"That I didn't know."

"You said nothing about the Seti statue?"

"No. I was afraid if I mentioned the statue, I'd be drawn into talking about Hamdi's murder."

"Did he say anything about the Seti statue?"

"Nothing."

"Erica, you are fantastic." Suddenly he leaned over the table, cradled Erica's face in his hands, and kissed her on both cheeks.

The exuberance of the gesture dumbfounded her, and she

felt herself blushing, something she hadn't done in years. Self-consciously she took a sip of the sweet coffee. "I don't think Ahmed Khazzan believed everything I said."

"What makes you say that?" asked Yvon. He went back to his dessert.

"When I returned to my hotel room this afternoon, I noticed some very subtle changes in my belongings. I think my room was searched. After Ahmed Khazzan had been in there the night before, the only thing I can imagine is that the Egyptian authorities returned. My valuables weren't touched. I wasn't robbed. But I have no idea what they could have been looking for."

Yvon chewed thoughtfully, looking directly at Erica. "Does your door have an extra night latch?" he asked.

"Yes."

"Use it," said Yvon. He took another bite of dessert and swallowed thoughtfully before he spoke again. "Erica, when you visited with Abdul Hamdi, did he give you any letters or papers?"

"No," said Erica. "He gave me a fake scarab, which looks real, and he did convince me to use his 1929 Baedeker instead of my own Nagel's."

"Where are these things?" asked Yvon.

"Right here," said Erica. She reached into her tote bag and extracted the Baedeker without the cover. It had finally detached, and Erica had left it in her room. The scarab was in her coin purse.

Yvon picked up the scarab and held it close to the candle. "Are you sure this is a fake?"

"Looks good, doesn't it?" said Erica. "I thought it was real too, but Hamdi insisted. Said his son made it."

Yvon carefully put the scarab down and picked up the guidebook. "These Baedekers are fantastic," he said. He flipped through the volume carefully, viewing each page. "They are the best guides ever written for the Egyptian sites, particularly Luxor." Yvon pushed the coverless book back toward Erica. "Do you mind if I have this authenticated?" he asked, holding the scarab between his thumb and forefinger.

"You mean carbon-dated?" asked Erica.

"Yes," said Yvon. "This looks very good to me, and it has the cartouche of Seti I. I think it's bone."

"You're right about the material. Hamdi said his son carved them of bone from mummies in the ancient public catacombs. So it will date properly. He also said that they make the cut surfaces look old by feeding them to turkeys."

Yvon laughed. "The antique industry in Egypt is extremely resourceful. Just the same, I'd like to have this scarab examined."

"It's fine with me, but I would like to have it back." Erica took a last sip of coffee but ended up with bitter grounds in her mouth. "Yvon, why is Ahmed Khazzan so interested in your affairs?"

"I think I worry him," said Yvon. "But why he spoke to you rather than to me, I cannot answer. He thinks of me as a dangerous collector of antiquities. He knows I've made some important acquisitions while trying to unravel the black-market routing. The fact that I am interested in doing something about the black market has no meaning. Ahmed Khazzan is part of the bureaucracy here. Rather than accept my help, they probably fear for their jobs. Besides, there is the lingering hatred of the British and the French. And I am French and a little English."

"You are part English?" asked Erica with disbelief.

"I don't admit it often," said Yvon with his strong French accent. "European genealogy is more complicated than most people think. My family residence is the Château Valois near Rambouillet, which is between Paris and Chartres. My father is the Marquis de Margeau, but my mother was from the English Harcourt family."

"Sounds a long way from Toledo, Ohio," said Erica quietly.

"I beg your pardon."

"I said, it sounds intriguing," said Erica, smiling as he settled the bill.

Leaving the restaurant Yvon slipped his hand around Erica's waist. It felt good. The evening air had cooled considerably and the almost full moon shone between the branches of the eucalyptus trees lining the road. A chorus of insects resounded

152

in the darkness, reminding Erica of August nights as a child in Ohio. It was a comfortable memory.

"What kind of important Egyptian antiquities have you purchased?" asked Erica as they drew near to Yvon's Fiat.

"Some wonderful pieces that I'd love to show you sometime," said Yvon. "I'm particularly fond of several small golden statues. One of Nekhbet and another of Isis."

"Have you purchased any Seti I pieces?" asked Erica.

Yvon opened the passenger door to the car. "Possibly a necklace. Most of my pieces are from the New Kingdom, and a number could be from the time of Seti I."

Erica entered the car and Yvon told her to use her seat belt. "I've done a little auto racing," said Yvon, "and I always use them."

"I could have guessed," said Erica, remembering the ride the day before.

Yvon laughed. "Everyone says I drive a little fast. I enjoy it." He reached for his driving gloves on the dash. "I suppose you know about as much about Seti I as I. It is curious. It is known very accurately when his fabulous rock-cut tomb was plundered in ancient times. The faithful priests in the twentieth dynasty were able to save his mummy, and they documented their efforts very well."

"I saw the mummy of Seti I this morning," said Erica.

"Ironic, isn't it?" asked Yvon, starting the engine. "The fragile body of Seti I comes down to us essentially intact. Seti I was one of the pharaonic mummies in that fabulous cache illicitly found by the clever Rasul family at the end of the nineteenth century." Yvon turned and leaned over the front seat to back up the car. "The Rasuls slowly exploited that find over a ten-year period before they were caught. An amazing story." He pulled away from the restaurant and accelerated toward Cairo. "A few people still think there are some Seti I belongings to be discovered. When you visit his enormous tomb in Luxor, you'll see places where people have obtained permits to cut tunnels during this century, trying to find a secret room. The stimulus for this has been occasional Seti pieces surfacing on the black market. But it's not surprising to see some Seti artifacts. He probably was buried with a staggering array of possessions. And even if his tomb was stripped, they often recycled funerary objects in ancient Egypt. The stuff was probably buried and robbed over and over again down through the years. Consequently a lot of it is most likely still under ground. Very few people have any idea how many peasants currently dig for antiquities in Luxor. Every night they shift the desert sand, and occasionally they find something spectacular."

"Like the Seti I statue?" said Erica, looking again at Yvon's profile. He smiled and she could see the whiteness of his teeth against his tanned skin.

"Exactly," he said. "But can you imagine what Seti's unplundered tomb must have looked like? My God, it must have been fantastic. The treasures of Tutankhamen dazzle us today, but they were insignificant compared to Seti I's."

Erica knew Yvon was right, especially after seeing the statue at Abdul Hamdi's. Seti I had been a major pharaoh who ruled an empire, Tutankhamen an insignificant boy king who probably never held any real power.

"*Merde!*" shouted Yvon as they hit one of the ubiquitous potholes. The car shimmied from the impact. As they entered Cairo, the road deteriorated and they had to slow down. The city began as pieces of cardboard propped up with sticks. They were the housing of the newly arrived immigrants. The cardboard gave way to sheets of metal and cloth and occasional oil barrels. Finally the shantytown was superseded by crumbly mud brick and eventually the city proper, but the feeling of poverty hung in the air like a miasma.

"Would you care to come to my suite for an after-dinner brandy?" asked Yvon.

Erica glanced over at him, trying to sort out her feelings. There was a good chance that Yvon's offer was not as innocent as it sounded. But she was definitely attracted to him, and after the appalling day, the idea of being close to someone was very appealing. Still, physical attraction was not always a reliable guide to behavior, and Yvon was almost too good to be true. Looking at him, she admitted that he was beyond her experience. It was too much too soon.

154

"Thank you, Yvon," said Erica warmly, "but I think not. Perhaps you'd like to have another drink at the Hilton."

"But of course." For a moment Erica felt a little disappointed Yvon wasn't more persistent. Perhaps she was a victim of her own fantasies.

Reaching the hotel, they decided a walk would be better than the smoke-filled Taverne. Hand in hand they crossed the busy Korneish-el-Nil Boulevard to the Nile and wandered out onto the El Tahrir bridge. Yvon pointed out the Meridien Hotel on the tip of Roda island. A lone felucca silently slipped through the dappled path of moonlight on the water.

Yvon put his arm around Erica as they strolled, and Erica allowed her own hand to cover his. Again she felt self-conscious. It had been a long time since she had been with any man besides Richard.

"A Greek named Stephanos Markoulis arrived in Cairo today," said Yvon, stopping by the balustrade. They gazed at the dancing lights reflected on the water's surface. "And I believe he will call and try to see you."

Erica looked up questioningly.

"Stephanos Markoulis deals in Egyptian antiquities in Athens. He rarely comes to Egypt. I don't know why he is here, but I would like to find out. Ostensibly he's come because of Abdul Hamdi's murder. But he might be here because of the Seti statue."

"And he wants to see me about the murder?"

"Yes," said Yvon. He continued to avoid looking at Erica. "I don't know how he is involved, but he is."

"Yvon, I don't think I want to have any more to do with the Abdul Hamdi affair. Frankly, the whole business frightens me. I've told you everything I know."

"I understand," said Yvon soothingly, "but unfortunately, you are all I've got."

"And what do you mean by that?"

Yvon turned to her. "You are the last connection to the Seti statue. Stephanos Markoulis was involved somehow with the sale of the first Seti statue to the man in Houston. I'm worried he's involved with the present statue. You know how important it is to me to stop this rape of antiquities."

Erica looked over toward the gay lights of the Hilton. "The man from Houston who bought the first Seti statue also arrived today. He was waiting for me in the Hilton lobby this afternoon. His name is Jeffrey Rice."

Yvon's mouth tightened perceptibly.

"He told me," continued Erica, "that he was offering ten thousand dollars to anyone who could merely tell him where this second Seti statue is so he could buy it."

"Christ," said Yvon. "That's going to turn Cairo into a circus. And to think I've been worried whether Ahmed Khazzan and the antiquities service were going to find out about the existence of this statue. Well, Erica, this means I've got to work fast. I can understand your feelings about involvement, but please do me the favor of seeing Stephanos Markoulis. I need to know more about what he's up to, and you may be able to help. With Jeffrey offering that kind of money, I think we can be sure the statue is still available. And if I don't move quickly, it too is going to disappear into some private collection. All I ask is that you see Stephanos Markoulis and then tell me what he says. Everything he says."

Erica looked at Yvon's pleading face. She could sense his commitment and knew how important it was that the fabulous Seti I statue be preserved for the public.

"You're sure it will be safe?"

"Of course," said Yvon. "When he calls, arrange to meet in a public place so you don't have to worry."

"All right," she said, "but you'll owe me another dinner."

"D'accord," said Yvon, kissing Erica—this time on the lips.

Erica studied Yvon's handsome face. A warm smile lingered at the corners of his mouth. She wondered for a moment if he wasn't using her. Then she chided herself for her own suspiciousness. Besides, it was possible she was using him.

Returning to her room, Erica felt better than she had during the whole trip. Yvon had aroused her in a way that she had not experienced for a long time, since even the physical aspect of her relationship with Richard had not been totally satisfying for a number of months. And Yvon was capable of making his sexual desires seem secondary to a meaningful relationship.

156

He was willing to wait, and that made her feel good. Outside her room she inserted her key quickly and swung the door open widely. Everything appeared in its place. Remembering hundreds of movies she'd seen, she wished she had made some provision to determine if someone had entered her room. Turning on the lights, she strode into the bedroom. It was empty. She checked the bathroom, smiling at her own sense of melodrama.

Then, sighing with relief, Erica gave her door a shove, and it closed with a resounding thud followed by the reassuring click of the American-made hardware. She kicked off her shoes, turned off the air conditioning, and opened the balcony door. The floodlights on the pyramids and sphinx had been turned off. Returning to her room, she took her jersey dress off over her head and hung it up. In the distance she could hear the traffic that still plied the Korneish-el-Nile, despite the hour. Otherwise the hotel was silent. It was while she was removing her eye makeup that she heard the first unmistakable sound at her door.

She stopped moving, staring at her image in the mirror. She was dressed in her bra and panties, with the eye makeup gone from one eye. In the distance the usual auto horns sounded, followed by silence. She held her breath, her ears straining. Again she heard the muted sound of metal hitting metal. Erica felt the blood drain from her face. Someone was pushing a key into the lock of her door. The realization made her turn slowly around. The night bolt on the hall door was undone. Erica was paralyzed. She couldn't make herself lunge for the dead bolt. She was afraid that she would not be able to close it before the door was opened. The tumblers in the lock clicked again.

Then, as she watched, the doorknob began slowly to turn. Erica looked at the lock on the bathroom door. It was a mere button on the handle, and the door itself was a thin panel. Again, the isolated sound of the key being forced made her look back at the slowly turning door handle. Like a frightened animal's her eyes raced around the room for escape. The balcony! Could she cross over to the neighboring terrace? No, she'd have to swing out over a nine-story drop. Then she remembered the telephone. She ran across the room on silent feet and yanked the receiver to her ear. She heard a distant ring. Answer, she shouted silently, please answer.

There were a few final clicks from the door, different from the others, heralding the full penetration and rotation of the key. The door was unlocked, and without another sound it cracked open, allowing a strip of harsh light fom the hall to knife into the room. Erica dropped on her knees. Throwing the phone receiver onto the bed and flattening herself on the floor, she wriggled under the bed.

From beneath the spread she could just see the base of the door as it opened. A buzzing sound came from the phone. Erica knew the phone would give her away, a telltale sign she was hiding! A man came into the room, quietly closing the door behind him. As Erica watched in an agony of terror he walked toward the bed and out of Erica's line of vision. She was afraid to move her head. Above her she heard the receiver replaced. The intruder then silently walked back into her line of vision and apparently checked the bathroom.

Cold sweat formed on Erica's face as she watched the feet go to the closet. He was searching for her! The closet door opened, then closed. Coming back to the center of the bedroom, the man stopped, his shoes no more than five or six feet from Erica's head. Then they came forward, step by step, stopping by the bed. She could have touched him—he was that close.

Suddenly the bedspread was pulled up, and Erica was looking up into a man's face.

"Erica, what in the world are you doing under the bed?"

"Richard!" Erica screamed, and burst into tears.

Although Erica was still too shaken to move, Richard pulled her from beneath the bed and dusted her off.

"Really," he said with a grin. "What are you doing under the bed?"

"Oh, Richard," said Erica, suddenly throwing her arms around his neck. "I'm so glad it's you. I can't tell you how glad I am." She pressed herself against him, holding him tight.

"I should surprise you more often," he said happily, putting his arms around her bare back. They stood together for a few moments as Erica collected herself and dried her tears.

158

"Is it really you?" she said finally, looking up into his face. "I can't believe it. Am I dreaming?"

"You're not dreaming. It's me. Maybe a little exhausted, but right here with you in Egypt."

"You do look a little tired." Erica brushed his hair off his forehead. "Are you all right?"

"Yeah, I'm okay. Just tired. Trouble with equipment, they said. We were delayed almost four hours in Rome. But it was worth it. You look wonderful. When did you start putting makeup on only one eye?"

Erica smiled and hugged him gently. "I would have looked better if you'd given me a little more notice. How could you get the time off?" She leaned back in his arms, her hands pressed up against his chest.

"I had covered for someone a few months ago when his father died. He owed me a favor. He'll see all the emergencies and in-house patients. The office will just have to wait. I'm afraid I wasn't very effective anyway. I've missed you terribly."

"I've missed you too. I guess that's why I telephoned."

"I was glad you did," said Richard, kissing her forehead.

"When I asked you a year ago about possibly coming to Egypt, you said there was no way you could take the time."

"Well . . ." said Richard, "I didn't feel as confident about the practice then. But that was a year ago, and now I'm here with you, in Egypt. I have trouble believing it myself. But, Erica, what were you doing under the bed?" A smile formed in the corners of his mouth. "Did I scare you? I didn't mean to, and I'm sorry if I did. I thought you'd be sleeping, and I wanted to come in quietly and awaken you as I used to do at home."

"Did you scare me?" questioned Erica. She laughed sarcastically. She pushed herself away to get her white eyelet robe from the closet. "I still feel weak. I mean, you terrified me."

"I'm sorry," said Richard.

"How did you get a key?" Erica sat on the edge of the bed, her hands in her lap.

Richard shrugged. "I just walked in and asked for a key to 932."

"And they just gave it to you? They didn't ask any questions?"

"Nope. It's not unusual in hotels. I was hoping they would, so I could really surprise you. I wanted to see your face when you first learned I was in Cairo."

"Richard, with what I've been through during the last few days, it was probably the worst possible thing you could have done." Her voice took on an edge. "In fact, it was pretty stupid."

"Okay, okay," said Richard, lifting his hands in mock defense. "I'm sorry if I frightened you. I didn't mean to."

"Didn't you think I'd be scared if you snuck into my room at midnight? Really, Richard, that's not too much to ask. Even in Boston, that would not be wise. I don't think you thought about my feelings at all."

"Well, I was excited to see you. I mean, I've come nineteen zillion miles." Richard's smile began to fade. His sandy hair was tousled, and his eyes were lined with dark shadows.

"The more I think about it, the more idiotic it sounds. God, I could have had a heart attack. You scared me to death."

"I'm sorry, I said I was sorry."

"'I'm sorry,'" repeated Erica testily. "I suppose saying I'm sorry is supposed to make it all okay. Well, it doesn't. It was bad enough to witness two murders in two days, but then to be subjected to an adolescent prank! Enough is enough!"

"I thought you were glad to see me," said Richard defensively. "You said you were glad to see me."

"I was glad you weren't a would-be rapist or murderer."

"Well, that certainly makes a fellow feel welcome."

"Richard, what in heaven's name are you doing here?"

"I'm here to see you. I came halfway around the world to this dusty, hot city because I wanted to show you how much I care."

Erica opened her mouth, but she didn't speak right away. Her irritation softened slightly. "But I specifically asked you not to come," she said, as if speaking to a naughty child.

"I know that, but I talked it over with your mother." Richard sat down on the bed and tried to take Erica's hand.

160

"What?" she questioned, eluding his grasp. "Tell me that again."

"Tell you what?" asked Richard, confused. He sensed her renewed anger but did not understand.

"You and my mother conspired."

"I wouldn't use that word. We discussed whether I should come."

"Wonderful," scoffed Erica. "And I'll bet it was decided that Erica, the little girl she is, is just going through a difficult stage and that she'll grow out of it. She just needs to be treated like a child and tolerated for the time being."

"Look, Erica. For your information, your mother has your best interests at heart."

"I'm not so sure about that," said Erica, getting off the bed. "My mother cannot distinguish between her life and mine anymore. She's too close and I feel as if she's sucking the life right out of me. Can you understand that?"

"No, I can't," said Richard, his own irritation beginning to surface.

"I didn't think you could. I'm beginning to think it has something to do with being Jewish. My mother is so intent on my following in her footsteps that she doesn't bother to find out who I really am. Maybe she does want what's best for me, but I also think she wants to justify her own life through mine. The trouble is that my mother and I are very different; we've grown up in different worlds."

"The only time I think of you as a child is when you talk like this!"

"I don't think you understand at all, Richard, not at all. You don't even know why I'm here in Egypt. No matter how many times I've explained it, you refuse to comprehend."

"I disagree. I think I know why you're here. You're afraid of a commitment. It's as simple as that. You want to demonstrate your independence."

"Richard, don't you dare turn this around. You were the one who was afraid of a commitment. A year ago you would not even discuss marriage. Now suddenly you want a wife, a house, and a dog, and I don't think the order makes much difference. Well, I'm not a possession, not for you, not for my mother. I'm not here in Egypt to act out my independence. If that's what I wanted, I would have fled to one of those canned vacation spots, like the Club Med, where you don't have to think. I've come to Egypt because I've spent eight years studying ancient Egypt and it's my life's work. It's part of me as much as medicine is a part of you."

"So you're trying to tell me that love and family are secondary to your career."

Erica closed her eyes and sighed. "No, not secondary. It's just that your current conception of marriage would mean a type of intellectual abdication. You have always viewed my work as a kind of elaborate hobby. You don't take it seriously."

Richard tried to disagree, but Erica continued. "I'm not saying you did not like the fact that I was getting an exotic doctorate. But it wasn't because you were happy for me. It just happened to fit some grand design you had for yourself. I think it made you feel more liberal, more intellectual."

"Erica, I don't think this is fair."

"Don't misunderstand me, Richard. I know I'm partly to blame. I never really made a point of communicating my enthusiasm for my work. If anything, I camouflaged it for fear that it would frighten you away. But it's different now. I recognize who I am. And it doesn't mean I don't want marriage. It means that I don't want the wifely role that you have in mind. And I've come here to Egypt to do something that involves my professional expertise."

Richard sagged under the weight of Erica's argument. He was too tired to fight. "If you're so intent on being useful, why did you choose such an obscure field? I mean, really, Erica, Egyptology! New Kingdom hieroglyphics!" Richard fell back on the bed, his feet still touching the floor.

"Egyptian antiquities generate a lot more action than you'd ever imagine," said Erica. Walking over to the bureau, she picked up the envelope containing the photos Jeffrey John Rice had given to her. "I've been painfully learning that fact during the last two days. Take a look at these!" Erica tossed the envelope onto Richard's chest.

162

Richard sat up with obvious effort and took out the photos. He looked at them rapidly, then replaced them. "Nice statue," he said noncommittally, falling back onto the bed.

"Nice statue?" said Erica cynically. "That could be the finest ancient Egyptian statue ever found, and I've witnessed two murders, at least one of which I believe involved that statue, and you just say nice."

Richard opened one eye and looked at Erica, who was defiantly leaning against the bureau. The tops of her breasts were visible through the eyelet embroidery of her robe. Without sitting up again, Richard took the photos back out of the envelope and looked at them more carefully. "All right," he said at length. "A nice deadly statue. But what do you mean, two murders? You didn't see another today, did you?" Richard pushed himself up to a half-sitting position. His eyes were only half-open.

"Not only did I see it, but the victim fell on top of me. It would be difficult to be any closer and not be involved."

Richard stared at Erica for several minutes. "I think you better come back to Boston," he said with as much authority as he could muster.

"I'm going to stay here," said Erica flatly. "In fact, I think I'm going to do something about the antiquities black market. I think I can help. And I'd like to keep that Seti statue from being smuggled out of Egypt."

Immersed in deep concentration, Erica was oblivious of the passage of time. Looking at her watch, she was surprised to see it was two-thirty in the morning. She had been sitting on her balcony at the small round table she'd dragged from inside. She'd also carried out the bedside-table lamp, which cast a bright puddle of light on the table, illuminating the photos of the Houston statue.

Richard was lying on the bed in a deep sleep, still fully clothed. Erica had insisted on trying to get him a separate room, but the hotel was full. So were the Sheraton, Shepheard's, and the Meridien. While Erica was trying to call a hotel on Gezira island, his breathing became stertorous and she realized he had passed out. Erica relented. She had not wanted him to spend the night with her because she did not want to risk making love to him. But since he was already asleep, she decided he could find himself a room in the morning.

Too overwrought to sleep herself, she had decided to work on the hieroglyphics in the photos. She was particularly interested in the short inscription containing the two pharaonic cartouches. Hieroglyphics were always difficult, since there were no vowels and directives had to be interpreted correctly. But this inscription on the Seti statue seemed more obtuse than usual, as if the original designer wanted to encode his message. Erica wasn't even positive in which direction the inscription should be read. No matter what she did, nothing made much sense. Why would the name of the boy king Tutankhamen be carved on the effigy of a mighty pharaoh?

The best interpretation of the phrase she could make was: "Eternal rest [or peace] given [or awarded] to his majesty, king of Upper and Lower Egypt, son of Amon-Re, beloved of Osiris, Pharaoh Seti I, who rules [or governs or resides] after [or behind or under] Tutankhamen." As far as she could remember, that was reasonably close to what Dr. Lowery had said on the phone. But she wasn't satisfied. It seemed too simple. Certainly Seti I ruled or lived after Tutankhamen by fifty years or so. But of all the pharaohs, why hadn't they picked Thutmose IV or one of the other great empire-builders? Also, the final preposition bothered her. She rejected "under" because there was no dynastic connection between Seti I and Tutankhamen. There were no family ties whatsoever. In fact, before Seti's time she was reasonably sure Tutankhamen's names had been obliterated by the usurper general, Pharaoh Horemheb. She rejected "behind" because of the insignificance of Tutankhamen. That left "after."

Erica read the phrase out loud. Again, it sounded too simple, and for that reason mysteriously complicated. But it excited her trying to pierce a human mind that had functioned three thousand years previously.

Looking back into the room at Richard's sleeping form, Erica realized more than ever the gulf that separated them. Richard would never comprehend her fascination with Egypt and the fact that such intellectual excitement was an important part of her identity.

She got up from the table and carried the lamp and the photos back into the room. As the light fell on Richard's face, with his lips parted ever so slightly, he suddenly appeared very young, like a boy. Erica remembered the beginning of their relationship and she longed for that simpler time. She really did care for him, but it was hard to face reality: Richard was always going to be Richard. His medical career kept him from viewing himself with any kind of perspective, and Erica had to face the fact that he was not going to change.

She switched off the lamp and stretched out beside him. He groaned and turned over, putting his hand on Erica's chest. Gently she replaced it at his side. She wanted to maintain her distance, and she did not want to be touched. She thought about Yvon, who she believed treated her as an intellectual equal and a woman at the same time. Looking at Richard in the dim light, Erica realized she was going to have to tell him about the Frenchman, and Richard would be hurt. She stared up at the dark ceiling, anticipating his jealous reaction. He'd say that all Erica wanted was to run off and find a lover. He would never understand the strength of her commitment to keep the second statue of Seti I from being spirited out of the country. "You'll see," she whispered to Richard in the darkness. "I'm going to find that statue." Richard groaned in his sleep and turned away.

Day 3

When Erica awoke the next morning, she thought she had again left the shower running, but she soon remembered Richard's unexpected arrival and realized that he had turned on the water. Pushing a stray wisp of hair off her forehead, Erica let her head flop over on the pillow so she could see out the open balcony door. The noise of the steady traffic below blended with the sound of the shower and was as soothing as a distant waterfall. Her eyes restfully closed again while she recalled her resolves the night before. Then the sound of the shower stopped abruptly. Erica did not move. Presently Richard came padding into the room, vigorously drying his sandy hair. Carefully turning, yet pretending to be asleep, Erica looked out of half-open eyes and was surprised to see him stark naked. She watched as he finished with the towel, advanced to the open balcony door, and began studying the great pyramids and the guardian sphinx in the distance. He did have a handsome body. She looked at the graceful curve of the small of his back; she felt the suggestion of power in his well-defined legs. Erica closed her eyes, afraid that familiarity and the sexiness of Richard's body would prove too much for her.

The next thing Erica knew she was being gently shaken awake. Opening her eyes, she looked directly into the faraway blue of Richard's. He was smiling impishly, dressed in jeans

167

and a fitted navy-blue knit shirt. His hair was combed as much as the natural curls would allow.

"Let's go, sleeping beauty," said Richard, kissing her forehead. "Breakfast will be here in five minutes."

While she was taking a shower, Erica debated how she could be firm without sounding insensitive. She hoped Yvon would not call, and thinking of him reminded her of the Seti I statue. It was one thing to declare a crusade in the middle of the night; it was quite another actually to begin. She knew she had to have a plan of some kind if she hoped to find the sculpture. Lathering up with the harsh-smelling Egyptian soap, Erica considered for the first time the continued danger of having witnessed Abdul's murder. Wondering why she had not considered this aspect of her position before, she rinsed off quickly and stepped out of the shower. "Of course," she said out loud. "Any danger would depend on the killers knowing that I had been a witness. And they did not see me."

Erica ran a comb through her damp hair to remove the tangles, and looked in the mirror. The pimple on her chin had involuted to a red blemish, and already the Egyptian sun had given her complexion an attractive glow.

Putting on her makeup, Erica tried to recall her conversation with Abdul Hamdi. He'd said the statue was resting before resuming its journey, presumably out of Egypt. Erica hoped the murder of Abdul Hamdi meant it had not left the country. Her supposition was supported by the fact that Yvon, Jeffrey Rice, or the Greek whom Yvon had talked about would have heard if the statue had resurfaced in some neutral country like Switzerland. All in all, she felt reasonably certain the statue was not only still in Egypt but also still in Cairo.

Erica inspected her makeup. It would do. She'd used just a small amount of mascara. There was something romantic about the fact that Egyptian women four thousand years ago had darkened their lashes in a similar fashion.

Richard knocked on the door. "Breakfast is being served on the veranda," he said, assuming an English accent. He sounded too happy, thought Erica. It was going to be harder to talk with him.

Erica called through the door that she'd be out in a few

minutes and then began to dress. She missed her drawstring cotton pants. She knew her jeans would be much warmer in the hot climate. Struggling with the tight legs, she thought about the Greek. She had no idea what he wanted from her, but maybe he could be a source of information. Perhaps she could exchange whatever he wanted for some inside information about how the black market worked. It was a long shot, but at least a place to begin.

Tucking in her blouse, Erica wondered if the Greek—or anyone else, for that matter—would understand the significance of the hieroglyphics she'd tried to translate the evening before. Overshadowing the missing statue was the mystery of Seti I himself. Three thousand years had passed since this ancient Egyptian had lived and breathed. Aside from conducting a very successful military campaign into the Middle East and Libya during the first decade of his reign, all Erica could remember about the mighty pharaoh was that he built an extensive temple complex at Abydos, added to the Temple of Karnak, and built the most spectacular cave tomb in the Valley of the Kings.

Recognizing that more significant information was available, Erica decided to return to the Egyptian Museum and use her professional letters of introduction. It would give her something to do while waiting for the Greek to contact her. The other person who might have information for her was the son Abdul Hamdi had mentioned, who had an antique business in Luxor. As Erica opened the bathroom door, she made up her mind. As soon as possible she was going to head up the Nile to Luxor, to Abdul Hamdi's son. She was convinced it was the best idea she'd had.

Richard had taken it upon himself to order a large breakfast. Like the previous morning, it had been served on the balcony. Beneath silver warmers were eggs, bacon, and fresh Egyptian bread. Slices of papaya nestled in ice chips. The coffee was waiting to be poured. Richard hovered over the table like a nervous waiter adjusting the position of the flatware and napkins.

"Ah, your Highness," said Richard, still in an English accent. "Your table is ready." Holding back one of the chairs, he beckoned for Erica to sit. "After you," he said, holding up each of the platters in turn.

Erica was genuinely touched. Richard had none of Yvon's sophistication, but his behavior was appealing. As tough as he liked to act under most circumstances, Erica knew he was rather vulnerable. And she knew what she was going to tell him could hurt him. She started: "I don't know how much you remember from our conversation last night."

"Everything," said Richard, holding up his fork. "In fact, before you go any further, I'd like to make a suggestion. I think we should march right over to the American embassy and tell them exactly what has happened to you."

"Richard," said Erica, knowing that she was being side-tracked, "the American embassy wouldn't be able to do anything. Be realistic. Nothing really has happened to me, just around me. No, I'm not going to the American embassy."

"All right," said Richard. "If that's the way you feel, then fine. Now, about the other things you said. About us." Richard paused and fingered his coffee cup. "I admit there's some truth in what you say about my attitude concerning your work. Well, I'd like to ask you to do something for me." He raised his eyes to meet Erica's. "Let's just have a day together here, in Egypt, on your turf, so to speak. Give me a chance to see what it's all about."

"But, Richard . . ." began Erica. She wanted to talk about Yvon and her feelings.

"Please, Erica. You've got to admit we haven't discussed this before. Give me a little time. We'll talk tonight, I promise. After all, I did come all the way here. That should count for something."

"It counts for something," said Erica tiredly. Such emotional moments were draining for her. "But even that kind of a decision was something we should have made together. I appreciate your effort, but I still don't think you understand why I came here. We seem to view the future of our relationship very differently."

"That's what we will discuss," said Richard, "but not now. Tonight. All I'm asking is to spend a pleasant day together so I can see something of Egypt and get a feeling for Egyptology. I think I deserve that much consideration."

"All right," said Erica reluctantly. "But we will talk tonight."

"Phew," said Richard. "With that decided, let's discuss our plans. I'd really like to see those babies." Richard pointed with a piece of toast toward the sphinx and the pyramids of Giza.

"Sorry," said Erica. "The day is already booked. We are going to the Egyptian Museum this morning to see what is known about Seti I, and this afternoon we are going to return to the scene of the first murder, Antica Abdul. The pyramids will have to wait."

Erica tried to speed up their breakfast and leave the room before the inevitable phone call. But she didn't make it. Richard was busy putting film into his Nikon as she picked up the receiver. "Hello," she said quietly. As she'd feared, it was Yvon. She knew she should not feel guilty, but she did just the same. She had wanted to tell Richard about the Frenchman but he had cut her off.

Yvon was cheerful and full of warm words about the previous evening. Erica acquiesced at appropriate junctures, but she knew she sounded stilted.

"Erica, are you all right?" Yvon finally asked.

"Yes, yes, I'm just fine." Erica tried to think of a way to end the conversation.

"You would tell me if something was wrong?" he asked, sounding alarmed.

"Of course," said Erica quickly.

There was a pause. Yvon knew something was wrong.

"We both agreed last night," said Yvon, "that we should have spent yesterday together. So how about today? Let me take you to some of the sights."

"No, thank you," said Erica. "I have a surprise guest who arrived last night from the States."

"No matter," said Yvon. "Your guest is welcome."

"The guest happens to be . . ." Erica hesitated. "Boyfriend" seemed so immature.

"A lover?" asked Yvon hesitantly.

"A boyfriend," said Erica. She couldn't think of anything more sophisticated.

*　　*　　*

Yvon slammed the phone down. "Women," he said with anger, pressing his lips together.

Raoul looked up from his week-old *Paris Match*, trying not to smile. "The American girl is giving you some trouble."

"Shut up," said Yvon with uncharacteristic irritation. He lit a cigarette and blew smoke up at the ceiling in turbulent blue billows. He thought it was entirely possible that Erica's guest had arrived unexpectedly. Yet there was a lingering doubt that she had purposely not told him, to lead him on.

He stubbed out his cigarette and walked over to the balcony. He was not accustomed to being upset about women. If they proved troublesome, he left. It was as simple as that. The world was full of women. He stared down at a dozen feluccas heading south before the wind. The placid view made him feel better.

"Raoul, I want Erica Baron tailed again," he called.

"Fine," said Raoul. "I have Khalifa on hold at the Scheherazade Hotel."

"Try to tell him to be conservative," said Yvon. "I don't want any more unnecessary bloodshed."

"Khalifa insists the man he shot had been stalking Erica."

"The man was working for the Department of Antiquities. It's inconceivable that he was stalking Erica."

"Well, I assure you Khalifa is first-class. I know," said Raoul.

"He'd better be," said Yvon. "Stephanos expects to meet with the girl today. Warn Khalifa. There might be trouble."

"Dr. Sarwat Fakhry can see you now," said a robust secretary with a bulging bosom. She was about twenty and brimming with health and enthusiasm, a relief from the otherwise oppressive atmosphere of the Egyptian Museum.

The curator's office was like a dim cave with shuttered windows. A rattling air conditioner kept the room cool. It was paneled in dark wood, like a Victorian study. One wall was dressed with a fake fireplace, certainly out of place in Cairo, the others completely covered with bookshelves. In the middle of the room was a large desk stacked with books, journals, and

172

papers. Behind the desk sat Dr. Fakhry, who looked up over the tops of his glasses as Erica and Richard entered. He was a small nervous man, about sixty, with pointed features and wiry gray hair.

"Welcome, Dr. Baron," he said without getting up. Erica's letters of introduction trembled slightly in his hand. "I'm always happy to welcome someone from the Boston Museum of Fine Arts. We are indebted to Reisner for his excellent work." Dr. Fakhry was looking directly at Richard.

"I'm not Dr. Baron," said Richard, smiling.

Erica took another step forward. "I'm Dr. Baron, and thank you for your hospitality."

Dr. Fakhry's look of confusion gave way to embarrassed understanding. "Excuse me," he said simply. "From your letter of introduction I see that you are planning to do some on-site translations of New Kingdom monuments. I am pleased. There is much to be done. If I can be of any assistance, I am at your service."

"Thank you," said Erica. "Actually I did want to ask a favor. I am interested in some background information on Seti I. Would it be possible for me to review the museum's material?"

"Certainly," said Dr. Fakhry. His voice changed slightly. It was more questioning, as if Erica's request surprised him. "Unfortunately, we don't know very much about Seti I, as you are undoubtedly aware. In addition to the translations we have of the inscriptions on his monuments, we do have some of Seti I's correspondence from his early campaigns in Palestine. But that's about all. I'm certain that you can add to our knowledge with your on-site translations. Those we have are quite old, and much has been learned since they were made."

"What about his mummy?" asked Erica.

Dr. Fakhry handed Erica's letters back to her. The tremor increased as he extended his arm. "Yes, we do have his mummy. It was part of the Deir el-Bahri cache illicitly found and plundered by the Rasul family. It is on display upstairs." He glanced at Richard, who smiled again.

"Was the mummy ever closely examined?" asked Erica.

"Indeed," said Dr. Fakhry. "It was autopsied."

"Autopsied?" asked Richard with disbelief. "How do you autopsy a mummy?"

Erica grasped Richard's arm above the elbow. He got the message and remained silent. Dr. Fakhry continued as if he had not heard the query. "And it was recently X-rayed by an American team. I will gladly have all the material made available to you in our library." Dr. Fakhry got to his feet and opened the office door. He walked partially bent over, giving the impression of a hunchback with his hands curled at his side.

"One other request," said Erica. "Do you have much material on the opening of Tutankhamen's tomb?"

Richard passed Erica and checked out the secretary with a sly sideways glance. She was busy leaning over her typewriter.

"Ah, there we can help you," said Dr. Fakhry as they emerged in the marbled hall. "As you know, we are planning to use some of the funds generated by the world tour of the 'Treasures of Tutankhamen' to build a special museum to house his artifacts. We now have a full set of Carter's notes from what he called his 'Journal of Entry' on microfilm, as well as a significant collection of correspondence among Carter, Carnarvon, and others associated with the discovery of the tomb."

Dr. Fakhry deposited Erica and Richard in the hands of a silent young man whom he introduced as Talat. Talat listened carefully to the doctor's complicated instructions, then bowed and disappeared through a side door.

"He will bring the material we have on Seti I," said Dr. Fakhry. "Thank you for coming in, and if I can be of further assistance, please let me know." He shook hands with Erica, keying off an involuntary facial spasm that pulled his mouth into a sneer. He left, his hands drawn up and his fingers rhythmically clutching at nothing.

"God, what a place," said Richard when the curator had left. "Charming fellow."

"Dr. Fakhry happens to have done some fine work. His specialty is ancient Egyptian religion, funerary practices, and mummification methods."

"Mummification methods! I could have guessed. I know a big church in Paris who'd hire him in a minute."

"Try to be serious, Richard," said Erica, smiling despite herself.

They took seats at one of the long battered oak tables that dotted the large room. Everything was covered with a fine layer of Cairo dust. Tiny footprints crossed the floor beneath Erica's chair. Richard told her it had been a rat.

Talat brought back two large red paper envelopes, each tied with a string. He gave them to Richard, who smiled scornfully and gave them to Erica. The first was marked "Seti I, A." Erica opened it and spread the contents on the table. They were reprints of articles about the pharaoh. A number of them were in French, a couple in German, but most were in English.

"Pssst." Talat touched Richard's arm.

Richard turned, surprised at the noise.

"You want scarabs from the ancient mummies. Very cheap." Talat extended a closed hand, palm up. While he glanced over his shoulder like a pornography peddler in the fifties, his fingers slowly opened to reveal two slightly damp scarabs.

"Is this guy serious?" asked Richard. "He wants to sell some scarabs."

"Undoubtedly they are fake," said Erica, not pausing from her work to look up.

Richard picked one of the scarabs from Talat's open palm.

"One pound," said Talat. He was getting nervous.

"Erica, take a look at this. It's a good-looking little scarab. This guy's got balls, carrying on business here."

"Richard, you can buy scarabs all over the place. Maybe you should wander around the museum while I get this work done." She looked up at him to see how he'd taken her suggestion, but he wasn't listening. He'd taken the other scarab from Talat.

"Richard," said Erica, "don't get fooled by the first peddler you meet. Let me see one." She took one of the artifacts and turned it over to read the hieroglyphics on the underside. "My God," she said.

"Do you think it's real?" queried Richard.

"No, it's not real, but it's a clever fake. Too clever. It has the

175

cartouche of Tutankhamen. I think I know who made it. Abdul Hamdi's son. Amazing."

Erica bought the scarb from Talat for twenty-five piasters and then sent the boy away. "I already have one made by Hamdi's son with Seti I's name on it." Erica made a mental note to get the fake scarab back from Yvon. "I wonder what other pharaohs' names he uses."

On Erica's insistence they went back to the articles. Richard picked up several reprints. There was silence for a half-hour. "This is the driest stuff I've ever read," said Richard finally, tossing an article onto the table. "And I thought that pathology was dull. God."

"It has to be put into context," said Erica condescendingly. "What you're looking at are bits and pieces that are being assembled about a powerful person who lived three thousand years ago."

"Well, if there was a little more action in these articles, it would be a lot easier." Richard laughed.

"Seti I reigned soon after the pharaoh who tried to change the Egyptian religion to monotheism," Erica said, ignoring Richard's comment. "His name was Akhenaten. The country had been plunged into chaos. Seti changed that. He was a strong ruler who managed to restore stability at home and through most of the empire. He assumed power around age thirty and ruled for approximately fifteen years. Except for some of his battles in Palestine and Libya, very few details are known about him, which is unfortunate, because he reigned during a very interesting time in Egyptian history. I'm talking about a period a little over fifty years long, from Akhenaten through Seti I. It must have been a fascinating era, full of turmoil, upheaval, and emotion. It's just so frustrating that we don't know more." Erica tapped the stacks of reprints. "It was during that time that Tutankhamen ruled. And strangely enough, there was one huge disappointment in the discovery of Tutankhamen's magnificent tomb. Despite all the treasures that were found, there were no historical documents. Not a single papyrus was found! Not one!"

Richard shrugged.

Erica realized he was trying, but he couldn't share her

excitement. She turned back to the table. "Let's see what's in the other folder," she said, and slid the contents of "Seti I, B," onto the table.

Richard perked up. There were dozens of photographs of the mummy of Seti I, including photos of X rays, a modified autopsy report, and several more reprinted articles.

"God," said Richard, feigning a horrified expression. He picked up a photo of the face of Seti I. "This looks as bad as my cadaver in first-year anatomy."

"It does horrify at first, but the longer you look at it, the more serene it seems."

"Come on, Erica, it looks like a ghoul. Serene? Give me a break." Richard picked up the autopsy report and started reading.

Erica found a full-body X ray. It looked like a Halloween skeleton with the arms crossed on the chest. But she studied it just the same. Suddenly she realized that something was strange. The arms were crossed, like all the mummies of the pharaohs, but the hands were open, not clenched. The fingers were extended. The other pharaohs had all been buried clutching the flail and the scepter, the insignia of office. But not Seti I. Erica tried to understand why.

"This is not an autopsy," said Richard, interrupting her thoughts. "I mean, they had no internal organs. Just a shell of a body. When a post is done, the shell is only cursorily examined, unless there is some specific indication. The autopsy is really the microscopic examination of the internal organs. Here all they did was take a little bit of muscle and skin." He took the X-ray photo from Erica and held it at arm's length to examine it. "Lungs are clear," said Richard, laughing. Erica didn't get it, so Richard explained that since the lungs had been removed in antiquity, the X ray showed the chest clear. It didn't sound so funny when he explained, and his laughter trailed off. Erica looked over Richard's arm at the photo. Seti I's open hands still bothered her. Something told her they were significant.

There were two printed cards in the large glass case. To pass the time Khalifa bent down to read them. One card was old and said: "Gold Throne of Tutankhamen, circa 1355 B.C." The other card was new and said: "Temporarily Removed as Part of World Tour of Tutankhamen's Treasures." From where Khalifa was standing, he had a full view of Erica and Richard through the empty display case. Normally he would never approach a quarry so closely, but he was now intrigued. He'd never been on such an assignment. The day before, he'd felt that he saved Erica from certain destruction, only to be lambasted by Yvon de Margeau. De Margeau had told him he'd nailed a measly civil servant. But Khalifa knew better. The civil servant had been stalking Erica, and there was something about this fresh American woman that intrigued Khalifa. He sensed big money. If de Margeau had been as mad as he sounded, he would have fired him. But he'd kept him on the two hundred-dollar-a-day payroll and stashed him at the Scheherazade Hotel. And now there was a new development that complicated the scene: a boyfriend named Richard. Khalifa knew that the boyfriend did not please Yvon, although the Frenchman had told him he did not believe Richard was a threat to Erica. But Yvon did tell Khalifa to be on guard, and Khalifa wondered if he should take it upon himself to get rid of Richard.

As Erica and Richard moved to the next exhibit, Khalifa stepped behind another empty case with a "Temporarily removed . . ." card. Hiding behind his open guidebook, he tried to catch the conversation. All he got was something about the wealth of one of the great pharaohs. But that also sounded like money talk to Khalifa, and he pressed closer. He liked the feeling of excitement and danger the proximity afforded, even though it was only imaginary danger. There was no way these people were an actual threat to him. He could kill them both in two seconds. In fact, the idea turned him on.

"Most of the really exquisite pieces are on exhibit in New York," said Erica, "but look at that pendant there." She pointed, and Richard yawned. "All this was buried with insignificant Tutankhamen. Try to imagine what was buried with Seti I."

"I can't," said Richard, shifting his weight onto his other foot.

Erica looked up, sensing his boredom. "Okay," she said consolingly. "You've been pretty good. Let's head back to the hotel for a bite of lunch and see if I've gotten any messages. Then we'll walk into the bazaar."

Khalifa watched Erica walk away, enjoying the tight curve of her jeans. His thoughts of violence merged with others more intimate and salacious.

There was a message and a number for Erica to call when they got back to the hotel. There was also a vacant room available for Richard. He hesitated and gave Erica a pleading look before going over to the registration desk to make the arrangements. Erica retired to one of the pay telephones but had no luck with the complicated machine. She told Richard that she'd make her call from her room.

The message had been simple. "I would like the pleasure of seeing you at your earliest convenience. Stephanos Markoulis." Erica shivered at the prospect of meeting with someone actually involved in the black market and possibly a murder. But he had sold the first Seti I statue and he could be important if she wanted to find its mate. She remembered Yvon's admonition to choose a public place, and for the first time she was actually glad that Richard was with her.

The hotel operator was infinitely more capable than the mechanical device in the lobby. The call went through quickly. "Hello, hello." Stephanos' voice had a commanding quality.

"This is Erica Baron."

"Ah, yes. Thank you for calling. I am looking forward to meeting you. We have a mutual friend, Yvon de Margeau. Charming fellow. I believe he told you that I would call and that I'd like to get together for a chat. Can we meet this afternoon, say, around two-thirty?"

"Where do you have in mind?" said Erica, mindful of Yvon's warning. She heard a deep rumbling sound in the distance.

"It's up to you, dear," said Stephanos, speaking louder over the background noise.

Erica bristled at the familiarity of the word. "I don't know," she said, looking at her watch. It was eleven-thirty. Richard and she would probably be in the bazaar at two-thirty.

"How about right there in the Hilton?" suggested Stephanos.

"I will be in the Khan el Khalili bazaar this afternoon," said Erica. She thought about mentioning Richard, but she decided against it. It seemed a good idea to retain some element of surprise.

"Just a minute," said Stephanos. Erica could hear a muffled conversation. Stephanos had put his hand over the receiver. "Sorry to have kept you waiting," he said in a voice that conveyed he was not sorry. "Do you know the Al Azhar mosque next to the Khan el Khalili?"

"Yes," said Erica. She remembered Yvon pointing it out to her.

"We'll meet there," said Stephanos. "It's easy to find. Two-thirty. I'm really looking forward to seeing you, dear. Yvon de Margeau had some nice things to say about you."

Erica said good-bye and hung up. She felt distinctly uneasy and even a little afraid. But she had made up her mind to go through with it because of Yvon; she was certain he would never allow her to meet with Stephanos if there was real danger involved. Nonetheless, she wished it was over.

Luxor 11:40 A.M.

Dressed in loose-fitting white cotton shirt and slacks, Ahmed Khazzan felt reasonably relaxed. He still was perplexed about Gamal Ibrahim's violent death but was able to ascribe the event to the inscrutable workings of Allah, and his sense of guilt abated. As a leader, he knew he had to face such episodes.

During the previous evening he'd made his obligatory visit to the home of his parents. He loved his mother deeply but disapproved of her decision to stay at home to care for his invalid father. His mother had been one of the first women in Egypt to obtain a university degree, and Ahmed would have preferred it if she had used her education. She was a highly intelligent woman and could have been a great help to Ahmed. His father had been critically injured in the 1956 war, the same war that had taken Ahmed's older brother. Ahmed did not know a family in Egypt that had not been touched with tragedy from the many wars, and when he thought about it, it made him tremble with anger.

After his visit to his parents, Ahmed had slept long and well in his own rambling mud-brick home in Luxor. His housekeeper had prepared a wonderful breakfast of fresh bread and coffee. And Zaki had called, reporting that two special plainclothes agents had been dispatched to Saqqara. Everything seemed quiet in Cairo. And perhaps most important, he had successfully handled a potential family crisis. A cousin, whom he had promoted to chief guard of the Necropolis of Luxor, had become restive and wanted to move to Cairo. Ahmed had tried to reason with him, but when that did not work, he had dispensed with diplomacy, and becoming angry, had ordered him to stay. The cousin's father, Ahmed's uncle-in-law, had tried to intervene. Ahmed had to remind the older man that his permit to run the concession stand in the Valley of the Kings could easily be revoked. That being settled, Ahmed had been able to sit down to some paperwork. So the world seemed better and more organized than the day before.

Placing the last of the memoranda he had brought to read in his briefcase, Ahmed had a sense of accomplishment. It would have taken him twice as long to go through the same material in Cairo. It was Luxor. He loved Luxor. Ancient Thebes. For Ahmed there was magic in the air that made him feel happy and at ease.

He stood up from his chair in the large living room. His home was dazzling white stucco outside, and although rustic inside, it was spotlessly clean. The building had been made by connecting a series of existing mud-brick structures. The result was a narrow house, only twenty feet wide, but very deep, with a long hall running on the left side. A series of guestrooms opened on the right. The kitchen was in the back of the house and was quite crude, without running water. Behind the kitchen was a small courtyard bounded by a stable for his prized possession, a three-year-old black Arabian stallion he called Sawda.

Ahmed had ordered his houseman to have Sawda saddled and ready by eleven-thirty. He planned to interrogate Tewfik Hamdi, Abdul Hamdi's son, at his antique shop before lunch. Ahmed felt it was important to do this himself. Then, after the midday heat had abated, he planned to cross the Nile and ride unannounced to the Valley of the Kings to inspect the new security system he'd put into effect. There would be time to return to Cairo in the evening.

Sawda pawed the ground impatiently when Ahmed appeared. The young stallion was like a Renaissance study, with each muscle defined in flawless black marble. His face was sharply chiseled, with flaring nostrils. His eyes rivaled

Ahmed's for their black watery depth. Once en route, Ahmed sensed the sheer power and life force in the exuberant animal beneath him. It was with difficulty that he kept the horse from exploding in a burst of thunderous speed. Ahmed knew that Sawda's unpredictable personality mirrored his own volatile passions. Because of their similarities, sharp words spoken in Arabic and forceful use of the reins were needed to control the stallion so that rider and horse could move as one in the sun-speckled shade of the palms planted along the banks of the Nile.

Tewfik Hamdi's antique shop was one of many nestled within a series of dusty crooked streets behind the ancient Temple of Luxor. They were all close to the major hotels and depended on the unsuspecting tourists for their continued existence. Most of the artifacts they sold were fakes manufactured on the West Bank. Ahmed did not know the exact location of Tewfik Hamdi's shop, so once he got in the area, he asked.

He was told the street and the number, and he found the shop without difficulty. But it was locked. It wasn't just closed for lunch. It was boarded up for the night.

With Sawda hitched in a patch of shade, Ahmed inquired about Tewfik in the neighboring shops. The answers were consistent. Tewfik's shop had not been open all day, and, yes, it was strange, because Tewfik Hamdi had not missed a day in years. One proprietor added that Tewfik's absence might have something to do with his father's recent death in Cairo.

Heading back toward Sawda, Ahmed passed directly in front of the shop. The boarded door caught his attention. Looking more closely, Ahmed found a long fresh crack in one of the boards. It appeared as if a portion had been torn off and then replaced. Ahmed inserted his fingers between the boards and pulled. There was no movement whatsoever. Looking up at the top of the crude shutter, Ahmed noticed that the boards were nailed to the doorjamb instead of being hooked from inside. He decided that Tewfik Hamdi must have left with the expectation of being gone for some time.

Ahmed stepped back from the building, stroking his mustache. Then he shrugged his shoulders and walked back toward Sawda. He thought that it probably was true that

Tewfik Hamdi had gone to Cairo. Ahmed wondered how he could find out where Tewfik Hamdi lived.

En route to his horse, Ahmed met an old family friend and stopped to chat; his thoughts, however, strayed beyond the exchanged pleasantries. There was something particularly unsettling about Tewfik nailing his door shut. As soon as he could, Ahmed excused himself, skirted the commercial block, and entered the maze of open passageways that led into the area behind the shops. The noontime sun beat down and reflected off the stuccoed walls, bringing perspiration to his forehead. He felt a rivulet of sweat trickle down the small of his back.

Directly behind the antique shops, Ahmed found himself in a warren of hastily made shelters. As he continued, chickens scattered and naked young children paused in their play to stare at him. After some difficulty and several false turns, Ahmed arrived at the rear door of Tewfik Hamdi's antique shop. Through the slats of the door he could see a small brick courtyard.

While several three-year-old boys watched, Ahmed put his shoulder against the wooden door and forced it open far enough to enter. The courtyard was about fifteen feet long, with another wooden door at the far end. An open doorway was on the left. As Ahmed returned the wooden door to its original position, he saw a dark brown rat dash from the open doorway across the courtyard into a clay drainage pipe. The air was heavy, hot, and still.

The open doorway led into a small room where Tewfik apparently lived. Ahmed stepped over the threshhold. On a simple wooden table a rotting mango and a wedge of goat cheese lay covered with flies. Everything else in the room had been opened and dumped. A cabinet in the corner had its door torn off. Papers were indiscriminately thrown about. Several holes had been dug in the mud-brick walls. Ahmed surveyed the scene with mounting anxiety, trying to comprehend what had happened.

Quickly he moved from the apartment to the door into the shop. It was unlocked and swung open with an agonized rasp. Inside, it was dark. Only small pencils of light penetrated the

184

slats of the boarded front doorway, and Ahmed paused while his eyes adjusted from the harsh sunlight. He heard the scurrying of tiny feet. More rats.

The disarray in the shop was much greater than in the sleeping room. Huge cabinets lining the walls had been pulled down, splintered, and thrown into a large pile in the center of the room. Their contents had been smashed and scattered. It was as if a cyclone had hit the shop. Ahmed had to lift portions of the broken furniture to enter. He picked his way to the center of the shop; then he froze. He'd found Tewfik Hamdi. Tortured. Dead. Tewfik had been pulled over the wooden counter, which was stained with dried blood. Each hand had been nailed palm down to the counter with a single spike, his arms spread apart. Almost all Tewfik's fingernails had been pulled out. Then his wrists had been cut. He had been forced to watch himself bleed to death. His bloodless face was ghostly pale, and a filthy rag had been stuffed in his mouth to silence his screams, making his cheeks bulge grotesquely.

Ahmed shooed away the flies; he noticed the rats had been feasting on the corpse. The bestiality of the scene revolted him, and the fact that it had occurred in his beloved Luxor enraged him. With the rage came a fear that the sicknesses and sins of urban Cairo would spread like a plague. Ahmed knew he had to contain the infestation.

He bent down and looked into the vacant eyes of Tewfik Hamdi. They mirrored the horror they had witnessed as their own life had ebbed. But why? Ahmed stood up. The stench of death was overwhelming. Carefully he picked his way back across the debris-strewn floor to the small courtyard. The sunlight fell warm on his face, and he stood there for a moment, breathing deeply. He knew he could not return to Cairo until he knew more. His thoughts turned to Yvon de Margeau. Whenever he was around, there was trouble.

Ahmed squeezed out through the door to the alley and pulled it shut behind him. He'd decided to go directly to the main police station near the Luxor railway depot; then he'd call Cairo. Mounting Sawda, he wondered what Tewfik Hamdi had done or what he'd known to warrant such a fate.

Cairo 2:05 P.M.

"Wonderful shop," said Richard as he entered from the busy alleyway. "Good selection of merchandise. I can do all my Christmas shopping here."

Erica could not believe the emptiness of the room. Nothing remained of Antica Abdul except for some bits of broken pottery. It was as if the shop had never existed. Even the front window glass had been removed. There were no beads in the entranceway; no rugs or curtains, not a piece of cloth or cabinetry remained.

"I can't believe this," said Erica, walking over to where the glass topped counter had been. Bending down, she picked up a potsherd. "Across here hung a heavy drape, dividing the room." She walked back to the rear and turned to face Richard. "I was in here when the murder happened. God, it was so awful. The killer was standing right where you are, Richard."

Richard looked down at his feet and stepped away from the guilty spot. "Looks like the thieves stole everything," he said. "With the poverty here, I suppose everything has a value."

"You're undoubtedly right," said Erica, taking a flashlight from her tote bag, "but the place looks more than just burglarized. These holes in the walls—they weren't here before." She flipped on the light and looked into the depths of some of the holes.

"A flashlight!" said Richard. "You're really prepared."

187

"Anyone who comes to Egypt without a flashlight is making a mistake."

Richard walked over to one of the fresh niches and scraped some of the loose dried mud onto the floor. "Cairo vandalism, I guess."

Erica shook her head. "I think this place has been searched very carefully."

Richard looked around, noting how the floor had been dug up in places. "Maybe, but so what? I mean, what could they have been looking for?"

Erica nibbled the inside of her cheek, a habit she had when concentrating. Richard's question was reasonable. Perhaps Cairenes regularly hid money or valuables in walls or under the floor. But the violation reminded her of her own room being searched. On impulse she mounted the flash attachment on her Polaroid and took a photo of the interior of the shop.

Richard sensed Erica's uneasiness. "Does it bother you to return here?"

"No," said Erica. She did not want to stimulate Richard's overprotectiveness. But in fact she did feel extremely uneasy within the remains of Antica Abdul. It emphasized the reality of Abdul Hamdi's murder. "We've got ten minutes to get to the Al Azhar mosque. I want to be on time for Mr. Stephanos Markoulis." She hurried out of the shop, glad to leave.

As they entered the crowded alleyway, Khalifa pushed off the wall he'd been leaning on. His jacket was draped again over his right hand, concealing the Stechkin semiautomatic. It was cocked. Raoul had told him that Erica was meeting Stephanos sometime during the afternoon, and he did not want to lose her in the confusion of the bazaar. The Greek was known for his ruthless violence, and Khalifa was being well-paid not to take chances.

Erica and Richard emerged from the Khan el Khalili at the west end of the crowded but sun-filled Al Azhar square. Its dusty heat made them appreciate the relative coolness of the bazaar. They headed across the square toward the ancient mosque, admiring the three needlelike minarets that rose into the pale blue sky. But the going became difficult in the milling crowds; they had to hold onto each other tightly to keep from being separated. The area directly in front of the mosque reminded Erica of Haymarket in Boston, with hundreds of vegetable and fruit vendors with their pushcarts, haggling with their customers over the price of the produce. Erica felt definite relief when she and Richard reached the mosque and slipped through the main entrance known as the Gate of the Barbers. The environment changed immediately. The sounds from the busy square did not penetrate the stone building. It was cool and somber, like a mausoleum.

"This reminds me of dressing for surgery," said Richard with a smile as he slipped paper covers over his shoes. They walked through the entrance vestibule, peering into the open doorways leading into darkened rooms. The walls were constructed of large limestone blocks, giving the appearance of a dungeon, not a house of God. "I think," said Erica, "I should have been a bit more specific about where in this mosque we were going to meet."

Passing under a series of archways, she and Richard were surprised to find themselves back in bright sunlight. They were standing at the edge of a vast rectangular colonnaded court surrounded on all four sides by arcades with pointed Persian arches. It was a strange sight, because the courtyard was in the heart of Cairo, yet was empty and almost totally silent. Erica and Richard stood in the shade and speechlessly surveyed the scene of exotic keel-shaped archways with scalloped parapets topped by arabesque crenellations.

Erica was uneasy. She was nervous about meeting Stephanos Markoulis, and now the alien surroundings increased her fears. Richard took her hand and led her across the rectangular court toward an archway slightly higher than the others, topped by its own dome. As they crossed the court, Erica tried to peer into the violet shade of the surrounding porticoes. There were a few white-robed figures reclining on the limestone floor.

Evangelos Papparis moved around the marble column very slowly, keeping Erica and Richard in view. His sixth sense warned him to expect trouble. He was in the northern corner of the courtyard, deep within the shade of the arcade. Erica and Richard were now heading diagonally away from him.

Evangelos was not sure that Erica was the woman he was awaiting, mostly because she was accompanied, but the description seemed to fit. So when the couple reached the entrance arch to the mihrab, he stepped back to the center of the arcade and waved his arm in a slow circular fashion, then held up two fingers. Stephanos Markoulis, standing deep in the vast columned prayer room about two hundred feet away, waved back. From their previous plans Stephanos now knew that Erica had come with another person. With this information he stepped around the column in front of him, then leaned against it, waiting. To his left was a group of Islamic students grouped around their teacher, who was reading from the Koran in a singsong.

Evangelos Papparis was about to walk down to the main entrance when he caught a glimpse of Khalifa. He pulled back into the shadows, struggling to place the profile. When he looked again, the figure was already gone, and Richard and Erica had entered the prayer area. Then Evangelos remembered. The man with the jacket suspiciously draped over his arm was Khalifa Khalil, the assassin.

Evangelos returned to the center of the arcade, but he could not see Stephanos. He was confused. Turning, he decided to see if Khalil was still in the building.

Erica had read about the Al Azhar mosque in the Baedeker, and she knew that they were looking at the original mihrab, or prayer niche. It was intricately constructed of minute pieces of marble and alabaster forming complicated geometric patterns. "This alcove faces toward Mecca," whispered Erica.

"This place is awesome," said Richard quietly. In the dim light, as far as he could see to the left or right was a forest of marble columns. His eyes wandered to the floor around the prayer niche, noticing it was covered with overlapping Oriental carpets.

"What is it that I smell," he asked, sniffing.

"Incense," said Erica. "Listen!"

There was a constant sound of muted voices, and from where they were standing they could see numerous groups of students sitting at the feet of their teachers. "The mosque is not a university any longer," whispered Erica, "but it is still used for koranic studies."

"I like the way he studies," said Richard, pointing toward

a sleeping figure curled up on an Oriental rug.

Erica turned and looked back through the series of arches to the sunlit courtyard. She wanted to leave. The mosque had a sinister, sepulchral atmosphere, and she decided it was an inappropriate spot to meet someone. "Come on, Richard." She took his hand, but Richard, interested in going deeper into the pillared hall, pulled back.

"Let's check out that tomb of Sultan Rahman you read about," he said, halting Erica's progress toward the sunlight.

Erica looked around at Richard. "I'd prefer . . ." She didn't finish. Over Richard's shoulder she saw a man walking toward them from between the columns. She knew it was Stephanos Markoulis.

Noticing her expression and following her line of vision, Richard turned toward the approaching figure. He could feel the tension in her hand. Knowing she wanted to meet with the man, he wondered why she was agitated.

"Erica Baron," said Stephanos with a broad smile. "I'd recognize you in a crowd of a thousand. You are far more beautiful than Yvon suggested." Stephanos did not try to conceal his appreciation.

"Mr. Markoulis?" questioned Erica, although there was no doubt in her mind. His unctuous manner and greasy appearance coincided with her expectations. What she didn't expect was the large gold Christian cross around his neck. Within the mosque its sheen seemed provocative of violence.

"Stephanos Christos Markoulis," said the Greek proudly.

"This is Richard Harvey," said Erica, pulling Richard forward.

Stephanos glanced at Richard, then ignored him. "I would like to speak to you alone, Erica." He extended his hand.

Ignoring Stephanos' gesture, Erica grasped Richard's hand more firmly. "I'd prefer Richard to stay."

"As you wish."

"This is a rather melodramatic spot," said Erica.

Stephanos laughed, and the sound echoed between the columns. "Indeed, but remember, it was your idea not to meet at the Hilton."

"I think we'd better make this short," said Richard. He had no idea what was going on, but he did not like to see Erica upset.

191

Stephanos' smile faded. He was not used to being opposed.

"What do you want to speak to me about?" said Erica.

"Abdul Hamdi," said Stephanos matter-of-factly. "Remember him?"

Erica wanted to give as little information as possible. "Yes," she said.

"Well, tell me what you know about him. Did he tell you anything out of the ordinary? Did he give you any letters or papers?"

"Why?" said Erica defiantly. "Why should I tell you what I know?"

"Perhaps we can help each other," said Stephanos. "Are you interested in antiquities?"

"Yes," said Erica.

"Well, then, I can help you. What are you interested in?"

"A large life-size Seti I statue," said Erica, leaning forward to gauge her words' effect on Stephanos.

If he were surprised, he did not show it. "You're speaking about very serious business," he said finally. "Have you any idea of the sums involved?"

"Yes," said Erica. Actually, she had no idea. It was hard to even guess.

"Did Hamdi talk to you about such a statue?" asked Stephanos. His voice had a new seriousness.

"He did," said Erica. The fact that she knew so little made her feel particularly vulnerable.

"Did Hamdi say from whom he'd obtained the statue or where it was going?" Stephanos' face was deadly serious, and Erica shivered a little despite the heat. She tried to decide what Stephanos hoped to learn from her. It had to be where the statue was going before the murder. It must have been on its way to Athens! Without looking up, Erica spoke softly. "He didn't tell me who sold him the statue . . ." She deliberately left the second part of Stephanos' question unanswered. She knew she was gambling, but if it worked, then Stephanos would think she had been told some secrets. Then perhaps she could get something out of him.

But the conversation was cut short. Suddenly a massive figure materialized from the shadows behind Stephanos. Erica saw a huge bald head with a gaping knife wound that ran from the crown down over the bridge of the nose onto the right cheek. The wound looked like it had been made with a razor; despite its depth, it was barely bleeding. The man's hand reached for Stephanos, and Erica gasped, digging her nails into Richard's hand.

With surprising agility Stephanos reacted to Erica's warning. He spun, falling to the right, his right leg cocked for what would have been a karate kick. At the last moment he checked himself, recognizing Evangelos.

"What happened?" asked Stephanos with alarm, regaining his feet.

"Khalifa," rasped Evangelos. "Khalifa is in the mosque."

Stephanos pushed the weakened Evangelos against a column for support and rapidly looked around. From beneath his left arm he extracted a tiny but lethal-looking Beretta automatic and snapped off the safety.

At the sight of the gun, Erica and Richard shrank against each other in total disbelief. Before they could respond, a bloodcurdling scream reverberated through the vast prayer hall. Because of the echoes, it was difficult to determine where it had come from. As it trailed off, the koranic murmuring stopped. There was a dreadful silence like the calm before a holocaust. No one moved. From where Erica and Richard were huddled they could see several groups of students with their teachers. They too reflected confusion and mounting fear. What was happening?

Suddenly shots rang out, and the deadly sound of ricocheting bullets echoed through the marbled enclosure. Erica and Richard as well as Stephanos and Evangelos ducked down, not even knowing in which direction the danger lay. "Khalifa!" rasped Evangelos.

Other screams penetrated the prayer room, followed by a kind of vibration. All at once Erica realized it was the sound of running feet. The groups of students had stood up and were facing north. Suddenly they turned and ran. Bearing down on her was a crowd of panicked people fleeing through the forest of columns. There were more shots. The crowd became a stampede.

Ignoring the two Greeks, Erica and Richard jumped to their feet and fled southward, racing hand in hand around the columns, trying to stay ahead of the panicky horde that pressed behind them. They ran blindly until they reached the end of the hall. A few of the students passed them, wide-eyed with terror, as if the building were on fire. Erica and Richard followed them as they ducked through a low door and ran down a stone passageway. It opened into a mausoleum; beyond was an opening where a heavy wooden door was ajar, leading to the outside. They ran out into the dusty street, where an excited crowd had already gathered. Erica and Richard did not join it, but slowed to a fast walk and left the area.

"This place is insane," said Richard, his voice more angry than relieved. "What the hell was going on in there?" He didn't expect an answer, and Erica did not respond. For three days in a row she had been forced to witness unexpected violence, and on each occasion the attack had seemed more closely associated with her. Coincidence was no longer a viable explanation.

Richard gripped her hand, pulling her behind him through the crowded streets. He wanted to put as much distance as possible between them and the Al Azhar mosque.

"Richard . . " said Erica finally, holding her side. "Richard, let's slow down."

They stopped in front of a tailor shop. Richard's mouth was set in anger. "This Stephanos, did you have any idea he'd be armed?"

"I was somewhat concerned about meeting him, but I—"

"Just answer the question, Erica. Did you think he would be armed?"

"I did not even consider it." She did not like Richard's tone of voice.

"Obviously it was something you should have considered. Anyway, who is this Stephanos Markoulis?"

"He is an antiquities dealer from Athens. Apparently he's involved in the black market."

"And how was this meeting, if you can call it that, arranged?"

"A friend asked me if I'd see Stephanos."

"And who is this wonderful friend who sends you into the hands of a gangster?"

"His name is Yvon de Margeau. He's French."

"And what kind of friend is he?"

Erica looked at Richard's face, now flushed with anger. Still trembling from their experience, Erica did not know how to cope with his emotion.

"I'm sorry about what happened," she said, with mixed feelings about apologizing.

"Well," said Richard crossly, "I could repeat what you said last night when I tried to apologize about scaring you. Saying 'sorry' is supposed to make everything okay, but it doesn't. You could have gotten us killed. I think your escapade has gone far enough. We're going to the American embassy and you're coming back to Boston if I have to drag you on the plane by your hair."

"Richard . . ." said Erica, shaking her head.

An empty taxi was slowly picking its way along the crowded streets. Richard saw the car over Erica's shoulder and hailed it as the crowds reluctantly parted. They climbed into the back seat without speaking, and Richard told the driver to go to the Hilton Hotel. Erica felt a combination of anger and despair. If Richard had taken it upon himself to direct the driver to the American embassy, she would have gotten out of the car.

After ten minutes of silence, Richard finally spoke. His voice had mellowed slightly. "The fact is that you are not equipped for this kind of affair. You have to recognize that."

"With my background in Egyptology," snapped Erica, "I think I'm superbly equipped." Locked in traffic, the taxi inched past one of Cairo's huge medieval gates, and Erica studied it first through the side, then the rear window.

"Egyptology is the study of a dead civilization," said Richard, lifting his hand in the air as if to pat her knee. "It has no relevance to the current problem."

Erica looked over at Richard. "Dead civilization . . . no relevance." The words confirmed Richard's concept of her work. It was belittling and infuriating.

"You are trained as an academician," continued Richard,

"and I think you should accept that fact. This cloak-and-dagger routine is childish and dangerous. It's a ridiculous risk for a statue, any statue."

"This isn't just any statue," said Erica angrily. "Besides, the issue is much more involved than you are willing to comprehend."

"I think it's all too obvious. A statue worth a lot of money is unearthed. Such sums can explain all sorts of behavior. But it's a problem for the authorities, not tourists."

Erica clenched her teeth, bristling at the label "tourist." As the taxi started to move more quickly, she tried to understand why Yvon had allowed her to meet with Stephanos. Nothing seemed to make any sense, and she tried to decide what to do next. She had no intention of giving up, no matter what Richard said. Abdul Hamdi seemed to be the pivot. Then she remembered his son and her earlier resolve to visit his antique shop in Luxor.

Richard leaned forward and tapped the driver on the shoulder. "Do you speak English?"

The driver nodded. "A little."

"Do you know where the American embassy is?"

"Yes," said the driver. He looked at Richard in the rearview mirror.

"We are not going to the American embassy," said Erica, pronouncing each word carefully and loudly enough for the driver to hear.

"I'm afraid I'm going to insist," said Richard. He turned to speak to the driver.

"You can insist on whatever you want," Erica said evenly, "but that's not where I'm going. Driver, stop the car." She moved forward on the seat, pulling her tote bag onto her shoulder.

"Keep driving," Richard instructed, trying to pull Erica back into her seat.

"Stop the taxi!" Erica shouted.

The driver complied, pulling over to the side. Erica had the door open before the car reached a standstill, and leaped to the sidewalk.

Richard followed, leaving the taxi unpaid. The irate driver

drove slowly alongside as Richard overtook Erica and caught her arm. "It is time to stop this adolescent behavior," he shouted, as if threatening an errant child. "We are going to the American embassy. You're over your head. You're going to get hurt."

"Richard," said Erica, tapping his chin with her index finger, "you to go the American embassy if you want. I'm going to Luxor. Believe me, the embassy can do nothing at all about this, even if they were so inclined. I'm going to go to Upper Egypt and do what I came here for."

"Erica, if you persist, I'm going to leave. I'll go back to Boston. I mean it. I've come all the way over here, and it doesn't seem to matter to you. I just cannot believe it."

Erica didn't say anything. She just wanted him to leave.

"And if I do leave, I don't know what will happen to our relationship."

"Richard," said Erica quietly, "I *am* going to Upper Egypt."

With the afternoon sun low in the sky, the Nile appeared like a flat ribbon of silver. Sudden highlights sparkled from the surface where gusts of wind stirred the water. Erica had to shield her eyes from the sun to distinguish the timeless form of the pyramids. The sphinx looked as if it were made of gold. She was standing on the balcony of her room at the Hilton. It was almost time to leave. The management had been over-joyed at her decision to vacate her room, because as usual, they had overbooked. Erica had packed and her single suitcase was ready. The travel desk in the lobby had arranged a booking for her on the seven-thirty sleeper south.

The thought of the trip managed to dull the fear of the last few days and alleviate her feelings about fighting with Richard. The Temple of Karnak, the Valley of the Kings, Abu Simbel, Dendera—these were the reasons she had come to Egypt. She would go south, see Abdul's son, but concentrate on viewing the fabled monuments at first hand. She was glad Richard had decided to leave. She would not think about their relationship until she returned home. Then they would see.

Checking the bathroom for the final time, Erica was re-warded by finding her cream rinse behind the shower curtain.

She shoved it in her bag and checked the time. It was a quarter to six. She was about to leave for the train station when the phone rang. It was Yvon.

"Did you see Stephanos?" he asked cheerfully.

"I did," said Erica. She allowed an awkward pause. She had not called because she was angry he had subjected her to such danger.

"Well, what did he say?" asked Yvon.

"Very little. It was what he did that was important. He had a gun. We had just met at the Al Azhar mosque when a huge bald man appeared who looked like he'd been beaten. He told Stephanos that someone named Khalifa was there. Then all hell broke loose. Yvon, how could you have asked me to meet such a man?"

"My God," said Yvon. "Erica, I want you to stay in your room until I call back."

"I'm sorry, Yvon, but I was just leaving. In fact, I'm leaving Cairo."

"Leaving! I thought you were officially detained," said Yvon with surprise.

"I'm not supposed to leave the country," said Erica. "I called Ahmed Khazzan's office and informed them I was going to Luxor. It was fine with them."

"Erica, stay until I call back. Is your . . . boyfriend planning on going with you?"

"He's returning to the States. He was as upset about meeting Stephanos as I was. Thanks for calling, Yvon. Keep in touch." Erica hung up the phone very deliberately. She knew Yvon had used her as bait in some way. Although she believed in Yvon's crusade against the antiquities black market, she did not like being used. The phone rang again but she ignored it.

It took over an hour for the taxi to go from the Hilton to the central railway station. Although Erica had carefully showered for the trip, within fifteen minutes her blouse was soaked with perspiration and her back stuck to the hot vinyl seat cover.

The railway station stood in a busy square behind an ancient statue of Ramses II, whose timeless appearance was in sharp contrast to the mad rush-hour commotion. The inside of the station was jammed with people, ranging from businessmen in

Western clothes to farmers carrying empty produce containers. Although Erica was aware of some stares, no one tried to accost her, and she moved easily through the crowds. There was a short line in front of the sleeping-car window, and Erica had no trouble purchasing her ticket. She planned to break her trip at a small village called Balianeh and do a little sightseeing.

At the large kiosk she bought a two-day-old *Herald Tribune*, an Italian fashion magazine, and several popular books on the discovery of Tutankhamen's tomb. She even bought another copy of Carter's book, even though she'd read it many times.

The time passed quickly, and she heard her train announced. A Nubian porter with a wonderful smile took her bag and stowed it at the foot of her berth. The porter told her that they did not expect the car to be full, so she could spread her things out over two seats. She put her tote on the floor and leaned back with the *Herald Tribune*.

"Hello," said a pleasant voice, slightly startling her.

"Yvon," she said, truly surprised.

"Hello, Erica. I'm amazed I found you. May I sit down?"

Erica picked up her reading material from the seat next to her.

"I took a chance you were going south by train. All the flights had been booked for some time."

Erica gave a half-smile. Although she was still angry, she couldn't help but be a little flattered that Yvon had followed her, obviously with some effort. His hair was disheveled, as if he had been running.

"Erica, I want to apologize for whatever happened when you met Stephanos."

"Nothing really happened. What bothered me was what could have happened. You must have had some idea, because you said to meet him in a public place."

"Indeed I did, but I was only concerned because of Stephanos' reputation with women. I didn't want you to be subjected to any uncomfortable overtures."

The train lurched slightly, and Yvon stood, looking up and down the aisle. Satisfied that the train was not pulling out, he sat back down.

"I still owe you a dinner," said Yvon. "That was our deal.

Please stay in Cairo. I have learned some things about the killers of Abdul Hamdi."

"What?" asked Erica.

"That they were not from Cairo. I have some photos I'd like you to see. Perhaps you could recognize one."

"Did you bring them?"

"No, they are at the hotel. There wasn't time."

"Yvon, I'm leaving for Luxor. I've made up my mind."

"Erica, you can go to Luxor whenever you wish. I have a plane. I can fly you there tomorrow."

Erica looked down at her hands. Despite her anger, despite her misgivings, she could feel her resolve weakening. At the same time, she was tired of being protected, taken care of.

"Thank you for the offer, Yvon, but I think I'll go by train. I'll call you from Luxor."

There was the sound of a whistle. It was seven-thirty.

"Erica . . ." said Yvon, but the train began to move forward. "All right. Call from Luxor. Perhaps I'll see you there." He dashed down the aisle and jumped from the train, which was now picking up speed.

"Damn," said Yvon as he watched the train slide from the station. He turned into the busy waiting room. By the exit he met Khalifa.

"Why aren't you on that train?" snapped Yvon.

Khalifa smiled slyly. "I was told to follow the girl in Cairo. Nothing was said about taking a train to the south."

"Christ," said Yvon, walking toward a side door. "Follow me."

Raoul was waiting in the car. He started the engine when he saw Yvon. Yvon held open a rear door for Khalifa then climbed in after him.

"What happened in the mosque?" asked Yvon as they pulled out into the traffic.

"Trouble," said Khalifa. "The girl met Stephanos, but Stephanos had posted a guard. In order to protect her, I had to break up the meeting. I had no choice. It was a bad location, almost as bad as the serapeum yesterday. But in deference to your sensibilities, there was no killing. I shouted a few times and fired off a couple of shots and cleared out the whole mosque." Khalifa laughed contemptuously.

"Thank you for considering my sensibilities. But tell me, did Stephanos threaten or make any move against Erica Baron?"

"I don't know," said Khalifa.

"But that was what you were supposed to find out," said Yvon.

"I was supposed to protect the girl, then learn what I could," said Khalifa. "Under the circumstances, protecting the girl took all my attention."

Yvon turned his head and watched a bicyclist go by, balancing a large tray of bread on his head and making better time than they were in the car. Yvon felt frustrated. Things were going poorly, and now Erica Baron, his last hope for the Seti statue, had left Cairo. He looked at Khalifa. "I hope you're ready to travel, because you're going to Luxor tonight by air."

"Whatever you say," said Khalifa. "This job is getting interesting."

Day 4

"Balianeh in one hour," said the porter through the curtain of her berth.

"Thank you," said Erica, sitting up and pulling back the drape covering a small window. Outside, it was very early daybreak. The sky was a light purple and she could see low desert mountains in the distance. The train was moving rapidly, with slight to-and-fro movements. The tracks ran right along the edge of the Libyan desert.

Erica washed at her small sink and put on a bit of makeup. The night before, she'd tried to read one of the books on Tutankhamen that she'd purchased at the station, but the train's movements had cradled her instantly asleep. It was some time in the middle of the night that she had awakened long enough to turn off the reading light.

They served an English breakfast in the dining car as the first tentative rays of sunlight cleared the eastern horizon. As she watched, the sky changed from purple to a clear light blue. It was incredibly beautiful.

Sipping her coffee, Erica felt as if a burden had lifted from her shoulders; in its place was a euphoric sense of freedom. She felt as if the train were hurtling her back in time, back to ancient Egypt and the land of the pharaohs.

It was a little after six when she detrained at Balianeh. Very few passengers got off, and the train departed as soon as the last foot touched the platform. With some difficulty Erica checked her suitcase at a baggage window, then walked out of the station into the bright bustle of the small rural town. There was a gaiety in the air. The people seemed much happier than the oppressive crowds of Cairo. But it was hotter. Even this early in the morning Erica could feel the difference.

There were a number of old taxis waiting in the shade of the station. Most of the drivers were asleep, their mouths gaping. But when one spotted Erica, they all got up and began chattering. Finally a slender fellow was pushed forward. He had a large untrimmed mustache and a ragged beard, but he seemed pleased with his luck and made a bow in front of Erica before opening the door to his 1940-ish taxi.

He knew a few words of English, including "cigarette." Erica gave him a few and he immediately agreed to serve as her driver, promising to return her to the station to catch the five-P.M. connection to Luxor. The cost was five Egyptian pounds.

They headed north out of the town, then turned away from the Nile to the west. With his portable radio lashed to the dash so that its aerial could stick out of the missing window on the right, the driver smiled his contentment. On either side of the road stretched a sea of sugarcane, broken by an occasional oasis of palm trees.

They crossed a foul-smelling irrigation ditch and passed through the village of El Araba el Mudfuna. It was a sorry collection of mud-brick huts built just beyond the reach of the cultivated fields. There were few people in evidence except for a group of women dressed in black carrying large water jars on their heads. Erica looked at them again. They were wearing veils.

A few hundred yards beyond the village the driver halted and pointed ahead. "Seti," he said without taking the cigarette from his mouth.

Erica climbed out of the car. So here it was. Abydos. The place Seti I chose to build his magnificent temple. Just as Erica started to get out her guidebook, she was set upon by a group of youths selling scarabs. She was the first tourist of the day, and only by paying her fifty-piaster entrance fee and advancing into the temple proper could she free herself from their insistent chatter.

With the Baedeker in hand she sat on a limestone block and read the section on Abydos. She was familiar with the site but wanted to be certain which sections had been decorated with hieroglyphics during the reign of Seti I. The temple had been finished by Seti's son and successor, Ramses II.

Unaware of Erica's plans to visit Abydos, Khalifa stood on the platform at Luxor waiting for the passangers to disembark. The train had pulled in on time and was greeted by a huge throng who eagerly pressed in on the train. There was a lot of commotion and shouting, particularly by the hawkers selling fruit and cold drinks through the windowless openings of the third-class coaches to the passengers continuing on to Aswan. Those people detraining and those boarding jostled each other in a mounting frenzy because whistles began to blow. Egyptian trains ran on time.

Khalifa lit one cigarette, and then another, allowing the smoke to snake up past his hooked nose. He was standing apart from the chaos at a place where he could view the entire platform as well as the main exit. A few late passengers scurried to catch the train as it began to pull out of the station. There was no sign of Erica. When he finished his cigarette, Khalifa left the building by the main entrance. He headed for the central post office to make a call to Cairo. Something was wrong.

Abydos 11:30 A.M.

Erica walked from one incredible room to the next as she
explored the temple of Seti I. At last she could experience all
the electrifying mystery of Egypt. The relief work was magnificent. She planned to return to Abydos in several days to do
some serious translation work on the wealth of hieroglyphic
inscription that covered the walls of the temple complex. For
the moment she just scanned the texts to see if the name
Tutankhamen ever appeared among Seti's inscriptions. It
didn't, except in the room called the Gallery of Kings, where
almost all the ancient Egyptian pharaohs were listed in
chronological order.

As she walked through the inner chambers, where the
roofing slabs were still in place, she used her flashlight to view
the hieroglyphics.

Silently Erica repeated an abbreviated translation of the
phrase on the Seti I statue: "Eternal rest granted to Seti I, who
rules after Tutankhamen." She admitted the phrase did not
make any more sense to her standing in Seti I's temple than it
did on the balcony of the room in the Hilton. Rummaging in
her bag, Erica pulled out the photo of the hieroglyphic
inscription on the statue. She looked about the temple for any
similar combination of signs. It was a slow process and
ultimately unrewarding. At first she couldn't even find Seti's
name written in the same way as it was on the statue, linked to

the god Osiris. In the temple it usually identified him with the god Horus.

Morning melted happily into afternoon, leaving Erica oblivious of the heat and of her appetite. It was after three when she passed through the chapel of Osiris into the god's inner sanctuary. It had once been a splendid hall whose roof had been supported by ten columns. Now sun drenched the room with light, illuminating the magnificent reliefs associated with the cult of Osiris, the god of the dead.

There were no other tourists in the ruined hall, and Erica moved slowly, undisturbed in her appreciation of the craftsmanship of the sculptured murals. At the far end of the empty hall she came to a low doorway. Inside it was dark. Consulting her Baedeker, she found the room beyond was described simply as a chamber with four columns.

Scoffing at her own misgivings, Erica took out her flashlight and ducked under the low door. Slowly she let the beam of light play upon the walls, columns, and ceiling of the deathly silent room. With great care she picked her way over the irregular floor and moved around the heavy columns. Against the far wall were the openings to the three chapels of Isis, Seti I, and Horus. Eagerly Erica entered the chapel of Seti I; its location within the sanctuary of Osiris was encouraging.

No daylight penetrated the small chapel. Erica's flashlight illuminated only a small area. The rest of the room was lost in darkness. She started to run the light around the room, but almost immediately glimpsed amid the hieroglyphics a cartouche of Seti I exactly as it had been written on the statue. It was Seti identified with Osiris.

Erica scanned the hieroglyphics in the neighborhood of the cartouche, guessing the text ran vertically from left to right. Without translating word for word, she quickly understood that the small chapel had been completed after Seti's death and had been used in the Osiris ritual. Then she came to something strange. It appeared to be a proper name. Incredible. Proper names did not appear on pharaonic monuments. Erica pieced together the sounds. Ne-neph-ta.

Erica moved the beam of light to the floor, preparing to put her bag down. She wanted a photo of the curious name. She started to bend over, but then froze. Within the circle of light was a cobra, its head raised and body arched, its forked tongue lashing out like a miniature whip, its yellow eyes with black slitlike pupils staring at her with deadly concentration. Erica was paralyzed with fear. It wasn't until the snake moved by lowering its head and sliding off its perch that Erica was able to look behind her toward the low door of the chapel. After another glance at the retiring snake, she fled out into the sunlight and returned to the ticket booth on shaky legs.

The guard thanked Erica for the information and told her that they'd been trying to kill that cobra for many years. The sanctuary of Osiris was then closed temporarily.

Despite the episode with the snake, it was with reluctance that she left the site for the drive back to Balianeh. It had been a wonderful day. Her only disappointment was that she'd have to wait for a photograph of the name Nenephta. Erica intended to cross-reference that name and wondered if it was one of Seti I's viziers.

The train for Luxor departed only five minutes late. Erica settled into her seat with the Tutankhamen books, but her attention was drawn to the scenery outside. The Nile valley began to narrow so that in places it was easy to see from one side of the area of cultivated fields to the other. As the sun neared the western horizon, Erica began to notice the people returning to their homes. Children riding on water buffalo. Men leading donkeys straining beneath their burdens. Erica could see into courtyards and wondered if the people in their mud-brick houses felt security and love like in the pastoral myths—or were they continuously aware of their precarious hold on life? In a sense, their lives were timeless, a borrowed moment of time.

At Nag Hammadi the train crossed the Nile from the West Bank to the East Bank and entered a long stretch of sugarcane that blocked any view of the countryside. Erica returned to her books, picking up *The Discovery of the Tomb of Tutankhamen*, by Howard Carter and A. C. Mace. She began reading, and despite her familiarity with the book, was immediately entranced. It was a recurrent surprise that the dry and meticulous Carter wrote with a genuine flair. The excitement of the discovery was communicated from every page, and Erica found herself reading faster and faster, as if it were a thriller.

As they occurred in the book, Erica studied the superb collection of photos taken by Harry Burton. She found the plate showing two life-size bituminized statues of Tutankhamen that guarded the sealed entrance to the burial chamber particularly interesting. Comparing them to the Seti statue, she comprehended for the first time that she was one of the few people who knew the Seti statues were a matched pair. That was very significant, because the probability of finding two such statues was very small, while the chance of other artifacts now being unearthed in the same location was very great. Suddenly Erica recognized that the site where the Seti statues had been found could be as important archaeologically as the statues themselves. Perhaps locating the site was a more reasonable goal than finding the statue. Erica looked out the window at the blur of the sugarcane, thinking.

Probably the best way of learning where the statues had been discovered was for her to pose as a serious antiquities buyer for the Museum of Fine Arts. If she could convince people she was willing to pay top dollar, she might be shown some valuable pieces. If more Seti material appeared, perhaps she could learn the source. There were a lot of ifs. But it was a plan, particularly if Abdul Hamdi's son could not provide further information.

The conductor came through the train announcing Luxor. Erica felt a thrill of anticipation. She knew that Luxor is to Egypt what Florence is to Italy: the jewel. Outside the station, there was another surprise. The only taxis left were horse-drawn carriages. Smiling with pleasure, Erica already loved Luxor.

When she arrived at the Winter Palace Hotel she discovered why it had been so easy to get a reservation despite the number of tourists. The hotel was being renovated, and to get to her room she had to walk down a carpetless hall on the second floor covered with piles of building blocks, sand, and plaster. Only a few of the rooms were being used. But the renovation did not dampen her spirits. She loved the hotel. It had an elegant Victorian charm. Across the formal garden was the New Winter Palace Hotel. In contrast to the building she was in, it was a modern high-rise structure with little character. She was pleased to be where she was. Instead of air conditioning, Erica's room had an extraordinarily high ceiling complete with a slow-moving large-bladed fan. A pair of French doors opened onto a graceful wrought-iron balcony that looked over the Nile.

There was no shower; the tiled bathroom was dominated by a huge porcelain bathtub that Erica immediately filled to the top. She had just managed to step into the refreshing water when the antique phone jangled in the other room. For a moment she debated not answering it. Then curiosity overcame inconvenience, and grabbing a towel from the rack, she walked into the bedroom and picked up the receiver.

"Welcome to Luxor, Miss Baron." It was Ahmed Khazzan.

For a moment his voice brought back all her fears. Even though she had decided to pursue the statue of Seti, she felt she had left the violence and dangers behind in Cairo. Now the authorities seemed to have already tracked her down. Still, his tone was friendly.

"I hope you enjoy your stay," he said.

"I'm sure I will," answered Erica. "I did notify your office."

"Yes, I got the message. That's why I'm calling. I asked the hotel to tell me when you arrived so that I could welcome you. You see, Miss Baron, I have a home in Luxor. I come here as frequently as possible."

"I see," said Erica, wondering where the conversation was leading.

Ahmed cleared his throat. "Well, Miss Baron, I was wondering if you would care to have dinner with me tonight."

"Is this an official or social invitation, Mr. Khazzan?"

"Purely social. I can have a carriage pick you up at seven-thirty."

Erica debated rapidly. It seemed quite innocuous. "All right. I'd be delighted."

"Wonderful," said Ahmed, obviously pleased. "Tell me, Miss Baron, do you like to ride?"

Erica shrugged. In truth she hadn't ridden a horse for a number of years. But as a child she had loved it, and the idea of seeing the ancient city on horseback appealed to her. "Yes," she said tentatively.

"Even better," said Ahmed. "Wear something you can ride in and I'll show you a little of Luxor."

Holding on for her life, Erica let the black stallion have his head as they reached the edge of the desert. The animal responded with a surge of speed and thundered up the small sand hill, galloping along the crest of the ridge for almost a mile. Finally Erica reined him in to wait for Ahmed. The sun had just set, but it was still light and Erica could look down onto the ruins of the Temple of Karnak. Across the river the mountains of Thebes rose sharply beyond the irrigated fields. She could even make out some of the entranceways to the tombs of the nobles.

Erica was hypnotized by the scene, and the heaving animal between her legs made her feel as if she had been transported into the past. Ahmed rode up beside her but did not speak. He sensed her thoughts and did not want to interrupt. Erica stole a quick glance at his sharp profile in the soft light. He was dressed in loose-fitting white cotton, with the shirt open to mid-chest and the sleeves rolled to the elbows. His black, shining hair was tousled by the wind, and tiny drops of perspiration lined his forehead.

Erica was still surprised by his invitation and unable to forget his official capacity. He had been cordial since her arrival, but not communicative. She wondered if his intent still lay with Yvon de Margeau.

"Beautiful here, isn't it?" he said at last.

"Gorgeous," said Erica. She struggled with the stallion, now eager to move on.

"I love Luxor." He turned to Erica, his face serious yet puzzled.

Erica was certain he was going to say something more, but he just looked at her for several minutes and then turned back to the vista over the Nile. As they watched in silence, the shadows within the ruins deepened, heralding the coming night.

"I'm sorry," he said finally. "You must be starved. Let's have our dinner."

They rode back toward Ahmed's rustic house, skirting the Temple of Karnak and riding along the Nile. They passed a felucca landing, where the men were singing softly while furling their sails for the night. When they arrived at Ahmed's house, Erica helped with the horses. Then they both washed their hands in a wooden tub in the courtyard before going inside.

Ahmed's housekeeper had prepared a feast and served it in the living room. Erica's favorite was ful, a dip made of beans, lentils, and eggplant. It was covered with sesame oil and subtly seasoned with garlic, peanuts, and caraway. Ahmed was surprised she'd not had it before. The main course was fowl, which Erica thought was cornish hen. Ahmed explained it was hamama, or pigeon. It had been grilled over charcoal.

Within his home Ahmed relaxed and conversation became easy. He asked Erica hundreds of questions about growing up in Ohio. She felt a little self-conscious when she described her Jewish background, and was surprised that it made no difference to Ahmed. He explained that in Egypt the confrontation was a political issue and involved Israel, not Jews. People did not think of them as synonymous.

Ahmed was particularly interested in Erica's apartment in Cambridge, and he had her describe all sorts of trivial details. Only when she had finished did he tell her he had gone to Harvard. As the meal progressed, she found him reserved but not secretive. He was willing to talk about himself if asked. He had a wonderful way of speaking, with a slight English accent from his days at Oxford, where he had gotten his doctorate. He was a sensitive man, and after Erica asked if he had dated any American girls, he told her about Pamela, with such feeling that Erica felt tears welling in her eyes. Then he shocked her with the ending. He had left Boston for England and just cut off the relationship.

"You mean you never corresponded?" asked Erica with disbelief.

"Never," said Ahmed quietly.

"But why?" pleaded Erica. She loved happy endings and abhorred unhappy ones.

"I knew that I had to come back here, to my country," said Ahmed, looking away. "I was needed here. I was expected to run the antiquities service. At that time, there was no room for romance."

"Have you ever seen Pamela again?"

"No."

Erica took a sip of her tea. The story about Pamela awakened uncomfortable feelings about men and abandonment. Ahmed did not seem the type. She wanted to change the subject. "Did any of your family visit you in Massachusetts?"

"No . . ." Ahmed paused, then added, "Actually, my uncle did come to the States just before I left."

"No one visited, and you didn't go home for three years?"

"That's right. It's a bit far, going from Egypt to Boston."

"Weren't you lonely and homesick?"

"Terribly, until Pamela."

"Did your uncle meet Pamela?"

Ahmed exploded. He threw his teacup against the wall, and it shattered in a hundred pieces. Erica was stunned.

The Arab dropped his head in his hands, and she could hear his heavy breathing. An awkward silence prevailed, as Erica sat torn between fear and empathy. She wondered about Pamela and the uncle. What had happened that could still evoke such passion?

"Forgive me," Ahmed said, his head still bowed.

"I'm sorry if I said something wrong," said Erica putting down her teacup. "Perhaps I'd better return to my hotel."

"No, don't go, please," said Ahmed, lifting his head. His face was flushed. "It isn't your fault. It's just that I've been under a certain strain. Don't go. Please." Ahmed jumped up to refresh Erica's tea and got another cup for himself. Then, in an attempt to lighten the atmosphere, he brought out some antiquities that the department had recently confiscated.

Erica admired them, especially a beautifully carved wooden figure. She began to feel more comfortable. "Have any articles from Seti I been confiscated from the black market?" She carefully put the pieces on a nearby table.

214

Ahmed looked at her for several minutes, thinking. "No, I don't think so. Why do you ask?"

"Oh, no real reason, except that I visited Seti's temple at Abydos today. By the way, are you familiar with a problem they have there with a cobra?"

"Cobras are a potential problem at all the sites, especially in Aswan. I suppose we really should warn the tourists. But it isn't a problem at the more popular sites. It can't compare with our difficulties with the black market. Only four years ago there was a major looting of carved blocks from the Temple of Hathor at Dendera, in broad daylight!"

Erica nodded her understanding. "If nothing else, this trip has underlined for me the destructive power of the black market. In fact, along with my translation work, I've decided to try to do something about it."

Ahmed looked up suddenly. "It's a dangerous business. I don't recommend it at all. To give you an idea, about two years ago a young idealistic American fellow came over here from Yale with similar goals. He disappeared without a trace."

"Well," said Erica, "I'm no hero. I just have some very tame ideas. I wanted to ask if you knew the location of Abdul Hamdi's son's antique shop here in Luxor."

Ahmed averted his face. The spectacle of Tewfik Hamdi's tortured body flashed in his mind. When he turned back to Erica, his face was strained. "Tewfik Hamdi, like his father, has recently been murdered. There is some trouble going on which I do not understand, but which my department and the police are investigating. You have already had your share of difficulties, so I implore you to concentrate on your translation work."

Erica was stunned by the news of Tewfik Hamdi. Another murder! She tried to think of what that could mean, but by now her long day had begun to take its toll. Ahmed noticed her fatigue and offered to accompany her to her hotel, to which Erica readily agreed. They reached the hotel before eleven, and after thanking Ahmed for his hospitality, Erica retired, carefully locking herself within her room.

She undressed slowly, anticipating bed. While removing her makeup, she thought about Ahmed. His intensity impressed her, and despite his outburst, she'd thoroughly enjoyed the evening. With her bedtime ritual accomplished, she crawled beneath the sheets. Just before sleep overcame her, she thought about Ahmed and Pamela; she wondered . . . But her last thought was a name from the ancient past: Nenephta.

Day 5

The excitement of being in Luxor woke Erica before sunrise. She ordered breakfast from room service and had it served on the balcony. With the breakfast came a telegram from Yvon: ARRIVING NEW WINTER PALACE HOTEL TODAY STOP WOULD LOVE TO SEE YOU TONIGHT.

Erica was surprised. She had been so sure the telegram was going to be from Richard. And after spending the evening with Ahmed, she was confused. It was incredible to think that only last year she had been anxiously hoping Richard would propose. Now she found herself attracted to three very different men at the same time. Although it was reassuring for Erica that she could be responsive, which had been a worry when her relationship with Richard began to crack, the present situation was also unnerving. She drank the rest of her coffee in one gulp and decided to put all emotional issues out of her head. Pushing back from the table, she returned to her room and prepared for the day.

Emptying her tote bag, she repacked it with the box lunch she'd ordered at the suggestion of the hotel, the flashlight, the matches and cigarettes, and Abdul Hamdi's 1929 Baedeker. The loose cover and other assorted papers were put on the bureau. Before she turned away, Erica again saw the name on the cover: Nasef Malmud, 180 Shari el Tahrir, Cairo. Her connection with Abdul Hamdi had not been completely

severed by Tewfik's murder! She would look up Nasef Malmud when she returned to Cairo. Carefully, she put the cover
in her bag.

It was a short walk from the Winter Palace Hotel to the
antiquities shops on Shari Lukanda. Some were still not open,
despite the fact that there already were a number of brightly
clad tourists in evidence. Erica chose one randomly and
entered.

The shop was reminiscent of Antica Abdul, but with
significantly more artifacts. Erica went over the more impressive specimens, isolating the real from the fake. The proprietor, a heavyset man named David Jouran, initially hovered
over her, but then retreated behind his counter.

Out of dozens of allegedly prehistoric pots, Erica found only
two she thought were real, and they were ordinary. She held
one up. "How much?"

"Fifty pounds," said Jouran. "The one next to that is ten
pounds."

Erica looked at the other pot. It had beautiful decorations.
Too beautiful: they were spirals, but going in the wrong
direction. Erica knew that predynastic pottery frequently had
spirals, but they were all counterclockwise spirals. The spirals
on the present pot were all clockwise. "I'm only interested in
antiques. Actually, I find very few genuine pieces in here. I'm
hoping to find something special." She put down the fake pot
and walked over to the counter. "I've been sent here to buy
some particularly good antiques, preferably from the New
Kingdom. I'm prepared to pay. Do you have anything to show
me?"

David Jouran regarded Erica for a few moments without
answering. Then he bent over, opened a small cabinet, and
heaved a scarred granite head of Ramses II onto the counter.
The nose was gone and the chin was cracked.

Erica shook her head. "No," she said, looking around. "Is
that the best you have?"

"For now." Jouran put the broken statue away.

"Well, let me leave my name," said Erica, writing on a slip
of paper. "I'm staying at the Winter Palace. If you hear of any
special pieces, get in touch with me." She paused, half-

expecting the man to show her something else, but he just shrugged, and after an awkward silence she left.

It was a similar story in the next five shops she entered. No one showed her anything extraordinary. The best piece she saw was a glazed ushabti figurine from the time of Queen Hatshepsut. In each shop she left her name, but she didn't feel very hopeful. Finally she gave up and walked to the ferry landing.

It cost only a few cents to cross to the West Bank on the old boat, which was crowded with camera-toting tourists. As soon as they landed, the group was set upon by an enormous band of taxi drivers, would-be guides, and scarab salesmen. Erica boarded a dilapidated bus with a "Valley of the Kings" painted haphazardly on a piece of cardboard. When all the ferry passengers had been absorbed in one way or another, the bus left the landing.

Erica was beside herself with excitement. Beyond the flat green cultivated fields, which ended abruptly at the desert's edge, stood the stark Theban cliffs. At their base Erica could see some of the famous monuments, like the graceful temple of Hatshepsut at Deir el-Bahri. Immediately to the right of Hatshepsut's temple was a small village called Qurna, built into the sloping hillside. The mud-brick buildings were set in the desert beyond the irrigated fields. Most were a light tan not too dissimilar from the color of the sandstone cliffs. A few buildings were whitewashed and stood out sharply, particularly a small mosque with a stubby minaret. In among the buildings were openings cut into the bedrock. These were doorways into the myriad of ancient crypts. The people of Qurna lived among the tombs of the nobles. Many attempts had been made to relocate the villagers, but the people had tenaciously resisted.

The bus careened around a sharp turn and then bore right at a fork. Erica caught a fleeting glimpse of the mortuary temple of Seti I. There was so much to see.

The desert began with a remarkably sharp demarcation line. Desolate rock and sand without a single growing plant replaced the verdant sugarcane fields. The road ran straight until it reached the mountains; then it became serpentine, leading into a progressively narrow valley. The ovenlike heat was intense and there was no wind to relieve the feeling of oppression.

After passing a tiny rock guard station, the bus pulled up in a large parking area already filled with other buses and taxis. Despite the 100-plus temperature, the area was dense with tourists. On a small rise to the left, a concession stand was doing swift business.

Erica donned a khaki-colored hat she'd bought as protection against the sun. It was hard for her to believe that she had finally arrived in the Valley of the Kings, the site of the discovery of the tomb of Tutankhamen. The valley was hemmed in by jagged mountains and dominated by a sharp, triangular peak that looked like a natural pyramid. Sheer rock faces of brown limestone dropped down into the valley and met the neat tracks lined with little stones that radiated from the parking area. At the juncture of the cliffs and the paths were the black openings of the tombs of the kings.

Although most of the passengers on the bus had repaired to the concession stand for cool drinks, Erica hurried to the entrance of Seti I's tomb. She knew that it was the largest and most spectacular in the valley, and she wanted to visit it first, to see if she could find the name Nenephta.

Catching her breath, she stepped over the threshold into the past. Although she had known the decorations were well-preserved, once she saw them herself, their pristine hues surprised her. The paint looked as freshly applied as yesterday. She walked slowly through the entrance corridor, then down another stairway, her eyes glued to the wall decorations. There were images of Seti in the company of the entire pantheon of Egyptian deities. On the ceiling were huge vultures with stylistically outstretched wings. Voluminous hieroglyphic texts of the Book of the Dead separated the images.

Erica had to wait for a large tour group before she could pass a wooden bridge spanning a deep shaft. Looking into the depths of the well, Erica wondered if it had been constructed to thwart tomb robbers. Beyond it was a gallery supported by four robust pillars. Then there was another stairway, which

220

had been sealed and carefully hidden in ancient times.

As she had descended ever deeper into the tomb, Erica marveled at the herculean effort it had taken to hand-carve the rock. By the time she had descended the fourth stairway and was several hundred yards into the mountain, she noticed that the air was considerably harder to breathe. She wondered what it had been like for the struggling ancient workmen. There was no ventilation despite the continuous stream of gawking visitors, and the low oxygen gave Erica a feeling of suffocation. She did not suffer from claustrophobia but was not fond of being closed in and had to consciously suppress her misgivings.

Once in the burial chamber, Erica tried to ignore her labored breathing and craned her neck to admire the astronomical motifs on the vaulted ceiling. She also noted one of the tunnels dug in relatively recent times by an individual who was certain he knew the location of additional secret rooms. Nothing had been found.

Although she was growing more and more anxious in the confines of the tomb, she convinced herself she should visit a small side room where there was a well-known representation of the sky goddess Nut, in the form of a cow. She navigated through the tourists to the doorway, but looking into the room, she could see that it was practically filled with people and decided to forgo seeing Nut. Turning suddenly, she bumped into a man entering the room behind her.

"I beg your pardon," said Erica.

The man flashed a smile before turning and walking back into the burial chamber. Another group of tourists entered, and Erica found herself forced against her will into the small room. Desperately she tried to calm herself, but the man who had blocked her way unnerved her. She'd seen him before—black hair, black suit, and a crooked smile revealing a pointed front tooth that she remembered from the Egyptian Museum in Cairo.

Knowing that tourists frequent the same places, Erica wondered why the man made her feel alarmed. She knew she was acting absurdly and that her fear was just a combination of the weird events of the last few days plus the hot, stuffy atmosphere of the tomb. Hiking her tote strap higher on her shoulder, Erica forced herself out into the burial chamber. The man was not in sight. A small flight of steps rose to the upper part of the room, leading to the exit. Erica started up the steps, her eyes scanning the area. She had to keep herself from running. Then she stopped. Moving quickly behind one of the square pillars on her left was the same man. It was just a fleeting glimpse, but now Erica was convinced she was not imagining things, that the man was acting strangely. He was stalking her. Impulsively she mounted the remaining steps and slipped behind a column. The room contained four pillars, each facade decorated with a colored life-size relief of Seti I before one of the Egyptian gods.

Erica waited, her heart pounding, unwillingly remembering the way violence had been exploding around her during the last few days. She did not know what to expect. Then the man appeared again. He walked around the pillar in front of her, looking at the giant mural on the wall. Even though his lips were only slightly parted, Erica could see that the right-front incisor came to a sharp point. He passed without looking at her.

As soon as her legs would move, Erica first walked, then ran, retracing her steps through corridors and up the stairways until she emerged into the shocking bright sunlight. Once in the open, her panic evaporated and she felt foolish. Her certainty of the man's evil intentions seemed like pure paranoia. She glanced back but did not return to Seti's tomb. She'd look for the name Nenephta on another day.

It was after noon, and the concession stand and rest house were jammed. As a consequence, Tutankhamen's comparatively meager tomb was almost empty. Earlier there had been a line to get in. Erica took advantage of the lull in the crowds and descended the famous sixteen steps to the entrance. Just before going in, she looked back toward Seti's tomb. She saw no one. While walking down the passageway, she considered the irony that the smallest tomb of the most insignificant pharaoh of the New Kingdom was the only one found reasonably intact. And even Tutankhamen's tomb had been broken into twice in antiquity.

As she crossed the threshold into the antechamber, she tried to recreate in her mind that wonderful day in November 1922 when the tomb was opened. How exciting it must have been when Howard Carter and his party stepped into the most dazzling archaeological treasure ever uncovered.

With her knowledge of the discovery, Erica could mentally place most of the objects found in the tomb. She knew that the life-size statues of Tutankhamen stood on either side of the burial-chamber entrance and that the three funerary beds stood against the wall. Then she remembered the strange disarray that Carter had found in the tomb. That was a mystery that never was explained. Presumably the chaos was from the tomb robbers, but why hadn't the funerary objects been put back to their original state?

Stepping out of the way of an exiting French tour group, Erica had to wait to enter the burial chamber. While she stood there, the man in the black suit who had frightened her in Seti's tomb entered, carrying an open guidebook. Involuntarily Erica stiffened. But she successfully fought her fear, convinced that she was just imagining things. Besides, the man did not seem to notice her as he passed. She got a good look at the hooked nose that gave him the appearance of a bird of prey.

Mustering her fortitude, she forced herself to enter the crowded burial chamber. The room was divided by a banister, and the only free spot at the railing was next to the man in the black suit. She hesitated for a moment but then walked up to the banister and looked over at Tutankhamen's magnificent pink sarcophagus. The wall paintings in the room were insignificant when compared with the stylistic perfection of those in Seti's tomb. As her eyes roamed the room, Erica happened to see the open page in the man's guidebook. It was the floor plan of the Temple of Karnak. It had nothing to do with the Valley of the Kings, and all Erica's fears returned with a rush. Quickly stepping away from the railing, Erica hurried out. Again she felt better in the sunlight and fresh air, but now she was convinced she was not paranoid.

There were no tables available in the concession stand, which stood a mere thirty feet from the entrance to Tutankhamen's tomb, but Erica was thankful for the crowd; it made her feel safe. She sat on the low stone wall of the veranda with a cold can of juice she'd purchased and her box lunch from the hotel. She'd kept her eye on the opening of Tutankhamen's tomb, and now as she watched, the man emerged and walked across the parking area to a small black car. He sat on the seat, leaving the door ajar, his feet on the ground. She wondered what his presence meant; if his intention had been to harm her, he'd had multiple opportunities. She concluded that he must be merely following her, perhaps working for the authorities. Erica took a deep breath and tried to ignore him. But she also decided to stay in the company of other tourists.

Her lunch consisted of several sliced lamb sandwiches, which she chewed thoughtfully while looking across the path to the nearby opening of Tutankhamen's tomb. It helped her to relax to think of the thousands of Victorian visitors to the Valley of the Kings who had unknowingly sipped their cool lemonade ten yards from the hidden entrance to the world's greatest buried treasure. The Seti I tomb was also reasonably close to the concesssion stand.

Biting into the second sandwich, she pondered the proximity of Ramses VI's tomb to Tutankhamen's. It was just above and slightly to the left. Erica remembered that it had been the workers' huts built during the construction of Ramses VI tomb over the entrance to Tutankhamen's which had delayed Carter's discovery. It hadn't been until he'd thrown a trench right into the area that he had found the sixteen descending steps.

Erica stopped eating, drawing the information together. She knew that the ancient plunderers had entered Tutankhamen's tomb through the original entrance, because Carter had decribed the breaks in the door. But because of the location of the workers' huts, the entrance to Tutankhamen's tomb had to have been covered and forgotten by the time the construction began on Ramses VI's tomb. This meant that Tutankhamen's tomb had to have been plundered in the early twentieth or perhaps the nineteenth dynasty. What if Tutankhamen's tomb had been plundered during the reign of Seti I?

Erica allowed herself to swallow. Could there be some connection between the defilement of Tutankhamen's tomb and the fact that Tutankhamen's name appeared on the Seti statue? While her mind wandered over these thoughts, Erica looked up and watched a lone hawk spiral on still wings.

She began putting her sandwich papers back into the box. The man in the car had not moved. A nearby table vacated, and Erica carried her belongings over to it, putting her tote bag on the ground.

Despite the heavy heat hanging over the valley like a thick blanket, Erica's mind kept racing. What if the Seti statues had been placed inside Tutankhamen's tomb after the tomb robbers had been caught? She immediately dismissed the idea as preposterous; it made no sense. Besides, if the statues had been in the tomb, they would have been cataloged by Carter, who had a reputation for being uncompromisingly meticulous. No, Erica knew she was on the wrong track, but she realized that the whole issue of robbers in Tutankhamen's tomb had been given short shrift because of the enormity of Carter's find. The fact that the boy king's tomb had been defiled might have significance, and the idea that the tomb had been entered during the reign of Seti I was intriguing. Suddenly Erica wished she were back at the Egyptian Museum. She decided she wanted to go over Carter's notes, which Dr. Fakhry said were on microfilm in the archives. Even if she did not learn anything astounding, it would be the subject of a good journal article. She also wondered if any of the people present during the initial opening of Tutankhamen's tomb were still alive. She knew Carnarvon and Carter had died, and thinking of Carnarvon's death, she remembered the "Curse of the Pharaohs" and smiled at the resourcefulness of the media and the gullibility of the public.

With her lunch finished, Erica opened the Baedeker to decide which of the many tombs she wanted to visit next. A German tour group went by, and she hurried to join. Above her the spiraling sparrow hawk abruptly dived to pounce on some unsuspecting prey.

Khalifa reached over and turned off the radio in the rented

car as he watched Erica trudge deeper into the white-hot valley. *"Karrah,"* he cursed as he heaved himself from the shade of the auto. He could not fathom why anyone would voluntarily subject herself to such merciless heat.

Luxor   8:00 P.M.

As Erica crossed the extensive gardens that separated the old Winter Palace from the new hotel, she could understand why so many wealthy Victorians had chosen to winter in Upper Egypt. Although the day had been hot, once the sun had set the temperature cooled gracefully. As she skirted the swimming pool she noticed it was still being enjoyed by a bevy of American children.

It had been a wonderful day. The ancient paintings she'd seen in the tombs had been outstanding, incredible. Then, when she had returned to the hotel from the West Bank, she had found two notes, both invitations. One from Yvon and one from Ahmed. The decision had been difficult, but she had agreed to see Yvon, hoping he might have discovered new information about the statue. On the phone he had told her that they would eat in the dining room of the New Winter Palace and that he would come by for her at eight. On an impulse she had told him that she'd rather meet him there in the lobby.

Yvon was dressed in a dark blue double-breasted blazer and white slacks, his fine brown hair carefully combed. He offered Erica his arm as they entered the dining room.

The restaurant was not old, but it appeared decadent, its unharmonious decor suggesting a failed attempt at a gracious continental dining room. But Erica soon forgot her surroundings as Yvon entertained her with stories of his European childhood. The way he described his formal and very cold relationship with his parents made it sound more funny than deplorable.

"And what about you?" asked Yvon, searching for his cigarettes in his jacket.

"I come from another world." Erica looked down and swirled her wine. "I grew up in a house in a small city in the Midwest. We had a small but very close family." Erica pressed her lips together and shrugged.

"Ah, there's more than that," said Yvon with a smile. "But don't let me be rude . . . and don't feel obligated to tell me."

Erica was not being secretive. She just didn't think that Yvon would be interested in hearing about Toledo, Ohio. And she didn't want to talk about her father's death in an air crash or the fact that she had trouble getting along with her mother because they were too similar. Anyway, she preferred hearing Yvon talk.

"Have you ever been married?" asked Erica.

Yvon laughed and then studied Erica's face. "I am married," he said casually.

Erica averted her eyes, certain that her instantaneous disappointment would be mirrored in her pupils. She should have known.

"I even have two wonderful children," continued Yvon, "Jean Claude and Michelle. I just never see them."

"Never?" The idea of not seeing one's own children was incomprehensible. Erica lifted her gaze; she was under control.

"I visit them rarely. My wife chooses to live in St. Tropez. She likes to shop and sun, both of which I find limiting. The children are at boarding school, and they like St. Tropez in the summer. So . . ."

"So you live in your château by yourself," said Erica, lightening the mood.

"No, it's a dreary place. I have a nice apartment on the Rue Verneuil in Paris."

It was only when they were drinking coffee that Yvon was willing to discuss the statue of Seti I or Abdul's death.

"I brought these photos for you to look at," he said, taking five pictures from his pocket and placing them in front of

Erica. "I know you saw the men who killed Abdul Hamdi for only a second, but do you recognize any of these faces?"

Taking each in turn, Erica studied the pictures. "No," she said at length. "But that doesn't mean they weren't there."

"I understand," said Yvon, picking up the photographs. "It was just a possibility. Tell me, Erica, have you had any problems since you've come to Upper Egypt?"

"No . . . except I'm quite sure I'm being followed."

"Followed?" said Yvon.

"That's the only explanation I can think of. Today in the Valley of the Kings I saw a man I believe I first saw in the Egyptian Museum. He's an Arab with a large hooked nose, a sneering grin, and one front tooth that comes to a point." Erica bared her lips and pointed to her right incisor. The gesture brought a smile to Yvon's face, although he was not pleased that she had spotted Khalifa. "This is not funny," continued Erica. "He scared me today, pretending to be a tourist but reading the wrong page in his guidebook. Yvon," she said, changing the subject, "what about this plane of yours? Do you have it here in Luxor?"

Yvon shook his head, confused. "Yes, of course. The plane is here in Luxor. Why do you ask?"

"Because I want to go back to Cairo. I have some work that will take about half a day."

"When?" asked Yvon.

"The sooner the better," said Erica.

"What about tonight?" He wanted Erica back in the city.

Erica was surprised at the offer, but she trusted Yvon, especially now that she knew he was married. "Why not?" she said.

Although she had never been in a small jet before, she had imagined there would be a lot more room than there was. She was strapped into one of the four large leather seats. In the chair next to Erica was Raoul, trying to carry on a conversation with her, but Erica was more interested in what was happening and whether they were going to get off the ground. She didn't believe in the principles of aerodynamics. In big planes it didn't worry her because the concept of the huge hulk ever flying was so preposterous that she refused to think about it. The smaller the plane, the more the issue was unwelcomely thrust into her awareness.

Yvon employed a pilot, but since he had trained to fly himself, he usually preferred to be at the controls. There was no air traffic and they were cleared immediately. The knifelike little jet thundered down the runway and leaped into the air as Erica's fingers blanched.

Once they were under way, Yvon relinquished the controls and came back to talk with Erica. Beginning to relax, she said, "You mentioned that your mother was from England. Do you think she might have known the Carnarvons?"

"Why, yes. I've met the present earl," said Yvon. "Why do you ask?"

"Actually, I'm interested to know if Lord Carnarvon's daughter is still alive. Her name is Evelyn, I believe."

"I haven't the slightest idea," said Yvon, "but I could find out. Why do you ask? Have you become interested in the 'Curse of the Pharaohs'?" He grinned in the half-light of the cabin.

"Maybe," answered Erica teasingly. "I have a theory about Tutankhamen's tomb that I want to investigate. I'll tell you about it when I get some more information. But if you could find out about Carnarvon's daughter for me, I'd really appreciate it. Oh, one other thing. Have you ever heard the name Nenephta?"

"In what context?"

"In relation to Seti I."

Yvon thought, then shook his head. "Never."

They had to fly a complicated pattern over Cairo before they were allowed to land, but formalities were brief, since the plane had already been cleared. It was just after one A.M. when they arrived at the Meridien Hotel. The management was extremely cordial to Yvon, and althogh they were supposedly full, they somehow managed to find an extra room for Erica next to his penthouse suite. Yvon invited her over for a nightcap after she had settled herself.

Erica had brought only her canvas tote bag, packing a minimum of clothing, her makeup, and reading material.

230

She'd left the guidebooks and flashlight in her room in Luxor. So there was little to do by way of "settling" herself, and she walked through the connecting door into the main room of Yvon's suite.

He had removed his jacket and rolled up his sleeves and was just opening a bottle of Dom Perignon when Erica entered. She took the glass of champagne, and for a moment their hands touched. Erica was suddenly conscious of his extraordinary good looks. She felt as if they had been moving toward this night since they first met. He was married, he obviously wasn't serious, but then, neither was she. She decided to relax and let the evening take its own course. But an excited pulse began between her thighs, and to distract herself she felt impelled to talk. "What makes you so interested in archaeology?"

"It started when I was still a student in Paris. Some of my friends talked me into going to the École de Lange Oriental. I was fascinated and worked like crazy for the first time. I'd never been much of a student. I studied Arabic and Coptic. It was Egypt that interested me. I guess that's more of an explanation than a reason. Would you like to see the view from the terrace?" He held out his hand to her.

"I'd love to," said Erica, the pulse quickening. She wanted this. She didn't care if he was using her, if he was simply compelled to take to bed any attractive woman he met. For the first time in her life she let herself be swept along by desire.

Yvon slid open the door, and Erica walked out under the trellis. She could smell the fragrant roses as she stared down at the whole city of Cairo spread out against the canopy of stars. The citadel with its bold minarets was still illuminated. Directly before them was the island of Gezira, surrounded by the dark Nile.

Erica could sense Yvon's presence behind her. When she looked up at his angular face, he was studying her. Slowly he reached out and drew the tips of his fingers through her hair, then cupped the back of her head and pulled her to him. He kissed her tentatively, sensitive to her emotions, then more fully, and finally with true passion.

Erica was amazed at the intensity of her response. Yvon was

231

the first man she had been with since knowing Richard, and she was not certain how her body would react. But now she opened her arms to Yvon, matching his excitement with her own.

Their clothes fell naturally as their bodies slowly sank to the Oriental carpet. And in the soft silent light of the Egyptian night they made love with intense abandon, the sprawling throbbing city serving as mute witness to their passion.

Day 6

Erica awoke in her own bed. She dimly remembered Yvon saying that he preferred to sleep alone. Turning over, thinking of the evening, she was amazed to find she felt no guilt.

When she emerged from her room it was about nine. Yvon was sitting on the balcony dressed in a blue-and-white-striped robe, reading the *El Ahram* newspaper in Arabic. The rays of the morning sun were broken into pieces by the trellis, splattering the area with bits of bright color like an impressionist painting. Breakfast lay waiting under silver serving dishes.

He got up when he saw her and embraced her warmly.

"I'm very glad we came to Cairo," he said, holding out her chair.

"So am I," said Erica.

It was a pleasant meal. Yvon had a subtle humor that Erica enjoyed immensely. But after the last piece of toast, she was impatient to continue her investigation.

"Well, I'm off to the museum," she said, folding her napkin.

"Would you care for some company?" asked Yvon.

Erica looked across at him, remembering Richard's impatience. She did not want to feel rushed. It was better to go alone.

"To be truthful, the kind of work I want to do is going to be a bit boring. Unless you want to spend the morning in the

233

archives, I prefer to go by myself." Erica reached across the table and touched Yvon's arm.

"Fine," he said. "But I'll have Raoul give you a ride."

"It's not necessary," she protested.

"Compliments of the French," said Yvon cheerfully.

Dr. Fakhry led Erica into a small stuffy cubicle off the main room of the library. On a single table against the wall was a microfilm reader.

"Talat will bring the film you desire," said Dr. Fakhry.

"I appreciate your help very much," Erica told him.

"What is it you are looking for?" queried Dr. Fakhry. His right hand suddenly shook spasmodically.

"I'm interested in the robbers who broke into Tutankhamen's tomb in ancient times. I don't think that aspect of the discovery has been given the attention it deserves."

"Tomb robbers?" he questioned, then shuffled from the room.

Erica sat down in front of the microfilm reader and drummed her fingers on the table. She hoped that the Egyptian Museum had as much material as possible. Talat appeared and gave Erica a shoe box full of film. "You buy scarab, lady?" he whispered.

Without even answering, Erica began to look through the microfilm canisters, conveniently labeled in English with cards from the Ashmolean Museum, which houses the original documents. She was genuinely surprised at the wealth of the material and made herself comfortable, since she was clearly going to be there for a while.

Flipping on the reader, Erica inserted the first roll of film. Fortunately Carter had written his journal in a compulsively neat script. Erica skimmed to the section describing the stonecutters' huts. There was no doubt that they had been built directly over the entranceway to Tutankhamen's tomb. Erica was now positive that the robbers had to have plundered Tutankhamen's tomb before the reign of Ramses VI.

She continued skimming until she came to the section where Carter listed the reasons he was sure before he discovered Tutankhamen's tomb that it existed. The piece of evidence that

234

Erica found the most fascinating was a blue faience cup with the cartouche of Tutankhamen, found by Theodore Davis. No one had ever wondered why the little cup was found hidden under a rock on the hillside.

When the first spool was finished, Erica put on the next. She was now reading about the discovery itself. Carter described at length the way the outer and inner doors of the tomb had been closed again in antiquity with a seal of the necropolis; the original Tutankhamen seal could only be found at the base of each door. Carter explained in detail why he was certain the doors had been breached and resealed twice, but offered no explanation why.

Closing her eyes, Erica rested for a few moments. Her imagination took her back to the solemn ceremony when the young pharaoh was interred. Then her mind tried to conjure up the tomb robbers. Had they been confident during their robbery, or had they been terrified at the possibility of angering the guardians of the netherworld? Then she thought about Carter. What was it like when he entered the tomb for the first time? From the notes Erica confirmed that he had been accompanied by his assistant, Callender; Lord Carnarvon; Carnarvon's daughter; and one of the foremen, named Sarwat Raman.

For the next several hours Erica scarcely moved. She could sense Carter's feeling of awe and mystery. With painstaking detail he described the location of each object: the alabaster lotiform cup and a nearby oil lamp took several pages. As she studied the material on the cup and the lamp, Erica remembered something she'd read elsewhere. On his lecture tour after the discovery, Carter had mentioned that the curious orientation of these two objects led him to conjecture that they were clues to some greater mystery that he hoped would be unraveled following a complete examination of the tomb. He'd gone on to say that the group of gold rings he had found discarded in cavalier manner suggested that the intruders were surprised in the middle of their brigandage.

Looking up from the machine, Erica realized that Carter assumed that the tomb had been burglarized twice, since it had been opened twice. But that was indeed an assumption, and there might be another equally plausible explanation.

After an initial reading of Carter's field notes, Erica put into the microfilm reader a roll of film labeled "Lord Carnarvon: Papers and Correspondence." What she found was mostly business letters concerning his support of the archaeological endeavors. She advanced the film rapidly until the dates coincided with the discovery of the tomb itself. As she expected, the volume of Carnarvon's correspondence increased once Carter had reported finding the entrance stairway. Erica stopped at a long letter Carnarvon had written to Sir Wallis Budge of the British Museum on December 1, 1922. In order to get the entire letter in one frame, it had been reduced considerably in size. Erica had to strain to read the script. The handwriting also wasn't as neat as Carter's. In the letter Carnarvon had excitedly described the "find" and listed many of the famous pieces Erica had seen in the traveling Tutankhamen exhibit. She read along quickly until a sentence leaped out at her. "I have not opened the boxes, and don't know what is in them; but there are some papyrus letters, faience, jewelry, bouquets, candles on ankh candlesticks." Erica looked at the word "papyrus." As far as she knew, no papyrus had been found in Tutankhamen's tomb. In fact, that had been one of the disappointments. It had been hoped that Tutankhamen's tomb would have afforded some insight into the troubled era in which he lived. But without documents, that hope had been destroyed. But here Carnarvon was describing a papyrus to Sir Wallis Budge.

Erica went back to Carter's notes. She reread all the entries made the day the tomb was opened and for the following two days: Carter did not mention any papyrus. In fact, he alluded to his disappointment that there were no documents. Strange. Going back to Carnarvon's letter to Budge, Erica was able to cross-reference with Carter's notes every other article he mentioned. The single discrepancy was the papyrus.

When Erica finally emerged from the dreary museum, it was early afternoon. She walked slowly toward the busy Tahrir Square. Although her stomach was empty, she wanted to accomplish one more errand before returning to the Meridien Hotel. From her tote bag she withdrew the cover of the

Baedeker and read the name and address, Nasef Malmud, 180 Shari el Tahrir.

Crossing the massive square was an accomplishment in itself, since it was filled with dusty buses and crowds of people. At the corner of Shari el Tahrir she turned left.

"Nasef Malmud," she said to herself. She did not know what to expect. Shari el Tahrir was one of the more fashionable boulevards, with smart European-style shops and office buildings; 180 was a modern marble-and-glass high-rise.

Nasef Malmud's office was on the eighth floor. Riding in an empty elevator, Erica remembered the long midday break and was afraid she would not be able to see Nasef Malmud until later in the afternoon. But his office door was ajar and she walked in, noting the sign that said "Nasef Malmud, International Law: Import-Export Division."

The reception area of the office was deserted. Smart Olivetti typewriters on mahogany desks proclaimed a flourishing business.

"Hello," called Erica.

A stocky man appeared in a doorway, dressed in a carefully tailored three-piece suit. He was about fifty and would not have looked out of place strolling in the financial section of Boston.

"Can I help you?" he asked in a businesslike voice.

"I'm looking for Mr. Nasef Malmud," answered Erica.

"I am Nasef Malmud."

"Would you have a few moments to talk with me?" asked Erica.

Nasef looked back into his office, pursing his lips. He had a pen in his right hand, and it was obvious he was in the middle of something. Turning back to Erica, he spoke as if he'd not quite made up his mind. "Well, for a few minutes."

Erica entered the spacious corner office with a view up Shari el Tahrir to the square and the Nile beyond. Nasef eased himself into his high-backed desk chair and waved Erica to a seat nearby. "What can I do for you, young lady?" he asked, putting the tips of his fingers together.

"I wanted to inquire about a man named Abdul Hamdi." Erica stopped to see if there was any response. There wasn't.

Malmud waited, thinking there was more. But when Erica did not continue, he said, "The name is not familiar. In which context might I know this individual?"

"I was wondering if by chance Abdul Hamdi was a client of yours," said Erica.

Malmud removed his reading glasses and put them on his desk. "If he were a client, I'm not sure why I would be willing to disclose such information," he said without malice. He was a lawyer and as such was more interested in receiving information than giving it.

"I have some news about the man that would interest you if he was a client." Erica tried to be equally evasive.

"How did you get my name?" he asked.

"From Abdul Hamdi," said Erica, knowing that it was a slight permutation of the truth.

Malmud studied Erica for a moment, went into the outer office, then returned with a manila file. Sitting behind the desk, he replaced his reading glasses and opened the file. It contained a single sheet of paper, which he took a minute to scan.

"Yes, it seems that I do represent Abdul Hamdi." He looked expectantly across at Erica over his glasses.

"Well, Abdul Hamdi is dead." Erica decided not to use the word "murdered."

Malmud thoughtfully regarded Erica, then reread the paper in his hand. "Thank you for the information. I will have to investigate my responsibilities to his estate." He stood up and extended his hand, forcing a rapid conclusion to the interview.

While walking to the door, Erica spoke. "Do you know what a Baedeker is?"

"No," he said, hurrying her through the outer office.

"Have you ever owned a Baedeker guidebook?" Erica paused at the doorway.

"Never."

Yvon was waiting when she returned to the hotel. He had another series of photos for Erica to examine. One man looked vaguely familiar, but she could not be sure. She felt the chances of her being able to recognize the killers were pretty slim, and tried to say as much to Yvon, but he just insisted, "I'd prefer if you'd try to cooperate rather than telling me how to proceed."

Walking out onto the beautiful balcony, Erica remembered the night before. Yvon's interest now seemed strictly business, and she was glad she had at least gone into the affair with her eyes open. His desires had been momentarily satisfied and his attention had reverted to the Seti statue.

Erica accepted the reality with equanimity, but it made her want to leave Cairo and return to Luxor. She walked back into the suite and told Yvon her plans. Initially he complained, but she derived a certain pleasure in denying him his way. He was obviously unaccustomed to such treatment. But in the end he relented, even offering Erica the use of his plane. He would follow her, he said, as soon as he could.

Returning to Luxor was a joy. Despite the memory of the man with the sharp tooth, Erica felt infinitely more comfortable in Upper Egypt than she did in the raw brutality of Cairo. When she arrived at the hotel, she found a number of messages from Ahmed, asking her to call. She put them by the phone. Walking over to the French doors to the balcony, she threw them open. It was just after five, and the afternoon sun had lost most of its heat.

Erica drew a bath to rinse off the dust and fatigue of travel, although the plane trip had been comfortingly short. When she got out of the tub she called Ahmed, who seemed both relieved and happy to hear from her.

"I was very worried," said Ahmed. "Especially when the hotel said you had not been seen."

"I went to Cairo overnight. Yvon de Margeau took me by plane."

"I see," said Ahmed. There was an awkward pause as Erica remembered that he had acted strangely about Yvon since their first conversation.

"Well," said Ahmed finally, "I'm calling to see if you'd enjoy visiting the Temple of Karnak tonight. There is a full moon, and the temple will be open until midnight. It is worth seeing."

"I'd like that very much," said Erica.

They made arrangements for Ahmed to pick her up at nine o'clock. They'd visit the Temple of Karnak, then eat. Ahmed said he knew a small restaurant on the Nile that was owned by a friend. He promised her that she'd like it, then hung up.

Erica dressed in her brown scoop-necked jersey dress. With her deepening tan and the light streaks in her hair, it made her feel very feminine. She ordered a glass of wine from room service and sat down on the balcony with the Baedeker, holding the torn cover in front of her.

The name carefully written on the inside of the separated cover of Abdul Hamdi's guidebook was Nasef Malmud. There had been no mistake. Why had Malmud lied? She picked up the book and examined it carefully. It was a well-constructed volume, actually sewn, not just glued. It had many diagrams and line drawings of the various monuments. Erica flipped through the pages, stopping frequently to look at an illustration or read a short section. There were also a few fold-out maps: one of Egypt, one of Saqqara, and one of the Necropolis of Luxor. She examined them in turn.

When she tried to refold the map of Luxor, she had difficulty returning it to its previous shape. Then she noticed the paper felt different from the other maps. Looking more closely, she saw it was printed on two sheets laminated together. Erica held the book up so that the map was between her eye and the setting sun: some sort of document was fused to the back of the map of the Necropolis of Luxor.

Going back inside the room, Erica closed one of the doors to the balcony, and placing the map against the glass, allowed the sun to backlight it. She could make out the letter sealed inside. The print was faint and small, but in English and legible. It was addressed to Nasef Malmud.

Dear Mr. Malmud:

This letter is written by my son, who express-es my words. I cannot write. I am an old man, so if you read this letter, do not grieve my fate. Instead use the information enclosed against those individuals who have decided to silence me rather than pay. The following routing is the way in recent years that all the most valuable ancient treasures have been removed from our country. I had been hired by a foreign agent (whose name I choose to withhold) to infiltrate the routing in order to allow him to obtain the treasures for himself.

Once a valuable piece has been found, Lahib Zayed and his son Fathi of the Curio Antique Shop send photos to prospective buyers. Those interested come to Luxor and view the pieces. Once a deal is made, the buyer must place the money on account with the Zurich Credit Bank. The piece is then routed north by small boats and delivered to the office of Aegean Holidays, Ltd., in Cairo, proprietor Stephanos Markoulis. The antiquities are there placed within the luggage of unsuspecting tour groups (large pieces disassembled) and flown with the tour group to Athens by Jugoslwenski Airlines. Airline personnel are paid to leave specific luggage on the aircraft for continuation to Belgrade and Ljubljana. Pieces are sent overland to Switzerland for transfer.

A newer route has recently been established via Alexandria. The cotton export firm Futures, Ltd., controlled by Zayed Naquib, packs antiquities in bales and sends them to Pierce Fauve Galleries, Marseilles. This route is untested as of the writing of this letter.

> Your faithful servant,
> Abdul Hamdi

Erica folded the map back into the Baedeker. She was stunned. Without doubt the Seti statue Jeffrey Rice had purchased had gone through the Athens connection, as she had guessed when she met with Stephanos Markoulis. It was clever, because tour-group luggage was never subjected to the same examination as the baggage of an individual traveler. Who'd guess that a sixty-three-year-old lady from Joliet would be carrying priceless Egyptian antiquities in her pink Samsonite suitcase?

Walking back onto the balcony, Erica leaned on the railing. The sun had reluctantly dipped behind the distant mountains. In the middle of the irrigated fields on the West Bank stood the colossi of Memnon, veiled in lavender shadow. She wondered what she should do. She thought about giving the book to either Ahmed or Yvon—probably Ahmed. But maybe she should wait until she was ready to leave Egypt. That would be the safest. Important as exposing the black-market routing was, Erica was also interested in the Seti I statue itself and the location in which it had been dug up. With excitement she dreamed of what else could be found at such a site. She did not want her own investigations cut off by the police.

Erica tried to be realistic about the danger of keeping the book. It was obvious now that the old man had been a blackmailer and things had closed in on him. It was equally obvious that Erica had been a last-minute addition to his plans. No one actually knew she had any information, and until a few minutes earlier, neither had she. She resolved again to ignore the information until she was ready to leave the country.

While evening crept slowly over the Nile valley, Erica reviewed her plans. She would continue her role as museum buyer and visit the Curio Antique Shop, which, for all she knew, she had already seen, since she did not remember the various names. Then she would try to find out if Sarwat Raman, Carter's foreman, was still alive. He'd have to be at least in his late seventies. She wanted to talk with someone who had entered Tutankhamen's tomb on that first day, and ask about the papyrus Carnarvon had described in his letter to Sir Wallis Budge. In the meantime, she hoped Yvon would make the promised inquiries about Lord Carnarvon's daughter.

"That's the Chicago House," said Ahmed, pointing to an impressive structure on the right. Their carriage was taking them peacefully up Shari el Bahr, along the tree-lined edge of the Nile. The rhythmic sound of the horses' hooves was comforting, like the fall of waves on a stone beach. It was very dark because the full moon had not yet crested the palms and

242

desert ridges. The slight wind that blew from the north was not enough to disturb the mirrorlike surface of the Nile.

Ahmed was again impeccably dressed in white cotton. When Erica looked at his deeply tanned face, she could see only his brilliant eyes and white teeth.

The more time she spent with Ahmed, the more confused she became about his reasons for seeing her. He was friendly and warm, and yet he maintained a sharp distance. The only time he had touched her was to help her climb into the carriage, holding her hand and giving the small of her back a very slight push.

"Have you ever been married?" asked Erica, hoping to learn something about the man.

"No, never," said Ahmed curtly.

"I'm sorry," said Erica. "I suppose it isn't any of my business."

Ahmed lifted his arm and put it behind Erica on the top of the seat. "It's all right. There's no secret." His voice was fluid again. "I've not had time for romance, and I suppose I became spoiled when I was in America. Things are not quite the same here in Egypt. But that's probably just an excuse."

They passed a group of fancy Western houses built on the Nile bank, surrounded by high whitewashed walls. In front of each gate was a soldier in battle uniform with a machine pistol. But the soldiers were not attentive. One had even put his weapon on top of the wall to talk with a passerby.

"What are these buildings?" asked Erica.

"They are the houses of some ministers," said Ahmed.

"Why are they guarded?"

"Being a minister can be dangerous in this country. You can't please everyone."

"You're a minister," said Erica, concerned.

"Yes, but the people unfortunately don't care so much about my department." They rode in silence as the first rays of moonlight fell through the rustling palms.

"That's the Department of Antiquities office for Karnak," said Ahmed, pointing to a waterfront building. Directly ahead, Erica could see the massive first pylons of the great Temple of Amon lit by the rising moon. They rode up to the entrance and climbed from the carriage. Walking up the short processional way lined with ram-headed sphinxes, Erica was spellbound. The half-light created by the rising moon hid the ruined aspect of the temple, making it appear still in use.

They had to walk carefully through the deep purple shadows of the entranceway to gain the main courtyard. Abruptly Ahmed took Erica's hand as they crossed the broad courtyard and passed into the great hypostyle hall. It was like being transported into the past.

The hall was a forest of massive stone columns that soared into the night sky. Most of the ceiling was gone, and shafts of moonlight plunged down, washing the pillars and their extensive hieroglyphic texts and bold reliefs with silver light.

They didn't talk; they just wandered hand in hand. After a half-hour Ahmed pulled Erica out through a side entrance and walked her back to the first pylon. On the north side was a brick stairway that took them the 140 feet to the top of the temple. From there Erica could see the entire mile-square area of Karnak. It was awe-inspiring.

"Erica . . ."

She turned. Ahmed's head was tilted to the side, his eyes enjoying her.

"Erica, I find you very beautiful."

She liked compliments, but they always made her feel a little self-conscious. She averted her eyes as Ahmed reached out and gently ran the tips of his fingers over her forehead. "Thank you, Ahmed," she said simply.

Looking up, she noticed Ahmed was still studying her. She could sense some kind of conflict. "You remind me of Pamela," he said finally.

"Oh?" said Erica. Reminding him of a former girlfriend was not what she wanted to hear about, but she could tell that Ahmed meant it as a compliment. She smiled weakly and looked off into the moonlit distance. Perhaps her similarity to Pamela was the reason Ahmed was seeing her.

"You are more beautiful. But it is not your appearance that reminds me of her; it is your openness and warmth."

"Look, Ahmed, I'm not so sure I understand. Last time we were together I asked some innocent question about Pamela and whether your uncle had met her, and you blew up. Now you insist on talking about her. I don't think that's very fair."

244

They stood in silence for a while. Ahmed's intensity was intriguing but also a little frightening, and the memory of the shattered teacup was sharp.

"Do you think you could ever live in a place like Luxor?" asked Ahmed without taking his eyes from the Nile.

"I don't know," said Erica. "The thought never occurred to me. It is very beautiful."

"It's more than beautiful. It's timeless."

"I'd miss Harvard Square."

Ahmed laughed, relieving the tension. "Harvard Square. What a crazy place. By the way, Erica, I have thought about your decision to try to do something about the black market. I'm not sure my warning was strong enough. It really frightens me to think of your becoming involved. Please don't. I cannot bear the idea of anything happening to you."

He leaned forward and gently kissed her on the temple. "Come. You must see Hatshepsut's obelisk in the moonlight." And taking her hand, he led her back down the brick stairway.

Dinner was marvelous. Having walked for over an hour within the splendor of Karnak, they did not start their meal until after eleven. The small Nile-side restaurant was built under an umbrella of tall date palms. The dates were almost ready for picking, and the globular red fruit was held up in the trees by pouches of netting.

The specialty of the restaurant was kebabs made with green peppers, onion, and lamb marinated in garlic, parsley, and mint. The dish was garnished with peeled tomatoes and artichokes, and served on a bed of rice. It was an open-air restaurant and obviously popular with the emergent middle class of Luxor, whose conversations were accompanied by hand gestures and laughter. No tourists were in evidence.

Ahmed had become considerably more relaxed since their conversation on the pylon. He stroked his mustache thoughtfully when Erica told him about her recently completed Ph.D. dissertation on "The Syntactical Evolution of New Kingdom Hieroglyphics." He laughed with pleasure when she told him that she used ancient Egyptian love poetry as her primary source. Using love poetry as the basis for such an esoteric thesis was wonderfully ironic.

Erica asked Ahmed about his childhood. He told her he had been very happy growing up in Luxor. That was why he liked to return. It wasn't until he had been sent to Cairo that his life had become complicated. He told her that his father had been wounded and his older brother killed in the 1956 war. His mother had been one of the first women from the area to obtain both a high-school and college degree. She had tried to work in the Department of Antiquities, but at that time she couldn't because of her sex. Now she lived in Luxor and worked part-time for a foreign bank. Ahmed said he had a younger sister who was trained as a lawyer and worked for the Department of the Interior in the customs division.

After dinner they had small cups of Arabic coffee. There was a natural lull in the conversation and Erica decided to ask a question. "Is there any central registry here in Luxor so that if someone tried to find another individual, they'd know where to look?"

Ahmed did not answer immediately. "We did try to have a census a few years ago, but I'm afraid it was not very successful. The information they obtained would be available in the government building next to the central post office. Otherwise, there is the police. Why do you ask?"

"Just curious," said Erica evasively. She debated telling Ahmed about her interest in the ancient tomb robbers of Tutankhamen, but she was afraid he might try to stop her, or worse, laugh at her if she told him she was looking for Sarwat Raman. When she thought about it, it did seem a bit far-fetched. The last reference she had for the man was fifty-seven years ago.

It was at that moment that Erica saw the man in the dark suit. She could not see his face because his back was to her, but the way he sat hunched over his food was familiar. He was one of the few people not in Arabic clothing. Ahmed sensed her reaction and asked, "What's the matter?"

"Oh, nothing," said Erica, coming out of her trance. "Really nothing."

But it was disturbing. Being with Ahmed cast grave doubts on her explanation that the man in the dark suit worked for the authorities. Who was he?

246

Day 7

The sound of the recorded voice coming from the small mosque built against the Temple of Luxor awoke Erica from a troubled dream. She had been running from some unseen but terrifying creature through a medium that progressively resisted her movement. When she awoke she was tangled in the bedcovers and realized she must have been tossing and turning.

She pulled herself up from the bed and opened the windows to the morning freshness. With the crisp air on her face, her nightmare vanished. She took a quick sponge bath standing in the large tub. For some reason there was no hot water, and she was actually shivering when she was through.

After breakfast Erica left the hotel to find the Curio Antique Shop. She had her tote bag with her flashlight, Polaroid camera, and guidebooks. She was comfortably dressed in new cotton slacks she'd purchased in Cairo to replace those that she'd ripped in the serapeum.

She strolled down Shari Lukanda and noted the names of the shops she'd already visited. Curio Antique Shop was not among them. One of the proprietors she recognized told her that the Curio Antique Shop was on Shari el Muntazah near the Hotel Savoy. Erica found the area and the shop very easily. Next to the Curio Shop was a store that was rudely boarded up. Although she could not read its full name, she saw the

247

word "Hamdi" and knew what she was looking at.

Clutching her bag tightly, she entered the Curio Shop. There was a good selection of antiquities, although on closer examination she could tell they were mostly fakes. A French couple was already in the shop and bargaining fiercely for a small bronze figure.

The most interesting piece Erica saw was a black mummiform ushabti figure with a delicately painted face. Its plinth was gone, so the statue was leaning against the corner of the shelf. As soon as the French couple departed without buying the bronze, the proprietor approached Erica. He was a distinguished-looking Arab with silver-grey hair and a neat mustache.

"I am Lahib Zayed. May I help you?" he said, switching from French to English. Erica wondered what made him guess her nationality.

"Yes," said Erica. "I'd like to look at that black Osiriform figure."

"Ah, yes. One of my best pieces. From the tombs of the nobles." He lifted the figure ever so gently with the tips of his fingers.

While his back was turned, Erica licked the tip of her finger. When he handed her the statue she was ready.

"Be very careful. It is a delicate piece," said Zayed.

Erica nodded and wiped her finger back and forth. The tip of her finger was clean. The pigment was stable. She looked more closely at the carving and the manner in which the eyes were painted. That was the critical area. She was satisfied the statue was an antique.

"New Kingdom," said Zayed holding the statue away from Erica so she could appreciate it at a distance. "I get something like this only once or twice a year."

"How much?"

"Fifty pounds. Normally I'd ask more, but you are so beautiful."

Erica smiled. "I'll give you forty," she said, knowing full well that he did not expect to get his initial price. She also knew it was a little more than she should be spending, but she thought it was important to prove that she was serious.

Besides, she liked the statue. Even if it later proved to be a very clever fake, it was still decorative. They concluded the deal at forty-one pounds.

"Actually, I'm here representing a large group," said Erica, "and I'm interested in something very special. Do you have anything?"

"I might have a few things you'd like. Perhaps I could show you in a more suitable place. Would you care for some mint tea?"

Erica felt a surge of anxiety as she stepped into the back room of Curio Antique Shop. She had to suppress the image of Abdul Hamdi's throat being slit. Fortunately the Curio Antique Shop was constructed differently, opening onto a courtyard with bright sunlight. It did not have the confining feeling of Antica Abdul.

Zayed called his son, a dark-haired, lanky facsimile of his father, and told him to order some mint tea for their guest.

Settling back in his chair, Zayed asked Erica the usual questions: if she liked Luxor, if she'd been to Karnak, what did she think of the Valley of the Kings? He told her how much he loved Americans. He said they were so friendly.

Erica added to herself, ". . . and so gullible."

The tea came, and Zayed produced some interesting pieces, including several small bronze figurines, a battered but recognizable head of Amenhotep III, and a series of wooden statues. The most beautiful statue was a young woman with hieroglyphics down the front of her skirt and a tranquil face that defied time. She was priced at four hundred pounds. After carefully examining the artifact, Erica was quite sure it was authentic.

"I'm interested in the wooden statue, and possibly the stone head," said Erica in a businesslike tone.

Zayed rubbed his palms together with great excitement.

"I'll be checking with the people I represent," said Erica. "But I know there is something they would want me to buy immediately if I were to see it."

"What is that?" asked Zayed.

"There was a life-size statue of Seti I bought a year ago by a man in Houston. My clients have heard that a similar statue has been found."

"I have nothing like that," said Zayed evenly.

"Well, if you happen to hear about such a piece, I'll be staying at the Winter Palace Hotel." Erica wrote her name on a small piece of paper and gave it to him.

"And what about these pieces?"

"As I said, I'll contact my clients. I do like the wooden statue, but I must check." Erica picked up her purchase, which had been wrapped in Arabic newspaper, and walked back to the front part of the shop. She felt confident she had played her role very well. As she left, she noticed Zayed's son bargaining with a man. It was the Arab who had been following her. Without breaking her stride or looking in his direction, Erica left the shop, but a shiver went up her spine.

As soon as his son finished with his customer, Lahib Zayed closed the front door to the shop and bolted it. "Come into the back," he commanded his son. "That was the woman Stephanos Markoulis warned us about when he was here the other day," he said, once they were in the security of the back room. He had even closed the old wooden door to the courtyard. "I want you to go to the central post office and call Markoulis and tell him that the American woman came into the shop and specifically asked about the Seti statue. I'll go to Muhammad and tell him to warn the others."

"What is going to happen to the woman?" asked Fathi.

"I think that's rather obvious. It reminds me of that young man from Yale about two years ago."

"Will they do the same to the woman?"

"Undoubtedly," said his father.

Erica was appalled by the chaos in the Luxor administration building. Some of the people had been waiting so long that they were sleeping on the floor. In the corner of one hall she saw a whole family camped out as if they'd been there for days. Behind the counters the civil servants ignored the crowds and casually talked among themselves. Every desk was a heap of completed forms awaiting some impossible signature. It was awful.

By the time Erica found someone who spoke English, she learned that Luxor was not even an administration center. The Muhāfazah for the area was located in Aswan, and all the

250

census data were stored there. Erica told the woman that she wanted to trace a man who lived on the West Bank fifty years ago. The woman looked at Erica as if she were crazy and told her it was impossible, though she might check with the police. There was always the possibility the person she sought could have had trouble with the authorities.

The police were easier to deal with than the civil servants. At least they were friendly and attentive. In fact most of the uniformed officers in the main room were watching her by the time she got to the counter. All the signs were in Arabic, so Erica just went to a location where no one else was waiting. A handsome young fellow in a white uniform came from behind one of the desks to help her. Unfortunately he did not speak English. But he found a man with the tourist police who did.

"What can I do for you?" he said with a smile.

"I'm trying to find out if one of Howard Carter's foremen by the name of Sarwat Raman is still alive. He lived on the West Bank."

"What?" said the policeman with disbelief. He chuckled. "I've had some strange requests, but this is certainly one of the more interesting. Are you talking about the Howard Carter who discovered Tutankhamen's tomb?"

"That's right," said Erica.

"That was over fifty years ago."

"I understand that," said Erica. "I'd like to find out if he's still alive."

"Madam," said the policeman, "no one even knows how many people live on the West Bank, much less how to find a specific family. But I'll tell you what I'd do if I were you. Go over to the West Bank and visit the small mosque in the village of Qurna. The imam is an old man, and he speaks English. Maybe he could help. But I doubt it. The government has been trying to relocate the village of Qurna and get those people out of the ancient tombs. But it's been a fight, and there's been some antagonism. They're not a friendly group. So be careful."

Lahib Zayed looked both ways to make sure he was not seen before entering the whitewashed alleyway. He scurried down it and pounded on a stout wooden door. He knew Muhammad Abdulal was at home. It was the noon hour and Muhammad always napped. Lahib pounded again. He was afraid he might be seen by some stranger before he'd have a chance to enter the house.

A small peephole opened, and a bloodshot sleepy eye looked out. Then the latch was lifted and the door opened. Lahib stepped over the threshold, and the door was slammed behind him.

Muhammad Abdulal was clad in a rumpled robe. He was a large man with heavy, full features. His nostrils were flared and highly arched. "I told you never to come to this house. You'd better have a good reason for taking this risk."

Lahib greeted Muhammad formally before speaking. "I would not have come if I did not believe it was important. Erica Baron, the American woman, came into the Curio Antique Shop this morning saying that she represented a group of buyers. She is very sharp. She knows antiquities and actually bought a small statue. Then she specifically asked for the Seti I statue."

"Was she alone?" asked Muhammad, alert now rather than angry.

"I believe so," said Lahib.

"And she asked specifically for the Seti statue?"

"Exactly."

"Well, that leaves us very little choice. I'll make the arrangements. You inform her that she can see the statue tomorrow night on the condition that she come alone and that she is not followed. Tell her to come to the Qurna mosque at dusk. We should have gotten rid of her earlier, as I wanted."

Lahib waited to be sure Muhammad was finished before he spoke. "I've also had Fathi contact Stephanos Markoulis and give him the news."

Muhammad's hand struck out like a snake, cuffing the side of Lahib's head. *"Karrah!* Why did you take it upon yourself to inform Stephanos?"

Lahib cowered, expecting another blow.

"He asked me to let him know if the woman appeared. He's as concerned as we are."

252

"You do not take orders from Stephanos," shouted Muhammad. "You take orders from me. That must be understood. Now, get out of here and deliver the message. The American woman must be taken care of."

Necropolis of Luxor Village of Qurna 2:15 P.M.

The policeman had been right. Qurna was not a friendly place. As Erica trudged up the hill separating the village from the asphalt road, she did not have the feeling of welcome that was apparent in the other towns she'd visited. She saw few people, and those she did pass glared, shrinking back into the shadows. Even the dogs were mangy, snarling curs.

She had begun feeling uncomfortable in the taxi when the driver objected to going to Qurna instead of the Valley of the Kings or some other more distant destination. He had dropped her off at the base of a dirt-and-sand hill, saying that his car could not make it to the village itself.

It was blazingly hot, well over one hundred degrees, and without shade. The Egyptian sun poured down, scorching the rock and reflecting brilliantly from the light sand color of the earth. Not a blade of grass or a single weed survived the onslaught. Yet the people of Qurna refused to move. They wanted to live as their grandfathers and their great-grandfathers had down through the centuries. Erica thought that if Dante had seen Qurna he would have included it in the circles of hell.

The houses were made of mud brick either left their natural color or whitewashed. As Erica climbed higher onto the hill she could see occasional hewn openings into outcroppings of rock among the houses. These were entrances to some of the ancient tombs. A number of houses had courtyards with curious structures in them—six-foot-long platforms supported about four feet from the ground by a narrow column. They were made of dried mud and straw similar to the mud bricks. Erica had no idea what they were.

The mosque was a one-story whitewashed building with a fat minaret. Erica had noticed the building the first time she'd seen Qurna. Like the village, it was constructed of mud brick, and Erica wondered if the whole thing would wash away like a sand castle with one good rain. She entered through a low wooden door and found herself in a small courtyard, facing a shallow portico supported by three columns. To the right of the building was a plain wooden door.

Unsure of the propriety of her entering, Erica waited at the entrance to the mosque until her eyes adjusted to the relative darkness. The interior walls were whitewashed and then painted with complicated geometric patterns. The floor was covered with lavish Oriental carpets. Kneeling in front of an alcove pointing toward Mecca was an old bearded man in flowing black robes. His hands were open and held alongside his cheeks as he chanted.

Although the old man had not turned, he must have sensed Erica's presence, because he soon bent over, kissed the page, and got up to face her.

She had no idea how to greet a holy man of Islam, so she improvised. She bowed her head slightly then spoke. "I would like to ask you about a man, an old man."

The imam studied Erica with dark sunken eyes, then motioned her to follow. They crossed the small courtyard and entered the doorway Erica had seen. It led to a small austere room with a pallet in one end and a small table at the other. He indicated a chair for Erica and sat down himself.

"Why do you want to locate someone in Qurna?" asked the imam. "We are suspicious of strangers here."

"I'm an Egyptologist and I wanted to find one of Howard Carter's foremen to see if he were still alive. His name was Sarwat Raman. He lived in Qurna."

"Yes, I know," said the imam.

Erica felt a twinge of hope until the imam went on.

"He died some twenty years ago. He was one of the faithful.

The carpets in this mosque came from his generosity."

"I see," said Erica with obvious disappointment. She stood up. "Well, it was a good idea. Thank you for your help."

"He was a good man," said the imam.

Erica nodded and walked back out into the blinding sunlight, wondering how she was going to get a taxi back to the ferry landing. As she was about to leave the courtyard, the imam called out.

Erica turned. He was standing in the doorway to his room. "Raman's widow is still alive. Would you care to speak with her?"

"Would she be willing to talk with me?" asked Erica.

"I'm sure of it," called the imam. "She worked as Carter's housekeeper and speaks better English than I do."

As Erica followed the imam higher up the hillside, she wondered how anyone could wear such heavy robes in the heat. Even as lightly dressed as she was, the small of her back was damp with perspiration. The imam led her to a whitewashed house set higher than the others in the southwestern part of the village. Immediately behind the house the cliffs rose up dramatically. To the right of the house Erica could see the beginning of a trail etched from the face of the cliff, which she guessed led to the Valley of the Kings.

The whitewashed facade of the house was covered with faded childlike paintings of railroad cars, boats, and camels. "Raman recorded his pilgrimage to Mecca," explained the imam, knocking on the door.

In the courtyard next to the house was one of the platforms Erica had seen earlier. She asked the imam what it was.

"People sometimes sleep outside in the summer months. They use these platforms to avoid scorpions and cobras."

Erica felt gooseflesh rise on her back.

A very old woman opened the door. Recognizing the imam, she smiled. They spoke in Arabic. When the conversation concluded, she turned her heavily lined face to Erica.

"Welcome," she said with a strong English accent, opening the door wider for Erica to enter. The imam excused himself and left.

Like the small mosque, the house was surprisingly cool.

Belying the crude exterior, the interior was charming. There was a wood floor covered with a bright Oriental carpet. The furniture was simple but well made, the walls plastered and painted. On three walls there were numerous framed photographs. On the fourth hung a long-handled shovel with an engraved blade.

The old woman introduced herself as Aida Raman. She told Erica proudly that she was going to be eighty years old come April. With true Arabic hospitality she brought out a cool fruit drink, explaining that it had been made from boiled water so that Erica need not fear germs.

Erica liked the woman. She had sparse dark hair brushed back from her round face and was cheerfully attired in a loose-fitting cotton dress printed with brightly colored feathers. Around her left wrist she wore an orange plastic bracelet. She smiled frequently, revealing that she had only two teeth, both on the bottom.

Erica explained that she was an Egyptologist, and Aida was obviously pleased to talk about Howard Carter. She told Erica how she had adored the man even though he was a little strange and very lonely. She recalled how much Howard Carter loved his canary and how sad he was when it had been eaten by a cobra.

As Erica sipped her drink, she found herself enthralled by the stories. It was obvious that Aida was enjoying their meeting just as much as she was.

"Do you remember the day when Tutankhamen's tomb was opened?" asked Erica.

"Oh, yes," said Aida. "That was the most wonderful day. My husband became a happy man. Very soon after that, Carter agreed to help Sarwat obtain the right to run the concession stand in the valley. My husband had guessed that the tourists would soon come by the millions to see the tomb Howard Carter had found. And he was right. He continued to help with the tomb, but he spent most of his effort on building the rest house. In fact, he built it almost all by himself, even though he had to work at night. . . ."

Erica allowed Aida to ramble on for a moment, then asked, "Do you remember everything that happened the day the tomb was opened?"

258

"Of course," said Aida, a little surprised at the interruption.

"Did your husband ever say anything about a papyrus?"

The old woman's eyes instantly clouded. Her mouth moved, but there was no sound. Erica felt a surge of excitement. She held her breath, watching the old woman's strange response.

Finally Aida spoke. "Are you from the government?"

"No," answered Erica.

"What makes you ask such a question? Everyone knows what was found. There are books."

Putting her drink down on the table, Erica explained to Aida the curious discrepancy between Carnarvon's letter to Sir Wallis Budge and the fact that Carter's notes listed no papyrus. She was not from the government, she added reassuringly. Her interest was purely academic.

"No," said Aida after an uncomfortable pause. "There was no papyrus. My husband would never take a papyrus from the tomb."

"Aida," said Erica softly, "I never said your husband took a papyrus."

"You did. You said my husband—"

"No. I just asked if he ever said anything about a papyrus. I'm not accusing him."

"My husband was a good man. He had a good name."

"Indeed. Carter was a demanding individual. Your husband had to be the best. No one is challenging your husband's good name."

There was another long pause. Finally Aida turned back to Erica. "My husband has been dead for over twenty years. He told me never to mention the papyrus. And I haven't, even after he died. But no one has mentioned it to me either. That's why it shocked me so much when you said it. In a way, it's a relief to tell someone. You won't tell the authorities?"

"No, I won't," said Erica. "It is up to you. So there was a papyrus and your husband took it from the tomb?"

"Yes," said Aida. "Many years ago."

Erica now had an idea what had happened. Raman had gotten the papyrus and sold it. It was going to be hard to trace. "How did your husband get the papyrus out of the tomb?"

"He told me he picked it up that first day when he saw it in the tomb. Everyone was so excited about the treasures. He thought it was some kind of curse, and he was afraid that they would stop the project if anyone knew. Lord Carnarvon was very interested in the occult."

Erica tried to imagine the events of that hectic day. Carter must have initially missed seeing the papyrus in his haste to check the integrity of the wall into the burial chamber, and the others had been dazzled by the splendor of the artifacts.

"Was the papyrus a curse?" asked Erica.

"No. My husband said it wasn't. He never showed it to any of the Egyptologists. Instead he copied small sections and asked the experts to translate them. Finally he put it all together. But he said it wasn't a curse."

"Did he say what it was?" asked Erica.

"No. He just said it was written in the days of the pharaohs by a clever man who wanted to record that Tutankhamen had helped Seti I."

Erica's heart leaped. The papyrus associated Tutankhamen with Seti I, as had the inscription on the statue.

"Do you have any idea what happened to the papyrus? Did your husband sell it?"

"No. He didn't sell it," said Aida. "I have it."

The blood drained from Erica's face. While she sat immobilized, Aida shuffled over to the shovel mounted on the wall.

"Howard Carter presented this shovel to my husband," said Aida. She pulled the wooden shaft from the engraved metal blade. There was a hollow in the end of the handle. "This papyrus has not been touched for fifty years," continued Aida as she struggled to extract the crumbling document. She unrolled it on the table, using the two pieces of the shovel as paperweights.

Slowly rising to her feet, Erica let her eyes feast on the hieroglyphic text. It was an official document with seals of state. Immediately Erica could pick out the cartouches of Seti I and Tutankhamen.

"May I photograph it?" asked Erica, almost afraid to breathe.

"As long as my husband's name is not blackened," said Aida.

"I can promise you that," said Erica, fumbling with her

Polaroid. "I won't do anything without your permission." She took several photos and made sure they were good enough to work from. "Thank you," she said when she was finished. "Now, let's put the papyrus back, but please be careful. This might be very valuable, and it could make the Raman name famous."

"I'm more concerned about my husband's reputation," said Aida. "Besides, the family name dies with me. We had two sons, but both were killed in the wars."

"Did your husband have anything else from Tutankhamen's tomb?" asked Erica.

"Oh, no!" said Aida.

"Okay," said Erica, "I will translate the papyrus and tell you what it says so you can decide what you want to do with it. I won't say anything to the authorities. That will be up to you. But for now, don't show it to anyone else." Erica was already jealous of her discovery.

Emerging from Aida Raman's house, she debated on how best to return to the hotel. The thought of walking five miles to the ferry landing oppressed her, and she decided to risk the trail behind Aida Raman's house and walk to the Valley of the Kings. There she could surely get a taxi.

Although it was a hot and tiring climb to the ridge, the view was spectacular. The village of Qurna was directly below her. Just beyond the village was the stately ruin of Queen Hatshepsut's temple, nestled against the mountains. Erica continued to the crest and looked down. The entire green valley was spread out in front of her, with the Nile snaking its way through the center. Shielding her eyes from the sun, Erica turned to the west. Directly ahead was the Valley of the Kings. From her vantage point Erica could look beyond the valley at the endless rust-red peaks of the Theban mountains as they merged with the mighty Sahara. She had a feeling of overwhelming loneliness.

Descending into the valley was comparatively easy, though Erica had to be careful about the loose ground on the steeper parts of the trail. The route merged with another path coming from the ruined Village of Truth, where Erica knew the ancient necropolis workers had lived. By the time she reached the floor of the valley, she was very warm and tremendously thirsty. Despite her wish to return to the hotel and get to work translating the papyrus, she walked toward the crowded concession stand for a drink. Climbing the steps of the building, she couldn't help but think of Sarwat Raman.

It was an amazing story indeed. The Arab had stolen a papyrus because he was afraid it would spell out an ancient curse. He had been worried that such a curse would stop the excavation!

Erica purchased a Pepsi-Cola and found an empty chair on the veranda. She glanced around the structure of the rest house. It was made of local stone. Erica marveled that Raman had built it. She wished she could have met the man. There was one question in particular she would have liked to ask. Why hadn't Raman found some way to return the papyrus after he learned it did not represent a curse? Obviously he did not want to sell it. The only explanation Erica could think of was that he had been afraid of the consequences. She took a large swallow of the Pepsi and pulled out one of the precious photos of the papyrus. The directives suggested it was to be read in the usual fashion, from lower right upward. She stumbled over a proper name at the beginning, almost not believing her eyes. Slowly she pronounced it to herself: "Nenephta. . . . My God!"

Noticing a group of tourists boarding a bus, Erica thought that perhaps she could get a ride to the ferry landing with them. She put the photos back into her tote bag and quickly looked for the ladies' room. A waiter told her the rest rooms were under the concession stand, but after finding the entrance, she was discouraged by the acrid smell of urine. She decided she could wait until she got back to the hotel. She ran down to the bus as the last passengers were getting on.

Luxor   6:15 P.M.

Standing at the edge of her balcony, Erica stretched her arms over her head and sighed with relief. She had finished translating the papyrus. It had not been difficult, although she was not sure she understood the meaning.

Looking out over the Nile, she watched a large luxury liner glide by. After her immersion in antiquity with the papyrus, the modern vessel looked out of place. It was like having a flying saucer land in the Boston Commons.

Erica went back to the glass-topped table she'd been working at, picked up the translation, and read it over:

> I, Nenephta, chief architect for the Living God (may he live forever), Pharaoh, King of our two lands, the great Seti I, do reverently atone for the disturbance of the eternal rest of the boy king Tutankhamen within these humble walls and with these scant provisions for all eternity. The unspeakable sacrilege of the attempted plunder of Pharaoh Tutankhamen's tomb by the stonecutter Emeni, whom we have rightfully impaled and whose remains we have scattered on the western desert for the jackals, has served a noble end. The stonecutter Emeni has opened my eyes to understand the ways of the greedy and unjust. Thus I, chief architect, now know

the way to ensure the eternal safety of the Living God (may he live forever), Pharaoh, King of our two lands, the great Seti I. Imhotep, architect for the Living God Zoser and builder of the Step Pyramid, and Neferhotep, architect for the Living God Khufu and builder of the Great Pyramid, used the way in their monuments, but without full understanding. Accordingly the eternal rest of the Living God Zoser and the Living God Khufu was disturbed and destroyed in the first dark period. But I, Nenephta, chief architect, understand the way, and the greed of the tomb robber. So it will be done, and the boy king Pharaoh Tutankhamen's tomb is resealed on this day.

Year 10 of Son of Re, Pharaoh Seti I, second month of Germination, day 12.

Erica put the page down on the table. The word she'd had the most problem with was "way." The hieroglyphic signs had suggested "method" or "pattern" or even "trick," but the word "way" made the most sense syntactically. But what it meant eluded her.

Translating the papyrus gave Erica a great feeling of accomplishment. It also made the life of ancient Egypt come amazingly alive, and she smiled at Nenephta's arrogance. Despite his supposed understanding of the greed of the tomb robber and the "way," Seti's magnificent tomb had been plundered within a hundred years of its closure, while the humble tomb of Tutankhamen had remained undisturbed for another three thousand years.

Picking up the translation again, Erica reread the section mentioning Zoser and Khufu. Suddenly she was sorry she'd not visited the Great Pyramid. At the time, she'd felt comfortably abstemious not rushing to the pyramids of Giza like all the other tourists. Now she wished she had. How could Neferhotep have used the *way* in constructing the Great Pyramid, but without full understanding? Erica stared off at the distant mountains. With all the mysterious meanings attributed to the shape and size of the Great Pyramid, Erica had uncovered another, more ancient one. Even in Nenephta's time, the Great Pyramid was an ancient structure. In fact, thought Erica, Nenephta probably did not know much more about the Great Pyramid than she did. She decided to visit it. Perhaps by standing in its shadow or by walking within its depths she might comprehend what Nenephta meant by the word "way."

Erica checked the time. She could easily make the seven-thirty sleeper to Cairo. With feverish excitement she packed her canvas tote bag with her Polaroid, the Baedeker, the flashlight, jeans, and clean underwear. Then she took a quick bath.

Before leaving the hotel she called Ahmed and told him she was going back to Cairo for a day or so because she had an insatiable desire to see the Great Pyramid of Khufu.

Ahmed was instantly suspicious. "There is so much to see here in Luxor. Can't it wait?"

"No. All of a sudden I have to see it."

"Are you going to see Yvon de Margeau?"

"Maybe," said Erica evasively. She wondered if Ahmed could be jealous. "Is there something you'd like me to tell him?" She knew she was baiting him.

"No, of course not. Don't even mention my name. Give me a call when you return." Ahmed hung up before she could say good-bye.

As Erica boarded the train for Cairo, Lahib Zayed entered the Winter Palace Hotel. He had a confidential message for Erica saying that she would be shown a Seti I statue the following night, provided she followed certain directions. But Erica was not in her room, and he decided he'd return later, afraid of what Muhammad would do to him if he failed to give her the message.

After the train to Cairo departed, Khalifa entered the main post office and cabled Yvon de Margeau that Erica Baron was on her way to Cairo. He added that she'd been acting very strangely and he'd await further instructions at the Savoy Hotel.

Day 8

The grounds of the pyramids of Giza opened at eight A.M. With thirty minutes to wait, Erica entered the Mena House Hotel for a second breakfast. A dark-haired hostess showed her to a table on the terrace. Erica ordered coffee and melon. There were only a few other people eating, and the pool was empty of bathers. Directly in front of her, above a line of palms and eucalyptus trees, was the Great Pyramid of Khufu. With an elemental simplicity its triangular form soared upward against the morning sky.

Since Erica had heard about the Great Pyramid since she was a child, she had prepared herself to be a little disappointed when she finally confronted the monument. But such was not the case. She was already moved and awed by its majesty and symmetry. It wasn't so much the size, although that contributed, as it was the fact that the structure represented an attempt by man to make an imprint on the implacable face of time.

Removing the Baedeker from her bag, Erica found the Great Pyramid and studied the schematic for the interior. She tried to think of Nenephta and how he'd look at the design. She realized that she probably knew something that Nenephta didn't. Careful investigation had shown that the Great Pyramid, like most of the other pyramids, had undergone significant modification in the course of construction. In fact, it had been hypothesized that the Great Pyramid had passed through three distinct stages. In the first stage, when a much smaller structure was planned, the burial chamber was to be underground, and it had been carved from the bedrock. Then, when the structure was enlarged, a new burial chamber within the building was planned. Erica looked at this room in the diagram. It was erroneously labeled the Queen's Chamber. Erica knew she could not visit the underground crypt unless she got special permission from the Department of Antiquities. But the Queen's Chamber was open to the public.

She checked her watch. It was almost eight. Erica wanted to be one of the first to enter the pyramid. Once the busloads of tourists arrived, she knew it would be unpleasant in the narrow passageways.

Turning down persistent offers of donkey and camel rides, Erica walked up the road to the plateau on which the pyramid stood. The closer she got to the structure, the more monumental it became. Although she could quote statistics on the millions of tons of limestone used in building it, such statistics had never moved her. But now that she was within its shadow, she walked as if she were in a trance. Even without its original facing of white limestone, the effect of the sun on the surface of the pyramid was painfully intense.

Erica approached the cave that had been enlarged from the opening Caliph Mamun had ordered dug in A.D. 820. There were no other people in the entryway, and she went in quickly. The glaring whiteness of the day was replaced by dim shadows and weak incandescent light.

The caliph's tunnel joined the narrow ascending passageway just beyond the granite plugs that had sealed it in antiquity and which were still in place. The ceiling of this ascending corridor was little more than four feet high, and Erica had to bend over to walk up it. In order to facilitate climbing, horizontal ribs had been set in the slippery paving. The passageway was about a hundred feet long, and when Erica emerged at the base of the grand gallery she was relieved to be able to stand upright.

The grand gallery sloped upward at the same ratio as the ascending passage. With its corbeled ceiling over twenty feet high, it was pleasantly spacious after the narrow confines of the corridor. To Erica's right a grating covered the entrance to the descending shaft, which connected to the underground burial chamber. Ahead of her was the opening she wanted. Erica bent over again and entered the long horizontal corridor leading to the Queen's Chamber.

Once there, she was again able to stand upright. The air was stuffy, and Erica remembered her uncomfortable feelings in Seti I's tomb. She closed her eyes and tried to collect her thoughts. The room was without decoration, as were all the interior walls of the pyramid. She took out her flashlight and ran it around the room. The ceiling was vaulted in a chevron formation with huge slabs of limestone.

Erica opened her Baedeker to the schematic of the pyramid. She tried again to imagine what an architect like Nenephta would think if he were within the Great Pyramid, keeping in mind that even in his day the structure was over a thousand years old. From the diagram she knew that standing in the Queen's Chamber she was directly above the original burial chamber and below the King's Chamber. It was during the third and final modification of the pyramid that the burial chamber was designed higher in the structure. The new room was labeled King's Chamber, and Erica decided it was time to visit it.

Bending over to enter the low passage back to the grand gallery, Erica saw that a figure was coming toward her. Passing someone in the narrow corridor would have been difficult, so she waited. With the exit momentarily blocked, she felt a rush of claustrophobia. Suddenly she was aware of the thousands of tons of rock above her. She closed her eyes, breathing deeply. The air was heavy.

"Christ, it's just an empty room," complained a blond American tourist. He wore a T-shirt that said "Black holes are out of sight."

Erica nodded, then started down the tunnel. When she reached the grand gallery, it was already crowded. She climbed to the top behind an obese German man and mounted the wooden steps to get to the level of the King's Chamber passage. Then she had to duck under a low wall. The grooves for huge sealing portcullises were visible on the sides.

Erica found herself in a pink granite room about fifteen by thirty feet. The ceiling was made from nine slabs laid horizontally. In one corner was a badly damaged sarcophagus. There were about twenty people in the room, and the air was oppressive.

Again Erica tried to imagine how the structure would suggest a way to thwart tomb robbers. She examined the area of the portcullises. Perhaps that was what Nenephta meant: granite closure of the tomb. But portcullises had been used in many of the pyramids. There was nothing unique about those in the Great Pyramid. Besides, they had not been used in the Step Pyramid, and Nenephta said that the *way* had been used in both.

Although the King's Chamber was a good-sized room, it was certainly not large enough to store all the funerary possessions of a pharaoh of the importance of Khufu. Erica reasoned that the other chambers had probably been used for the pharaoh's treasures, particularly the Queen's Chamber, which was below her, and perhaps even the grand gallery, although many Egyptologists suggested that the grand gallery was constructed to store the sealing blocks for the ascending passage.

Erica had no idea how to explain Nenephta's comments. As with all its other mysteries, the Great Pyramid remained mute. More and more people pressed into the King's Chamber. Erica decided she needed some air. She put away her guidebook, but before leaving the chamber she wanted to see the sarcophagus. Gently pushing her way across the room, she peered into the granite box. She knew there was a good deal of controversy about its origin, age, and purpose. It was quite small to accommodate the royal coffin, and a number of Egyptologists doubted that it was a sarcophagus at all.

"Miss Baron . . ." a high-pitched but resonant voice said softly.

Erica turned, stunned to hear her name. She scanned the people nearest her. No one seemed to be looking at her. Then she glanced down. An angelic-looking boy of about ten, wearing a soiled galabia, was smiling at her.

"Miss Baron?"

"Yes," said Erica hesitantly.

"You must go to the Curio Shop to see the statue. You must go today. You must go alone."

The boy turned and disappeared into the crowd of people.

"Wait!" called Erica. She pushed her way through the crowd and looked down the sloping grand gallery. The boy was already three-quarters of the way down. Erica began the descent, but the wooden ribs were more difficult to handle going down than coming up. The boy seemed to have no trouble, and quickly disappeared into the opening of the ascending passageway.

Erica slowed to a safe speed. She knew she'd never catch him. She thought about his message and felt a rush of excitement. The Curio Shop! Her ruse had succeeded. She'd found the statue!

Luxor 12:00 P.M.

With a violent tug Lahib Zayed felt himself pulled to his feet. Evangelos had an iron grip on the front part of his galabia. "Where is she?" he growled into the Arab's frightened face.

Stephanos Markoulis, dressed casually in an open-necked shirt, put down the small bronze figure he'd been examining and turned to the two men. "Lahib, I cannot understand why, after letting me know Erica Baron came into your shop asking for the Seti statue, you hesitate to tell me where she is."

Lahib was terrified, uncertain who scared him the most, Muhammad or Stephanos. But feeling Evangelos' fingers tighten on his galabia, he decided it was Stephanos. "All right, I'll tell you."

"Let him go, Evangelos."

The Greek released his grip abruptly so that Lahib staggered backward before regaining his balance.

"Well?" asked Stephanos.

"I don't know where she is at the moment, but I know where she is staying. She has a room at the Winter Palace Hotel. But, Mr. Markoulis, the woman will be taken care of. We have made arrangements."

"I would like to take care of her myself," said Stephanos. "To be sure. But don't worry, we'll be back to say good-bye. Thanks for all your help."

Stephanos motioned to Evangelos, and the two men walked out of the shop. Lahib did not move until they had gone from

273

view. Then he ran to the door and watched them until they had disappeared.

"There is going to be big trouble here in Luxor," said Lahib to his son when the two Greeks were out of sight. "I want you to take your mother and sister to Aswan this afternoon. As soon as the American woman appears and I give her the message, I'll join you. I want you to go now."

Stephanos Markoulis had Evangelos wait in the outer lobby of the Winter Palace Hotel while he approached the registration desk. The clerk was a handsome Nubian with ebony skin.

"Is there an Erica Baron staying here?" Stephanos asked.

The clerk turned to the daily ledger, running his finger down the names. "Yes, sir."

"Good. I'd like to leave a message. Do you have a pen and paper?"

"Of course, sir." The clerk graciously gave Stephanos a piece of stationery, an envelope, and a pen.

Stephanos pretended to write a message. Instead he just scribbled on the paper and sealed it in the envelope. He gave it to the clerk, who turned and put it into box 218. Stephanos thanked him and went to get Evangelos. Together they walked upstairs.

There was no answer when they knocked on the door to 218, so Stephanos had Evangelos work on the lock while he stood guard. The Victorian hardware was easy to manipulate, and they were inside the room almost as fast as if they'd had the correct key. Stephanos closed the door behind him and eyed the room. "Let's search it," he said. "Then we'll wait here until she comes back."

"Am I going to kill her immediately?" asked Evangelos.

Stephanos smiled. "No, we'll talk to her for a little while. Only, I get to talk with her first."

Evangelos laughed and pulled open the top drawer of the bureau. There in neat stacks were Erica's nylon panties.

Cairo   2:30 P.M.

"Are you certain?" asked Yvon in disbelief. Raoul looked up from his magazine.

"Almost positive," said Erica, enjoying Yvon's surprise. After receiving the message in the Great Pyramid, Erica had decided to see Yvon. She knew he'd be pleased about the statue, and she was quite sure he'd be willing to take her to Luxor.

"It is almost unbelievable," said Yvon, his blue eyes shining. "How do you know they plan to show you the Seti statue?"

"Because that's what I asked to see."

"You are incredible," said Yvon. "I have been doing everything possible to find that statue, and you locate it just like that." He waved his hand in an easy gesture.

"Well, I haven't seen the statue yet," said Erica. "I must get to the Curio Shop this afternoon, and I must go alone."

"We can leave within the hour." Yvon reached for the phone. He was surprised the statue was back in Luxor; in fact, it made him a little suspicious.

Erica stood up and stretched. "I've just spent the night on the train, and I'd love to shower, if you don't mind."

Yvon gestured toward the adjoining room. Erica took her tote bag and went into the bathroom while Yvon was talking with his pilot.

Yvon completed the plans for transportation, then checked the sound of the shower before turning to Raoul. "This possibly could be the opportunity we've been hoping for. But we need to be extremely careful. Now is when we must rely on Khalifa. Get in touch with him and let him know we'll be arriving around six-thirty. Tell him that Erica will be meeting tonight with the people we want. Tell him that there will undoubtedly be trouble and that he should be prepared. And tell him that if the girl is killed, he's finished."

The small jet rolled slightly to the right, then banked gracefully, passing over the Nile valley in a wide curve about five miles north of Luxor. It passed through one thousand feet, then straightened on a heading due north. At the correct moment, Yvon cut the air speed, pulled up the nose, and landed smoothly over a cushion of air. The reverse thrust of the engines shook the plane and brought it down to taxi speed in a very short distance. Yvon left the controls to come back to talk with Erica while the pilot taxied toward the terminal.

"Now, let's go over this once more," he said, turning one of the lounge seats around to face Erica. His voice was serious, making her uncomfortably anxious. In Cairo the idea of being taken to see the Seti statue had been exciting, but here in Luxor she felt the rumblings of fear.

"As soon as we arrive," Yvon continued, "I want you to take a separate taxi and go directly to the Curio Antique Shop. Raoul and I will wait at the New Winter Palace Hotel, suite 200. I'm positive, though, that the statue will not be at the shop."

Erica looked up sharply. "What do you mean it won't be there?"

"It would be too dangerous. No, the statue will be somewhere else. They will take you to it. It's the way it's done. But it will be all right."

"The statue had been at Antica Abdul," protested Erica.

"That was a fluke," said Yvon. "The statue was in transit. This time I'm sure that they will take you somewhere else to see the statue. Try to remember exactly where, so you'll be able to return. Then, when you are shown the statue, I want you to bargain with them. If you don't, they will be suspicious. But remember, I'm willing to pay what they ask, provided

276

they can guarantee delivery outside Egypt."

"Like via the Zurich Credit Bank?" said Erica.

"How did you know that?" asked Yvon.

"Same way I knew to go to the Curio Antique Shop," said Erica.

"And how is that?" asked Yvon.

"I'm not going to tell you," said Erica. "Not yet, anyway."

"Erica, this is not a game."

"I know it's not a game," she said heatedly. Yvon had been making her more and more anxious. "That's exactly why I'm not going to tell you, not yet."

Yvon studied her, perplexed. "All right," he said at length, "but I want you to come back to my hotel as soon as possible. We can't allow the statue to go underground again. Tell them that the money can be on account within twenty-four hours."

Erica nodded and looked out the window. Even though it was after six, shimmering heat still radiated from the tarmac. The plane came to a stop, and the engines died. She took a deep breath and unhooked her seat belt.

From an observation post near the commercial terminal, Khalifa watched the door to the small jet swing open. As soon as he saw Erica, he turned and walked quickly to a waiting car, checking his automatic before climbing into the driver's seat. Certain that tonight he was going to earn his two hundred-dollar-a-day salary, he put the car in gear and drove toward Luxor.

Inside Erica's room at the Winter Palace, Evangelos drew his Beretta from beneath his left arm and fingered the ivory handle. "Put that thing away," snapped Stephanos from the bed. "It makes me nervous for you to be fumbling with it. Just relax, for Christ's sake. The girl will show up. All her stuff is here."

Driving into town, Erica considered stopping at her hotel. There was no use carting around her camera and extra clothes. But worrying that Lahib Zayed might close his shop before she got there, she decided to go directly there, as Yvon had suggested. She had the driver stop at one end of the crowded Shari el Muntazah. The Curio Antique Shop was a half-block away.

Erica was nervous. Yvon had unknowingly magnified her misgivings about the affair. She could not help remembering that she had seen a man murdered because of this statue: what was she doing going to see it? As she drew nearer, she could see that the shop was filled with tourists, so she walked past. A few shops down, she stopped and turned, watching the entrance. Soon a group of Germans emerged, joking loudly among themselves as they joined the late-afternoon shoppers and strollers. It was now or never. Erica breathed out through pursed lips, then strode toward the shop.

After all her worry, she was surprised to find Lahib Zayed ebullient instead of furtive or surreptitious. He came out from behind the counter as if Erica were a long-lost friend. "I'm so happy to see you again, Miss Baron. I cannot tell you how happy I am."

Erica was initially wary but Lahib's sincerity was apparent and she allowed herself to be gently hugged.

"Would you care for some tea?"

"Thank you, but no. I came as quickly as possible after I got the message."

"Ah, yes," said Lahib. He clapped his hands with excitement. "The statue. You are indeed very lucky, because you are to be shown a marvelous piece. A statue of Seti I as tall as yourself." Lahib closed an eye, estimating her height.

Erica couldn't believe he was so blasé. It made her fears seem melodramatic and childish.

"Is the statue here?" asked Erica.

"Oh, no, my dear. We are showing it to you without the knowledge of the Department of Antiquities." He winked. "So we must be reasonably careful. And since it is such a large and marvelous piece, we don't dare have it here in Luxor. It is on the West Bank, but we can deliver it wherever your people wish."

"How do I get to see it?" asked Erica.

"Very simple. But first you must understand that you have to go alone. We cannot show this type of piece to many people, for obvious reasons. If you are accompanied, or even followed, you will lose your chance to view it. Is that clear?"

"It is," said Erica.

"Very well. All you have to do is cross the Nile and take a taxi to a small village called Qurna, which is located—"

"I know the village," said Erica.

"That makes it easier," Lahib laughed. "There is a small mosque in the village."

"I know it," said Erica.

"Ah, marvelous, then you should have no trouble at all. Arrive at the mosque tonight at dusk. One of the dealers like myself will meet you there and show you the statue. It's as simple as that."

"All right," said Erica.

"One other thing," said Lahib. "When you reach the West Bank, it's best to hire a taxi that will wait for you below the village. Offer him an extra pound. Otherwise you'll have trouble later getting one back to the ferry landing."

"Thank you very much," said Erica. Lahib's concern pleased her.

Lahib watched Erica walk down Shari el Muntazah toward the Winter Palace Hotel. She turned once, and he waved. Then he quickly closed the door to the shop and secured it with a wooden beam. In a recess below one of the floorboards he hid his best antiques and ancient pottery. Then he locked the back door and left for the station. He was certain he'd make the seven-o'clock train for Aswan.

As Erica walked along the waterfront toward her hotel, she felt significantly better than she had before visiting the Curio Antique Shop. Her cloak-and-dagger expectations were unfounded. Lahib Zayed had been open, friendly, and thoughtful. Her only disappointment was that she couldn't see the statue until evening. Erica looked up at the sky, estimating the time until sunset. She had another hour, plenty of time to return to the hotel to change into jeans for the journey to Qurna.

Approaching the majestic Temple of Luxor, which was now surrounded by the modern town, Erica suddenly stopped. She had not given any thought to her being followed. If she were, it would ruin the whole plan. Turning around quickly she scanned the street for her shadow. She'd completely forgotten the man. There were many pedestrians in sight, but no hooked-nosed man in a dark suit. Erica checked her watch again. She had to know if she was being followed. Turning back to the temple, she quickly bought a ticket and walked through the passageway between the towers of the front pylon. Entering the court of Ramses II, majestically surrounded by a double row of papyrus columns, she turned immediately to the right and stepped into a small chapel for the god Amon. From here Erica could see the entrance as well as the courtyard. There were about twenty people milling around, photographing the statues of Ramses II. Erica decided to wait fifteen minutes. If no one appeared, she would forget her shadow.

She peered into the chapel to look at the reliefs. They had been carved during the time of Ramses II and lacked the quality of the work she'd seen at Abydos. She recognized the images of Amon, Mut, and Khonsu. When Erica turned her attention back to the courtyard, she was startled. Khalifa had rounded the edge of the pylon no more than five feet from where she was standing. He was equally surprised. He shot a hand into his jacket to grasp his pistol, but caught himself and withdrew his hand as his face contorted into a half-smile. Then he was gone.

Erica blinked. When she had recovered from the shock, she ran from the chapel and looked down the corridor behind the double row of columns. Khalifa had disappeared.

Pulling the strap of her bag up onto her shoulder, Erica hurried from the temple grounds. She knew she was in trouble, that her pursuer could ruin everything. She reached the esplanade along the Nile and looked both ways. She had to lose him, and checking her watch, she realized she was running out of time.

The only time Khalifa had not followed was when she had visited the village of Qurna and hiked over a desert ridge to the Valley of the Kings. Erica thought that she could use the route in reverse. She could go to the Valley of the Kings now, then use the trail to visit Qurna, telling her taxi to wait for her at the base of the village. Then she realized the plan was ridiculous. Probably the only reason Khalifa had not followed her to the Valley of the Kings was that he knew where she was going and did not want to subject himself to the heat and effort. He'd not been fooled. If she were to really lose Khalifa, it would have to be in a crowd of people.

Checking her watch again, she had an idea. It was now almost seven. There was a seven-thirty express train to Cairo, the same train she'd taken the previous night. The station and the platform had been jammed. It was the best idea she'd had. The only trouble was that it would keep her from seeing Yvon. Perhaps she could call from the station. Erica hailed a carriage.

As she had expected, the station was swarming with travelers, and she moved with difficulty to the ticket windows. She passed an enormous stack of reed cages filled with clucking chickens. A small herd of goats and sheep were tethered to a column, and their plaintive bleating merged with the cacophony of voices that echoed in the dusty hall. Erica bought a one-way first-class ticket to Nag Hamdi. It was seven-seventeen.

It was even more difficult to walk down the platform than it had been to get to the ticket window. Erica did not look behind her. She pushed and squeezed past crying relatives until she reached the comparative quiet alongside the first-class coaches. She climbed aboard coach two, flashing her ticket to the conductor. It was seven-twenty-three.

Erica went directly to the toilet. It was closed and locked. So was the one opposite. Without hesitation she turned into coach three and hurried down the central aisle. A toilet was free, and she entered. Locking the door and trying to breathe as little of the stench as possible, Erica undid her cotton slacks and pulled them off. Then she pulled on her jeans, banging her elbow on the sink as the wriggled into them. It was seven-twenty-nine. She heard a whistle.

Almost in a panic, she changed into a blue blouse, hastily pushed up her luxurious hair, and pulled her khaki sun hat over her head. Glancing into the mirror, she hoped her appearance had changed enough. Then she left the toilet and literally ran down the aisle to the next coach. It was second-class and more crowded. Most of the occupants had not taken their seats yet and were busy placing their belongings in the overhead racks.

Erica continued from coach to coach. When she reached third-class, she found the chickens and cattle had been loaded between the coaches and progress became impossible. Looking out, she assessed the milling crowd. It was seven-thirty-two. The train lurched and began to move as she climbed down to the platform. There was a sudden increase in the murmur of voices, and several people shouted and waved. Erica worked her way from the platform into the station, and for the first time looked for Khalifa.

The crowd began to disperse. Erica allowed the press of people to sweep her to the street. Once outside, she hurried across to a small café and took a table with a view of the station. Ordering a small coffee, she kept her eyes on the entrance.

She did not have to wait long. Pushing people rudely aside, Khalifa stormed from the station. Even from where Erica was sitting she could sense his anger as he leaped into a taxi and headed down Shari el Mahatta toward the Nile. Erica gulped down her coffee. The sun had set and dusk was falling. She was late. Picking up her bag, she hurried from the café.

"Christ almighty!" yelled Yvon. "Why am I paying you two hundred dollars a day? Can you tell me that?"

Khalifa frowned and examined the fingernails of his left hand. He knew he really did not have to suffer this tirade, but his assignment fascinated him. Erica Baron had tricked him, and he was not accustomed to losing. If he were, he would have been dead a long time ago.

"All right," said Yvon with a disgusted tone. "What are we going to do?"

Raoul, having suggested Khalifa, felt more responsible than Khalifa himself.

"You should have someone meet the train," said Khalifa. "She bought a ticket to Nag Hamdi, but I don't think she actually left. I think it was all a trick to get away from me."

"All right, Raoul, have the train met," said Yvon decisively.

Raoul went to the phone, glad to have something to do.

"Listen, Khalifa," said Yvon, "losing Erica has put this whole operation in jeopardy. She got her instructions from the

Curio Antique Shop. Get over there and find out where she's been sent. I don't care how you do it, just do it."

Without saying a word, Khalifa pushed off the bureau on which he'd been leaning and left the hotel, knowing that there was no way the shop owner was going to keep information from him unless he was willing to die.

Under the towering sandstone cliffs, the village of Qurna was already shrouded in darkness when Erica climbed the long hill from the road. The taxi she had hired for the evening waited below, its door ajar.

She trudged past the somber mud-brick houses. Cooking fires of dried dung could be seen in the courtyards, illuminating the sharply grotesque summer sleeping platforms. Erica remembered the reason they were built—cobras and scorpions—and shivered despite the warmth of the night.

The darkened mosque with its whitewashed minaret looked silver. It was about a hundred yards ahead. Erica paused to catch her breath. Looking back at the valley, she could see the lights of Luxor, particularly the high-rise New Winter Palace Hotel. A string of colored lights like Christmas decorations marked the area of the Abul Haggag mosque.

Erica was about to continue walking when there was a sudden movement in the darkness near her feet. Uttering a cry of fright, she leaped back, almost falling in the sand. She was about to run when a bark, followed by an angry growl, pierced the air. A small pack of snarling dogs suddenly surrounded her. She bent down and picked up a rock. It must have been a familiar gesture, because the dogs scattered before she could throw the stone.

About a dozen people walked by Erica as she passed through the village. They were all dressed in black gowns and black shawls, silent and faceless in the darkness. Erica realized that had she not passed through Qurna during the day, she probably would have been unable to find her way at night. A sudden raucous cry of a donkey shattered the silence, then stopped as abruptly as it had begun. From where she was walking, Erica could see the outline of Aida Raman's house high up against the hillside. The faint glow of an oil lamp shone from her windows. Rising behind the house, Erica could see the trail to the Valley of the Kings etched against the mountains.

She was now within fifty feet of the mosque. There were no lights. Her steps slowed. She knew she was late for the rendezvous. It was not dusk; it was night. Perhaps they had decided she was not coming. Maybe she should turn and go back to her hotel or visit with Aida Raman and tell her what she had learned from the papyrus. Erica stopped and looked at the building. It appeared deserted. Then, remembering Lahib Zayed and his casual attitude, she shrugged her shoulders and started toward the door.

It opened slowly, affording a view of the courtyard. The facade of the mosque seemed to attract and reflect the starlight, and the courtyard was brighter than the street. She saw no one.

Silently Erica stepped inside, closing the door behind her. There was no sound or motion from the mosque. All she could hear was an occasional dog barking in the village below. Finally she made herself walk forward beneath one of the archways. She tried the door to the mosque. It was locked. Walking along the small portico, she knocked on the door to the imam's quarters. There was no answer. The place was deserted.

Erica stepped back into the courtyard. They must have decided she was not coming, and she eyed the door to the street. But instead of leaving right away, she walked back under the portico and sat down, her back against the front of the mosque. In front of her the dark archway framed a view of the courtyard. Beyond the walls Erica could see the eastern sky, which brightened in anticipation of the rising moon.

Erica rummaged in her tote bag until she found a cigarette. She lit one to salvage her courage, and looked at her watch with the aid of a match. It was eight-fifteen.

As the moon rose, the shadows in the courtyard grew paradoxically darker. The longer Erica sat, the more her imagination played tricks on her. Every sound from the village made her jump. After fifteen minutes she'd had enough. She stood up and dusted off the seat of her pants. Then she walked back across the courtyard and yanked open the wooden door to the street.

"Miss Baron," said a figure in a black burnoose. He was standing in the dirt street just outside the door to the courtyard. With the moon directly over his shoulder, Erica could not see his face. He bowed before continuing. "I beg your pardon for the delay. Please follow me." He smiled, revealing huge teeth.

There was no more conversation. The man, who Erica guessed was a Nubian, led her up the hillside above the village. They followed one of the many trails, and the going was easy with the moonlight reflecting from the light rock and sand. They passed a few rectangular openings of tombs.

The Nubian was breathing heavily now, and it was with obvious relief that he stopped by a sloping cut into the mountainside. At the base of the slope was an entrance closed with a heavy iron grille. The number 37 hung on the gate.

"I beg your pardon, but you must wait here for just a few minutes," said the Nubian. Before Erica could respond, he started back toward Qurna.

Erica watched the retreating figure, then glanced at the iron gate. She turned, started to say something, but the Nubian was already so far away that she would have had to shout.

Walking down the ramp, Erica grasped the iron gate and shook it. The number 37 rattled but the gate did not budge. It was locked. Erica could just make out some ancient Egyptian decoration on the walls.

She walked back up the ramp, and the anxiety she had felt before entering the Curio Antique Shop swept over her. She stood on the lip of the tomb, watching the Nubian entering the village below. In the distance a few dogs barked. Behind her she could feel the ominous presence of the overhanging mountain.

Suddenly she heard a sharp metallic click behind her. Fear made her legs weak. Then she heard an agonizing grating of steel on steel. She wanted to run but was unable to move as her imagination conjured horrid images issuing from the tomb. The iron gate closed behind her, and she heard steps. Slowly she forced herself to turn around.

"Good evening, Miss Baron," said a figure coming up the ramp. He was dressed in a black burnoose like the Nubian's but with the hood over his head. Beneath the hood he wore a white turban. "My name is Muhammad Abdulal." He bowed, and Erica regained some composure. "I apologize for these delays, but unfortunately they are necessary. The statues you are about to see are very valuable, and we were afraid you might have been followed by the authorities."

Erica again realized how important it had been for her to lose her shadow.

"Please follow me," said Muhammad as he passed Erica and began climbing higher on the slope.

Erica cast a last glance at the village below her. She could barely make out her taxi waiting on the asphalt road. She had to hurry to catch up to Muhammad.

He turned to the left when they reached the very base of the sheer cliff. Trying to look up the rock face, Erica practically fell over backward. They walked for another fifty feet and rounded a huge boulder. Again she had to hurry after Muhammad. On the other side of the rock was a ramp similar to that for tomb 37. There was another heavy iron grille, but this time without a number. Erica stopped behind Muhammad as he fumbled with a large ring of keys. She had lost her nerve but was now equally afraid to show fear.

She had had no idea the statue would be stored in such an isolated location. The iron gate squealed on its hinges, unaccustomed to being opened.

"Please," said Muhammad simply, motioning for Erica to enter.

It was an undecorated tomb. She turned and watched Muhammad close the door behind him. There was a resounding click as the lock engaged. Anemic moonlight filtered in through the iron bars.

Muhammad lit a single match and pushed past Erica, moving down a narrow corridor. She had no choice but to stay close behind. They moved in a small sphere of light, and she had a helpless feeling that events were far beyond her control.

They entered an antechamber. Erica could make out dim line drawings on the walls. Muhammad bent down and touched his match to an oil lamp. The light flickered, making his shadow dance among the ancient Egyptian deities on the walls.

A sharp gilded reflection caught Erica's eye. There it was, the Seti statue! The burnished gold radiated a light more powerful than the lamp. For the moment awe conquered fear, and Erica walked over to the sculpture. Its alabaster-and-green-feldspar eyes were hypnotic, and she had to force herself to look below at the hieroglyphics. There were the cartouches of Seti I and Tutankhamen. The phrase was the same as that on the Houston statue: "Eternal life granted unto Seti I, who ruled after Tutankhamen."

"It is magnificent," said Erica with sincerity. "How much do you want for it?"

"We have others," said Muhammad. "Wait until you see the others before you make your choice."

Erica turned to look at him, intending to say she was satisfied. But she did not speak. Once again she was paralyzed by fear. Muhammad had flipped back his hood, revealing his mustache and gold-tipped teeth. He was one of the killers of Abdul Hamdi!

"We have a wonderful selection of statues in the next room," said Muhammad. "Please." He half-bowed and gestured toward the narrow doorway.

A cold sweat chilled her body. The grate to the tomb was locked. She had to play for time. She turned and started toward the doorway, not wanting to go deeper into the tomb, but Muhammad came up behind her. "Please," he said, and pushed her gently forward.

Their shadows moved grotesquely on the walls as they walked down the sloping corridor. Ahead, Erica could see a recess that extended on both sides of the passageway. A stout beam ran from the floor up into the alcove. As Erica passed, she realized that the beam supported a huge stone portcullis.

Just beyond, the passageway ended and a flight of stairs hewn from the rock led steeply downward into darkness.

"How much farther?" she asked. Her voice was higher than usual.

"Just a little way."

With the light behind her, Erica's shadow fell onto the stairs in front of her, blocking her vision. She felt ahead with her foot. It was at that point she felt something on her back. She first thought it was Muhammad's hand. Then she realized he had centered his foot in the small of her back.

Erica only had time to throw her hands out against the smooth walls of the stairway. The force of the kick had knocked her feet out from under her, and she began falling. She landed on her buttocks, but the stairs were so steep that she continued sliding, unable to stop her downward motion into absolute blackness.

Muhammad quickly put down his oil lamp and pulled a stone sledge from the recess. With several carefully directed blows he dislodged the supporting beam, triggering the balanced portcullis. In slow motion the forty-five-ton granite block slid down a short incline, then fell into place with a deafening crash that sealed the ancient tomb.

"No American woman got off the train at Nag Hamdi," said Raoul, "and there was no one that even came close to Erica's description on the train. It looks like we've been tricked." He was standing at the door to the balcony. Across the river the moonlight was bright on the mountains above the necropolis.

Yvon was sitting rubbing his temples. "Am I always destined to come so close, only to see success slip through my fingers?" He turned to Khalifa. "And what has the mighty Khalifa learned?"

"There was no one at the Curio Antique Shop. The other shops were still open and there were plenty of tourists. Apparently the shop had closed right after Erica left. The proprietor's name is Lahib Zayed, and no one seemed to know where he'd gone. And I was quite insistent." Khalifa smiled.

"I want the Curio Antique Shop and the Winter Palace watched. I don't care if you both have to stay up all night."

When Yvon was alone, he walked out onto the balcony. The night was peaceful and soft. The sound from the piano in the dining room drifted up through the palms. Nervously he began pacing the small terrace.

*   *   *

Erica ended in a sitting position at the bottom of the stairs, with one leg tucked under her. Her hands were badly scraped, but otherwise she was unhurt. Most of the contents of her tote bag had fallen out. She tried to look around in the Stygian darkness, but she could not even see her hand directly in front of her face. Like a blind person, she groped in her bag for the flashlight. It was not there.

Struggling to her hands and knees, she felt along the paving stone. She found her camera, which seemed intact, then her guidebook, but still no flashlight. Her hand hit a wall, and she recoiled in fear. Every phobia she'd ever had about snakes, scorpions, and spiders emerged to frighten her. The image of the cobra at Abydos plagued her. Groping back along the wall until she found the corner, she felt her way back to the stairway and found the pack of cigarettes. The book of matches was pushed beneath the cellophane cover.

She struck a match and held it away from her. She was in a room about ten feet square, with two doorways, plus the stairway behind her. The walls were plastered with painted scenes of everyday life in ancient Egypt. She was in one of the tombs of the nobles.

Against the far wall Erica caught a glimpse of her flashlight before the match singed the tips of her fingers. She lit another, and in its hesitant light walked over to retrieve the flashlight. The front glass had broken, but the bulb was still in place. Erica pressed the switch and it leaped to life.

Without allowing herself time to think about her situation, she returned to the stairs, climbed to the top, and ran the beam of the flashlight around the perimeter of the portcullis. The granite plug fit into its slot with incredible precision. She pushed against it. It was cold and motionless, like the mountain itself.

Returning to the base of the stairs, she began to explore the tomb. The two doorways from the antechamber led into a burial chamber on the left and a storeroom on the right. She entered the burial chamber first. Except for a rough-hewn sarcophagus, the room was empty. The ceiling was painted dark blue with hundreds of gold five-pointed stars, and the walls were decorated with scenes from the Book of the Dead. From the back wall Erica could read whose tomb she was in. Ahmose, scribe and vizier to Pharaoh Amenhotep III.

Moving her light about the sarcophagus, Erica saw a skull lying amid rags on the floor. Hesitantly she moved closer. The eye sockets were darkened pits and the lower jaw had separated, giving the mouth an expression of continued agony. All the teeth were in place. It was not that old.

Standing over the skull, Erica realized that she was looking at the remains of a whole corpse. The body had been curled up beside the sarcophagus, as if in sleep. Ribs and vertebrae could be seen through the decaying clothing. Just under the skull Erica saw a flash of gold. Falteringly she reached down and lifted the object. It was a 1975 Yale ring. Gingerly Erica replaced it and stood up.

"Let's see the next room," she said out loud, hoping the sound of her voice would reassure her. She did not want to think, not yet, and as long as there were places to explore, she could keep her mind from the reality of the situation. Acting like a tourist, she passed into the next and last chamber. It was the same size as the burial chamber, and completely empty save for a few rocks and a little sand. The decorations were of everyday life, as in the antechamber, but they were unfinished. The wall to the right had been prepared for a large harvest scene, and the figures were drawn in red ocher. There was a broad band of white plaster, prepared for hieroglyphics, running along the bottom. After shining her light around the room, Erica returned to the antechamber. She was running out of things to do, and a cold fear threatened to surface. She began to pick up the rest of her things from the floor and replace them in the tote bag. Thinking she might have probably missed something, she climbed the long flight of stairs to the granite plug. An overwhelming sense of claustrophobia swept over her, and vainly trying to control her emotions, she pushed at the stone with both hands.

"Help!" she shouted at the top of her lungs. The sound reverberated against the rock faces and echoed within the depths of the tomb. Then the silence closed in on her again, smothering her with its absolute stillness. She felt as if she needed air. Her breathing became labored. She slapped the granite plug with an open palm, harder and harder, until she could feel pain. Tears welled up and overflowed her eyes, and she continued to pound the stone, sobs racking her body.

The exertion exhausted her, and she slowly sank to her knees, still crying uncontrollably. All her fears of death and abandonment rose from the recesses of her mind, causing renewed spells of sobbing and shaking. She had suddenly realized that she was buried alive!

Having faced the grim reality of her situation, Erica began to recover a modicum of rational thought. She picked up the flashlight and descended the long flight of stone steps to the antechamber. She wondered when Yvon would begin to worry that something might have happened. Once he became suspicious, he would probably go to the Curio Antique Shop, but did Lahib Zayed know where she was? Would her taxi driver ever think of reporting that he had taken an American girl to Qurna, who had failed to return? Erica had no answers to these questions, but the mere asking of them revived a glimmer of hope that supported her until her flashlight perceptibly dimmed.

She switched it off and rummaged through her bag until she found three books of matches. It wasn't much, but while looking for the matches she came across a felt-tip pen. Touching the pen gave her an idea. She could leave some sort of message on the wall of the unfinished chamber, explaining what had happened to her. She could write it in the form of hieroglyphics so that her captors would probably not recognize its significance. She did not delude herself into believing that such an act would have any value short of giving her mind something to do. But that was something. Fear had given way to despair and bitter regret. Doing something would at least distract her.

With the flashlight propped up with several rocks, Erica began to space out her message. The simpler the better, she thought. Once the spacing was accomplished, she began to outline the figures. She was about halfway through when the flashlight suddenly dimmed markedly. It came back on again, but only for a moment. Then it dimmed to a red ember.

Once again Erica refused to contemplate her plight. She struck matches to continue the hieroglyphic text. She was crouching down at the base of the wall on the right, the text running in columns from the floor to the bottom of the unfinished harvest scene. She still suffered intermittent bouts of tears as she admitted to herself that her cleverness had been just enough to get her into inescapable trouble. Everyone had warned her about the involvement, and she had listened to no one. She'd been a fool. Training in Egyptology had not equipped her to deal with criminals, especially someone like Muhammad Abdulal.

With only one pack of matches left, Erica did not want to think about how much time she had left . . . about how long the oxygen would last. She bent down near to the floor to draw a bird. Before she could outline the figure, the match suddenly went out. It had gone very fast, and Erica cursed in the darkness. She struck another, but as she bent to write, this also went right out. Erica lit a third and very carefully approached the area where she was working. The match burned smoothly, then suddenly wavered, as if in a wind. Licking her fingers, Erica could feel a stream of air coming from a small vertical crack in the plaster, close to the floor.

The flashlight still glowed very slightly in the darkness, and Erica used it as a beacon to fetch one of the rocks she'd used to prop it up. It was a piece of granite, probably part of the sarcophagus lid. Erica carried it over to the draft and struck another match.

Holding the meager light in her left hand, she hit the plaster in the area of the crack. Nothing happened. She continued to hit the area as hard as she could until the match went out. Then, locating the crack in the darkness by feel, Erica pounded the spot blindly for more than a minute.

Finally calming down, she lit another match. At the spot where the crack had been, now there was a small hole, big enough for her to insert her finger. There was a space beyond, and more importantly, a current of cool air. Unseeing, Erica continued to pound the area with the piece of granite, until she could feel movement beneath the stone. She lit a match. A crack now ran along the juncture of the floor and the wall before arching back to join the slowly enlarging opening. Erica concentrated on pounding this area, holding the match with her left hand. Suddenly a large piece of plaster broke free and disappeared. After a moment, Erica heard it hit the ground. The hole was now about a foot in diameter. When she tried to light another match, the air current put it out. Gingerly she stuck her hand into the hole, as if she were reaching into the mouth of a wild beast. She could feel a smooth plastered surface on the inside. Turning her palm up, she could feel a ceiling. She had discovered another room built diagonally below the room she was in.

With renewed enthusiasm Erica slowly enlarged the opening. She worked in the dark, not willing to sacrifice any more matches. Finally the hole was deep enough to allow her to stick her head in. After locating a few pebbles, she lay prone on the floor of the chamber, shoving her head into the opening. She let the pebbles go and listened for the impact. The room did not seem deep, and appeared to have a floor of sand.

Erica emptied her cigarettes from the pack and lit the paper. When it was flaming, she pushed it into the hole and let it go. The flames went out, but the ember sank in a spiral. When it landed, it was about eight feet away. Erica found more stones, and with her head in the hole she tossed them in various directions, trying to get some idea of the space. It seemed to be a square room. And what pleased Erica, there was a constant movement of air.

Sitting in the inky blackness, she debated what she should do. If she lowered herself into the room she'd found, there was a chance she would not be able to get back into the tomb she was in. But what difference did that make? The real problem was finding the courage to go into the hole. She had only half a pack of matches left.

Erica picked up her tote bag. Counting to three, she forced herself to drop it through the opening. On all fours she backed up to the wall and lowered her legs into the hole. She had an image of being swallowed. Slowly she wriggled farther and farther into space, until the tips of her toes touched a smooth plastered wall. Like a diver trying to get himself to plunge into cold water, Erica forced her body to slide through the hole into the black void. As she fell for what seemed forever, her arms flailed in the air, attempting to keep her feet first. She landed off balance but unhurt, and fell over backward on a rubble-strewn sand floor.

Fear of the unknown made her stumble to her feet, only to lose her balance again and sprawl forward. There was a tremendous amount of dust choking her. Her outstretched right hand fell on an object that she thought was a piece of wood. She held onto it, hoping it would ignite like a torch.

Finally she managed to stand up. She switched the piece of wood to her left hand in order to get her matches from her jeans pocket. But the object no longer felt like a piece of wood. Touching it with both hands, she realized she was holding a mummified forearm and hand, trailing wrappings in the darkness. With disgust she threw the object away from her.

Shaking, Erica pulled the matches from her pocket and struck one. As its light filtered outward in the dust, Erica found herself in a catacomb with bare, unadorned walls and filled with partially wrapped mummies. The bodies had been broken apart and stripped of any valuables, then rudely discarded.

Turning around slowly, Erica saw evidence that the ceiling had partially caved in. In the corner she saw a low dark doorway. Grabbing her tote bag, she struggled forward in the knee-deep debris. The match burned her fingers, and she shook it out, moving forward with her hands groping for the wall, then the doorway. She passed into the next room. Lighting another match, she found herself in a room filled with equally grotesque images. A niche in the wall was filled with decapitated mummified heads. There was evidence of more cave-ins.

On the wall opposite Erica were two widely separated doorways. She worked her way into the center of the room, and holding the match ahead of her, decided the air was coming from the smaller passage. The match went out, and she moved forward with her hands ahead of her.

Suddenly there was a great commotion. A cave-in! Erica

threw herself forward against the wall, feeling particles hit her hair and shoulders.

But there was no crash. Instead the commotion in the air continued and the atmosphere became saturated with dust and high-pitched screeches. Then something landed on Erica's shoulder. It was alive and clawing. As her hand swept the animal off her back, she touched wings. It wasn't a cave-in. It was a million disturbed bats. She covered her head with her arm and crouched low against the wall, breathing as best she could. Gradually the bats quieted and she was able to move into the next room.

Erica slowly realized that she had fallen into a maze of tombs of the common people of ancient Thebes. The catacombs had been progressively cut into the mountainside in the form of a labyrinth to make room for the millions of dead. Sometimes they had inadvertently connected with other tombs, in this case with the tomb of Ahmose, in which Erica had been interred. The connection had been plastered over and forgotten.

Erica pushed on. Although the presence of the bats was horrifying, it was also encouraging. There had to be a connection with the outside. Eventually she tried lighting the mummy wrappings and discovered they burned briskly. In fact, Erica found that the pieces of mummies with their wrappings burned like torches, and she forced herself to pick them up. The forearms were best, because they were easy to hold. With the help of better light she worked her way through many galleries and up several levels until she felt fresh air. Dousing her torch, Erica walked the last feet by the light of the moon. When she emerged into the warm Egyptian night, she was several hundred yards from the place she had entered the mountain with Muhammad. Directly below her was the village of Qurna. There were very few lights.

For a time Erica stood trembling at the entrance to the catacomb, appreciating the moon and the stars in a way she'd never done. She knew she was enormously lucky to be alive.

The first thing she needed was a place to rest, pull herself together, and have a drink. Her throat was raw from the suffocating dust. She also wanted to wash, as if the experience clung to her like dirt, and most of all she wished to see a friendly face. The closest source of all these comforts was Aida Raman's house. She could see it up against the hillside. A light still shone in the window.

Stepping from the seclusion of the catacomb, Erica walked warily along the base of the cliff. Until she got back to Luxor, she would take no chance on being seen by Muhammad or the Nubian. What she really wanted to do was get back to Yvon. She'd tell him as best she could the location of the statue and then get out of Egypt. She'd had enough.

When she was directly above Aida Raman's, Erica began the descent. For the first hundred yards it was deep sand, then loose gravel, which frightened her by shifting noisily in the bright moonlight. Finally she reached the back of the house.

Erica waited for a few minutes in the shadows, watching the village. She saw no movement. Satisfied that it was all clear, she walked around the building into the courtyard and knocked at the door.

Aida Raman shouted something in Arabic. Erica responded by calling out her name and asking if she could talk with her.

"Go away," shouted Aida through the closed door.

Erica was surprised. Aida had been so warm and friendly. "Please, Mrs. Raman," she said through the door. "I need a drink of water."

The door unlatched and swung open. Aida Raman was clad in the same cotton dress she had on for their first meeting.

"Thank you," said Erica. "I'm sorry to trouble you. But I am very thirsty."

Aida looked older than she had two days previously. Gone was the apparent humor. "All right," she said, "but wait here by the door. You cannot stay."

While the old woman fetched a drink, Erica looked around the room. The familiar sight was comforting. The long-handled shovel nested in its brackets. The framed photos hung neatly on the wall. Many were of Howard Carter with a turbaned Arab Erica thought had to be Raman. There was a small mirror among the photos, and Erica was shocked by her appearance.

Aida Raman brought some of the juice she'd given Erica on

her first visit. Erica drank slowly. Swallowing hurt her throat.

"My family was very angry when I told them you tricked me into revealing the papyrus to you," said Aida.

"Family?" said Erica, the drink reviving her. "I thought you said you were the last of the Ramans."

"I am. My two sons died. But I also had two daughters, who have families. It was one of my grandsons I told about your visit. He became very angry and took the papyrus."

"What did he do with it?" asked Erica, alarmed.

"I don't know. He said it had to be treated very carefully and that he would put it somewhere safe. He also said that the papyrus was a curse, and that now that you have seen it, you must die."

"Do you believe that?" Erica knew that Aida Raman was no fool.

"I don't know. It's not what my husband said."

"Mrs. Raman," Erica said, "I translated the whole papyrus. Your husband was right. There was nothing about a curse. The papyrus was written by an ancient architect for Pharaoh Seti I."

A dog barked loudly in the village. A human voice shouted in reply.

"You must go," said Aida Raman. "You must go in case my grandson returns. Please."

"What is your grandson's name?" asked Erica.

"Muhammad Abdulal."

The news hit Erica like a slap in the face.

"You know him?" asked Aida.

"I think I met him tonight. Does he live here in Qurna?"

"No, he lives in Luxor."

"Have you seen him tonight?" asked Erica nervously.

"Today, but not tonight. Please, you must go."

Erica hastened to leave. She was more nervous than Aida. But at the doorway she paused. Loose ends were beginning to merge. "What kind of work does Muhammad Abdulal do?" Erica was remembering that Abdul Hamdi had written in the hidden letter in the guidebook that a government official was involved.

"He is the chief of the guard of the necropolis and he helps his father run the concession stand in the Valley of the Kings."

Erica nodded in understanding. Chief of the guards was the perfect position from which to mastermind a black-market operation. Then Erica thought about the concession stand and Raman. "And that concession stand is the same one that your husband, Sarwat Raman, built?"

"Yes, yes. Miss Baron, please go."

All at once everything became clear. All at once she believed she could explain everything. And it all depended on the concession stand in the Valley of the Kings.

"Aida," said Erica with feverish excitement, "listen to me. As your husband said, there is no 'Curse of the Pharaohs,' and I can prove it, provided you will help. I just need time. All I ask is that you do not tell anyone, not even your family, that I have returned to see you. They will not ask, I can assure you. So all I'm begging is that you do not bring it up. Please." Erica grasped Aida's upper arms to emphasize her earnestness.

"You can prove my husband was right?"

"Absolutely," said Erica.

Aida nodded her head. "All right."

"Oh, there is something else," said Erica. "I need a flash-light."

"All I have is an oil lamp."

"That will be fine," said Erica.

As she left, Erica gave Aida a hug, but the old woman remained passive and withdrawn. Holding the oil lamp and several books of matches, Erica stood in the shadow of the house watching the village. It was deathly still. The moon had passed the zenith and was now in the western sky. The lights of Luxor were still bright with activity.

Taking the same path she had two days previously, Erica hiked up the spur of the mountain. It was a much easier climb in the moonlight than in the hot sun.

Erica knew she was violating her recent resolve to leave the rest of the mystery to Yvon and the police, but the conversation with Aida had rekindled her intoxication with the past. Going from the tomb of Ahmose down into the public catacombs had offered her a single explanation for all the disparate events, including the mystery of the inscription on

298

the statue and the meaning of the papyrus. And with the knowledge that Muhammad Abdulal would never imagine she was free, Erica felt reasonably safe. Even if he wanted to check the Ahmose tomb, it would probably take days to raise the portcullis. Erica believed she had time, and she wanted to visit the Valley of the Kings and the concession stand of Raman. If she was right, she would discover a truth that would make Tutankhamen's tomb pale to insignificance.

Reaching the summit of the ridge, she paused to catch her breath. The desert wind softly whistled among the naked peaks, adding to the feeling of desolation. From where she was standing she could see into the dark and barren Valley of the Kings with its network of etched paths.

Erica could see her goal. The concession stand and rest house stood out clearly on its small rocky promontory. Seeing it encouraged her, and she pushed on, descending carefully to keep from setting off small avalanches of pebbles. She did not want to disturb anyone who might be in the valley. Once she had joined the route to the ancient necropolis workers' village, the trail flattened out and she could walk much more easily. Before entering one of the carefully scraped pathways lined with stones that ran between the tombs, Erica waited and listened. All she could hear was the wind and the occasional screech of a bat in flight.

With a light step Erica walked to the center of the valley and mounted the front steps of the concession stand. As she expected, it was tightly shuttered and locked. Walking back out onto the veranda, Erica let her line of vision trace the triangle made by Tutankhamen's tomb, Seti I's tomb, and the concession stand. Then she walked around to the rear of the rock building, and steeling herself against the foul odors, pushed her way into the ladies' room. Putting a match to Aida Raman's oil lamp, she checked out the room, following the foundation line. There was nothing strange about its construction.

Within the men's room, the pungent smell of urine was much more intense. It came from a long urinal made from fired brick built along the front wall. Above the urinal was a two-foot-high crawl space that extended forward under the veranda; the men's room did not abut the front foundation of the building. Erica walked toward the urinal. The lip of the crawl space was at shoulder height. Holding the oil lamp into the opening, she tried to look in, but the light penetrated for only five or six feet. She could see an opened sardine can and a few bottles strewn on the dirt floor.

With the help of the waste barrel Erica climbed up into the crawl space. She left her tote bag on the edge. Avoiding the debris, she crawled forward like a crab until she came to the front masonry wall. The smell of the toilet was worse in the confined space, and Erica's enthusiasm rapidly waned. But having come this far, she forced herself to check the rough stone wall from one end to the other. Nothing!

Resting her head on her wrists, Erica admitted that she'd been wrong. It had seemed so clever. She sighed deeply, then tried to turn around. It was difficult, so she began to worm her way backward toward the toilet. Holding the oil lamp in one hand, she attempted to push herself backward with the other, but the earth under her was loose and gave way. She tried to gain a better purchase on the ground, and when she pushed, she felt something smooth under the dirt.

Erica twisted herself and looked down. Her right hand was touching a metallic surface. Scraping away some of the dirt, she exposed a piece of sheet metal. She put the lamp down and with both hands began to clear away the loose earth. At the perimeter of the metal she could see that it had been set down into a carved bed in the rock. She had to clear away all the dirt before she could lift the edge of the metal and work it up over the mounds of surrounding earth. Beneath the sheet of metal a yawning shaft had been cut into the bedrock.

Holding the light over the hole, Erica could see that it was about four feet deep and was the beginning of a tunnel that headed toward the front of the building. She had been right! Her head slowly rose, and she stared into the gloom. A sense of satisfaction and excitement gripped her. She knew how Howard Carter had felt in November 1922.

Quickly she pulled her tote bag into the depths of the crawl space. Then she lowered herself backward into the shallow pit and held the oil lamp to the mouth of the tunnel. It slanted downward and immediately enlarged. Taking a deep breath, she moved forward. At first she had to practically crawl on all fours, but soon she was able to walk partially bent over. As she advanced, she tried to estimate the yardage. The tunnel was heading directly for Tutankhamen's tomb.

Nassif Boulos crossed the dark empty parking area of the Valley of the Kings. He was seventeen years old and the youngest of the three nighttime guards. As he walked, he hiked up the shoulder strap of his aged rifle, which had been abandoned in Egypt during the First World War. He was angry because it was not his turn to walk up to the end of the valley and back to the guard house, where he could rest and get a drink. Once again his colleagues had taken advantage of his youth and lack of seniority by ordering him to make the rounds.

The moonlit night soon soothed his anger, leaving him merely restless and anxious for something to break the boredom of his watch. But the valley was quiet, and each of the tombs was sealed by its stout iron gate. Nassif would have loved to use his rifle against a thief, and his mind wandered into one of his fantasies in which he protected the valley against a band of brigands.

He stopped across from the entrance to Tutankhamen's tomb. He wished the tomb were being found now instead of a half-century before. He looked up at the concession stand, because that was where he'd have been on guard in Carter's day. He'd have hidden behind the parapet on the veranda, and no one would be able to approach the tomb without succumbing to his murderous fire.

Looking up, Nassif noticed the door to the lavatories was ajar. He realized it had never been left open before, and he debated whether he wanted to walk up to the building. Then he looked up into the valley and decided he'd check the lavatory on the way back. While he walked, he pictured himself traveling to Cairo with a group of men he'd arrested.

Erica estimated that she should be very close to Tutankhamen's tomb. Progress had been slow because of the rounded, uneven floor of the tunnel. In front of her there was a sharp turn to the left, and she could not see ahead until she had rounded the corner. The floor of the passageway then slanted steeply down and entered a room. With her hands pressed against the rough, rock-hewn sides of the tunnel, she inched herself downward until her feet rested on a smooth floor. She had entered an underground chamber.

Now Erica guessed she was directly below the antechamber of Tutankhamen's tomb. She lifted the oil lamp above her head, and the light spread out, illuminating smoothly finished but unadorned walls. The room was about twenty-five feet long and fifteen feet wide, with a ceiling made of a single gigantic limestone block. As Erica's eyes dropped to the floor, she saw an enormous tangle of skeletons, some with varying amounts of naturally mummified tissue. Holding the light a little closer, she could see that each one of the skulls had been fractured and penetrated by the blow of a heavy blunt instrument.

"My God," whispered Erica. She knew what she was looking at. This was the remains of the massacre of the ancient workers who had dug the chamber in which she was standing.

Slowly she passed through the room with its gruesome reminder of ancient cruelty, and began to descend a long flight of steps that led to a masonry wall. Raman had opened a large hole, and Erica stepped into another, much larger room. When the light penetrated the darkness, Erica gasped for breath and steadied herself against the wall. Spread out in front of her was an archaeological fairyland. The room was supported by massive square columns. The walls were painted with exquisite images of the ancient Egyptian pantheon. In front of each deity was the image of Seti I. Erica had found the pharaoh's treasure. Nenephta had realized that the safest spot for one treasure was below another.

Gingerly Erica advanced, holding her oil lamp so that the flickering light could play upon the myriad objects carefully stored within the room. In contrast to Tutankhamen's small tomb, there was no disarray. Everything had its place. Entire gilded chariots were standing as if waiting to be harnessed to a horse. Huge coffers and upright chests fashioned from cedar and inlaid with ebony lined the right wall.

One small ivory chest was open, and its contents—jewelry made with unparalleled elegance—had been carefully laid out on the floor. Obviously it had been a source of plunder for Raman.

Wandering around the central pillars, Erica discovered there was another stairway. This led to a further room of the same dimensions, also filled with treasure. There were several passageways leading to still more rooms.

"My God," said Erica again, only this time with astonishment, not horror. She realized that she was in a vast complex of chambers extending downward and outward in bewildering directions.

She knew she was gazing on a treasure beyond comprehension. As she wandered on, she thought of the famous Deir el-Bahri cache discovered in the late 1800's and carefully plundered by the Rasul family for ten years. Here the Raman family and then the Abdulal family were apparently doing the same.

Entering another room, Erica stopped. She was standing in a chamber that was relatively empty. There were four matching chests of ebony built in the form of Osiris. The decorations on the walls were from the Book of the Dead. The vaulted ceiling was painted black with gold stars. In front of Erica was a doorway carefully blocked with masonry and sealed with the ancient necropolis seals. On each side of the doorway were alabaster plinths with hieroglyphics carved in high relief along the front. Erica could read the phrase instantly. "Eternal life granted to Seti I, who rests under Tutankhamen."

All at once it was clear to Erica that the verb was "rest," not "rule," and the preposition was "under," not "after." She also realized she was looking at the original location of the two Seti statues. They had been standing across from each other in front of the masonry wall for three thousand years.

Suddenly Erica realized that she was standing at the unopened entrance to the burial chamber of the mighty Seti I. What she had found was not just a treasure trove, but an entire pharaonic tomb. The statue of Seti she had seen had been one of the guards of the burial chamber, like the bituminized statues found in Tutankhamen's tomb. Seti I had not been buried in the tomb constructed in a pattern of the other New Kingdom pharaohs. It had been Nenephta's final ruse. A substitute body had been buried in the tomb publicly proclaimed to be Seti's, when in actuality Seti had been buried in a secret tomb below Tutankhamen. Nenephta had pleased both sides. He gave the professional thieves a tomb to rob, and his sovereign protection that no other pharaoh had been given. Nenephta probably also believed that even if someone stumbled into Tutankhamen's tomb, they would never imagine that it would serve as a shield for the mighty treasure below. He had understood "the ways of the greedy and unjust."

Shaking the lamp to check the oil, Erica decided that she'd better begin the journey back. Reluctantly she turned and retraced her footsteps, continuing to marvel at Nenephta's scheme. He had indeed been clever, but he'd also been arrogant. Leaving the papyrus in Tutankhamen's tomb had been the weakest link in his elaborate plan. It had provided the clue for the equally clever Raman to solve the mystery. Erica wondered if the Arab had gone to the Great Pyramid as she had, and if he noticed that the chambers had been built one on top of the other, or if on visiting one of the tombs of the nobles he had found a tomb below it.

Walking up the narrow passage, Erica thought of the enormity of the discovery, and the huge stakes involved. No wonder there had been a murder. The thought brought Erica to a stop. She wondered just how many murders there had been. For more than fifty years the secret had to have been kept. The young man from Yale . . . All at once Erica began to question the association of the so-called Curse of the Pharaohs. Perhaps the people had been killed to protect the secret. What about Lord Carnarvon himself? . . .

Reaching the uppermost chamber, Erica paused to glance at the jewelry taken from the ivory chest. Although she had been scrupulously careful not to touch anything for fear of disturbing the archaeological aspects of the tomb, she felt comfortable touching something already disturbed. She picked up a pendant with a cartouche of Seti I rendered in solid gold. She wanted to have something in case Yvon and Ahmed refused to believe her story. So she took the pendant with her as she mounted the steps to the room filled with skeletons of the luckless ancient workers.

Climbing up into the tunnel was much easier than the descent. At the end she placed the oil lamp on the dirt and pulled herself into the crawl space under the concession stand. She had to decide the best way to return to Luxor. It was just past midnight, so the chances of running into Muhammad or the Nubian were much less. Her biggest worry was the government guard who worked under Muhammad. On the asphalt road into the valley she remembered seeing a gatehouse. Consequently she could not leave via the road, but would have to take the trail back to Qurna.

Manipulating the piece of sheet metal was difficult in the confined space. Erica had to slide it over the dirt and allow it to drop into its bed. Then, with the sardine can she'd seen earlier she began to scoop the loose dirt over the metal cover.

Nassif was several hundred feet away from the concession stand when he heard the clank of metal against stone. Immediately he pulled the rifle from his shoulder and dashed toward the partially open doorway to the lavatories. With the butt of the rifle he pushed the door completely open. Moonlight filtered into the small entryway.

Erica heard the door opening and smothered the oil lamp with her hand. She was about ten feet from the edge of the men's room. Her eyes quickly adjusted to the dark, and she could see the doorway to the vestibule. Her heart began to pound as it had when Richard entered her hotel room.

While she watched, a dark silhouette slipped into the room. Even in the partial light Erica could recognize the rifle. A feeling of panic began to grip her as the man slowly moved directly toward her. He was hunched over, moving like a cat stalking its prey.

With no idea what the man could see, Erica hugged the ground. He appeared to be looking directly at her as he reached the wall of the urinal. Then he stopped, and for what seemed like hours he stood there intently staring. Finally he reached out and grabbed a handful of loose dirt. Cocking his arm, he tossed the dirt into the recess. Erica closed her eyes as a portion of it hit her. The man repeated the action. Some of the pebbles clanked against the still-exposed sheet metal.

Nassif stood up. *"Harrah,"* he muttered. He was angry because he did not even get to shoot a rat.

Erica felt a small amount of relief, but noticed the man did not move away. He stood there looking at her in the darkness with his rifle back on his shoulder. Erica was perplexed until she heard the trickle of urine.

There was enough moonlight reflecting from the sail of the felucca for Erica to see the time. It was after one. The passage across the Nile was so smooth that she could have dozed. Crossing the river was the last hurdle, and she allowed her body to relax. She was sure Luxor was safe. The excitement of her discovery had superseded the harrowing experience in the tomb, and it was her anticipation of revealing her find that kept her awake.

Looking back toward the West Bank, Erica felt pleased. She'd climbed from the Valley of the Kings, passed the sleeping village of Qurna, and crossed the cultivated fields to the banks of the Nile without any problems. A confrontation with some dogs had been solved by merely bending down to pick up a stone. She stretched her tired legs.

The boat heeled against a puff of wind, and Erica looked up at the graceful curve of the sail across the star-strewn sky. She was not sure who she'd enjoy telling her discovery to the most: Yvon, Ahmed, or Richard. Yvon and Ahmed would be the most appreciative, Richard would be the most surprised. Even her mother would for once be genuinely pleased: she would never again have to make excuses at the country club for her daughter's career choice.

Back on the East Bank, she was pleased to find the lobby of the Winter Palace Hotel deserted. She had to call out at the desk to raise a clerk.

The sleepy Egyptian, although taken aback by her appearance, gave her a key and an envelope without saying a word. Erica started up the broad carpeted stairway while the clerk looked after her, wondering what she could have been doing to get so dirty. Erica glanced at the envelope. It was Winter Palace stationery, addressed to her in a bold, heavy hand. When she reached the corridor, she put her finger into the corner of the envelope. tearing it open while she navigated around the remnants of the hotel construction. At her door, she was about to insert the key when she unfolded the letter. It was a meaningless scribble. Looking at the outside of the envelope, Erica wondered if it were some kind of joke. If so, she did not understand it or appreciate it. It was like getting a phone call and hearing the person hang up without speaking. It was somehow unnerving.

Erica looked at her door. If there was one thing she'd learned during the trip, it was that hotels were not safe places. She remembered finding Ahmed in her room, Richard's arrival, her room being searched. With a renewed sense of uncertainty she pushed her key into the door.

Suddenly she thought she heard a noise. In her present state of mind, that was all she needed. Leaving the key dangling in its slot, Erica fled down the corridor. In her haste, her tote bag hit against a stack of building blocks with a resounding crunch. Behind her she heard her door being rapidly unlocked from within.

When Evangelos had heard the sound of the key, he had jumped up and rushed to the door. "Kill her," shouted Stephanos, awakened by the noise. Drawing his Beretta, Evangelos whipped open the door in time to see Erica disappear down the main stairway.

She had no idea who was in her room, but she had no illusions about being protected by the sleeping clerk. Besides, he wasn't even at the desk. She had to get to Yvon at the New Winter Palace. She ran out the back of the hotel into the garden.

In spite of his size, Evangelos could move like a hawk on the attack, especially when he concentrated. And when given an order for violence, he was like a rabid dog.

Erica ran through a flowerbed and reached the edge of the pool. Trying to run around it, she slipped on the wet tiles, falling on her side. Scrambling to her feet, she discarded her bag and began to run again. Footsteps were gaining on her.

Evangelos was close enough for an easy shot. "Stop," he yelled, leveling his gun at Erica's back.

Erica knew it was hopeless. There was still another fifty yards to the New Winter Palace. She stopped, exhausted, her chest heaving, and turned to look at her pursuer. He was only thirty feet away. She recognized him from the Al Azhar mosque. The huge laceration he had that day was now sutured, making him look like the Frankenstein monster. His gun was pointed at her, the muzzle hidden by an evil silencer.

Evangelos tried to decide what kind of shot he'd make. Finally, holding the gun out at arm's length, he aimed for Erica's neck and slowly began to pull the trigger.

Erica saw his arm extend slightly, and her eyes widened as she realized he was going to shoot even though she'd stopped as commanded. "No!"

The gun muffled by the silencer gave a soft thump. Erica felt no pain, and the image in front of her remained clear. Then the strangest thing happened. A small red flower blossomed in the center of Evangelos' forehead, and he fell forward onto his face, the gun dropping from his hand.

Erica could not move. Her hands were motionless at her sides. Behind her she heard movement within the bushes. Then a voice: "You should not have been so clever about losing me."

Erica slowly turned. In front of her was the man with the pointed tooth and hooked nose. "That was very close," said Khalifa, motioning toward Evangelos. "I assume you are on your way to Monsieur de Margeau's. You'd better hurry. There will be more trouble."

Erica tried to speak but couldn't. She nodded and stumbled past Khalifa, her gait unsteady on rubbery legs. She did not remember how she got to Yvon's room.

The Frenchman opened the door, and she collapsed into his arms, mumbling about the shot, about being sealed in the tomb, about finding the statue. Yvon was calm, stroking her hair, sitting her down, telling her to start from the beginning.

She was about to begin when someone knocked at the door.

"Yes," called Yvon, instantly alert.

"It is Khalifa."

Yvon opened the door, and Khalifa propelled Stephanos into the room.

"You hired me to protect the girl and get the person who tried to kill her. Here he is." Khalifa pointed toward Stephanos.

Stephanos looked at Yvon, then at Erica, who was surprised that Khalifa had been hired by Yvon to protect her, since Yvon had deliberately downplayed her risk. Erica began to feel uncomfortable.

"Look, Yvon," said Stephanos at length. "It is ridiculous for you and me to be at odds with each other. You're angry at me because I sold the first Seti statue to the man from Houston. But all I did was get the statue from Egypt to Switzerland. There really is no competition between us. You want to control the black market. Fine. I just want to protect my corner. I can get your stuff out of Egypt with a time-tested method. We should work together."

Erica looked quickly at Yvon to see his reaction. She wanted to hear him laugh and tell Stephanos that he was all wrong, that he, Yvon, wanted to destroy the black market.

Yvon ran his fingers through his hair. "Why were you threatening Erica?" he asked.

"Because she had learned too much from Abdul Hamdi. I wanted to protect my route. But if you two are working together, then everything's fine."

"You didn't have anything to do with Hamdi's death and the disappearance of the second statue?" asked Yvon.

"No," said Stephanos. "I swear it. I hadn't even heard about the second Seti statue. That was what worried me. I was afraid I was being closed out and that Hamdi's letter would get to the police."

Closing her eyes, Erica let the truth sweep over her. Yvon was no crusader. His idea of controlling the black market meant controlling it for his own ends, not for the benefit of science, Egypt, or the world. His passion for antiquities superseded any moral issue. Erica had been duped, and more aggravating still, she could have been killed. Her fingernails dug into the couch. She knew she had to get away. She had to tell Ahmed about Seti's tomb.

"Stephanos did not kill Abdul Hamdi," said Erica suddenly. "The people who killed Abdul Hamdi are the people here in

Luxor who control the source of the antiquities. The Seti statue was brought back here to Luxor. I've seen it and I can lead us to it." She was careful to use the word "us."

Yvon looked back at Erica, a little surprised by her sudden recovery. She smiled at him reassuringly. Her instincts for self-preservation gave her unexpected power. "Furthermore," said Erica, "Stephanos' route through Yugoslavia is far better than trying to get things from Alexandria in cotton bales."

Stephanos nodded as he began talking with Yvon. "Smart woman. And she's right. My method is far better than packing antiquities in cotton bales. Was that really what you had planned? My God, it would last for one or two shipments at the most."

Erica stretched. She knew that she had to convince Yvon that she had personal interests in antiquities. "Tomorrow I can show you the location of the Seti statue."

"Where is it?" asked Yvon.

"In one of the unmarked tombs of the nobles on the West Bank. It is very difficult to describe its location. I'll have to show you. It's above the village of Qurna. And there are a number of other very interesting pieces." Erica fished in the pocket of her jeans for the gold Seti pendant. She pulled it out and tossed it casually onto a table. "My fee for finding the Seti statue will be for Stephanos to get this pendant out of the country for me."

"This is exquisite," Yvon said, examining the necklace.

"There are many more pieces there, some much better than that. The pendant was the one I could afford. Now, I for one would like to bathe and get some rest. In case you haven't noticed, I've had quite a night." Erica went over to Yvon and gave him a kiss on the cheek. It was the hardest thing she'd done. She thanked Khalifa for helping her in the garden. Then she boldly walked to the door.

"Erica . . ." said Yvon calmly.

She turned. "Yes?"

There was a silence. "Perhaps you should stay here," said Yvon. It was apparent he was debating what to do with her.

"Tonight I'm too tired," said Erica. The implication was obvious. Stephanos smiled behind his hand.

"Raoul," called Yvon, "I want you to make sure Miss Baron is safe tonight."

"I think I'll be fine," said Erica, opening the door.

"Just to be sure," said Yvon, "I want Raoul to go with you."

Evangelos' body was still lying in the moonlight by the pool as Erica and Raoul walked back toward the Winter Palace. He looked like he was sleeping, except for the pool of dark blood that ran from under his head and dripped into the water. Erica averted her face as Raoul went over and checked to see if Evangelos was really dead. Suddenly she noticed Evangelos' semiautomatic pistol still lying on the tiles.

Erica stole a glance at Raoul. He was struggling to turn Evangelos over. Without looking at Erica, he spoke. "God, Khalifa is fantastic. He got him between the eyes."

Erica reached down and picked up the gun. It was heavier than she expected. Her finger curled around the trigger. She detested the instrument, and it frightened her. She had never held a gun before, and the knowledge of its lethal capabilities made her tremble. She did not delude herself. She knew she could never pull the trigger, but she turned and looked at Raoul, who was standing up and brushing his hands. "He was dead before he hit the ground," said Raoul, turning toward Erica. "Ah, I see you found his gun. Hand it to me and I'll put it in his hand."

"Don't move," said Erica slowly.

Raoul's eyes danced back and forth between the gun and Erica's face. "Erica what—?"

"Shut up. Take off your jacket."

Raoul complied, tossing his blazer on the ground.

"Now, pull your shirt over your head," commanded Erica.

"Erica . . ." said Raoul.

"Now!" She extended Evangelos' gun to arm's length.

Raoul yanked his shirt from his trousers and with some difficulty pulled it over his head. Beneath his shirt he had on a sleeveless undershirt. Strapped under his left arm was a small pistol. Erica moved around behind him and took the gun from the holster. She threw it into the pool. Hearing it hit the water, she hesitated, fearful Raoul would be angry. Then the absurdity of the idea caught her. Of course he was going to be

311

angry. She was holding a gun on him!

She had Raoul replace his shirt so he could see where he was going. Then she ordered him to walk around to the front of the hotel. He tried to talk, and she told him again to shut up. Erica thought how ridiculously easy it was in gangster movies to incapacitate a man by hitting him on the head to knock him out. In reality she could do nothing. If Raoul had turned around, he could have taken the gun. But he didn't, and they walked single file through the shadows around to the front of the hotel.

Several antique street lights cast a pale glow over a row of taxis parked along the curb of the curved driveway. The drivers had long since departed for the night, their principal job being to run back and forth between the hotel and the airport. But since the last flight arrived at nine-ten P.M., there was nothing for them to do. Tourists preferred the romantic carriages for transport in and around the town.

With Evangelos' gun trembling in her hand, Erica marched Raoul along the line of aged taxis, glancing in at the ignitions. Most of the keys were in place. She wanted to get to Ahmed, but had to decide what to do with Raoul.

The lead car was similar to the others, with the exception of tassels lining the rear window. The keys were in the ignition.

"Lie down," commanded Erica. She was terrified someone would walk out of the hotel.

Raoul took it upon himself to step sideways onto the close-clipped lawn.

"Hurry up!" said Erica, trying to sound angry.

Leaning on his palms, Raoul lay down. He kept his hands under him, ready to spring, his confusion dissolving into anger.

"Arms out in front of you," said Erica. She opened the door to the taxi and got in behind the vinyl-coated steering wheel. A pair of soft red plastic dice hung from the dash.

The engine turned over agonizingly slowly, belched black smoke, then caught. Keeping the gun on Raoul, Erica searched for the headlight switch and flipped it on. Then she threw the pistol on the seat next to her and put the car in gear. It lurched forward and bucked dramatically, bouncing the pistol from the seat to the floor.

Out of the corner of her eye Erica saw Raoul leap to his feet and rush toward the taxi. She played with the accelerator and clutch, trying to ease the bucking and gain speed as he jumped on the back bumper and grabbed the closed trunk.

The car was in second gear when Erica pulled out onto the broad illuminated boulevard. There was no other traffic, and she accelerated as fast as she could past the Temple of Luxor. When the motor was racing, Erica forced the gearshift into third. She had no idea of the speed because the speedometer was not functioning. In the rearview mirror she could see Raoul still clinging to the trunk. His dark hair was blowing wildly in the wind. Erica wanted to get him off the car.

She threw the steering wheel from side to side. The taxi careened in a serpentine manner, its tires screeching. But Raoul pressed himself against the back of the car and managed to hold on.

Erica put the car in fourth gear and pressed on the accelerator. The taxi leaped forward but developed a shimmy in the right-front tire. The vibration was so violent that she had to hold the steering wheel tightly with both hands as she shot past the two ministers' houses. The soldiers on guard just smiled at seeing the shuddering taxi speed by with a man clinging to the trunk.

Jamming on the brakes, Erica brought the car to a sudden stop. Raoul slid up onto the back window. Downshifting to first, Erica again accelerated, but Raoul continued to hang on, grasping the rear doorframes. Erica could still see him in the mirror, so she deliberately drove onto the shoulder of the road, seeking out potholes, which the car hit with jarring force. The passenger door on the right sprang open. The red dice fell from the dash.

Raoul was now lying on the trunk with his arms spanning the back window, each hand holding a doorframe through the missing windows of the rear doors. The impact with each pothole made his head and body slam up against the back of the car. He was determined to stay with Erica. He thought she'd gone crazy.

At the turnoff to Ahmed's, the headlights of the taxi illuminated a mud-brick wall at the side of the road. Erica screeched to a stop and threw the car into reverse. The sudden stop caused Raoul to slide up on top of the car. He grabbed for a handhold, his left hand grasping the doorframe next to Erica's face.

Erica accelerated backward, the car weaving wildly before ramming the wall. Her neck snapped back like a whip. The right-front door swung open to its limit, almost pulling it from its hinges. Raoul hung on.

Throwing the shift into first, Erica forced the car to leap forward. The sudden acceleration caused the right front door to close, slamming on Raoul's hand.

He cried out from the pain and jerked his hand back by reflex. At the same moment, the car hit the asphalt lip of the road, and the jolt tossed Raoul into the sand by the roadside. Almost the instant he hit the ground he regained his feet. Supporting his throbbing hand, he ran after Erica, noticing that she was pulling up at a low whitewashed mud-brick house. He came to a stop as she dashed from the car toward the front door. After making sure he knew exactly where he was, he turned around and headed back to get Yvon.

Erica was afraid Raoul was right behind her when she reached Ahmed's door. It was unlocked, and she burst through, leaving the door ajar. She had to convince Ahmed as quickly as possible of the conspiracy so that adequate police protection could be arranged.

Running directly into the living room, she was overjoyed to see Ahmed still up, conversing with a friend. "I'm being followed," shouted Erica.

Ahmed leaped to his feet, dumbfounded when he recognized Erica.

"Quickly," she continued, "we must have help."

Ahmed recovered enough to dash past her and out the open doorway. Erica turned to Ahmed's companion to ask him to summon the police. Her mouth started to open, but then her eyes widened with astonishment and fear.

Closing the door behind him, Ahmed returned and swept Erica into his arms. "It's all clear, Erica," he said. "It's all clear and you are safe. Let me look at you. I don't believe it; it is a miracle."

But Erica didn't respond, just strained to see over Ahmed's

shoulder. Her blood ran cold. She was looking at Muhammad Abdulal! Now both she and Ahmed would be killed. She could tell that Muhammad was equally astonished to see her, but he collected himself and unleashed a torrent of angry Arabic.

At first Ahmed ignored Muhammad's raving. He asked Erica who had been following her, but before she could respond, Muhammad said something that triggered in Ahmed the same suppressed violence Erica had seen when he smashed the teacup. His eyes darkened and he whirled to face Muhammad. He spoke in Arabic, and at first his voice was low and threatening, but it gradually rose in pitch until he was shouting.

Erica looked back and forth between the two men, expecting Muhammad to pull out a weapon. To her relief she noticed that instead he was cowering. Apparently he took orders from Ahmed, because he sat down when Ahmed pointed to a chair. Then with relief came fear. When Ahmed turned back to Erica, she looked into his powerfully deep eyes. What was happening?

Ahmed spoke softly. "Erica, it is truly a miracle that you have returned. . . ."

Erica's mind was beginning to scream that something was wrong. What was Ahmed saying? What did he mean, return?

"It must be Allah's wish that you and I should be together ' he continued, "and I am willing to accept his decision. I have been talking with Muhammad for many hours about you. J was going to come to you, to talk with you, to plead with you."

Erica's heart pounded; her whole sense of reality was disintegrating. "You knew about my being sealed in the tomb?"

"Yes. It was a difficult decision for me, but you had to be stopped. I ordered that you would not be hurt. I was going to come to the tomb to convince you to join us. I love you, Erica. One other time I had to give up the woman I loved. My uncle made sure I had no choice. But not this time. I want you to become part of the family—my family and Muhammad's family."

Closing her eyes for a moment, Erica tried to deal with all

her conflicting thoughts. She could not believe what was happening and what she was hearing. Marriage? Family? Her voice was uncertain. "You are related to Muhammad?"

"Yes," said Ahmed. He led her slowly to the couch and sat her down. "Muhammad and I are cousins. Our grandmother is Aida Raman. She is my mother's mother." Ahmed carefully described the complicated genealogy of their family, starting with Sarwat and Aida Raman.

When he finished speaking, Erica threw a frightened glance at Muhammad.

"Erica . . ." said Ahmed to regain her attention. "You have been able to do something no one else has been able to do for fifty years. No one outside of the family has seen the Raman papyrus, and anyone with even the slightest idea of its existence has been dealt with. Thanks to the media, the deaths have been ascribed to some mysterious curse. It's been most convenient."

"And all the secrecy is to guard the tomb?" asked Erica.

Ahmed and Muhammad exchanged glances. "What tomb are you referring to?" asked Ahmed.

"The real Seti tomb under Tutankhamen's," said Erica.

Muhammad jumped up and treated Ahmed to another stream of harsh Arabic. Ahmed listened this time and did not shut him up. When Muhammad was finished, Ahmed turned back to Erica. His voice was still calm. "You are indeed a marvel, Erica. Now you know why the stakes are so high. Yes, we are guarding an unplundered tomb of one of the great Egyptian pharaohs. With your training you know what that means. Unbelievable wealth. So you can understand that you have put us in an embarrassing position. But if you marry me, then it is part yours and you can help clear this most spectacular archaeological find."

Erica tried again to think of a way to escape. First she'd had to get away from Yvon, now Ahmed. And Raoul was probably going back to Yvon. There would be a horrible confrontation. The world was crazy. To stall for time she asked, "Why hasn't the tomb been cleared already?"

"The tomb is filled with such riches that removing any required careful planning. My grandfather Raman knew it would take a generation to set up the machinery to market the treasures from such a tomb and to place the family in positions where they could control moving the priceless objects from Egypt. During the latter part of his life, we only took from the tomb enough to educate the next generation. It has only been within the last year that I have become director of the Department of Antiquities and Muhammad chief guard of the Necropolis of Luxor."

"So it's like the Rasul family in the nineteenth century," said Erica.

"There is a superficial resemblance," said Ahmed. "We are working on a very sophisticated level. The archaeological interests are being carefully considered. In fact, Erica, you could be instrumental in that aspect."

"Was Lord Carnarvon one of the people that had to be 'dealt with'?" asked Erica.

"I'm not certain," said Ahmed. "It was a long time ago, but I think so." Muhammad nodded. "Erica," continued Ahmed, "how did you learn what you did? I mean, what made—?"

Suddenly the lights in the house went out. The moon had set and the darkness was absolute, like a tomb. Erica did not move. She heard someone pick up the phone, then slam it down. She guessed Yvon and Raoul had cut the wires.

She heard Ahmed and Muhammad speak swiftly in Arabic. Then her eyes began to accustom themselves to the darkness so she could see vague forms. A figure loomed toward her, and she shrank back. It was Ahmed, and he grasped her wrist and pulled her to her feet. She could see only his eyes and his teeth.

"I ask you again, who was following you?" His voice was an urgent half-whisper.

She tried to speak, but she stumbled over her words; she was terrified. She was caught between two horrid forces. Ahmed yanked on her wrist impatiently. Finally Erica managed to say, "Yvon de Margeau."

Ahmed did not let go of Erica's wrist while he conversed with Muhammad. Erica caught the gleam from the barrel of a pistol in Muhammad's hand. She had the helpless feeling that events were again beyond her control.

Without warning Ahmed pulled Erica across the living room and down the long darkened hallway toward the rear of the house. She struggled to free her hand, unable to see and fearing she was going to trip and fall. But Ahmed's grip was like steel. Muhammad ran behind.

They exited from the house into the courtyard, where there was slightly more light. They skirted the stable, reaching the back gate. Ahmed and Muhammad spoke quickly; then Ahmed opened the wooden door. The alley beyond was deserted and darker than the courtyard because of a double row of date palms. Muhammad carefully leaned out with his gun poised, his eyes searching the shadows. Satisfied, he stepped back, making room for Ahmed. Without releasing her wrist, Ahmed urged Erica forward, pushing her through the doorway into the alley. He followed close behind.

The first thing Erica was aware of was a sudden tightening of Ahmed's hold on her wrist. Then she heard the report of the gun. It was the same dull thud she'd heard when she faced the crazed Evangelos. It was the sound of a gun with a silencer. Ahmed fell sideways, back through the doorway, pulling Erica off her feet on top of him. In the meager light she could see he'd been shot like Evangelos, between the eyes. Bits of brain tissue had spattered on the side of her face.

Erica pushed herself up to a kneeling position in a state of catatonia. Muhammad lunged past her, running across the alley to the safety of the rows of palm trunks. Erica blankly watched him turn and fire his pistol down the alley. Then he turned and fled in the opposite direction.

In a daze Erica stood up, her eyes riveted to the lifeless Ahmed. She backed up into the shadows until she hit against the wall of the stable. Her mouth was open and her breathing was in shallow gasps. From the front part of the house she could hear a sharp splintering sound followed by a crash that had to be the front door. Behind her she could hear Sawda nervously stir in his stable. She was immobilized.

Directly in front of her and framed by the doorway to the alley, Erica saw a crouching figure run past. Almost immediately, more shots rang out on the right. Then behind her she heard the sounds of running in the house, and her numbness began to revert to terror. She knew that it was she that Yvon wanted. He was desperate.

Erica heard the back door to the house swing open. She held her breath as a silent figure came into view. It was Raoul. She watched as he bent over Ahmed, then exited into the alley.

Erica's paralysis lasted for another five minutes, the sound of the firefight fading in the alley. Suddenly she pushed away from the wall and stumbled back through the dark house and out the front door.

She crossed the road and ran down a passageway made of mud bricks. She passed through a yard, then another, causing a few lights to come on in her noisy wake. She crashed through debris, a chicken coop, and splashed through an open sewer. In the distance she could hear more shots and a man shouting. She ran on until she felt she was going to collapse. But it wasn't until she stumbled onto the Nile that she allowed herself to rest. She tried to think of where to go. No one could be trusted. Since Muhammad Abdulal was chief of the guards, she was even afraid of the police.

It was at that point that Erica remembered the two houses of the ministers guarded by the casual soldiers. With effort she heaved herself to her feet and began walking south. She remained in the shadows away from the road until she had reached the guarded properties. Then, like an automaton she walked out into the lighted street and rounded the front wall of the first house. The soldiers were there, conversing with each other across the fifty feet that separated the two entrance-ways. They both turned and watched as Erica walked directly toward the first. He was young, dressed in loose-fitting brown uniform with highly polished boots. A machine pistol hung from a shoulder strap. He moved the weapon around, and as Erica came closer, he started to say something.

With no intention of stopping, Erica walked right past the surprised youth into the grounds of the house. *"O af andak!"* yelled the soldier, coming after Erica.

Erica stopped. Then, after mustering her resources, she yelled as loud as possible, *"Help!"* and kept screaming until a light came on in the darkened house. Soon a robed figure appeared at the door—bald, overweight, and shoeless.

"Do you speak English?" asked Erica breathlessly.

"Of course," said the man, surprised and slightly irritated.

"Do you work for the government?"

"Yes. I'm deputy assistant defense minister."

"Do you have anything to do with antiquities?"

"Nothing."

"Wonderful," said Erica. "I have the most incredible story to tell you. . . ."

Boston

The TWA 747 banked gently, then made its graceful approach to Logan Airport. With her nose pressed up against the window, Erica stared out on the vista of Boston in the late fall. It looked very good to her. She felt a true excitement about coming home.

The wheels of the huge jet touched down, sending a slight shudder through the cabin. A few passengers clapped, happy that the long transatlantic flight was at an end. As the plane taxied toward the international-arrivals building, Erica marveled at the experiences she'd had since her departure. She was a different person than when she'd left, feeling that she'd finally made the transition from the academic to the real world. And with the invitation by the Egyptian government to play a major role in clearing the tomb of Seti I, she felt confident of a promising career.

There was a final lurch as the plane came to the gate. The sounds of the engines died away, and the passengers began opening overhead storage bins. Erica stayed in her seat and looked out at the crisp New England clouds. She remembered Lieutenant Iskander's immaculate white uniform when he'd come to see her off from Cairo. He had told her the final result of that fateful night in Luxor: Ahmed Khazzan had died from gunshot wounds—a fact she'd known from the moment he'd been hit; Muhammad Abdulal was still in a coma; Yvon de

Margeau had somehow received clearance and had flown out of the country, becoming a persona non grata in Egypt; and Stephanos Markoulis had just disappeared.

It all seemed so unreal now that she was in Boston. The experience saddened her, especially about Ahmed. The experience also made her question her ability to judge people, especially because of Yvon. Even after what had happened, he had had the nerve to telephone her from Paris when she'd returned to Cairo, offering her large sums to provide inside information about the tomb of Seti I. She shook her head in dismay as she gathered her carry-on belongings.

Erica allowed herself to be carried along by the crowd. She passed through the immigration control quickly and retrieved her baggage. Then she pushed out into the waiting area.

They saw each other at the same moment. Richard ran up and hugged her as Erica dropped her bags, forcing the people behind her to step over them. They held each other without speaking, their emotions balanced. Finally Erica pulled away. "You were right, Richard. I was over my head from the start. I'm lucky to be alive."

Richard's eyes filled with tears, something Erica had never seen. "No, Erica, we were both right and both wrong. It just means there is a lot we need to learn about each other, and believe me, I'm willing."

Erica smiled. She wasn't sure what it meant, but it made her feel good.

"Oh, by the way," said Richard, picking up her bags. "There's a man here from Houston who wants to see you."

"Really?" asked Erica.

"Yeah. He apparently knew Dr. Lowery, who gave him my phone number. He's over there." Richard pointed.

"My God," said Erica. "It's Jeffrey John Rice."

As if on cue, Jeffrey Rice came over, taking off his stetson with a flourish.

"Sorry to interrupt you two at this time, but, Miss Baron, here's your check for finding that Seti statue."

"But I don't understand," said Erica. "The Egyptian government now owns the statue. You cannot buy it."

"That's just the point. It makes mine the only one outside of

Egypt. Because of you it's worth tons more than it was before. Houston is mighty pleased."

Erica looked down at the ten-thousand-dollar check and burst out laughing. Richard, who did not really understand what was happening, saw her amazed expression and began laughing too. Rice shrugged, and still holding the check, led them out into the bright Boston sun.